CW01472053

ROGER McDONALD is the author of six novels: *1915*, *Slipstream*, *Rough Wallaby*, *Water Man*, *The Slap* and *Mr Darwin's Shooter*. His account of travels with New Zealand shearers in the Australian outback, *Shearers' Motel*, won the 1993 National Book Council Banjo Award for non-fiction and has been republished by Vintage. The internationally acclaimed *Mr Darwin's Shooter* was awarded the New South Wales, Victorian and South Australian Premiers' Literary Awards, and won the National Fiction Award at the 2000 Adelaide Writers' Week.

Roger McDonald (signature)

1915

— A NOVEL —

ROGER McDONALD

V

VINTAGE

A Vintage Book
Published by
Random House Australia Pty Ltd
20 Alfred Street, Milsons Point, NSW 2061
http://www.randomhouse.com.au

Sydney   New York   Toronto
London   Auckland   Johannesburg

First published in Australia by University of Queensland Press 1979
This Vintage edition first published 2001

Copyright © Roger McDonald 1979

All rights reserved. No part of this publication may be reproduced,
stored in a retrieval system, or transmitted in any form or by any
means, electronic, mechanical, photocopying, recording or otherwise,
without the prior written permission of the publisher.

National Library of Australia
Cataloguing-in-Publication Entry

McDonald, Roger, 1941- .
1915.

ISBN 1 74051 129 8.

1. World War, 1914-1918 – Fiction. I. Title. II. Title: Nineteen fifteen.

A823.3

Cover image courtesy of Australian War Memorial
Cover design by Greendot Design
Typeset by Press Etching Pty Ltd, Brisbane
Printed and bound by Griffin Press, Netley, South Australia

10 9 8 7 6 5 4 3 2 1

Come to the stables all men that are able
and give your poor horses some hay and some corn...

To my wife Sue

Part One

1
After a Fall

It was inconceivable to Walter that a person could be well educated yet morally bad. But in the district hospital he met a woman who was said to be both, a governess from a station on the Condobolin line. People said she had tried to drown herself in a dam.

"The doctor says I need a rest," she told Walter. "I went for a swim and got into trouble. Don't let anyone tell you otherwise."

"Cripes no, Miss Davis."

She sat on the end of his bed while he avoided her eye. She discovered his enthusiasm for geology, and for half a day talked of nothing else.

Yet things she said disturbed him.

"It's a cow," she whined in her English accent. "The way things hang over me. *Or*stralia."

Nurse Armitage was different. She was rounded and warm as she sat on the bed or leant over him, and he closed his eyes wondering what he might dare.

Then late one night he was woken by a whisper: *"It's Edie Davis."* She was standing by his bedside, her silk dressing gown smelling of camphor. "Are you awake?"

He leapt upright, his shoulder jarring painfully. For a long time she said nothing. He heard her catch her breath. "What do you want?" he asked. "Will I call the nurse?" His hand groped for the bedside bell and knocked it to the floor.

"I'm sorry." She was already leaving. "I lost my way in the dark." She gave a high-pitched laugh that relieved him, because now she sounded happy, and it had all been a mistake.

But in the morning she ignored him. She returned a stack of *Knowledge* magazines by dumping them on the foot of his bed, and he began to believe everything that was said about her. It was the day of his operation. The image of her bitter eyes stayed with him until the last minute, bearing down with the chloroform mask as he slipped into oblivion.

When he regained consciousness, fighting against a nightmare, he found restraining bars on the sides of the bed and the matron holding him. The pain in his arm and shoulder was worse than it had been at the time of his accident, when Coalheap had viciously shied and flung him against a tree. Through the dark doorway of the ward he thought he saw Edie Davis's faintly pockmarked face, but she might have been part of his dream — everything unpleasant and unexplained was mixed up in it. At the end of the dream he had found himself trapped in a stone tomb with no means of escape. Rough walls had pressed on him from all sides. This terrible place was a vision of fate drained of hope. He could imagine nothing worse.

When he tried to tell his parents they smiled:

"The doctor says you'll be all right now."

"You're ruined for work," laughed his father.

Billy Mackenzie, the son of their nearest neighbour, was the only visitor to listen to him. In town delivering his father's hay he came in the evening and again the next morning. It was no secret that Billy enjoyed seeing a boastful rider brought low by a fall, but he was affable about it. From now on, Walter decided, they would be friends again.

4

"I had the same feeling the time you pushed the wheat sacks on me," said Billy. "Remember? We had our share of fights."

He stood on the gauzed veranda and smoked, turning to stare at Nurse Armitage whenever she passed.

The break in Walter and Billy's friendship had come four years before.

"There's a war," Walter had said, "and we're scouts." He and Billy squatted behind a rock at the edge of the rabbit-proof fence. "If we're caught we'll be shot, so keep it quiet."

"Git going," said Billy, but as he spoke he leapt up and went first himself, making Walter feel stupid.

When they reached the top of the ridge the homestead could be seen glinting through the greenery far below, its roof a tarnished silver tray. Walter pulled two apples from his haversack and handed one to Billy: "Rations." After a while one and then the other apple-core flew into the air and spun out of sight over the tops of the trees. "Let's go to the pool," said Walter, watching Billy flick a caterpillar onto a rock and squash it with his thumb, where it arched, fierce and hairy.

The far side of the ridge fell steeply. Now Billy leapt in places where Walter lowered himself gingerly, and soon he was well ahead. Walter was scratched by sharp branches, and slowing down, maddeningly wedged a boot in a crevice. "Wait on!" he called to Billy.

A hawk glided in circles over the treetops. Down in the gully a wallaby crashed with one noisy leap and was still. And he was sure that Billy was no longer moving either, but crouched somewhere far below. So he decided to stalk him.

Because the game forced him to travel slowly he found the going easier. He dangled down a rock on his belly, finding suction by spreading his arms. He discovered a split in the cliff-face wide enough to fit into, its base jammed with small boulders forming a steep descending staircase.

Suddenly Walter saw water. And just as he was about to let fly with a warlike yell he noticed Billy sitting on a stone near the edge of the creek. Something odd was going on. His boots and trousers were in a pile beside him. His right hand was between his legs moving rapidly up and down. After a moment he leaned forward, moved his hand even more rapidly, slowed it and stopped, examined something in the water, and then glanced around to see if anyone was watching. Then he removed his shirt and lowered himself into the pool. He floated face down, lifting his head now and again to breathe, shaking it from side to side, spluttering like a dog. Walter dropped to the ground and crossed the intervening patch of tussocky grass without being seen. He sat on the rock and glanced at the point where Billy had been peering, but saw only the gritty curve of stone and the gently lapping water.

Billy gave a shout, his round head breaking from the water with slicked-down hair, his eyes, always oddly Chinese, now screwed tight against the glare and his wide-open mouth releasing a cry of alarm.

"How long have you been there?"

"Long enough."

"How long?"

"I told you."

"What do you mean?"

"Long enough to put a bullet between your eyes. If we'd had men with us yours would be dead." Billy waded unsteadily ashore. The stones at the edge of the pool clacked like billiard balls.

"I'd probably have you confessing by now."

Billy hauled on his trousers: "Give it a rest."

"I'd've taken you back to HQ as a prisoner," insisted Walter. "You'd be shot as a spy."

Billy sat in the grass lacing his boots. "I'm sick of all these games."

"What were you doing on the rock?"

"When?"

"Before. I could see you doing something with your cock." Walter had not meant to say anything, but if Billy was no longer playing, all right, he wouldn't play either, even if it meant fists.

"I was pulling my pud."

"What's that?"

"You saw, so you ought to know. You play with yourself till something happens." Now Billy was angry again, on his feet and shouting through the cracks and sudden bullfrog-descents of his voice. "But you wouldn't know," he yelled. "You can't do nothing properly. I can do anything better than you."

"You can't!" But it was true, though never something that had bothered him. "You can't!" Walter's voice rose screaming till it hurt.

Billy was now harsh and parental: "Damn you."

Walter swooped and grabbed a stone, and Billy taunted him: "You couldn't if you tried," he sneered, at the same time collecting a rock himself and feinting a sudden throwing action. This caused Walter to let his go, but it curved wide and missed. "Right-oh," shouted Billy, "now get back, go on, get back!" He advanced with threatening jerks of his throwing arm, the stone in his fist as big as a cricket ball. "Get back or I'll kill you!" Walter retreated to the edge of the water.

"Get in!"

"No."

"Get in!" Billy's stone sparked on the rock six inches in front of his boots leaving a white streak of powder. He stumbled into the water and waded out.

Billy stood with a pile of stones at his feet and one by one hurled them into the pool.

"Stop it will you! Quit it up!"

When Walter was wet all over and crying and falling down and balancing himself on one hand while shielding his eyes with the other, Billy ran to a pine tree near an overhanging rock, clambered up its branches, and disappeared without a backward glance.

Walter was aware of light attempting to penetrate his tightly closed lids, and opened them to find Billy once again standing beside the bed.

"Mum said you'd like these." He tipped half a dozen oranges from his pockets.

"I was dreaming." Walter wondered if he had shouted and made a fool of himself.

"Don't get into a sweat." Billy sat on the bed and peeled an orange. "They say you'll be home soon. Next week?" But before Walter could answer he changed tack: "I never dream interesting things. All I ever get when I'm asleep is the same thing over and over. If I've been ploughing it's the bloody horse and plough stuck up there in front of me. Same with sowing, clearing, going to town, the lot." He glanced out the door and whispered: "There's only one thing I wish'd come up true to life," and he winked, accompanying the batted eye with a click of the tongue. An adult smell of beer and sweat emanated from him, full of the threat of the town, but also a mark of Billy's break from the mistrustful silence between them. They were no longer the same: that was good. His move in a rougher direction allowed space for Walter, and his visits and increasing talkativeness were as good as a handshake.

"I hear your Miss Davis's done a bunk."

"Mine?" Walter laughed, and Billy smacked a hand on his knee. Edie Davis had walked out of the hospital the night before without saying a word to anyone.

"She's a pal of yours, ain't she?" Billy now sucked his fingers after finishing the orange, wiped them dry on a large handkerchief, took out pipe and tobacco. "I'll tell you something," he lowered his voice, "I got the drum on her from Eric Waterhouse."

"Make it quick," said Walter, who feared that the bright and suspicious Edie Davis might step through the door.

"She was governess for the Keith Fryers out at Windy station, but that's only the start. Eric maintains the minute she set eyes on Fryer it was plain what would happen. First thing when she arrived, she had him in the Royal lapping up port wine like a puppy. Right off the train. His poor bloody wife didn't get a look-in. They were soon at it like a couple of mad things. They seemed to think the place was run by blind men. But it couldn't last. One night there'd been a lot of drinking and it ended with her hitting him around the face with a cane basket. If it had been me," mused Billy, "I would have given her the boot early on."

"What did Fryer do?"

"The same as any man. So she went off her cracker

and threw herself in the dam. You know the rest," he nodded quickly as Nurse Armitage came in, tut-tutting over the unlit lamp. She told Billy to leave the ward at once. "I was just going," he said, but sat there, knocking out his pipe. "Now?" asked the nurse as she made her final snaps and tucks of the bedcover. "I'm off," said Billy, and stood, his slit eyes following her movements like a cat's, his smooth skin soapy like a fat child's in the lamplight.

Next morning the news came that Edie Davis's body had been found in an abandoned mine shaft at the back of the hospital hill.

When the matron arrived to take Walter's evening details he wriggled away. "I'm all right," he snapped, hardly aware of his irritation.

When his mother came, urging a prayer, they argued.

"It was no accident," said Walter.

"Where's the note? I saw myself how she looked better."

"I know she meant to do it."

"Those mines are a disgrace. Oh dear, if she suicided she won't be buried with the rest."

"She shouldn't be," said Walter with force, and this shocked his mother so much that he wondered himself at the asperity of his judgment. But was he mad at Miss Davis! She was the reason for his bad temper. What business did she have blinking out like that when she had the opportunity to go on? He knew, having surfaced from his fall, that there was something unforgivable about staying down there by choice.

2
Hotel Albion

Billy saw small grey shapes moving, stopping, edging along the strip where the cut of the plough ended and the native grasses began. From his seat on the dunny he raised an arm and fired an imaginary rifle. The shapes wriggled on the blurred green horizon like tiny water creatures in a fish tank. He tore a rectangle from the *Western Champion* and hastily splashed a half-dipper of ash in the pit. Rising, trouserless, he lifted his arm and again squeezed the trigger. "Crack," he said in a whisper, "crack, crack." Although the wallabies were a mile or more distant, and would not have noticed even if Billy had leapt outside with a shout, he hung back, listening to his heartbeat and watching, poised in an emotion that belonged not to work, nor to play either, but to another function of himself, nameless, that brooded over and was greater than both.

He fetched his rifle from the house and set off in a northerly direction in order to circle round, moving in a diagonal line across furrows. Here he stumbled, causing the rifle barrel to jab for a second into the soil, so that when he reached the grass under the mountain he squatted for a few minutes to clean it.

When he raised his head he found a huge kangaroo, a Blue Flyer, staring at him across the tall grass.

Without standing he brought the rifle round and slipped the safety catch. Then, while the animal stared and Billy whistled, he fired, keeping the shot low so that it lashed through the hundreds of intervening grass stalks towards the kangaroo's hidden chest. Hardly anything happened. The animal lifted her head, sniffed, then slumped as if inside an overcoat of fur, yet remained upright.

Billy giggled because he wanted to go up and shake a paw (he would have in company), and might have even so, only he saw blood pump from the chest. The sporting chance he offered (*go!* under his breath) was not to be taken. The wet nose, the wet eyes, the beautiful set-back ears that twitched: a lovely face that Billy wanted to nuzzle, as often he had nuzzled Yabbie, dog and man-dog growling in the clean-swept ring under the peppercorn tree.

"What do you want, 'roo?"

In the ring of grey silence, the sun gone, his own voice startled him. Then a thought rattled through him; he wished to erase that lovely face for ever — this gaze of his, that gaze of hers, the trembling mirage of contact between them. The joining of thought to action was everything to Billy; finger on metal, thought thus cracking into life: a harsh word to bark out and settle something.

In the yard the dogs threw bodiless yelps through the blackness as they leapt on their chains. Though it was still early the darkness was complete, and because he could not be bothered fixing a lamp, Billy did everything by feel. The back door swung open, his mother called "Is that you?" and from the old meat safe, head surrounded by hessian flaps, hands placing the slippery kangaroo meat on trays, he shouted a reply that mixed in with the animal yelps and satisfied her. More and more these days his mother disliked being left alone, especially on Saturday nights when travellers, drunk or sober, sometimes wandered in from the road with terrible thirsts. Later tonight, in the midst of these fears, her husband would arrive home reeking of whisky and cheerful, scorning his wife's timidity. As he washed at the tankstand Billy glanced up at the stars and around the dark line of hills and bush. At night even cleared land seemed inhabited by trees, with hunched forms wavering and creeping forward, putting the land back the way it was before the plough came.

Over dinner Billy said, "I might ride across and say hello to Wal tonight." It was the first week of the school holidays, Walter Gilchrist's last before he finished school at the end of the year.

"You be careful in the dark." But Billy knew that his mother thought of the Gilchrists as a civilizing influence: the whisky decanter on their sideboard barely sank over the space of a year. Still, she had to be gloomy: "Just remember Arnold Scott."

"Arnie was a mug."

Arnie! — his horse had tripped, falling on top of him while he was out rabbiting, crushing his stomach and injuring his spine.

"And Walter," she warned, recalling his accident of three years before, "his arm still gives him trouble in winter."

"Soon be summer," said Billy. And to celebrate his joke he splashed a thick crust of bread into his gravy. Three years! It was just like Walter to complain about something for a lifetime.

"You're all we've got, me and Dad." Her hand rested on Billy's as they drank their tea.

"Don't I know it."

On the way to the Gilchrists' the cleared land narrowed to a track and wound to the top of the ridge through boulders and thickening pines. Up there Billy dismounted and led Ginger at a slow walk, though usually he liked to take the track at a gallop. After rain, on frosty nights, water froze here in great sheets. Dawdling, smoking his pipe, he thought about his mother, her unhappiness a twisted burden, a sheet poled wearily from the copper. The track was stony now, dropping steeply, the Gilchrists' house a smudged brass fragment that signalled from the distance and then went black. "Who ain't unhappy?" Billy asked the stars. His father could wander miles and come home late, sometimes days late, with a head battered from whisky; his mother could sit at home staring at the fire; and Billy himself could head off on his own expeditions through the district. But when you fitted it all together, there they were, all three proud of each other. They kept their chins up.

He set Ginger free in the yard near the gate and walked whistling to the house. Firelight flickered through the living room windows, so he crept up and peered in. Mrs Gilchrist was knitting, the boss reading the paper, Walter and Douggie sitting cross-legged on the floor playing draughts. They weren't even talking. They might have been dead. Then Billy reached over and with tight knuckles rapped three times on the glass, at the same time laughing a hair-raising laugh in the cold garden. Walter and Douggie rushed out to tackle him and pummel his back while he rolled roaring in the icy grass.

When the others had gone to bed Billy and Walter sat deep in armchairs watching a new log being swallowed in flames. A piece of burning wood popped, a cinder flew in an arc to ding the kettle on the hearth.

Finally Billy asked, "How's school?"

"I feel like Methuselah."

"Me too, sometimes. The smelly old bugger," said Billy, recalling a dog of that name that had lolled for years around the house.

"I'll be coming back here after, for good." The decision had not been finally taken, but Walter read his father's mood.

"I'll show you a time. But listen," Billy blew a whistle of breath as he looked around to see if any of the family had sneaked back, "you haven't, I s'pose, I mean you haven't been gettin' yourself into trouble."

"Me?"

"Girls and that, down there in the city." The leather of Billy's tobacco pouch, like his hands, was supple and work-worn, already old. "Want the makings?"

"Talk," pronounced Billy, when the cigarettes were aglow, "that's the way to get 'em." He poured two mugs of tea from the warming pot, conjuring with a black column of liquid that spat wads of leaves. "Let me give you some advice. Find a widow, a new widow who ain't so old, and call on her when you can."

"A schoolboy?" asked Walter, though he and Billy were the same age.

"Where there's a will," said Billy, running a hand around his clean-shaven chin. A thought occurred to Walter:

"*Mrs Scott!*" he breathed in astonishment, and Billy almost sent his tea flying.

"How did you know?"

"It just added up." Walter needed a second to overtake his own lightning calculation: a widow who wasn't so old, who might see Billy now and again, who was fair game — Arnie Scott's wife who now ran the post office at Cookamidgera.

"But only me and her know."

Walter swirled his tea around the bottom of his mug and stared at it.

"All right," said Billy with a sigh, "you'd better swear to that one. If Arnie's brothers find out I'm a goner. They've all got their eyes on her." He sank deep in his chair. "What a life, eh?" Then he laughed. "Swear?"

When Billy left at midnight it was frosty. At the stockyards he formed a giant cut-out against the stars. Ginger had been frightened by something, and shuffled nervously, rattling the bit. Then, at a word, horse and rider flung themselves through into blackness with a hoofbeat-studded voice flinging back, "See you Saturday!"

Billy took the long way home. He rode at a canter, making a song out of the night and the regular pounding underfoot. The song had no sensible words, though Billy thought it did, for while he mumbled or let fly with torn rags of sound his mind was clear about the story it told itself, with the accompanying drumbeat of the horse keeping perfect time. Horse, horse,

horse, went the song: night, frost: if I die my mum will be sad and so will my dad and so will I! But I'll ride like mad till Ginger gets me home. Horse! And as he sang, his thoughts about Mrs Scott and the pestering Scott brothers, and his thoughts about the Parkes show the following Saturday worked their way in. After the ring events he wanted to take Walter into the town to meet the Reid boys and Eddie Harkness, and let him taste the atmosphere of the Royal just before dark on a Saturday night. Horse! he'd had some times there.

But when Billy saw Walter at the show he had his doubts. There he was with his father, tall rakes both of them, but Walter with an unfinished look about him: knobbly wrists like the sap-bumps on gum trees, and his hair, frizzy and overlong, flying out where it had been wetted and fiercely combed. Father and son were leaning over a sheep pen parting the depth of fleece of an indolent ram. Bent like this, Walter's trouser cuffs came above the tops of his high laced boots. He looked every inch the boarding school son, and Billy hung back for a moment, picking a burr from his coat. But when they turned, he could see how the differences between them dissolved, with Walter foreshadowing the work-cured depth of his father. Billy hailed them.

Together they toured the pigs and the produce. The Mackenzies had won second prize for their wheaten hay, so Billy stood for a while beside a tagged sheaf with his hands behind his back chatting about the achievement to all comers. When his father arrived Walter and Billy went off towards the sideshows. On the way they were captured by Billy's Aunt Bea and her two girls.

"Have you seen the boy with the dog's head?" asked Lottie.

"Why bother now we've seen you?" said Billy, and the skinny fifteen-year-old punched him in the stomach. In a crush near the entrance to the exhibits Walter felt Ethel leaning against his shoulder. He stepped from the flow and absorbed himself in the display of horseshoes and tanned leatherwork. Billy always said that the eighteen-year-old Ethel was a "good sport", and here she was making Walter nervous.

"Billy's coming to the Bindogundra hop. Are you?"

"Oh, sure," said Walter, knowing he'd be back at school.

When Billy put his arms round Ethel's waist from behind she shrieked. All four went to hear the man from the *Titanic*, and emerged blinking in the arctic white light of noon.

"I think Ethel likes me," said Walter later.

"She'd like a tree if it wore trousers," said Billy. "But you should try kissing her some time." He might have been recommending a brand of tobacco.

"I'd like to," concluded Walter, "I definitely will." He spoke with such force, yet so disdainfully, that Billy laughed.

"You'd better have a hot bath first to loosen up."

It was then that Mrs Fox the minister's wife came running from group to group dragging her whimpering daughter, asking in a voice dried raucous from tears if anyone had seen her husband.

"He's down yonder," said Billy, pointing past a striped tent awning, and as Mrs Fox scuttled away he lifted his finger to point at the sky: "Up yonder, with his boss," but by then she had gone, "no, around the bend," he finished, circling a finger around his ear and raising his eyebrows at Walter to give an opinion.

"Don't forget about later. You'll like Blacky and Ned."

Walter drowsed, sitting motionless on Peapod during the interminable judging of dairy cattle. Voices drifted from the crowd at the railings, and when someone said, "Walter?" he missed the connection to himself until, lazily turning, he saw Mr Fox. A veined hand strayed to Peapod's mane and stroked it. "One of the breed of Diomedes, no doubt," said Mr Fox through gingery lips. Walter said, "Pardon?" As the minister spoke he brushed the side of the mare's head (with his lips!) and laughed alarmingly: "Thou shalt not have me." Peapod wrenched her head as Mr Fox fought to hold it steady.

"Is that from the Bible?" The dairy men were staring.

"No," said the minister flatly. "Earlier trouble than that." And he strode back into the crowd. No wonder Mrs Fox had been worried. For the rest of the afternoon, clipped remotely high on the mare as he walked and trotted among shining horses, Walter felt irritatingly at fault. He felt guilty for withholding himself from the pain that had swirled momentarily at his feet. The show seemed a luxury after that, a ceremony for the fit. Thoroughbred stallions and mares followed the cows, then an army of draught horses with their owners swathed in hygienic white coats. They seemed invincible, but so had the *Titanic,* which had fallen to something as simple as frozen water. The minister's unstable rushing about was not just a rebuke to the organized display of the district's achievements, it was a threat, weaving in and out of the tents, ducking under the railings, being sighted, confronted, then sliding off again, dominated overwhelmingly by the weight of produce, by the dreadnought power of Suffolk Punch, Clydesdale and Percheron — yet persisting.

"What was biting old Foxy?" asked Billy as they left for town. Walter shrugged, then tapped his forehead: but felt cowardly for doing so.

Billy found his mates in the back bar wedged tight among a show crowd that had long since abandoned the show.

"Who's the young 'un?" asked the elder Reid. He extended a forge-hammered hand. "Blacky and Ned," explained Billy as one and then the other took delight in crushing Walter's fingers. Blacky was aged thirty, with a face of intense black stubble and caterpillar-like eyebrows. His younger brother was also black-haired, but somehow the shade was unremarkable.

"Drink up," said Blacky. He raised his glass in a toast to nothing in particular and tipped back his head.

After the third beer Walter felt that he understood a great many things. The back bar with its cream-painted walls and its grey kangaroo dog asleep in the corner under a Beck's Beer placard ("With horse in check, They called for Beck's . . ."), this seemed the pleasantest place in the world.

Soon after five Blacky drained his beer. "I'll see you fellows back here in half an hour."

"Have one for me," sniggered Ned.

"Where's he going?" asked Walter, surprised that anyone would want to let this pleasant occasion slide. Blacky jammed a wide hat on his head and winked at the barmaid.

"Off for some horizontal refreshment," said Ned as his brother shouldered his way out.

"We'll smoke out Eddie and then head for home," Billy nodded to Walter. "I don't want to be blamed by your dad."

"Still a nipper, eh?" said Ned, dragging a damp belch from his hidden chest. Walter pumped his hand in the rediscovered glow of the last beer. "Very pleased to have met you," he gushed, "you and your brother. Two of the nicest blokes I've ever met."

"We're all right, I s'pose," Ned responded. With a barely nodded "Good-on-you, mate," to Billy he switched to another group of drinkers.

Walter stood in the grass at the rear of the hotel, his head tipped back. Looking at the stars he thought: Yes, the universe is one complete whole, and I'm part of it. He sniffed dust in the frosty air and laughed companionably to himself as pleasant thoughts spread through the cold night. Friends! That was one thought. And women! He remembered the barmaid's eyes.

"What do you think of the Reids?" he called to Billy.

"What did you think of 'em?" They were passing the gloomy stand of pines near the racecourse where a swagman had recently been murdered.

"They're all right."

"Ned?"

"I liked his brother better."

"Blacky won't take nonsense from no-one." A light flickered far back in the pines, though each pretended not to notice. "He's showed me a thing or two."

"About where he went tonight?"

"The brothel?"

"Yes," Walter shaped the word for himself, "the brothel."

"Nah," but that was a lie.

Road and railway ran together, and a goods train drew alongside, chuffing and clattering, making the horses restless. At the rise above the creek they looked back on the faint lights of town: a column of smoke at the railway yards suddenly lit by sparks, a lantern faint as a star on a hillside. Then the road took another turn and they were in their own country. Walter climbed down several times to relieve himself, the reins looped over his arm. Once Peapod took off into the darkness without him, and Billy galloped away to fetch her back. Overhead the stars seemed thicker than anywhere.

They parted at the ten-mile.

"See you sometime," said Billy. "I've got to go down to Forbes next week for sheep."

"November at the latest, eh?" Walter thrust out a hand. They shook. It seemed the thing to do, now they were men.

Parkes was Billy's town, but he liked going to Forbes. When he reached the Eugowra road and entered the big river gums of the Lachlan he knew he was on foreign soil. Forbes hung together, it was solid, with its numerous hotels saluting each other across corners. Billy's place by contrast was barely a town at all, more a collection of small settlements with shops and hotels grown up somewhere in the middle. Away from home Billy was a complete stranger, anonymous as a stray dog, and like a stray dog on the lookout for pleasure.

He left his horse at the stockyards, and with Yabbie

at his heels walked the rest of the way into town. He carried a change of clothes and a razor rolled in a swag. Ambling along he broke a switch from a peppercorn tree and flicked it from side to side. "Nineteen's enough," he had said on his birthday a few days before. "It'll do me." He walked on, whistling, with Yabbie dashing left and right.

When he saw the Albion he paused to admire its size — three stories of brick and iron veranda, with blunt but royal-looking flagpoles surmounting a row of towers. He noticed a girl standing on the upper veranda. She was dressed for hotel work but not so plainly as to be mistaken for a maid, for she wore red beads and a short-sleeved blouse with a lace collar. Her face was hidden, turned half-in to the building. Black hair dropped in a long pigtail.

The day ended as Billy entered the hotel, a brown and shining darkness swallowing everything. Yabbie slithered on the polished linoleum of the hall while Billy scrutinized a row of hunting prints, disbelieving the horses' long necks. Out the back a yardman showed him a corner for Yabbie. Near the back door he found a lavatory, and there he sat with the door of his booth wide open, thinking of the girl, wondering what her face was like, imagining himself reaching from behind and making her squeal with surprise.

"Here long?" A man joined Billy at the handbasin. He spoke indistinctly, as if talking to himself. "Henry Kroner," he said, extending a hand. His eyes were the milky red of diced carrots in rabbit poison.

"You must have a drink, no?" Now he stood blocking the way.

"I s'pose so. When I've seen about my room."

"At the bar," said the old foreigner, "you can do it there."

The private bar was empty except for the barman and two stock agents from Weaver & Co who sat at a table at the far end. One raised a finger to his red nose in recognition of Billy.

"The young gentleman wants a room, Mr Reilly. And I want another beer."

Reilly extended a hairy hand: "Heinrich will tell you I can throw an eighteen gallon keg farther than you can spit."

Billy said: "I'm not troublesome."

The hotelkeeper reached behind the bar and rang a small handbell which dribbled its sound away into the depths of the building. "You'll have your room in a flash. What's your poison?"

"Beer."

Reilly hesitated for a second before reaching for a pint mug. "It's on the house."

Billy drank it down in half a dozen thumping gulps.

"You're a big drinker."

"Thirsty."

"You're not from round here, are you?"

Reilly stood with folded arms, his black hair dusted with silver. Dark circles under his eyes gave him a wise look.

"My dad is Hugh Mackenzie."

The hotelkeeper lifted the empty mug and slapped a piece of damp towelling along the bar. "The Hugh Mackenzie I know isn't a drinking man."

"No," said Billy. "Dad ain't." And they both laughed.

Henry Kroner had shifted to the near corner of the bar where he sat half-smiling with two fingers just touching the base of his glass.

"Why do you call him Hen-rick," whispered Billy.

"*Heinrich*," said Reilly. "That's his proper name. He likes to be called Henry so I take the mickey out of him."

"A Dutchman?"

"One of the Kaiser's crowd."

"Ah," said Billy. Then: "Who's the Kaiser?"

"He's the boss cocky of Germany."

The girl from the veranda poked her head through the servery.

"Is Dad there?"

"Dad?" Her dark eyes startled him.

"You're the one for the room. Come on!"

"My daughter," explained Reilly, pointing to the door. "She won't wait around."

The girl was standing in the foyer with her arms embracing his swag. His hat dangled from a free finger.

"My name's Frances. What's yours?"

Billy was reminded of a face that peered invitingly from the family's *Arabian Nights*. Even the shawl fitted.

"William," he said clumsily, "Billy. Billy Mackenzie."

"Billy big-ears," said the girl, and giggled.

On the first landing she stopped and chatted about the "turmoil" of life in Forbes and how this was an oddly quiet night. "We get everyone here, all the best quality." Billy kept close behind as she climbed the remaining stairs, noting how fully-shaped she was, sweeping her bottom from side to side like a woman. She was fifteen, probably sixteen, with smooth white skin against the lace of her collar and the smell of scented soap drifting around.

An elderly couple passed them, the woman steadying one heavy-booted foot in the air before

25

planting it with a crash on the stair. Her white haired husband guided her. "Good evening your honour, and Mrs Ward," said Frances, arching over the bannister to let them pass. But as soon as their backs were turned she poked out her tongue.

The upstairs corridor was gloomy and deserted. Frances led the way to the end door and fumbled with the key. The chance of putting his arms right round her presented itself now, but instead Billy found himself merely running the palm of his hand under her shawl and up her bare arm.

Nothing happened.

She stood there, not looking at him, her fingers on the iron key and the swag still clutched tightly. So he closed his fingers around the lace on her upper arm because there was nowhere else to go, sensing the chill of her response but needing all of a sudden to resolve something that stretched a long way past the rush of his desire.

"You must never mistake good will for anything else," she muttered, and with that the door swung open and she almost fell inside — throwing the swag on the bed and turning up the lamp, unclipping the outside double doors.

"That's it. Dinner's on till seven-thirty."

Billy moved to the centre of the room while Frances, smiling, backed onto the veranda.

"You get a splendid view of the town from up here." Just enough light remained to pick out phantom shapes. A corrugated iron stable peered from the lane, its rickety yards formed by uneven logs. The post office opposite was a substantial white-painted stone building.

Yabbie howled from the yard and Frances shivered:

26

"It's getting cold."

Then a shape stirred in the post office's recessed doorway. A woman. She seemed to be keeping watch on the front door of the hotel, and as she shifted position Billy saw that she wore a yellow dress and held something dark over one arm, a coat or a blanket. A dark woman, an Aborigine.

"Who's that down there?"

"Where?"

Before he could point her out Frances darted away through his room and down the corridor.

For a while, before he washed and changed for dinner, the odour of Frances's scented soap lingered in the room. Before going downstairs he kicked the wall angrily and then sat on the bed for a minute and laughed. Thinking about things might have helped someone else, but not Billy. If he acted, and the result went against him, he could only act again.

"You're good at this waitering caper," said Billy at dinner.

"Waitressing," Frances corrected, and primly set his things down. "It's just for the holidays. Next week I'll be back at St. Catherine's."

"I didn't know you were Catholics," said Billy with relief. He felt less stupid. Small wonder she had confused him. He could never fathom a Catholic.

"I'm not." Without explaining she went on: "There's a choice of vegetable soup or liver and bacon to start, but you can have both if you want to."

"Both."

A male voice at his shoulder made him jump: "How

27

do you like the food?" The silverware tinkled as Mr Reilly bumped the table with his stomach. "Nothing for me, dear," he called to Frances. "And how do you like our Franny?" he asked. "A happy girl."

Billy smelt whisky.

"Her mother insists on the city." He leaned forward, revealing tufts of unshaven beard in the dents of his face. "The bush doesn't agree with her — too hot in summer, too cold in winter." Mr Reilly lifted a piece of meat from Billy's plate and dropped it whole into his mouth. "Franny's going to have looks. I'll need to be on my guard against fellows like you," and he reached across to rap a finger on Billy's chest. "You're not a Catholic, are you?"

Billy made a noise with his mouth full.

"That's a good thing, a Catholic Mackenzie."

"I never said I was."

But Reilly was on his feet, swaying.

"I may not see you in the morning." They shook hands. "Tell your father you ate with Pat Reilly, eh?" He straightened chairs across the room as he left, shouldering aside the glass doors with a thump.

Frances was at his elbow tidying up. "You mustn't mind Dad."

"He reckons I'm a danger," he grinned.

"What to?"

"Ar," he looked up from a preoccupation with the sugar bowl, "to you."

"Dad's awfully good at running this hotel though you'd never think so sometimes. But he doesn't know the first thing about what a girl thinks, or why she thinks what she thinks. Do you?"

Billy played with the sugar bowl until she lifted it out of his hands.

"No-one's a danger to me," she concluded with kindness. "Do you understand?"

Then she spoke to him in a dream. The situation was exactly the same — dining room, Frances's black hair spilling down towards the waist of her starched pinny — and the words were the same too, except that Arnie Scott's widow was sitting at the table as well. When Frances asked, "Do you understand?" Mrs Scott said, "Of course he understands, my dear. I've been wife and mother to Arnie Scott and he knows it. Now don't you think you've been silly enough?" With that Billy felt intensely relieved. In the shifting planes of his dream he found himself tilted out of the dining room and poised on the crest of a wave, he *was* the wave, swaying backwards and forwards, ready to swoop down and run foaming along a human beach which suddenly was the naked body of Frances.

But why was Yabbie howling endlessly at the far reach of everything?

Damn!

He rolled out of bed and stood naked in the cold room, wide awake, his erection standing out like a stick. The municipal gaslamps threw planks of artificial moonlight on the wall. Yabbie now yap-yapped, holding at bay whatever she'd howled at earlier. As he dressed he heard the rattle of a distant window and a male voice cutting through the angry bark.

In the corridor the polished boards shone like water below the night lamps at either end. Someone coughed in the bowels of the hotel — the old German. And light flickered from under the door of the bar, though it must have been two in the morning. At the foot of the stairs Billy paused and heard a muffled conversation. "A thousand pounds," it was Reilly's voice; and another laughed: "That's between the four of us." Then Billy went outside to find Yabbie circling excitedly at the end of her chain.

"What is it, girl?"

The woman in the yellow dress was crouched against the wall of the stable.

"That's a mean dog, she wouldn't let me past."

"What are you doing here anyway?"

"Waitin'."

Billy knelt and stroked Yabbie's muzzle until she quietened, then walked across to where the woman squatted. She was barefooted and slightly built, just a girl. He could see she was terrified.

"Who're you waitin' for?" he softly asked.

"A friend."

"Any friend, eh?"

"You've got me wrong." She was close enough for Billy to see her eyes defiantly holding his in the cold starlight. "Peter Crane's in there doing business with Mr Reilly."

"Peter Crane?" said Billy in a bullying tone. "There ain't no such person." But he knew him by sight — a middle aged dairy farmer who lived alone on the flats near the river. The girl was very young, perhaps only fourteen, and pretty enough too. Billy tried to touch her but she drew back.

"Come in the grass with me."

"You don't understand. I'm just waitin'."

"Then wait along with me," Billy fiercely told her. He reached out and touched her breast, which was like re-entering the dream of minutes before. Everything that had then seemed possible now came to life.

"Don't do it, boss." Though she threatened to call out he twisted her arm and forced her down a grassy corridor between two outbuildings. The grass was long, thickly matted as a nest. When they reached a deep pool of shadow against the fence Billy put his arm around her neck, pushed himself hard against her, and forced her down into the icy grass. She gave a breathless whimper as she fell, landing on all fours. Billy dropped with her.

Now there was her blanket caught up in things, sometimes shifting under an elbow and sometimes not there at all, and a strangely wordless struggle which at first was with the yellow dress, then with bones and hard lumps of earth that gradually acquired flesh, and finally, rising above the cold smell of ashes from a nearby rubbish pile, a soft darkness that seemed to spread across the entire landscape, muffling the frost, the town, the entire continent underneath him as Billy pushed and the girl hissed with hatred through clenched teeth.

Then it was very cold.

Billy stood and pulled up his trousers at the same time. He found a half-crown piece folded in his ten shilling note. He wanted to obliterate her.

"*Thanks,* mister." She tossed the coin back.

Billy looked away and spat. The girl followed him into the open. A window rattled shut, a tin roof thumped in the cold, and far away a catfight erupted and as suddenly ceased.

"You go home." But the girl started to move in the direction of the hotel. "Not that way." He pushed her towards the back lane, but she objected.

"My place is through there."

"Not tonight it ain't." Again he pushed her and again she stepped sullenly forward.

So he punched her on the mouth.

"Do what I say."

A smudge of blood widened on her lower lip. She sat down in a heap and lowered her head to the ground. Yabbie, who all this time had been quiet, jangled her chain and Billy walked over to pat her. When he looked up, the girl was trotting down the drive and out the back gate.

Billy climbed the stairs carrying his boots. When he reached the first landing the door of the bar opened and he saw Reilly stare up at him through the gloom.

3
The Girl on the Night Mail

"A man can't help feeling attached to a place," Mr Gilchrist began, and spoke to the rhythm of the sulky's lurching, "with all the work I've put into it, and grandpa too. Y'see that old box tree? There was a swarm of bees there last spring." Walter saw six trees at once, but Douggie piped a muffled "I can" from his pile of blankets. "Wally, when Pa started it was just for the stock. Then me. I was part of the place. We knew the blacks here for a bit. They camped on this corner. Now how come you feel like you do, and want to get off what we've made? The bank owns a lot of the places around here. But not us. They'd need a hundred bullocks to root me out."

Walter grasped at the similarity: "It's the same for me."

"Then what's all the carry on?"

"Dad," and he risked the truth, silly as it sounded: "The difference is I could go away, and still be like you."

"I can't spot that. No sir." His father turned to him in the dark, bitter tobacco and the warm stink of spittle forcing Walter to gulp a quiet breath and hold it. "The point is you've got to go on a bit. How old are you now? Ideas are all right, but work," he concluded, "it brands something in that wasn't there. Or brands it deeper if it was. You have to find out for sure. What do you say? Your mother says yes to the university, y'know. But not yet. We want to give Douggie a couple more years away at school. Two or three, then if you're still in the same frame of mind you can go off. That's fair."

At the station Douggie called: "Hey! There's Billy."

Under the station lamps Walter felt exposed: he had none of the grit of his old man.

"I won't wait. I know you'll do well. Behave yourself on the train, boy."

Well, that's ended, Walter thought. He thudded the cases to the ground, the sulky grated off into darkness, and Billy whistled him over.

"Back to school with the kid, I see."

"He's on his own from now on," said Walter, thrusting his brother's case into his hand and giving him a push past Ozzie Deep at the ticket barrier.

Billy's riding boots were polished like apples. He wore a dark jacket and freshly-laundered moleskins.

"I thought you were fetching sheep?"

"Got 'em. I've only just cleaned up." Billy extended white scrubbed hands, which were trembling.

Ozzie Deep the porter punched Walter's ticket with scrupulous slowness, saying "Oi" and sparring with his ticket punch at the ready when Walter tipped his cap over his eyes — an exchange carried through ritually at the end of every holiday. Away from Ozzie, Billy suddenly became agitated, guiding Walter past the crowd and nudging him into a cul-de-sac of wicker baskets.

"Wally," he looked around for eavesdroppers, "there's a Mick girl on the train going back to school. Will you do something for me? Willya? When the bloody train gets in I'll introduce you." He cleared his throat. "This is the drill: when you get on the train ask her if she likes me."

"Who says she'll even talk to me?"

Suddenly the train hissed and clanked along the platform. Billy shouted: "When you get to Sydney write me a bloody letter. If she don't shape up, I won't care!"

The fireman on the footplate stared at him. A carpet of steam rose from the platform, warming them, clinging like cotton to their clothes, leaving them damp and chilled.

Walter saw her first, from behind. How did he know for sure? He *knew*.

"That's her," said Billy.

The train was still moving, but the girl stepped to the platform and ran a couple of feet before slowing to a walk. When she turned around Walter wondered why Billy was so interested in her.

She seemed quite ordinary. Her eyes were very dark, her hair black and unshining. Her nose was rather big.

She saw Billy and raised a hand.

"There she is," said Billy again, as though the two views of the girl had been aspects of different people. He set off along the platform and Walter followed.

"Isn't it cold." When she hugged herself Walter could see her body outlined under the overlarge St. Catherine's jacket and skirt.

Billy launched into introductions. As he spoke, Walter felt amusement dart from the girl: amusement at Billy, at the cold air, at being a castaway on the next town's station platform, alone and so young.

She was more attractive than Walter had at first thought, though he could not see in what way. Her nose seemed even bigger from the side. When she laughed she finished by drawing in her lower lip in a half-nervous, half-irrepressible way.

"I'd better climb back or they'll leave me behind. We couldn't have that," she said to Billy, holding his eye for a sober second. Then she swung herself up the two steps in a movement that left Billy stranded. Too late he whipped his hands from his pockets, then jammed them away again in frustration, for he had intended not merely to help her up, but also to squeeze her elbow and watch her face for a sign.

"Don't forget," hissed Billy. Walter found himself propelled aloft, with his suitcase skidding in behind.

"Half a mo', where's Douggie?"

"I saw him further back. *Hey Douggie!*" shouted Billy, and gave a thumbs up. "He's safe."

As Walter hoisted his suitcase overhead the compartment's other occupant spoke: "What a racket!"

"Oh, Mrs Stinson," apologized Frances. Walter scooped up a black-gloved hand.

"We're in for a cold trip," said the old lady, who sat almost submerged in blankets and cushions presided over by several chins the colour of orange cake. "Give the heater a shake, like a good boy." Her pearl-studded slippers, flashing green under the gaslamps, slipped from the footwarmer which Walter then rolled and waddled around the floor to agitate the chemicals.

Frances withdrew while the guard shouted "stand back" and thick wood — broad as the door of a cold-room — shut them in. But all the coldness was outside.

Billy was being left behind. He paced the carriage for a few feet and then slowed and stopped. He raised his hand — a dignified salute — looking glum. He slid backwards with all the other bits and pieces on the platform — the wicker baskets in their untidy stacks, empty luggage trolleys, milk cans, the black and silver platform scales, the dirty moon of the station clock. He was overtaken by two railway clerks with thumbs in waistcoat pockets, by a signalman lowering his lamp from an arm-high position to place it at his feet, by half-lit bushes at the end of the platform, by the blackness beyond.

As they turned from the window Walter and Frances caught each other's eye. The glance lasted half a second before Walter fell-to brushing soot from his knees and straightening his tie.

Mrs Stinson sighed and hummed: "I was a bride in Melbourne and a bride in Forbes, and widow in both places too." She spoke these words to Frances while addressing something like a cackle to Walter. "Us Victorians — but goodness, it's forty years since I left Ballarat. We outlast the men. We leave 'em behind: remember that —"

"I've got plenty of time," Walter spoke directly to the old lady, raising his voice, "though I'm going on for nineteen."

"When it's too late you'll want to spend it. My cushion, dear boy. Up a little. Across. Push it *down*." He almost fell, grabbing the luggage rack, when with a fleeting upward dart she bestowed a powdery kiss.

"She likes you." The old lady was instantly asleep, but her octogenarian authority prevailed. "I feel sorry for men," Frances relaxed in her seat, "there's so much duty for them."

"Look," Walter said, "Billy asked me — if I'd keep you company."

"Really?" She shifted away from Mrs Stinson,

leaning a shoulder on the glass, confronting Walter with unsmiling directness. "I don't know him all that well. We only met once. Did he really say that? I wish people wouldn't try to run my life for me."

It was then, right at that moment, that his idea of her changed. This was when it started, the murmur of sensation that was to accompany him all night, then for months, years — it began with her manner, then her voice, her withheld opinions, then the opinions themselves opening out, then his hunger for everything about her — open-mouthed.

"I shouldn't have done what he said. I shouldn't have joined you, eh?"

"Oh, no. I didn't mean you. How could I? I meant — everyone else." She was suddenly amused again. "Except Mrs Stinson. She's so old nothing bothers her. There's nothing she doesn't know — about people, that is. Do you like people?"

He had never considered it.

"I sometimes think people and art are all that matters."

"Art?"

"I mean the theatre. Bernard Shaw. Shakespeare." She had never seen any, but *Twelfth Night* was coming up. "Adeline Genée." She described the "wheatsheaf" adagio, in which the star pirouetted within the embrace of her partner's arms, yet so exactly on the one spot that he never really touched her.

"That's art all right."

"Mrs Stinson was on the stage," Frances whispered, suggesting an intensely important past which the old lady confirmed by her physical attitude, nodding monumentally under the rugs which descended in a dark masonry of lumps and folds. "She sings beautifully." Walter stared respectfully at the sleeping figure. Such achievements alarmed his Presbyterian soul a little, but if Frances saw her as grand so would he.

Now Frances was preoccupied, searching for a handkerchief, wetting her lips with a curved tongue, blinking. Her half turned face revealed a shining corner of eye, a clear curve of cheekbone, a mouth poised to speak lucidly — Walter thought — for an entire self.

"I've got a coal in my eye," she mumbled.

She twisted a corner of handkerchief and used the window as a mirror. "Nearly . . .", tugging her lower lid to reveal a reddened hollow, running the handkerchief along a blood-coloured edge. Walter, reclining on an elbow, could see Mrs Stinson's reflection past Frances's doubled head. The old lady seemed to be sitting far outside the train.

"There."

Frances held out the rolled up handkerchief like a wand, with a black speck visible on the wet tip of cloth.

"Billy told Dad he was a Catholic, but I knew better." Frances settled back in her seat and smiled a level somehow mocking smile.

"Did you like him?"

After hurling the question at Frances he peered out the window, cupping a hand over his eyes to disown any but the mildest interest in her reply. "He's a bit of a —", he paused, looking from the window to Frances and back again, blowing mist on the glass, attempting to smear Billy out of favour. "I don't know —"

"I'm not sure I like him. He's very direct." She shot a glance at the slumped heap that was Mrs Stinson, and whispered: "He tried to kiss me."

"Oh."

"He only tried. Beery men have tried before."

Walter felt impossibly clean and young in his newly pressed and odourless school outfit. "We were at school together," he caught Frances's view of Billy and tried to worsen it, "primary school. He left early."

But Frances talked on: "Something else happened." Now she peered out the window herself, blowing an oval of mist, erasing it line by line with a gloved finger. The train slowed through a long curve before entering a tunnel. "He and Dad were friendly enough at dinner, but the next morning Dad was angry with him." Her voice trailed. "Something horrible happened. I don't know what."

With a gulp the compartment filled with noise and they were in the tunnel. Frances prepared to shout the beginnings of an explanation and then thought better of it. She unfolded her travelling rug and arranged it on her lap. The overhead lamps wasted away as blue licks of flame guttered in the mantles. She dropped her shoes to the floor and tucked her feet under the rug. Walter fetched his own rug from the luggage rack, in the process leaning over her. Sleepily she readjusted her position and bumped him on the knee. "Sorry," she mouthed. Goose-bumps climbed the inside of his leg. Deep ahead the engine puffed breathlessly through constricted space. The wheels ground and squeaked, the air swirled and peppered them with soot. Frances huddled into herself, the blanket crept higher. Walter gazed at dark lashes on pale skin, at hands in an oddly formal clasp peering from a gap of blanket, at a hump formed by swaying knees.

Abruptly they slid from stuffy darkness onto a frosted upland. The silence after the underground roar was almost complete: a faint click-click of wheels, a murmur of movement — that was all. The effect was of bodiless gliding across vast sheets of phosphorescent water. The women slept and Walter sat guarding them — he was happy. Whenever he opened his eyes — Frances. Billy receded to a tiny dot under a remote pool of light on Parkes station, which then sank below the horizon.

At a late, indeterminate hour Walter woke again. He listened for a while to the knock of steel on steel. The figures of Frances and the old lady were like exhibits of exhausted life in a museum, making the same repeated movements — the tremble of a chin, the sway of a loose strand of hair — over and over as though controlled by a system of rods and wires.

When Walter woke at five in the morning clusters of houses, mysterious candleflame, dived at the train and drifted back into obscurity. Occasionally a light flashed in the distance keeping pace for a few minutes before looping behind. With a premonitory rattle of windows and then a loud bang a dark goods train rushed past. The cold of the outside world had now completely taken over from the airless cold of the compartment. Icy air slipped through hidden crevices in the floor. Walter stood and stamped his feet, rubbed his hands and hitched his blanket more securely around his shoulders. As he did so he noticed that Frances's blanket had slipped, so he slowly drew it up again, daring her not to wake. He stayed looking at her face: and suddenly she woke. Her black shining eyes stared as though she had been awake all along behind carved lids.

41

"Thanks."

He was close enough to feel the puff of breath that formed the word, a sweet-smelling association of saliva and warmed air. "That was kind of you," she said in the next breath, while his heart pounded.

"Oh, I'm stiff," Mrs Stinson spoke from her corner, "and freezing cold." She thumped herself into a new position. The tail-end of Frances's gaze disappeared into a secret hiding place that closed over. "Nobody will sleep now that I'm awake," commanded the old lady. She revealed a florid capability that had not been visible the night before, pointing to her hamper on the luggage rack and directing Walter to fetch it down. "Let's have breakfast!" The giggle of her youth had aged to a hum of glee.

They picnicked.

Walter displayed a vast appetite.

Mrs Stinson talked. All she did was babble about the district and town, yet with little thrusts of comment she accentuated their differing backgrounds: commercial and pastoral, Catholic and Protestant (though here Frances revealed that she wasn't a "real" Catholic, it was her father), their difference in age, their geographical separation. Her talk of marriages made Frances seem more desirable but remoter than ever. Walter's gloomy disposition wove a meaning that for the old lady was not there at all. "Men are never what you expect," she finished, "it's the best and worst thing about 'em." Walter remembered afterwards how Frances had looked at him then. But no rescue was possible — the grey dawn nailed his isolation down in unadventurous light as the train slid through Redfern.

What should he say to Frances? "I'm sorry I ate so much," he said, and immediately cursed himself. "I enjoyed the trip."

"Thanks for keeping us company," she smiled.

"Perhaps we could — ?" Walter heard himself talking through cotton wool. He wanted to say something about the Christmas holidays, but at Central a tall nun with half a dozen St Catherine's girls swept along the platform. What could be said that would not take minutes even to get started on? The girls carried her away.

4
Theatre

"The Duke was a bore."

"Fran!"

"I'm all for excitement and impulse." Frances tied
the belt of her seventeenth birthday present, a kimono,
and perched on a stool.

"So am I. But Antonio, how could you have liked
him?" Diana consulted her *Twelfth Night* programme,
"A sea-captain." Through the dressing table mirror she
watched Frances uncap a jar of Mrs Reilly's face cream,
then pegged her flannelette nightdress out like a tent
and collapsed inside it. "I'm all for the mind."

She flopped on her back and bicycled somewhat
stocky calves. "I can see through you, Franny. It was
just the actor, you babbled about him all the way to the
ferry."

"Harcourt Beatty is an artist."

"Would you really run off with — Antonio?"

"For a night or two."

"Fran!"

"I'm old enough." And Diana squeaked again.

While spreading clots of face cream Frances asked:
"How old is the Maharanee of Tikari?"

"The same as you. No, a year younger."

"The Maharanee of Tikari," Frances read from the
folded *Herald*, "danced a cakewalk with her father and
then with her bright engaging Indian secretary Miss
Knighton."

"I say."

"But," Frances's all-white face looked ghastly as she turned to raise a finger, "finally she danced with Mr Niblo."

"Mr Niblo."

"Upstairs," dared Frances, masked and reckless.

"Stop!"

"*In bed.*" That was the finish.

Later when the lights were out they talked again.

"Fran? Do you know what they do?"

"Niblos and Maharanees? Oh, Di. I thought you were all for the mind?"

"I am." A longer silence, then: "Remember when Olivia says wilt-though-go-to-bed-Malvolio? I know what happens."

So Frances breathlessly asked the ceiling: "How?"

Her father, a captain at Victoria Barracks, and her mother, Diana explained, were just mad some nights about getting to bed early. She and her brother could see everything through the big iron keyhole. Some of these things Frances had guessed. How could it be otherwise? But the tangled clash of anatomy, the fever, the uncouth cries, the extension and the parting of skin and the mounting clamour of ecstasy — she felt tumbled and tossed in the same process, for Diana had spared nothing, shocking them both to silence.

When the clock below chimed midnight Diana said, "Fran? Are you awake?"

Frances had been thinking of candid modern girls in books. How astonishing that Diana, not Frances herself, might be like them.

"Fran? Are we still friends?"

In the morning they ate a late breakfast while Mrs Reilly went to church with Harry Crowell.

"I'll bet Adeline Genée's got a lover," stated Diana.

"She's impossibly dedicated — she says." Frances scraped her chair, curtsied, and danced Genée's part around the sunlit kitchen: first to fifth positions, pointing in first and second positions, fourth position on the points, adagio, watching or seeing ("Where's Mum and Harry?"), listening pose ("What's Harry saying to Mum now?"), fingers to eyes, fingers to ears. How silly!

"That's your future!" clapped Diana.

"You're just saying it." Frances was puffed. "Anyway — I want to be — more serious." She sat again at the table.

"What's this?"

"More serious." Frances saw herself as she spoke: flushed, sounding false. "Even Genée, I know she's supposed to be a great artist, but she's not, is she? That's only what the papers say."

"She says it too."

"The trouble is I can't *do* anything. Look at my dance." She flapped a hand dismissively. "Why is Genée spending all this time in Australia if she really is great? I should stick to the piano."

Diana floated her pink face over the shattered eggshells and stared: "Do you ever feel, vaguely, that you're *bound* to do something in the end? Fated?"

"Why, yes."

"Do you ever feel, whatever comes, that bad things are going to happen to other people, but not to you?"

"Yes I do." She looked at Diana respectfully. Then with suspicion.

"That you're special. Really special?"

"Mmm. Now for the catch."

"There isn't one. It's just that everyone feels like that, up to a point. We might or we mightn't, *you* might or you mightn't. Nature wants us to try. It's one of the tricks of evolution."

"What do you think personally? About me."

Diana peered into her tea leaves: "I see a man, a handsome squatter from the western plains, broad verandas — wait! — here he comes, leather leggings, moustache — crikey, that's bad — he's not even taking them off."

"What?"

"The leggings."

"This started seriously."

Diana lowered the cup. "I'll be someone's governess, or a nun, eh?" She smiled sourly. "Sister Bernadette thought I was plain enough to be a nun."

"They wanted that for all of us. Anyway you're not plain."

"You'll be a wife, Fran."

Sometimes Diana was too disappointingly realistic. Yet in all this Frances saw her friend's defences: the moats and walls of an intelligent girl who considered herself unattractive, though she wasn't.

"Let's go for a walk," Frances suggested. Arm in arm, their diverging destinies reunited. Both wore button-up boots, long dark skirts, wide sleeved cotton blouses and straw hats with the brims tipped back: they might have been sisters. In the park Frances ran ahead to untangle a small boy's kite from a bush, becoming friendly enough in the end to send him off with a kiss — at which Diana laughed. When two young men passed and lifted their hats (but really, they seemed more interested in each other: some men were), Frances muttered "smile, smile" through a tortured mouth while Diana reddened. After a while they settled themselves on a bench near the water and listened to the smack of wavelets.

"I love it here," said Frances, conscious of using the same phrase every time she came. She believed Sydney Harbour to be a concentration of desirable — or bearable — Australianness: grand houses among gum trees, the glittering antipodean sunlight on desperately deep green water, all within sight of art galleries, theatres, institutes of music, literature, and languages. Here the freight of Europe was unloaded and displayed for the first time: hats and gowns, books, plays, dances, songs. And ideas. Diana, who was "all mind" no longer, had first interested her in talking about imponderables.

"Di," she heard herself saying, "aren't we fools?"

"Speak for yourself." Diana the botanist scrutinized a tuft of banksia blossom.

"Do you think we're just meant for men?"

"In natural respects, yes. Or them for us." Down corkscrewed the blossom.

"What a complication other people are."

"Oh, yes." Now Diana sighed, seeing her multitude of eagerly pursued scientific rules float into society where they lost their power. In this resided a bitter magic. She cursed the way underlying rules were no help in dealing with the phenomena they sprang from.

"I think Harry likes Mum."

"It's plain."

"How pathetic. He's reached the age, Mum says, when people feel sorry for a man."

"He's kind of sapless." They giggled, and glanced back through the park because church was well and truly over.

"Boccaccio! Boccaccio!" sang Frances, alluding to the Mosman Musical Society's production, in which Harry had played a stockinged, floppy-hatted, rather wet Leonetto, despite his muscular torso.

"*Nulli Secundus!*" boomed Diana, the motto of the Alexander School of Arms and Physical Culture where Harry "toned up". They had rendezvoused with him at its door the night of *The Devil's Disciple,* Harry rouge-red from a vapour bath, and he had spoken of the atmosphere of "airy persiflage" with which his "fellow-scholars of Hercules" tackled their tasks. Frances had tripped along behind holding her nose, while her mother and Diana flanked and flattered him.

Walking back to the house Frances suddenly thought of Walter Gilchrist. Diana knew all about Billy and the attempted kiss, she'd known right from the start of term; and she knew about Walter too. "He's respectful," Frances had said, "but dull."

"Oh gosh," now in the middle of everything Frances jerked to a stop and bit her fingers. "He was there!"

"Where? Who?"

"Walter Gilchrist was at the play." She saw again the frizzy-headed youth who had twice turned and stared at her during the brief interval before the last act.

"Remember?"

"Me? Why should I?"

Frances again reviewed the train trip. He could have been — was! — handsome. On the train he had seemed boyish, angular, unformed. But his stare at the theatre really had cut through her. She had felt it as the steely investigation of a stranger. No words, no polite concessions: a cut so deep that only now, twelve hours later, did it arrive on her nerves.

"Piffle," said Diana at the gate.

Frances creaked the hinges back and forth. "Mrs Stinson wanted me to like him."

"Is that important?" Diana disliked Mrs Stinson. The old lady had too much time for Frances. "Franny, you blow so hot and cold I can't keep up."

"Here's the remarkable pair!" beamed Harry as Frances and Diana burst through the door. The girls quizzed him, why "remarkable"? one on either side, elbows on table, faces mockingly up-close, while Mrs Reilly dispensed cold meat and tomatoes, relish, bread, butter, and thick-lipped teacups. She bubbled, a thin woman, brown, still with her daughter's very black hair: "Yes Harry, you'll have to tell them."

"Why, you'll take on anyone, gods and kings." For a moment his chair rocked backwards as he withdrew from their gaze.

"Tell us about your God, Harry."

"Frances," warned her mother from the pantry, but without force.

"Describe him," urged Diana.

"How could I? He's more, you know, everywhere."

"Like the wind? You're one of us!"

"A pantheist," said Diana.

"If I could put my finger on it I'd tell you."

"Has he ever spoken to you?"

"Or you to him?"

Diana giggled, spraying flecks of pink tomato on her white plate.

Mrs Reilly cleared her throat. "Harry's God lives in England, eh Harry?" She meant to be kind.

"Now that's unfair." He pointed his knife, not miffed but welcoming mature debate. "I've a great admiration for the English. Which of us here isn't scrubbed by John Bull's brush, heh?"

"We're Irish," Frances asserted, choosing her father's side of the family.

"We're — Italian!" announced Diana, choosing her great-grandfather's.

"Seriously," asked Frances after a break. "Why is England superior?" She believed it herself, everyone did, but resented Harry's bumbling arguments.

"You ask me?" Now, excitedly, the pointing knife swung in his own direction. Butter smeared his waistcoat. "Without England, all of this" — he indicated the harbour which glittered through three of six windows — "might be French or German or Chinese!"

During the baked custard Harry suddenly stopped eating. "You girls don't like me, do you." He held up a hand against their protests, "No" — folding his napkin, "Mrs Reilly" — scraping his chair and stiffly bowing, "I'd better be off, what-ho?" — making a last brave exit which Mrs Reilly pursued.

They were ages at the gate. When Mrs Reilly came back she sat the girls down.

"The world is full of Harrys. He means well, but you can't expect him to be — intellectual."

Her choice of word flattered them.

"What can't stand must give way." Frances used Diana's phrase (from Evolution), though Diana wouldn't have dared it herself, not at the moment.

"No — " Diana wanted peace. She stirred the pages of an encyclopaedia, head down.

"He's mushy as wet bread."

"That's Franny's cruel streak," said her mother, dealing coolly with a fact.

Standing with her back to the room Frances looked at the harbour; Diana sat stranded between the forces of loyalty and those of politeness; Mrs Reilly, after her pronouncement, toyed with objects in the room — examined a painted glass vase, straightened a picture, plumped cushions. Then she raised the heavy shell of the piano lid and pounded (to Diana's ears) a set of heavy scales. "Schubert," she smiled. At first the notes seemed of the same length, firmness, colour, but they altered as they ascended, reaching a point where the lunch and its aftermath were taken care of — shaved flat, shaped anew, and distributed to the floor, the walls, the ceilings of a house made over again, bearing no trace of dissension.

Hearing her mother play reconciled Frances to their differences. One mother retreated, the cloudy one, another advanced, the beautiful one: clear as her vases. The familiar Schubert impromptus did this, with their hesitations, their rollicking advances. And then the way Mum started again, Schubert started again — art started again! — swirling the tiny coloured pieces of the world's vast jigsaw-puzzle into their correct positions. A cloud here, there the churned wake of a ferry — but soon the notes alone inhabited Frances's head and she stopped thinking. She bobbed on a phrase, then stroked elatedly up harbour-reaches of sound to a place where emotion needed no object to fix on, but simply was.

At four thirty Amos Hart came, a man more to their taste: solid as cedar, and intelligent under his uncomplicated manner. Monday being a holiday Diana was to stay on. Music had transformed their inner clashes, and seemed effective on the world as well: the late afternoon glowed deep as a domed jelly, now with lime and lemon, later with raspberry and the sunken port wine colours of evening.

Amos was a traveller for a brewery, and had just come from Forbes where Pat Reilly had entertained him.

"How was the menu?" asked Frances, who was able to conjure the mood of the kitchen, the shape of a day at the Albion, from the conjunction of entrée and main course, main course and pudding, pudding and its accompanying sauce.

"As good as ever, but Mavis," said Amos, "is not so good."

"Her heart," Frances whispered to Diana, who had heard countless stories of the Albion's saintly cook.

"Now here's the worst news about her, "not the heart, but her old man. He just can't get work, and it's killing him. Mavis has to find for all six kids and she won't take a scrap from the hotel unless Pat forces it on her."

"He'd have to," Frances agreed. She loved Mavis, the warm slab of her body shuffling round the kitchen in slippers which she wrapped in newspaper and tucked beside the stove ready for the next day, the pink leather of her cheeks — above all Frances loved her good will, her unwillingness to be drawn, her slow refusal to be unkind — even when pecked. You couldn't argue with Mavis, or even talk to her much. But the kitchen would be cold and practical without her: the objects there took on warmth, the scrubbed wooden handles she gripped, her particular care with knives, her chair and fraying cushion. Mavis counted, not to millions, but to her flock of children and her unlucky husband alone. Amos had seen the husband on the river road, axe on shoulder, a dray of shingles grating along behind. Mavis counted to the hotel too, but not momentously. Outside her family the world dived into darkness. Were the true saints those who never would be? No-one ever saw Mavis coming to work at five in the morning through frost leaving a hot breakfast at home for her family, few even saw her at nine at night heading back, a boulder of a woman in a man's over-coat. Frances had caught her during her siesta on the daybed off the storeroom, panting like a dog at the end of a chase, and talked to her there. And it seemed that Mavis alone held the secret of goodness, closing her fingers around Frances's unblemished wrist, gripping it for the blunt duration of a breath, saying, "Dear, don't you never think I'm unhappy." That was the only thing that ever passed between them, except for kitchen talk. Her burden showed up her goodness, and she treasured it, otherwise there would have been no test; and she thanked Frances with those few words for her recognition of the virtue that floweres in rough places. Frances needed her own test — longed for it — but it would occur a thousand miles from Mavis's. It would have colour, romance, display, those things for sure. Certainly no silence. Stubbornness? But for setting-out, not for digging-in. Kindness? Now Frances reached difficult ground.

She looked at her mother, at Diana, at the solid shape of Amos Hart as he talked. They don't realize how worthless I am, she thought, these people who love me. Yet there was no self-condemnation in this feeling of worthlessness. It was a practical inadequacy — a mark of the distance ahead. Under everything Frances argued her way towards an outcome in which she would have pride. And the world — it must! — would spin its head around to take a look.

5
Shadows

Examinations were over: Walter had taken his last
tram ride from school. In the luggage room at Central
station, dumping his bags, he thought of a momentous
act to suit his circumstances — a lightning trip to
Cremorne Point to say hello to Frances Reilly. He had
two hours to kill, why not? But he bought a pie and a
cup of tea and leaned on the counter, numbly alone,
denying the warming impulse to go. By the time he
finished he had reduced the thought by ridicule.
Months ago at the theatre she had ignored him. He did
not exist.

On arrival that night he had nervously scanned the
audience, knowing she would be there, but then the
flute and drum began, the lights dipped, and the curtain
split open: and Walter had gasped (as Buck the English
master said he would) at those walls of pastel brick, the
arbour of velvet roses, and stiff clouds floating across a
fabric sky. The stage world was soft as a cushion:
people when they sneaked on were gentle, their feet
made no noise — only a whisper now and then, and a
timbery thud when they leapt: the land of Illyria had
been all female, and it instructed him.

Then, in the brief interval before Act Five, Walter
saw her. He'd been looking for a St Catherine's
uniform — but she wore blue velvet, looking somehow
sunken and younger than he'd remembered. He stared

across twelve rows and their gazes linked. He tried again after half a minute and by God she must have seen! Buck elbowed him, so he stopped, thankful for the fading lights and the stir of programmes. Darkness dissolved his alarm that hundreds of faces had seen him turn, and must have whispered to their companions about his predicament.

When he looked again, at the end, she had gone.

The Sunday after the play he had decided to write the promised letter to Billy. He told him everything, filling three pages with a blunt confession. But long before the end he knew the letter was not for posting. Still, he wrote furiously for his own benefit. How had it helped? It was like scratching at hives. During prep he'd smoothed the letter out, then screwed it up, compacting it like a stone, and thrust it deep in a pocket. It would never have done for anyone to find it, this erotic concentration, there in the senior's room or anywhere. After the letter he'd attempted calculus — hopeless — and opened Guerber's *Myths* for history revision, then flung it closed, but wait, there (he cut back to the page that caught his eye): "Diomedes, King of Thrace, a cruel and eccentric prince, was wont to feed his horses upon human flesh. The Eighth Labour of Herakles was to obtain and bring to Eurystheus these famous though fierce animals. This he accomplished ..." Walter's mind stuck on the strange words, now momentarily lucid, spoken by Mr Fox at the Parkes Show: "From Eurystheus I come." He took out the letter and unwrinkled it.

But suddenly the letter's heat had gone. Walter's

words were the scratch-marks of prodigal emotions lying in the shadow of something greater. Out in the darkness Mr Fox went about his burdensome task. For a moment Walter glimpsed the pain of a man for whom even a light remark demanded courage: he seemed bent over, with a wedge of the curved earth on his back, in a search for the key to something the rest of them — Walter, Billy, the town — already had in their keeping. The puzzle led further on, though its clues were carried in things as ordinary as horses and horsemen.

That night Walter had written to Billy after all:

Sunday
29th September 1913

Dear Billy,

You asked me to write so here goes.
Report: Regret to inform that young lady in question not overly conversational. In reference to your stay at Albion Hotel I would say doubtful if young lady's view and yours match. Exchange limited by presence in carriage of ancient female and night passed uneventfully.

Better luck next time round.

Sincerely in friendship &
anticipation of good times soon,

Your spy,

Wal.

Billy's reply shot back:

W'day October the second '13

Dear Wal,

Thanks for your trouble I smiled to read

it. Why worry thats life. Country here-abouts
green as can be.

Until your return.

Sincerely,

Wm.

After Walter's all night train trip his father handed
him the reins of the sulky and asked him to drive his
mother home while he set off separately in a wagon
loaded with twine, poison, and grease-clotted harvester
parts. Down past the racecourse Walter gave the horse
its head and ya-hooed until his mother objected,
quietening him with news of district "developments",
reddening enthusiastically over the Bindogundra New
Year Dance (he was expected), then describing a
missionary meeting as she probed uncertainly towards
a change of subject: Billy's mother was in hospital with
something serious. Billy — he'd been found drunk in a
horse-trough in October — now had himself well in
hand for the harvest, and Mr Mackenzie had been at
church every week since Elsie's illness. (*What* was
wrong with her?). Oh yes you'll be interested to hear
that Mrs Scott at Cookamidgera has married one of her
late husband's brothers.

When Walter persisted she told him: a cancer.

They were on a side-track because of the washaway
at Cobblestone Creek. From here, half a mile off-
centre, the familiar countryside looked strange, like
somebody else's. He missed none of the landmarks he
knew — the six white ringbarked trees, the decayed
cottage where rabbiters camped, the thirty-foot dip
they called "the plate" where the soil changed and their

wheat paddocks began — but farther off the suddenly-revealed distant view was altogether new. Where had the red gash in the hills come from? That lone pine standing above the rest, he'd never before seen it. And whose house was that, lying like a bent nail under the blue-hazed ridges?

"Ours," said his mother.

The imminence of death, Billy's mother's death, distorted his apprehension of familiar places and things.

Later, eating lunch without much appetite, Walter heard his mother say, "Elsie doesn't have long. A month at best." She performed plain tasks as she spoke: but the bread board, thought Walter, the cold mutton and the tea caddie would be remarkable to Mrs Mackenzie now.

That afternoon Walter wandered for miles around the wheat, skirting the edges then plunging in. The harvest would soon bear it away, this stalk-town of heat and dust and pale light, but for the moment it was endless. On all fours no-one could tell where he was, except the quail that skimmed between glassy stems and disappeared, except the nesting rabbits, the mice, the worms in the dry ground, the sparrowhawk twitching overhead. Emerging under the box tree at the centre of the paddock he rested in its unrelieving iron shade, where in a week or two waterbags would hang dripping from branches. With his hat on his knees Walter was itchy from the straw, messing his hair as he scratched, still unsurprised that at nineteen he should be engrossed in a game that had absorbed him at ten. Someone else might have said that the paddock murmured in the heat, but having crawled under its roof Walter heard each click and hiss and screech separately. The house was out of sight along with fences and out-buildings. Wheat alone dropped away in all directions: and he saw himself at an elevated point at the top of a ripening world. Soon the life of the paddock would go down before the blades of the harvester: then it would rise again. Here at least there was a pattern to hold to. Fear, which in the city was abstract and confusing and could conjure brick walls only, had ground to contend with in the bush, and on the ground life. It was good that Mrs Mackenzie would be able to see all that if she looked out the hospital window.

The place crackled with work towards Christmas. His mother, he now noticed, was indeed distressed about Mrs Mackenzie. She asked Billy and his father over for meals when they could manage and then the strain showed. Mr Mackenzie had sworn off the bottle (Billy confirmed it), but when Walter and Billy strolled down to the yards to look at the new draught horses, and Walter led with his question about the old man's whisky habits, Billy deflected from the unspoken fact of his mother and swore instead about Arnie Scott's double dealing widow.

For three weeks Walter finished work at midnight and started again at dawn. His energy seemed inex-haustible. When Douggie arrived home with John, his school friend who was to stay till Christmas, Walter found time among everything else to saddle horses and take them shooting. The harvest began and it was like a solid dream repeated day after day. He did the sewing when he wasn't handling one of the harvesters and went at it so fiercely that his father left him there — with a leather hand-pad, loops of twine on his belt, and a canvas hat pulled low over his eyes to cut the smashed-glass glare of the fallen wheat. Blacky and Ned Reid shared the work (they brought their machinery, and would have the Gilchrists' help next).

So when the Gilchrists' harvest was finished Blacky called up to the house to discuss his arrangements. He came on a day when the last bags had waddled away on wagons for the siding, when the pace of work dipped and they found time to look about. Douggie and his friend took off for the hills (John was to leave for home on the night train), Mr Gilchrist eyed his empty paddocks, and his wife cooked for Christmas.

Blacky was tall, but looked even taller at the cane veranda table with his battered thumbs embracing Mrs Gilchrist's Karlsbad china and his long legs knifed up practically to chest height. As he drank, it was as though he'd hauled the cup down from an elevated position (like the handle on a bagging shute) to work the tea in, wave by wave, rather than taking it in sips, so that his every gesture, like his conversation, flowed to himself.

"We don't live so good as this over our way." He took a slice of sponge cake and licked extruded cream from its compressed waist before taking a bite.

"It *is* Christmas," said Mrs Gilchrist, who was hovering at his side with a fresh pot.

"Work don't stop for Santa Claus, Mrs Gilchrist."

"Surely you'll take a rest on Christmas Day, it's the one day, here."

"No fear. Come the twenty-fifth the wheat'll be busting to hop in the bag."

"When do you want us?" Walter did the asking.

"Aw, about six in the morning will do. After you've been to church at the latest." He slapped his leg. "Fell for it!"

"This year," said Mrs Gilchrist with a cold smile, "the Christmas service is on the Sunday before."

Her husband collected crumbs from his knee. He and Blacky shook hands: "Until later, Stan." The proper name somehow subtracted the scaring factor — Blacky looked vaguely light weight.

"Boxing Day, then," Blacky winked. But he couldn't have cared less about Mrs Gilchrist when he thanked her for the morning tea.

"Don't take any notice of Mum," said Walter as they crossed the yard.

"Eh?" said Blacky. Then he snapped his fingers: "I don't go for this religion malarkey."

"Why not?" It seemed out of character that Blacky with his animal appetites and machine-like constitution built for work should touch the philosophical.

"It's all words. All bloody hot air. You've only got to look at a dead cow some time. That's us, boy, skin and bones and guts that go off just like a cow. I want to meet the man who digs out the eternal bloody soul. I'll shake his hand. Christ, we've been waiting long enough to see it."

Blacky grinned as he swung a leg over the saddle and bent to click the petrol cock. "It all fits. Christmas Day and the eternal soul mumbo-jumbo. Scratch one, you'll find the other." He unhitched his goggles from the handlebars. "But you're right," and he paused to let the adjective spit its opposite: *wrong* — "Christmas Day ain't for that. I reckon at lunch I'll be stuffing it down in the shade along with the best of 'em. The harvest be buggered." He kicked the motor and it spluttered. He pulled the goggles down and looked straight at Walter. "Right-oh, sonny. See you Boxing Day." And he roared off with coils of dust bounding along behind.

Walter took Douggie and his young school friend John to town in the sulky. From the last rise they saw the headlamp of the train on its way up the line from Forbes. "I hope I miss it," said John, but Walter snapped the whip. In the early dark they held a race with the miles-off engine, the boys cheering when the light slipped from view (now they were sure to miss it), and arguing with Walter as he forced the pace — even though the light wobbled, blinked, hovered as far away as ever.

When they reached the station there was no sign of the train. They quizzed Ozzie Deep but he shrugged. While Walter smoked a cigarette Douggie and John ran to the end of the platform to keep a look-out and listen for the singing rails. After another five minutes it occurred to Walter that the light they'd been competing against had been a star: the evening star, the planet Venus. He braced his mind on the thought: there was something magnificent about pitting a horse and sulky against a planet.

And suddenly the train from Forbes came right at him: waddling down the platform making friendly "oof-oof" noises. Douggie and John ran with it, then the train windows were dribbling past: deep golden pictures of glass and varnish which framed among much else a sudden flutter of white that was Frances Reilly. A man stood beside her wearing a drooping felt hat and a pin-striped suit. Now their door swung open. Walter froze. Frances carried a yellow straw hat with a red ribbon. She jumped down and led the man over.

"Dad, this is the Walter Gilchrist I told you about."

"It's a pleasure," said Walter, hearing his voice boom.

"Charmed," said Mr Reilly, fanning himself with his hat.

"I last saw your daughter at a play in Sydney," Walter addressed Reilly man-to-man, then clumsily added: "Though she was too high and mighty to notice me."

"That's not true!"

"Terrible weather," puffed her father. He studied the clock and made a decision. "If you'll bear with me I'll slip out for a minute and say hello to a colleague." He joined the stream of brisk-walking men that flowed towards the Railway Hotel.

When he'd gone Walter heard himself say: "I'm pleased to see you again."

She frowned: "I *did* see you at the theatre."

"I don't mind."

Somehow he'd said the right thing. Then she fired interested questions at him: asking about things he thought he'd covered during the cold night's trip to the coast — where their farm was, what his parents were like, even which school — no, she remembered. "But I do recall you don't like theatre."

"No, I'm theatre-mad," said Walter. He indicated his work-clothes: "Straight after the train I'm off to a show."

"I've finished with school," Frances informed him as they strolled with the train stretching ahead and the long asphalt pavement of the platform widening to the darkness of infinity. "From now on I'll be helping Mother with her piano classes. Come and see us when you're down?" For a second her hand touched his arm, just lingering there. "I'll be running the little ones through their scales." She played a tune on the brim of her hat, and with the help of her other hand danced the hat ahead, investing it with life. "I'd love to be interrupted."

What would Billy have replied to this invitation?

"Then I'll come and interrupt you," said Walter gruffly.

"Do," she pleaded. "I want the whole world to come."

Then she ran ahead to fetch pencil and paper from the compartment to give him the address, and at that moment Douggie and John decided to latch on.

"Hoi, Wally, what're you doing?" They swarmed like sly half-backs through a ruck of legs. John braked and stood with hands on hips, a miniature rooster: "Who's the *girl,*" he crowed. Walter grabbed him by the ear and twisted it till he squawked.

"I'm sorry." Walter squatted. "Look, when you blokes get a bit older you won't make jokes like that. They get a fellow fighting mad." He found a three-penny bit. "Here, get some lollies."

"Thanks, Wal, you're a sport," said John. But Douggie called back, "Hello Miss!" — Walter stood to find Frances standing behind him holding a piece of notepaper.

"You can come by ferry."

The paper was the colour of butter: the colour of her hat: and the hat shone its buttery yellow onto her bare lower arm. So he folded part of her away when he slipped the note in his pocket.

"I don't know when it will be," he shrugged. "Soon, I'm sure. Keep an eye out for me. What if I write you a letter?"

"I'd like you to. I like letters."

"From the whole world?"

"Well, you could write," she stated. And the words were so quietly inviting that she seemed to be saying, "From this part, especially."

Walter just stared at her until she fiddled with her ribbon in embarrassment.

The whistle saved them: at its summons the stream of men flowed in reverse from the hotel.

"We're away," announced Mr Reilly, "about half a minute to go." He looked cheerily at the train, smelling of whisky.

Then Frances's hand was in Walter's: "Write?"

The guard was bad-tempered slamming doors and Douggie called from farther down the platform: "*Waltah!*"

He remembered how Billy had looked, stranded on the platform. He stepped back in order to wave and watch for John at the same time. Frances and her father were framed for a moment in the window, a white figure and a black figure in a yellow square. After a second this picture dissolved and the figures swam away in a confusion of glass and varnished wood, their places taken by gliding mantles of molten light.

"I've got a message to deliver," Walter told Douggie as they drove from the station to the Royal Hotel. There was no message, except what he now told himself: he had captured Frances's interest.

The barmaid remembered him: "It's Walter, isn't it?"

The rum shrieked at him and then changed its mood: embraced him fiercely, and rippled aside to regard him with soft kindness. He must have gasped at the start, because the barmaid laughed.

"Blacky Reid was here," she told him. Walter should have guessed already. This was Blacky's lair. He imagined a smell, virulence reeking of motor spirit, and heard Blacky retelling the clash with his mother while his mates guffawed. At the end of these thoughts he was surprised to see only a splash of rum left so he asked for another. The spirits no longer bit: he read the name "Bundaberg" on the bottle and breathed the distant sugary air of Queensland.

She asked him why he was in town, and he found himself telling her about Frances. When he finished she said: "It's easy to see you're in love."

"She's good looking," he boasted.

On the way home the effects of the drinks wore off, leaving the events of the evening as sealed in as those of a play. Falling stars slipped from the sky one after the other, blinking out behind the dark heap of Mt Cookapoi. He made a wish to accompany each one: *Her.*

In the secrecy of his bedroom he scrutinized the note, holding it up to the hurting light of the lamp. Her touch had been dry as this paper, though underneath something had rippled like silk and skimmed the surface when their eyes met. Turning the paper edge-on (to find the night's code greeting him again: black, white, yellow) he saw faint hairs of fibre rising from the small furrow of her pencil-marks. She had written her name. Using his magnifying glass, the furrow deepened to a ditch. It was like the dropped edge of a sand pile, only it never moved. Here he located the very instant when she had impressed her whole self in a line leading unvaryingly to him.

6
Divine Service

When Billy laughed these days and said, "I'm a bad
bugger, eh?" he meant it. While he believed in God
and, as far as he cared to notice them, the laws of the
church, he saw himself standing off to one side. The
laws were all right — he'd pay some day for breaking
them — but for the moment they were for other
people and got in the way.

Billy saw heaven as a place full of ladies from town
dressed up as if waiting for the train. He saw Christ
babbling on over their bent heads while they crept forward, all those old ducks, and tugged at the hem of his
gown. There was nothing to be said to that weak and
bearded figure. But if Billy could make contact with the
Old Chap — he got on well with old men — he was
sure the two of them would hit it off and get to the
bottom of things. He wanted somewhere decent for his
mother to go when she died. She'd like somewhere
with a bit of grit in it. Why shouldn't she get a heaven
right here among the paddocks and hillsides she loved?
He wondered what would happen if he prayed at
white-hot heat and asked God for a bargain. He'd do
anything to make her happy. So as the church at the
crossroads came into view and he cantered to catch up
to his father he was impatient for the service to get
started and that moment of blunt contact to begin.

"It'll be hot later," he greeted Mr Gilchrist, then

clamped Walter by the elbow and urged: "Come on over and say g'day to the girls."

Walter found himself in view of those "good sports", Billy's cousins, puffing out his chest, hooking his thumbs in his belt. The cousins, sixteen and nineteen, with small chins, narrow chests, eyes as quick as pullets', glanced from one male to the other as if they had special food hidden about their persons. Then Ethel cocked her head to avoid the sun and bowled Billy a difficult question, something about "May".

For some reason the query rang in the air like a shout.

"Who?" asked Walter.

Billy bit a fingernail and grunted.

"Someone in hospital," Ethel confided.

At last Billy answered: "The police think it was the same shearer that pole-axed Albert Telford last Easter." After saying "a funny show all right" he excused himself and joined his father, who had signalled.

Ethel wrinkled her nose as if at a bad smell. "A nurse at the hospital got followed one night and attacked." She maintained the furrowed nose, but now seemed to be asking: do you think wrinkled noses are pretty?

Lottie pitched in: "The police quizzed Billy."

The Reverend Fox and his wife stood to one side under a copious yellow box tree. As the worshippers filed past they shot the couple shyly curious glances.

"Merry Christmases" multiplied from pew to pew: the phrase increased until it became a murmur, releasing a flow of small talk that ebbed only when Mrs Fox fussed her way to the organ. The cousins after a last peek around buried their hands in their laps feeling satisfactorily observed. The older women prayed by squeezing the bridges of their noses with thumb and forefinger, as if a root lived there that must be pinched to encourage the growth of the spirit. The prayer over, they took out raffia fans and cooled themselves rapidly. Where did the mothers go in these brief journeys? Walter had difficulty enough framing one clear hope from the many of his own that contended. But the women knew what they wanted.

Then he saw Billy at prayer also, and stared surprised at a thick yellow ear clutched devotedly in a red hand. The prayer went on and on through the neutral minutes of Mrs Fox shuffling sheets of music while bottoms made their last heaving adjustments, noses were blown, children silenced, knuckles cracked, yawns stifled. The varnished pews were already sticky. Then the corrugated iron of the roof gave a muffled thud as if God had knocked from above to say, "I am ready."

Billy looked up with a defensive set to his features. He had been exposing himself to another's will. It was not so much a matter of pushing in his prayer for what he wanted as a placement of himself and his intentions across from the might-be's of a force yet to reveal its hand. Billy's mental stance was like a boxer's at the ready.

The youthful Mr Fox started the service by gripping the pulpit and exposing white knuckles. He chose a couple of people in the congregation and looked them in the eye: Billy, who tried not to poke out his tongue, Mrs Gilchrist, who fanned herself in reply with the strength of tight-wound clockwork, embarrassed that a man not much older than her son should presume to seek out her soul. Then a child dropped a coin which gave out a long looping noise until the clap of a foot extinguished it. And just as throats were tickling and the impulse to clear them became irresistible, Mr Fox grinned mechanically, threw up his hands, and yelled:

"*Rejoice!*"

Ethel Mackenzie stifled a squeal and many others started at this piece of ecclesiastical theatre.

On signal the organ took a succession of deep breaths accompanied by regular wooden bumps from the foot-pedals. And at the first dustily-trumpeted chord the congregation rose: "Hark! the herald angels sing, 'Glory to the new-born King, Peace on earth, and mercy mild, God and sinners reconciled' —

> *Mild he lays his glory by,*
> *Born that man no more may die,*
> *Born to raise the sons of earth,*
> *Born to give them second birth.*

In the silence for breath that followed, a falling pine cone clattered in the guttering. Walter saw a tangle of green branches high up in a clear pane of window. Most of the windows were frosted over with white-wash, but here and there a pane had been left clear. In one of these the square of green hung like a painting in an otherwise bare room.

"Let us pray."

The minister's gaze wandered on a cobbled square of bent backs and bowed heads. Again the women pinched the bridges of their noses, while the men held their hands over their foreheads and looked at the floor as if shading themselves from an earthbound sun.

Billy swallowed a yawn. At the start of the prayer he had peered at a cup-hook of hair dangling on the lace collar of his older cousin. On this he built a rapid dream of defilement: yet his cousin became someone else — only the lace and the hair remained of her — he wanted the dream to be pure-someone, but it swelled — who was she? No face — he needed a face, but not Ethel's, and he raised his hand prayer-like to disguise his hunt for other possibilities, and as he glanced around, finding nothing, he heard his amplified breath rising from the palm of his hand: a thin cooling intake of air followed by a thick expulsion. The repeated sound was hypnotic. It caused his thoughts to step back from his body, so that he saw himself as a sleeping shape of flesh. And he disliked what he saw. Not the shape itself, not the work-thickened fingers or scrubbed-clean neck, but the immobile prison his thoughts had suddenly escaped from. In that second or two he conceived the idea that other people were not so trapped, and he envied them. When he tried to stay with the idea, to discover it properly, the tone of his breath changed, flapped wetly, and abolished the spell. He fell back to noting his boots dusty from the ride — he'd been up early polishing them — and he saw again that his fingernails were getting long. So he bit them.

"Amen."

After the children's address Mr Fox invited the younger ones to leave the church for Bible class. Douggie slipped away, and Mrs Gilchrist's hand, which seconds before had been resting on his knee, now lay flat on the empty seat. Father and son folded their arms, bumping elbows.

Mr Fox reminded the congregation that the year had been one of rich blessings. He spoke of grapes and melons, figs and honey, bread and milk — as if the produce of Palestine and the produce of Parkes were the same. The hoped-for rains had come, but elsewhere others had not been so fortunate. He referred to distant parishes. We must think of these less fortunate places as we garner our harvest, said Mr Fox, and thereby make a storehouse for the well-being of our souls.

Billy's mind now wandered the district, starting far away from the hospital, then coming closer, yet never actually entering the room where his mother lay. He felt for a bruised thumbnail and pressed it till it hurt. He thought of the silver roofs of Forbes, brick chimneys, the Bible class outside gathered in the shade of the tankstand — then far-off things again. Suddenly something forced him to view his mother walking the track near Pine Creek as she loved to in spring. But he wrenched that picture aside. He saw May Armitage escorted down a rocky laneway to a spot where an overhanging pepper tree plunged the track into utter darkness. She was black and blue now, and wouldn't be kissed by choice for ages.

Ethel thought Billy knew more than he said, which was true.

The police had walked him down the lane and asked what he'd seen that night, where he'd stopped. Near the pepper tree they tried to be clever:

"Remember how dark it was. Did she run?"

"Come off it!"

He'd been unable to help because what he knew and what they wanted to know would never fit together. They wanted the culprit — who wasn't Billy. But Billy knew something all right. He had kissed May Armitage the night before she'd been bashed, and he could have told the police why it happened and how. But that would have been about May, not the culprit.

Billy had half jokingly thought of getting Walter together with May some time, she would have been a treat for his innocent soul. The plump Baptist kindliness held surprises, though you had to be daring to track them down because she never offered a thing. When they kissed a suddenly fierce contest of limbs occurred and it took Billy a minute to realize that her cry was not "You're hurting me," but a plea for rougher treatment. Then a light had spilt from the kitchen door of the nearby rectory. "Spot?" called an approaching voice: "Here, Spot — Spotty Spotty Spotty — Oh!"

Billy wondered about his cousins, if any bloke would be tempted to get rough with them: and decided they were too jolly. Though Ethel wanted things, and demanded them smartly enough with her sinewy body, they weren't peculiar needs like May Armitage's. Nor did they catch at some half-buried need in Billy himself. He lifted his rump from the hot seat and unpeeled his sticky trouser-bottoms. In the deepening boredom of the service his thoughts now changed direction as abruptly as a horse's swinging head: his mind galloped everywhere. He dropped Ethel and shouted himself a tall glass of beer, he swung from a rope and splashed in the Lachlan, he scrutinized May Armitage's damaged body under the sheets and studied her swollen lips as they crackled madly with an electric phrase: "Kiss me."

Because the church encased these thoughts in its stone frame the idea of being trapped in his body came back, and he crossed and uncrossed his legs in frustration.

The cattle and sheep are finding the festive season a

little dry, said Mr Fox, so we must pray for fresh growth. The hot weather — and he unfurled a white handkerchief from the arm of his cassock and dabbed his forehead — is a burden to us all. Mrs Fox left the organ and took her seat in the front row. Her husband retreated from the prow of the pulpit and polished his spectacles on the sleeve of his gown.

He referred to notes.

The women, like a field of straw-winged butterflies, fanned their glowing throats rapidly. The men braced their shoulders as if for duty.

He spoke the text: "When they saw the star, they rejoiced with exceeding great joy."

Christmas, purred Mr Fox, is indeed a time of great rejoicing. Today we have sung carols and heard the Christmas story from the word of God Himself. Yet the festival would be without meaning if we failed to look beyond it. The annunciation and the birth, the bearing of gifts to the child, all these are wonderful in themselves, but their full importance lies in the future. Those coming events in the life of Christ, those bursts of light as he grows and the falling shadows on the road to Golgotha — these are the things that complete the meaning of Christmas. Look at Christ the Child in the old paintings. He is beckoning us with his raised hand to look at the life ahead.

Billy sank as Mr Fox spoke, sliding to a position where only his legs locked on the rung of the pew in front prevented his slipping off altogether. And at the same time Walter was raised up.

Pews creaked, and Mr Fox beckoned on behalf of a distant truth.

But suddenly he turned strange and difficult to follow. His spectacles reflected the frosted glare of a window as he steadied his head, and the effect of a brief, isolating blindness caused Walter to lose track, and then to feel mistrustful. The minister paused and lifted his chin as though listening to an instructing, inhuman voice from elsewhere. It was the same manner he adopted sometimes away from the church when you could tell he wasn't listening at all. Yet here he was asking the congregation to follow him who was following Christ. What if he was just — mad! His tense mouth pursed like a fish's . . . Mrs Fox half-rose from her seat as her husband manipulated his jaw, loosening a streak of foam-coloured light at one wet corner.

We do not store our grain without preparing for the next season — he leaned from the pulpit — we do not, we shall not sit down at our full tables on Wednesday unmindful of the tasks of the morrow. Therefore he proposed to look forward to a time of tribulation when God was inwardly to be called upon and blessed.

But for most this was Christmas, or near enough — no time to wrestle with the troubles of the future. Wednesday loomed, as far forward as anyone wished to look. Mr Fox pleaded with God from his lonely height while dozens of dinners sat ready in hot kitchens. Heads drooped, the old and careless dozed, the busy fans creaked right and left.

And now, well beloved father — he quoted from somewhere — what shall I say? I am taken among anguishes. Save me in this hour. Please it thee, Lord to deliver me, for I am poor and what shall I do and whither shall I go without thee.

A wasp's nest high on a lamp chain held Walter's

attention for a minute, and the creeping heat that advanced from outside cradled him. Then he heard Mr Fox talking a kind of sense — and he understood. For as we are taken, said the minister, and destroyed, so we shall glimpse the destination.

Walter clenched one hand in the other and bent his head as if in prayer.

Mr Fox returned to the Christmas scene but it sounded merely everyday. He rattled through its moral as if the thing he really believed in was lightning, and it had cracked once to show a black torrent and glistening rocks and bobbing white faces: and that was that. He seemed to have discovered something for himself in the sermon, and now he could feel it slipping away. But he squared up to his obligations and presented a sensible gift to a parish that had more than once addressed veiled queries about his capacity to the moderator. He called the nativity a light, the star over all our dark nights no matter how gloomy. This is what Christmas means when we recall it in our worst hours, as we should — as, if we are to find the Lord, we must. For He is the Shelter in the storm, the Lamp in the depth of night, the Beacon on the dangerous shore.

There was more of this, but the Christ part meant nothing to Walter — though heads nodded wisely and booted feet scraped on the gritty boards in agreement. He watched a line of dust motes climbing to the bare window pane — pollen-coloured swirling atoms held to the shape of a plank. Again through the glass he saw the dense cross-hatching of pine needles, and suddenly the tree moved. The needles shook as if a current of air were striking the tree continuously in one place. Wind? But wind moved around, wind went everywhere: then a glimmer of white appeared among the green. It grasped a small branch and pulled it aside. Douggie's face peered down, a white disc that had floated up from Bible class and was now suspended bodiless in the branches. Then the face and hand just as suddenly disappeared, and the tree was still.

All this time Billy had been asleep. As the congregation made its finishing up noises a dream flew from him in which his mother — to be buried in the small graveyard outside — thanked him for his concern and said, "God will speak to me in his sauce bottle."

He woke infuriated.

Mr Fox removed his glasses and slipped them away through a rent in his cassock.

"Therefore, *Rejoice!*"

The word travelled slowly this time and padded on the hot underside of the roof.

After a pause he uttered a low whispered "Amen".

The organ in the corner gasped with relief.

After the service Walter posed with one foot propped on a pine root.

"I saw you up the tree."

"What tree?" Douggie adopted the "at ease" position of a well-behaved Great Public Schoolboy.

"This tree."

"I didn't climb a tree."

"You did."

"I didn't."

"You did, you little liar."

"Don't call me a bloody liar."

"You're a liar. And don't swear."

"*Bloody.* I'm not a liar."

"Who's a liar?" asked Billy. He approached Douggie from behind. "You've got pine needles stuck in your hair."

"Dunno how I got those."

"You'll be at the Bindogundra hop, won't you? Aunty Bea and Uncle Len will be there" — he lowered his voice to exclude Douggie — "but a short leash never worried Ethel."

Walter glanced at Ethel who was perched on a shaded ledge of the tankstand: she fluttered a hand, made to get down, but was intercepted by Duncan Grieve who blocked her with a massive palm resting on the tank's rust-streaked corrugations.

"He treats her with respect," observed Billy, sneezing and flinging a string of snot to the grass — the rest was carried into his pocket. "Nothing turns off a good sport quicker."

All this talk about Ethel made it hard to bring up the name of May Armitage. Walter opened his mouth to ask but Billy elbowed him — "Just watch her."

Though Ethel rolled her eyes at Walter and had butted his hip at the show, and, he supposed, would do with him all those things Billy promised she would, still he felt she disliked him. But he said: "I wouldn't miss it for the world."

"He's already got a girl," intruded Douggie.

"Oh yeah?"

"Scamper!" Walter raised an arm to threaten his brother who sauntered off, but called back, "The girl on the train," then ran.

"Who?"

"No-one."

"Go on," Billy taunted. "Just the kid talking, eh? Or did you make it up to impress him?" He searched for his cigarette papers and finished off a laugh by hawking drily — nothing came out. "The harvest always gets me like this." He wiped his nose with the back of his hand and stuck a dampened corner of cigarette paper to his lower lip, letting it dangle while he rubbed a leathery strip of tobacco until it expanded into a ball.

"Well?" he mumbled.

Until he spoke Walter had no idea what might come out. He intended denying everything.

"Ar," he confessed, "Douggie meant the Reilly girl. We bumped into her at the station the other night. You know what kids are like."

Billy rolled his cigarette with great care. "I should have guessed you'd like that one." After he'd licked the glued edge, which was when most people looked up, his eyes remained hidden.

"It was only hello."

"Who knows who she'd go for, eh? But you'd be near enough her type for starters." Billy struck a match which popped and hissed. With the cigarette wedged in his mouth he now looked Walter in the eye: "The educated type," he enunciated. The cigarette waved around as he spoke, and the corners of his mouth gave a twitch that converted to a smile. "She'd always be looking for what she could say about a bloke to her friends, don't you think?"

Billy had spent a lot of time thinking about her.

Walter lied again, to throw him off the trail:

"She mentioned blokes in Sydney."

"She knows her onions, that one does."

"I got the impression she had some bloke down there she was especially sweet on."

"All the same, you'd do all right with her," Billy persisted — though he was suddenly tired of putting things on a plate for Walter and then having him hold off. He decided he'd like to punch him instead — and hard — so he laughed.

"What's so funny?"

"You couldn't guess." Billy looked around for his father, and it was easy for Walter to see everything: all the old resentment from years ago. "We're off to sit with Mum. See you at Blacky's."

"Merry Christmas" Walter called.

"It'd better be."

7
Harvest

To avoid a three hour ride before dawn on Boxing Day they spent the night at the Reids. Billy had ridden across from Bindogundra and when Walter got there was lying on his stomach on a camp bed on the veranda with his boots off and a wet towel draped over his head for the heat. His hands dangled from the end of the bed holding something — a stone — swaying it in blunt arcs which now and then scraped the floor.

After freeing Peapod and lugging the saddle to the veranda Walter asked for a look.

The stone was grey and slightly carrot-shaped. Billy rolled it between his palms, examined it as if for the first time, tapped its thick middle, then handed it across. "An Abo thing I found by the creek."

Walter rotated the stone and followed a vein of lighter colouring which petered out towards one end. Then, wetting it with spit, he noticed dozens of faint marks tilted this way and that, numerous small deliberate scratches.

"What about these marks?"

"Yeah, Abo writing."

When Walter had finished Billy held the stone tight in his hand and thought about his mother, who was now unconscious, and had kissed them both that afternoon with great weariness: it had been goodbye, he was certain. Yet she had managed to say: "Go to the

Reids' ", and his father had nodded, holding her yellow hand.

Blacky and Ned were still asleep on the veranda on the other side of the house when Mrs Pepper, who was to cook for the harvest, arrived at dusk with her husband. They unloaded boxes of food from their dray and a pot of stew ready for that night. Then Mrs Pepper set about gathering up the empty beer bottles from the dining room and the drained rum bottles from beside the beds where the Reids and their departed cronies had let them fall after their Christmas dinner. Old Pepper leaned on a veranda post until his wife brought out a pot of tea, then he sat on Walter's bed. "Queer," he said, examining the stone by lamplight. Mr Pepper blamed the Aborigine for not being a military fighter like the Maori. "Of course, they're a blacker race here," he explained, returning the stone to Billy. "And the professors at the university — you'd know all about this, Wally — they definitely put 'em low in the scale of black races."

No-one spoke up for the departed blacks, but Billy gripped the mysterious stone and mourned his mother angrily, for nothing in his world was able to offer the kind of consolation he demanded.

Blacky was up at four thirty to feed the horses. Walter woke to hear the lick and munch of a massive mouth and peered into the gloom to see the head of Flower, who had followed Blacky on his return to the house, elongated by her nose bag to the snout of something prehistoric.

At breakfast Paul Scott arrived, and the remaining helpers, the Lutheran Schulers, turned up just as the hot clamp of the sun finished its drying out of the wheat. It was the best moment of the day — as it turned out, the best for Walter in the entire harvest, for things were soon to turn sour. The horses champed away at a last minute feed, rigged powerfully in their leather collars and iron hames. The trace chains hung slack, but in a minute they'd clank and stiffen, and the clatter and swish of machinery would eat its way across the yellow and blue haze. But nothing could happen until Blacky surged back from his look at the wheat — there he was, giving his signal, a scarecrow in white shirt and stained waistcoat — and with his shout everything began.

Walter would be alone until the first harvester arrived ready to unload at the bagging point. He squatted, nibbled a straw, and spat. Old Pepper had fixed on the idea that he was a "scholar", but his only contact with the university he was supposed to know all about was a fading ambition, which the old-timer had picked up God knows when from his parents. At tea the night before when Walter ambled in, Mr Pepper had drawn attention to his "scholar's stoop". This had given Billy the chance to make a crack:

"What does he know?"

Mr Pepper considered the brown depths of his teacup. "I believe in an education. It can change a man's fortune without half-killing him. Why, you tell 'im, Wally."

"I don't know anything."

"Modest," nodded the old man, and swung round to confirm the virtue with his wife, who was checking the stew for the Reids — who'd woken with fearful bad tempers and immediately disappeared down to the yards. Mrs Pepper said nothing. Sometimes even her silence healed things, but not now.

"What I know isn't much use around here. Besides,"

Walter insisted, "the more you know, the more you realize you've got to learn."

"Do tell," sneered Billy.

Walter had meant to make a gift to Billy's point of view. Out here on the plains there existed only the equality of hands. But he had sounded merely priggish.

Billy mopped his plate with bread and swigged his remaining tea. "No pudding for me," he told Mrs Pepper.

Her husband now addressed Walter with a sharpened curiosity. "Look here, what happened to Ian Gillen's boy, eh? At twenty-five or thereabouts he's got nineteen thousand acres producing like his father never could."

"His Dad had the money to start with."

"Science, that's what done it," said Mr Pepper, and nothing would shift him. Suddenly Billy appeared to be holding everything against Walter, as if he had been getting away without scars, and would have to be wounded to make things equal. If it came to a fight, Walter's only weapon, words, would be next to useless. Billy's weapons, sharpened on rough experience, could do their work swiftly.

Even now, as Billy cajoled the horses from his high seat on a harvester, something was building up. Walter had no sense of a special quality which he had held over Billy to cause all this: as far as he could see it was himself, the accidental *he* that all his life had shaped, which had mysteriously become a point of contention. Two hares dashed by his boots, and the painted shells of quail scuttled from the path of approaching horses: all the disturbed life of the wheat paddocks flew out again as it had when Walter felt worst about Mrs Mackenzie, barely two weeks before. But now, instead of brooding, he stretched, gave a wave to the Schulers, and adjusted his hat for the job ahead.

The morning's work soon took over. Dust and chaff flew, Blacky shouted — you could hear him a mile off — Paul Scott and Eric Schuler swore and grunted as they hefted the granite-hard wheat bags onto the wagon. Blacky and Ned and Billy drove the harvesters, wheeling up to the bare apron of paddock where the bags sat ready, checking harness while Walter and Otto Schuler clipped empty bags to the bins and opened the shutes, guiding the dry torrent of wheat downwards. Then they took the bags by the ears and lugged them aside and got on with the sewing: six high-armed stitches, a ram of the funnel, and the wrinkled top of the bag swelled with extra wheat — then the final stitches, and the next bag and the next.

It seemed the Peppers would never arrive with morning tea, but at last their dray crept around the stubbled edge of the paddock and stopped under the lone tree on the fence.

For a few minutes no-one but Mrs Pepper spoke, and she said only "tea", "sugar", "buns" — these were yellow rock-cakes — and clicked the tin billy on the enamel mugs as they were held out for more. Then everyone had their breath back, and spoke at once. Finally Blacky's voice overrode the rest:

"Nobody," he said, "is working hard enough."

Otto and the other Schulers stared humourlessly across the rims of their mugs. Walter sensed that Blacky was working around the half-circle of reclining men to take a crack at him, so he waited while the

Lutherans were reassured by Blacky's wink and his "never mind", and a poke in the stomach for Otto, and then he was forced to take it on the chin.

"I think young Wally's tired himself in town."

"That'd be right," sniggered Ned.

"Wally," crooned Mrs Pepper, "a sweetheart?" Mrs Pepper habitually wore her hair coiled in a black and silver pile and had the energy of someone much younger: it was this — the breath of delight in others' lives — that kept her young. She pounced on Walter and poured him a fresh mug of tea, and urged another bun. The dry crumbs refused to go down when he swallowed.

"Well?"

"There's the daughter of a certain publican in Forbes, Mrs P, and she and Wally I understand are very thick." Blacky used his white mug as a pointer, though to Walter's eyes it butted the air like a fist.

"Whatsername," slurred Ned, and snapped his fingers as if he'd stated something.

Walter shot Billy a hot look which said: if you wanted to, you could stop this silly carry-on. But while Billy wasn't smiling and laughing like the rest, it was plain that he wanted things to get worse.

"Yeah, I hear Wally's 'in love'."

"Go on," breathed Ned with thick wonder.

"Oh, he told a friend of mine all about it," said Blacky, "and a very touching tale it was too. The only thing is" — and here he spoke to Mrs Pepper alone — "the lass herself ain't sure it's mutual."

"Stanley Reid!" admonished the woman, realizing too late what had happened. Walter gave Blacky a hard stare, and from the corner of his eye saw Billy slip from the dray and head back to his horses.

"A barmaid is a wonderful talker," observed Blacky to the world. He poured his tea-leaves clot by clot to the ground and rested his mug upside down on the dray.

The Schulers seemed barely aware of what had happened. They nodded to each other and thanked Mrs Pepper with pleasureless smiles. For the rest of the day, though, Walter took refuge in their company. He was wild at himself for not hitting back straight away, yet any attempt at redress would have been hopeless — he felt himself floundering at the centre of a ring of raised and mocking eyebrows.

Still, at dusk, when he and Billy sat on the veranda after their wash, he tried to wrest things back.

"What's Blacky been saying, eh?"

But Billy merely shrugged, sneezed, and cursed the wheat dust.

At tea-time Eddie Harkness rolled up to the front of the house driving his father's "Hudson 33", a motor car as sleek as a dressed plank.

The inspection called for several lamps to be lit, and a rag to wipe clean the inquisitive paw marks of old Pepper.

"Who wants a run to town?" Eddie beamed, showing his white teeth, and exhausted as they were, Blacky, Ned and Billy piled in, leaving Mrs Pepper's apple pie untasted in the kitchen.

"What about you?" asked Eddie as he fiddled with his expensive gloves. His father owned the general store. Eddie took what he wanted.

"I'm buggered," said Walter.

Off they went shouting and singing — someone yodelled "Ta-ta my bonnie Maggie darling" down at the gate, and Walter knew he was the cause of the laughter that followed. The acetylene headlamps peered weakly back as the car swung around and negotiated the dry creek.

With its owners gone the house seemed friendly. When the table was cleared and the dishes washed and stacked away, and her old man gone outside to fetch wood, Mrs Pepper apologized for getting things wrong at morning tea.

"It wasn't you," said Walter, staring at the stains on the bare wood table: cigarette burns, the brown rings of hot saucepans, dark clouds of liquid drifting down the years.

"You're not like the others, I can see that now."

"Aren't I." It was a dull statement, not a question.

"They're just a mob of no-goods." She spoke with fire. "I could tell you things about Blacky Reid that ought to hang him."

It appeared she was serious.

"Take Ned," she continued, "he's not lazy, but he's got no purpose. Which is the worst? He's Blacky's dog."

"Why do you help them out?"

"For his sake," she nodded to the thump, thump coming from behind the kitchen wall as her husband stacked wood. "You're a hard worker too," she smiled, "but you've got something better than this life on your mind."

"No," contended Walter, but he couldn't work out what to say. Would Mrs Pepper understand dreams — the "maybe" of not ever shifting, but scrutinizing the life that swirled under motionless things? Walter mistrusted his own convictions.

And Frances — he wasn't going to talk about her.

"I *know* Martha Bryant," said Mrs Pepper, referring

to the barmaid at the Royal. "She was married to a parson, did you know? But ran off with a train driver. Doesn't *everyone* know?" Mrs Pepper gave Walter the kind of look she might have reserved for Rip Van Winkle. "Then she came home to Parkes. Her dad was the straightest man in town, Eris Bryant the saddler. Trust Martha to shame him: she was bold, even as a kiddie."

Mrs Pepper then seemed to change the subject, but really it was the same story: "You're the type of boy who doesn't want to hurt people."

Walter nodded sleepily, she had him exactly.

"But you will, and you do."

"No — "

"You see," Mrs Pepper insisted, "you have an independent mind."

The solid-armed woman had turned florid in the practice of her intelligence. "And it's not just that you seem to have a certain attitude. You *do* have it."

She let the pronouncement sink in. A nightbird shrieked across the silent paddocks, and suddenly the house seemed not free of the Reids at all: inside and out it reeked of their ownership. Slowly Walter saw what Mrs Pepper was saying, and the injustice of it pricked him.

"You mean Blacky might have been getting back at *me*?" He scraped his chair signalling offence, but she restrained him with a rough hand.

She held on. "I can see what's happening between you and your friends. They're taking something from you after you took something from them."

"What?"

"I don't know." She poured herself a fresh cup.

"Blacky and Martha, are they, you know, engaged?"

"Well, they'll never marry," observed Mrs Pepper tactfully, plunging her hands into a mountain of dough as she prepared the next day's bread.

Walter was asleep when the others arrived home, though behind a tattered dream of crouching against a fence while Blacky rode at him on his motorbike he was dimly aware of low voices, dropped boots, and the distant whine of an engine.

The next day they all complained of headaches, and worked sullenly and hard. Walter yarned with the Schulers at morning tea, at dinner and at afternoon tea as well. The Reids and Billy flopped into bed straight after the evening meal. Even between themselves sociability seemed to have evaporated, and the split that Blacky had opened with his jab at Walter mattered less, though it remained. Billy was not unfriendly, but he stopped short of the way things had been before. At the end of each day he rode in to see his mother, but refused to respond with more than a word even to Mrs Pepper's gentle enquiries.

Something had diverted them on their outing to Forbes with Eddie, but it was not until Walter and Billy rode home together at the end of the fourth and last day that Walter learned about it.

The horses, head to tail, held Billy's voice behind. Walter scanned the lumpy blackness ahead, or just looked up at the stars. A storm was coming. Intermittent sheet-lightning showed high above Canowindra, over thirty miles away.

"We settled into the pub. Later Eddie got so drunk that Ned had to drive back. But first Blacky started roasting an old German, one of the Kaiser's crowd, you know, their king-bloke. Blacky told him all the Germans were sausage-eaters who'd put their mothers into sausages if they got half a chance. When the old German was hopping mad Blacky told him he knew for a fact he'd put his own mother into a sausage and brought her out to Australia in a suitcase. Things ran hot, Blacky nearly got a faceful of beer, but he bought the old geezer a drink — you know Blacky — they got to be good mates."

Ginger followed Peapod in a wake of horse smells. Lightning flickered closer now, so that a hump of black cloud was outlined. A curlew called eerily from far off.

"He said there was going to be a war."

"Who with?"

"Germany and England. He was all for England. For Australia, anyhow. He would not stick up for his own country at all — he spat."

"Australia wouldn't be in it," said Walter. "Never," he repeated firmly, because he was suddenly nervous. Though the peaceable bush nearby had hushed, the curlew faintly cried away to the west, where the stars, streaks of ash, burnt themselves out.

Billy urged Ginger alongside. Spittle and iron, clanked teeth, and the kick of boot-leather on horse-hide held him there.

"We're too far from anywhere," Walter concluded.

"You could be right."

Now they were at the crossroads, and Billy worked hard to hold in Ginger, who sensed the coming gallop along the sandy track. Walter said:

"There was nothing in what Blacky said about the Reilly girl, you know."

"Good-oh."

94

Though darkness was between them, and only the scrape of hoofs gave them away, Walter felt they saw each other clearly. And it wasn't friendship, nor was it shared interest that caused this peculiar flow of recognition. It was as though different nationalities had been declared. When had the declaration been made? The more Walter claimed to himself their differences didn't matter, the greater they loomed.

"The barmaid's just a trouble-maker."

"She's that all right."

Then they talked about Billy's mother — just a couple of words. Finally they agreed that hard work could kill a man, and they were dog tired. At last, each one echoing the sentiments of the other, they parted.

Both were home and asleep before the storm struck, though their parents saw everything. At the Gilchrists' the wind poured from the hills with the grinding sound of a huge axle. Over at the Mackenzies', Billy's father slammed doors and witnessed in a triple succession of lightning flashes the curtain of rain as it swayed just beyond the edge of the veranda.

That night in Parkes hospital Billy's mother died.

8
The Uninvited Guest

"Franny, this admirer of yours — "

"Admirer!"

"Walter whoever-he-is."

"Gilchrist," mouthed Frances, speaking at Walter's letter, which under its own power had raised two thick folds to form a triangle. Until this moment it had been paper alone. Now her mother was giving it importance. "He wrote, I didn't."

Mrs Reilly sat erect and prim, not at all herself. "I can see this Walter in a couple of years. He's ghastly enough now with his loathsome New Year dances and funerals and mud — heavens, he's trying so hard and all he can rise to is crudeness."

Frances saw the letter as inoffensive, even dull, compared with her mother's own quick-tongued picture of things on other occasions. What about the "full story" of her marriage, which she'd revealed over the queer week following New Year when Pat Reilly had again left for Forbes? There had been moments then, many of them, when Frances had wanted to cry *Stop,* either because she couldn't bear to see her father so unfairly investigated, or because she was in stitches. But she said nothing now, not because of this shared "cruel streak", but because staring at the letter she felt a need to rouse opposition, and form from the swirling nothingness of her emotions a definite attitude.

"Wide hat, red face, arms like sides of beef, thick shoes. Boots! Spilling tea all over the carpet," Mrs Reilly paused — having splashed a drop herself.

"Here?"

"Nothing to talk about but the price of wool, or cattle, or rabbits or whatever it is they kill and sell off. Asking about your music, as if he cared, producing a couple of tickets for the theatre — something awful, you can be sure — and clod-hopping with you down Pitt Street. And then, like a bull at a gate, producing a ring and asking you to cook hot dinners for ever in a tin shed."

"He's not like that," said Frances, at last meeting the force which gave Walter a shape. "He *won't* be like that," she added, surprising herself by thinking about him in the future.

"He'd ask you to play something for him in the living room. And after Debussy, if he were awake, he'd ask for something jolly. 'Polly Wolly Doodle', or 'Two Little Girls in Blue'."

Frances giggled. Her mother's secret was exaggeration — she loved to pound the heavy notes. "He's much finer than you think." She swallowed, and took more tea.

But her mother had not, as usual, taken this flight of fancy the extra distance and elevated it to the cosmically absurd, where peculiar figures with familiar faces were made to behave uproariously — Dad as an angel with dangling braces, Amos a possum with silver fur, Harry at the beach learning to talk under water.

"I don't think he should be encouraged. My strong advice would be to take your time before replying. *Intend* to, of course."

Frances looked obediently into her cup, but thought her mother hypocritical.

"At your age I was married. There's a lesson I hope won't escape you."

Then Mrs Reilly rounded the table and kissed Frances on the crown of her head. She whispered: "You've got a guardian angel who'll never stand in your way, darling."

Frances stayed on, not moving, staring at the letter, too listless in the gathering heat to make an effort. She admired her mother. Yet now, perversely, she wished after all that she could have come to a less fair conclusion. An outright condemnation of Walter, a final shriek of forbidding, would have been exciting. That was her nature — to crave extremes. But the outlook indicated by those parting words left her once again drifting. She found it boring to be left holding a choice. She dropped the letter into the copious pocket of her pinafore, and after stacking the cups and saucers floated to the hall mirror and gazed at herself in the hot half-dark. Overhead the rattle of windows and knock of brooms proceeded among grunts and shouts, and soon Frances would join in. But her dark face in the mirror shifted intriguingly. She cupped her hair and raised it, turning almost side-on yet holding her own returning gaze. Now that a hint of Arabia was not unfashionable she liked her profile. As might a stranger's, her face beckoned with the possibility of sensation, and brought her closer to an understanding of her inner nature.

Then in the midst of this reverie she heard the telephone give its faint click preliminary to ringing, and alertly she reached across to unhook the receiver.

"Mosman 343."

"Hello," drawled a male voice.

"Frances Reilly speaking."

Then there was silence, and she realized that the

voice had been hesitant. Now it seemed gone altogether: she heard other voices in the distance, as if the line were an empty tunnel crowded against busy ones.

"Hello-hello?" The exchange girl cut in. "Are you there?"

"Who is it?" asked a wide-awake Frances.

The voice had been familiar. She knew it from somewhere — Forbes? Climbing to help the others she found herself able to summon up an atmosphere. Cold air crowded against the outline of a figure in her mind, and she knew that floor polish, the squeak of hinges, and the creak of the Albion's stairs were all involved.

"Mother!" At the top of the stairs she wanted to tell her, and almost did while accepting the cobweb broom.

"Do the ceilings and hurry along, then we can all have a rest."

In all the houses up the hill wives and their maids sat hoarding the last puddles of coolness left over from the night before. At Mrs Reilly's, as with the rest, blinds were drawn, curtains pulled, doors closed. But now and again, as if this house alone was incapable of containing the energy within, a door would fly open and a mop shake its head in the molten sunlight, or an upstairs window rattle wide to enable female head to call to female head somewhere down below.

In the afternoon they slept, the first pupil not being due until four. Frances had made up her mind: she would not reply to Walter's letter. Why hurry? Why even bother. She parted the drapes and peered outside. When her eyes adjusted to the glare she could make out a smoulder of red tiles in the far distant eastern suburbs. In between, the harbour flowed nowhere, a broad stilled cauldron of heated glass. Then a ship hove into view, a passenger liner with the clear outlines of an

Orient Line boat on a painted postcard. It seemed the only real object in the world. Frances perched on the windowsill oblivious to the heat. The ship made her feel remote, tiny, stranded at the most distant corner of the globe. She imagined a dotted line leading down the harbour, through the Heads, around the underside of Australia and across the Indian Ocean — gesturing towards Ceylon and India as it progressed — spilling in its wake successive, endless *O's* of possibility: *Orvieto, Orsova, Otway, Orantes, Osterley, Otranto, Orana, Omrah, Ormonde* — then heading up through the Red Sea and Suez Canal where other lines jostled but failed to deter it, across the Mediterranean, past Gibraltar, until England loomed like a storybook illustration of a land in the sky, pastel-coloured and cool.

Over there, things *happened*. Would her parents let her go? With its smart lines and swept-back confident funnels, with its tiny figures of sailors stowing ropes or merely draped on the shaded port railings, the ship unbearably provoked her restlessness. She let the curtains flop and turned back the cover of the bed, and lay in her underclothes on the cool sheet. After a minute she took even these off.

Certainly it would be glorious to have a tragic blow struck by an enraged and madly obstructive parent — many artists sprang from such fires — but *her* parents? They loved her with too much kindness. Or perhaps they failed to love her enough, and finally would let her loose in a world where she'd struggle, cry for help, and disappear, and they wouldn't care.

She woke when Helen arrived with a cup of tea, and propped herself on an elbow. From below came the rattle of a duster playing scales and the drum of cushions as her mother tidied the music room. From outside came the heat-oppressed scrape of sparrows. She sweated with the tea and felt cooler, stretching an arm and shaking globes of perspiration onto the sheet. She supposed Walter's letter was intense enough. Her own brand of intensity seemed out of place in Australia, which loosened one's grip on things, never allowing one to — she grabbed the letter and sank back on the bed to read it again — to fly?

She had put it to Diana, mentioning his reserve, his consideration, his manners. And under these things, had she actually spoken this out loud? — he's very intense. He thinks. He's got his own life going on somewhere underneath. And then he looks at you.

Respectful and dull. To be truthful, that had been her first impression.

When talking to Amy Castle, who was more hard-bitten than Diana and not really a friend, though someone to be impressed, Frances had replied to her question "Is he handsome?" with "Yes, no. He'll be more handsome when he's older." Amy had been interested. "He laughs, he can see the funny side of things, but not the way those country boys usually do. When he laughs there's something there to laugh about." By then Frances was practically inventing him, and Amy was near enough bursting with curiosity. "When he laughs you don't feel left out," she said. "Oh, he'd create a stir at — the Governor's Ball," she managed, because that year Amy was going. And a final invention: "He does well at school. He could be anything he wanted." Amy asked: "A rich lawyer or a rich farmer?" Frances had said: "I don't know. Not a farmer."

Yet there he had been at Parkes station just before Christmas, looking like one. Not a fully made farmer, but going that way. The physical change was not what Frances had minded. She had rather liked the definite thickening of the frame from the stringy schoolboy of a few months before. It was a kind of sullen wariness that she noticed. It may have been tiredness. But it might just as easily have been a shadow of his future self — the kind of man who sat on the bench outside the pub on sale days, a beer in one hand and a stick in the other, wide awake but drowsing. The kind of man who spent so much time mending the edges of his own world that he would never want to go any further. Who was balding at twenty-nine, who spat, who went to church but had no religion, who made no changes in his life and expected those around him to make none either.

I'm unfair, she suddenly decided as she dressed. Just like mother, who loves to take a person and lean and lean until cracks appear, then force those cracks apart until nothing survives in one piece.

But Frances was also uncertain, not just of Walter — who was practically invisible on those millions of acres of western plain. Suddenly she glimpsed a life of unhappiness, wherein the choice not-made invariably would be the exciting one after all. She ought to be taking care of herself and not existing on dreams alone! In the cushioned square of her yellow-painted room she experienced the beginnings of a turn against herself, an unhappy dispersal not of fate, but of will.

I'll write, she decided, and did so straight away.

The cool change arrived and because the five thirty pupil was ill, Mrs Reilly suggested a walk.

"Pat was awfully romantic once," she took Frances's arm. "At least I thought he was." In an aside she said: "The mistakes women make about men populate the world" — and gave a bitter laugh, but then talked about secret mementos in locked drawers, hand-delivered letters brought in the dead of night, pebbles scattered on windows, even the dot-dot-dot from the signal lamp of a cutter on the bay . . . a load of silly talk about midnight occasions when anything could happen, though of course it never had.

"You don't mean Daddy," said Frances. They had reached their favourite seat by the harbour.

"To hear him talk you'd have thought so. It astonishes me what a man can get away with. I trusted him to be wild as the wind, and what happened?"

These days Mrs Reilly had her admirers, and though Frances mostly disliked them there was still an air of rivalry in the house. Harry Crowell, Amos Hart, Mr Tratinor the piano tuner whom Frances had caught one day with his chin resting un-innocently on the piano stool as if he'd just delivered it a kiss — not to mention the cheeky strangers who lifted their hats and won from the handsome music teacher a promising beam of recognition.

As they sat together in the park Frances twisted the corner of her handkerchief around her thumb, a nervous habit from childhood. Her mother tapped her on the hands.

"You mustn't."

"I wrote to him."

"That was quick."

"I kept it chatty. I told him about the concert last

103

week, what we wore, the ice creams; coming home on the last ferry."

"What about Harry?"

"Who'd want to know about old Harry? But I left it understood we must have gone with someone."

"Understood! Harry arranged the whole evening — bought the tickets, the refreshments, the supper. He *was* the outing."

Frances said slyly, "The full story might have been provoking."

"Still — "

The ferry tooted twice as it surged into view, a bow wave curving back on either side like blades of ice. With the engine cut, the wave slid to a snowy streak which disintegrated as the boat knocked the heavy stumps of the wharf. In a grinding moment of contact the ferry chugged black smoke, creating a drowned giant of a cauliflower astern while rope thudded and a flimsy gangplank rattled to the shore.

"Harry Crowell!" called Mrs Reilly when one of the passengers raised his arms theatrically.

"Some surprise," muttered Frances. Harry rarely failed to turn up on this ferry, but on weekdays he was a different-enough person to be bearable — dressed in a glum suit, with his idiotic flourishes kept in check by a day among the no-nonsense types at Goldsborough Mort's.

"Ian Gillen was in," said Harry, fidgeting with his red and gold ring.

"Who's he?" asked Frances.

"He had his boy with him — by golly he's a handsome type, smart as they come." In some detail Harry described a person called Robert until Frances burst out: "Could he possibly be a Greek god?" — Harry's enthusiasms ran on such lines.

"They own 'Westbury' near Condobolin, and innumerable places elsewhere," explained Mrs Reilly.

"Clever and rich, damn them," said Harry with a laugh.

"Pat and I knew them ages ago. Before you were born, when the Austrian prince went shooting with the Narromine Macks."

The story of the prince had whiskers on it, but who had ever talked about these Gillens? "Why does Harry know these things when I don't?"

"Any girl who marries into the Gillen crowd is in for a hot old time," said Harry. "South America — they're sailing today — you name it, interests everywhere."

He then cupped an arm around two waists and they set off up the hill.

When the crowd dispersed from the ferry a lone figure had been left on the wharf. Any watcher who cared to observe would have seen straight away that this remaining passenger came from out of town. His concentration as he fixed a pipe was too nonchalantly oblivious to the diversions all round. A local would have given the ferry a long and approving look of farewell, and would have taken in the tableau of the two women and the man with frank interest. Certainly noone but a stranger would have been downright furtive, and slipped as this one did into the shaded mouth of the shelter shed. Harry, tossing his head exaggeratedly to three points of the compass during a bout of laughter was the only one to notice. But if Frances had turned she would have recognized Billy Mackenzie immediately: he slouched with the same immobile expectancy that had characterized her last sight of him on Parkes station.

Yet after a minute this changed, and his manner became craftily decisive. When the trio moved another fifty yards he moved also, seeming to dawdle as he puffed his pipe and shifted his coat from the crook of one arm to the other. When the three slowed approaching the Reilly's place he plumped himself on the stone fence of a for-sale house, thus becoming one of an elongated crowd: up the road other figures hung over gates or sat on fences enjoying the cool change. When Frances did in fact look straight at him she registered no-one at all, seeing just another inhabitant of a street turned inside out for coolness.

Billy was ready to greet the females now, but preferred to see whether the man would go away. Also the harbourside evening had at last begun to work on him. He was strong willed enough to suspend his purpose in coming here and give himself over to a glimpsed extension of yellow rock just where a low shaft of sun illuminated the point, and wonder if it was a good fishing spot.

With Harry, Frances found herself enmeshed in ambiguous gestures. He was difficult. Not in manner, but in purpose. He seemed to want all the trappings of a close relationship — the roses, the theatre, the flirtatious gestures, the quick sexless kisses of farewell — but they merely duplicated themselves, becoming nothing sensible. And when he fell into one of his "slush" moods, losing all control of his pride as he had that night with Diana, he was impossibly weak, and all one could do was assist in his self-defeat.

Now irritated at the man's hanging on, it was another Harry that spurred Billy's envy — the man who on evenings like this could be fun of a sort. He was, as her mother said, "grand to be seen with". Some of this reached Billy and he repeatedly chopped a swinging heel against the stone fence. After absorbing the remaining glory of the evening — an empty tram braking its hollow-lit shell to the water — he turned his glance with increasing impatience towards the women and their imposing companion. The fellow's lithe physique would be handy in a fight.

Harry, who was never in a hurry, had by now started on scandalous stories of the theatre. He was not himself at such moments, but a mouthpiece for attenuated rumour. He whispered a name, and Frances skipped a couple of steps around to ask, "What? Who?" But they refused to say.

This evasiveness was pleasant.

It was almost dark and Mrs Reilly asked him in.

"Thanks, no. I've a man to see about a dog up at the Junction. Gotta be there now, won't make it." He consulted his watch and caught Frances's eye for a rolling fraction of a second, and she thought: Weak old Harry, he's only off because the cafe closes at seven and he wants a quick dinner, then he'll go to his flat and iron collars all night. She was about to tease him, but thought better of it in case he changed his mind. Instead she asked:

"Will you post a letter for me?"

"Don't bother Harry when he's going."

"No bother."

"Right — " Frances streaked down the side path.

"She's bored. And along comes a strange sheaf of writing from one of her train friends, urging a romance."

"Well, well," said Harry in his gossip's voice as Frances reappeared.

The pale blue envelope was swallowed by the slit mouth of his inside pocket — the last glimpse anyone was to have of it. "Top priority," he assured the world, tapping his coat where the hollow rap of paper could be heard. He grinned at Frances, for once failing to hide his badly-aligned teeth, which were starch-white but "falling all over each other", as Frances liked to say.

After the women had disappeared inside, and the tram had whined two stops uphill to collect Harry, Billy sauntered to the ornate brown door holding a lily ripped from the garden of the old Konrad place.

When Frances answered the doorbell she was quite unsurprised. "I knew it'd be you," she said: yet even as she spoke the different sources of her intuition had barely clicked into place . . . the voice on the telephone, the coatless figure perched on the fence. "Our visitors usually let us know first," she continued abruptly. Billy thrust the yellow flower into her hands, forgetting in the face of her rudeness the speech he'd prepared.

"Oh dear, come in." And after a pause, "*Mother?*"

When Mrs Reilly bustled down the hall Billy knew at once how to treat her. She was an older version of Brigid Scott, right down to the way she took his hand at waist-level, and stayed close as she spoke.

"How nice you should know Pat," she said after explanations. They tracked down the hall, Billy bumping his shins on a carved chest, and emerged in the kitchen where Helen was about to set the table for steak and kidney pudding. Mrs Reilly found Billy a glass of stout and took one herself. "I was sorry to hear about your mother." She leaned across, she actually touched his hand.

"How did you know?"

"I heard from Walter Gilchrist," said Frances, "we correspond, you know."

Billy launched into a version of his visit to Sydney while Helen darted in at his elbow with a fistful of cutlery. "Tah," said the visitor. Frances seemed bent on discovering the exact time needed for the smudged heat of her thumb to fade from the crook of a spoon handle: but all the while she wondered how Billy had landed so quickly at the heart of her family.

"After Mum died I felt low. I ended up at Wellington — d'you know it? — I knew a bloke's name there and we got on well enough, so I helped him out for a couple of weeks. For money." He jangled a hidden pocket. "I sold my horse. We was glad to see the last of each other. Nine pound, and the bloke must be hopping." He laughed with a sniffle, and began eating his pie before the others, then remembered himself and settled his implements quietly.

"What about your father?" asked Mrs Reilly.

"He don't need me, except," and the bluntness softened, "as a hand."

"So you're going back," Frances spoke more easily.

"Tomorrow," said Billy, who had no such intention.

He named a "swells' hotel" in Sussex Street. Mrs Reilly happened to know of it, though she kept the knowledge to herself — it was a cheap and cramped last resort for debris from the bush.

"It's not as roomy as your old man's place but it's real snug." He had been on the verge of lying expansively — just as the story of his stay at Wellington would need to be lies, if they wanted more details. Mrs Reilly's smile was that of an ally — he could get away with murder in her company but he sensed the difference between distorting hard facts and the allowable charm of other whoppers. So he winked, and concluded: "Snug enough for this character."

From Frances's point of view the wink practically froze: it created a multi-folded seal of flesh across Billy's left eye, held long enough to shift from the quick and commonplace gesture it might have been, to something coarse and vociferous, then plain arrogant. She was astonished to hear her mother laugh and say, "I can imagine!"

"Do you know Sydney well?" asked Frances.

"Never been here before."

She watched him as he talked on. The roughness and the ignorance and the self-confidence, she saw, were not anything like they would be if Billy had been, say, a character on the stage. No Australian audience would believe in a person who was so originally from the bush, yet subtly in charge of himself — and others. Bert Bailey would have had him all at sea, knocking things over, fuddled with inferiority, chewing with his mouth open, gazing at everyday objects as if they'd dropped from the moon. Instead, his directness unsettled her. When he turned as he did every now and then to shoot her one of those enquiring looks she felt helpless in a way that was quite new. Lately Frances had sensed a third or fourth version of herself waiting deep-down. Billy, she could tell, saw her as a finished person: all her doubts and hesitations were held still. And the person he saw was one of those third- or fourth-level ones. It was a limiting regard, yet she was suddenly caught by it.

At that moment both she and her mother shared the same feeling — Frances slowly becoming aware, her mother plainly aware of and even encouraging the queer pleasure to be got from Billy's company.

After the pudding, while Helen fetched tea, he talked about his mother. His clipped account of the funeral — "a wet day, Mum hated 'em" — gave the occasion a dignity which Walter's long description had lacked. Plainly Walter had no deep feelings engaged in the burial, whereas Billy spoke as someone who had lost almost everything.

"I — I —," he fumbled for his cup, intending to confess without actually detailing the red panic that had sent him flying with only a change of clothes the day after the funeral, when his father had bellowed from the veranda an enraged order for his return — holding his beltless trousers with one hand and asking if Billy knew where his wife had put his gum-boots.

Then Walter's name came up, just as the doorbell rang and Helen went to usher the evening's adult pupil into the music room. "Five minutes!" yelled Mrs Reilly, clutching her third cup of tea impatient for Billy's opinion.

"He's not cut out for the farm."

"Oh?" Mrs Reilly let the query rise and fall through three syllables in the manner of someone who all in one receives desired information, ironically underlines it, then urges for more.

"He's always wanted to be a geologist. I've learnt a bit myself through talking to him. Any old rock," he said in an aside to the ceiling, "can be millions of years old."

Frances breathed, "Truly?"

"Wally's always got a book somewhere handy. You can't do that on a farm, can you?"

"Geology books," the daughter supposed.

"All varieties — even Charles Dickens."

"Who hasn't," said Mrs Reilly in a tone of contest.

"Me," said Billy unabashed.

Frances fought an impulse to side with such candour.

"His dad sent him out to look for stragglers one shearing time, but he settled under a tree and read up on bones. He got whipped for that."

"Bones?" Mrs Reilly hastily concluded that Walter, and now Billy, was entirely boring.

"Just about all the animals that ever lived," Billy instructed her, "are dead." They waited politely while he sorted out his meaning. "If you want to find out what the world was like before we come on it, how do you?" Again he worked hard at a thought but the thread dangled out of his reach, so Frances grabbed it. She spoke to her mother: "Of all the different species that have ever existed, most are extinct. Extinction" — she quoted Diana — "is the common fate of all species."

"Don't tell me you're on top of all that stuff," Billy blurted. After his fair and even admiring account of Walter the outburst came as a surprise. Frances saw his hostility — it snared her together with Walter in the same net — so she stared back.

"Franny's got a science-mad friend," explained Mrs Reilly. She consulted her watch and leapt up. "I mustn't keep Mr Abbott." Frances waited for her to say goodbye. But she took Billy's hand and asked: "Shall you stay for supper?"

"Too right."

Helen started the dishes but Frances took over, leaving Billy to shout at the deaf girl for a minute.

"Do you live in?"

"Here."

"Where're you from?"

"*Here.*" Kneeling at a cupboard, she looked up at him as though from a deep hole from which she would never emerge.

"Holy smoke," Billy threw to Frances. He stared at the maid as he had stared that afternoon at a negro off an American whaler.

"You'd be surprised how much I hear," said Helen suddenly, making one of her longer speeches, each word bent back on the previous one, but with a tortured kind of amusement in the tone.

"Allow me," Billy said when Helen picked up a tea towel. Helping with the dishes kept him close to Frances, enabling him to move round behind and rake her outline with a hungry gaze. He found himself caught again by the smoulder that had ignited at Forbes, and blazed many times since in his imagination. "This science-mad friend of yours — what's his name?"

"Diana."

"Ah. What's she like?"

"Do people interest you? I wouldn't have thought so."

"Huh."

"She's bright as a button. You ought to meet her."

"Is that so?" Pleased with himself, Billy fastidiously

dabbed a floral tea towel around the inside of the crockery pie dish.

"You've done that before," observed Frances.

"I like to take care."

"Diana is man-mad as well as a scientist. *Scientiste,*" she added experimentally.

"She sounds dangerous."

"Only to herself — she doesn't know she's man-mad."

"She needs instruction, eh?" That coarseness again.

"Only in self-protection."

"I told Wally you knew your onions," said Billy complacently.

"*Onions?*" Frances turned with dripping hands.

Billy held a white shield of dinner-plate in rag fists. "You know what I mean — how many beans make five."

Frances flicked water from the dishmop in a vertical whipstroke, leaving a spatter of suds down his trousers. "Watch out, Mr — Mr Fat Sheep." The words spat, but hadn't Billy meant the phrase as a mark of admiration? This low kind of regard sprang from the physical, and called up a physical response. It could scarcely be answered by a retreat into indignation.

She went at him again, sloshing the mop on the plate when he parried. "Idiot," she heard herself giggle. Suddenly close, Billy's free arm snaked on an inside track to escape the mop, and tickled. Frances squirmed and hunched head down, defending herself like a child by a direct rush into the arms of the attacker. Still laughing, she dropped to one knee as the mop skidded senselessly away, and Billy found himself with his arms right round her.

The piano's rising clatter took care of the mother,

and the maid had gone off upstairs. Therefore Billy made certain Frances knew what he was about. He urged one hand upwards, penetrating a fold of protecting limbs until it reached her chin: then he followed through for a kiss.

"No —"

This denial was a pretence, though forcefully spoken. Frances heard a distant voice — Diana's — saying, "Go on, go on, you should have," as if what she was allowing hadn't happened, and already she was forward in the future regretting a lost chance at discovery.

Billy's lips now settled on hers — the cold lips of the surly blockhead who had prowled after her in Forbes. His mouth scraped and tickled, articulating as though in speech, while a disturbing slide of spittle somewhere intruded.

And yet —

Her head, being ground by another person's head smelling of tobacco and cheap soap, was no longer in command. Lack of air created a kind of drunken carelessness. Or was it that Billy's immoderate manner simply cancelled her out, and she was no-one, merely this fluttering sensation that might have been a heartbeat wildly racing, except that her heart — it registered on her now — boomed separately a dispassionate accompaniment.

Oh God — a hand of Billy's was travelling serenely up the inside of a leg, advancing to the very mark where she felt sick and unrestrained at the same time: where her being fluttered. Where victim and captor, if this horrible wrestling was to continue, must unite in complicity.

She heard Billy snort, *snort!* And it was over.

"You pig!" she managed. The thistle-patterned linoleum stretched to infinity as she rolled and then kicked clear. The world sprang back to its correct social shape of four walls and a doorway, of a piano talking once in the firm tones of the teacher, then many times in those of the awkwardly-responding pupil. The hall clock dizzily bonged eight.

Frances sat at the kitchen table straightening her dress, adjusting a tangled skein of hair, sniffing once and scratching the tip of her nose with a thumbnail. She felt as if she'd swum a creek which turned out to be wider and deeper than she'd imagined. There was also the pall of something murky in the air, not a smell — but a threatened mood oppressive as creek mud all the same.

"How shameful," she threw at Billy's smug shape, which stood with its back to the wash basin regarding her. "How *dare* you?"

Billy regarded the flushed and quick-breathing Frances without answering. She was less desirable now than before. His grab for her had been a lustful impulse overlain by something more calculating. By the time his lips touched hers he had been thinking: *I've beaten Wally good and smart.* So the pleasure he should have had from her was all absorbed in this vengeful impulse. Something else had intruded. On feeling the tell-tale acquiescence of Frances's body — just a second or two of surrender had been enough — he'd been alarmed. His hand curving upwards did so almost unwillingly, and dreaded to reach its destination. The trouble was, having got this impudent girl where he wanted her, where he'd got plenty of other girls before, he baulked. What if she'd just gone on giving in? Hell, what a handful. It was then that he had snorted.

116

Still . . . she was all right. His eyes couldn't leave her alone.

"Don't," she hissed.

Frances's thoughts narrowed to the problem of getting rid of him. He seemed unaware of any offence, having burst in uninvited to gulp a dinner and do what he liked. Was this all that men wanted from her — would ever want? At least Billy had done her the service of sneaking past the dithering and wasteful pretence of other men, but the bleak offering required of her at the end — to be a body — drew a curtain of despair over the future. Yet — there had been that sensational letting go.

Billy straddled a chair, chin on folded forearms, regarding her as if from the top of a fence.

"This isn't a sale."

"Huh?"

She hadn't expected him to understand. Didn't want him to. She just wanted him out. So she said with all the sourness she could muster:

"I suppose you're quite nice in your way."

He didn't mistake her hostility, but the sharpest edge of her meaning all the same whizzed through the jammed-wide window at his back and disappeared into the harbour night.

"Thanks," mumbled Billy in an imitation of gentlemanly lack of complication.

She spoke more softly: "Please, don't ever do that again." She had not intended to be conciliatory, but here she was — bother — almost making up.

"I promise."

She could see he'd sworn the formula before. "I just don't know what come over me — you're a temptation," he explained finally. His rancourless grin blamed her in a way she appeared to accept.

"Don't you think you should go? There's a boat at nine," suggested Frances. She heard her mother fare-welling her pupil at the front door. Billy anticipated Mrs Reilly's entry into the kitchen by standing, fingers drumming the back of his chair. The sexual contest died away to be once more replaced — on Billy's side — by something larger: the set Frances and her kind seemed to have against his nature.

Mrs Reilly entered to take his arm and steer him through to the parlour. She called back to Frances who replied, "Coming!" in the brightest tone she could manage, though by then tears were streaming down her cheeks and she sat gulping helplessly in an attempt to thrust back a threatened downpour.

Part Two

9
Late Quaternary

At the Gilchrists' polite table a new Billy chewed open-mouthed without caution. He had arrived at tea time with the latest talk from town. Half was about a social event, the Roller Skaters Fancy Dress Ball. The rest was war talk.

Until the week before Billy had rarely opened a newspaper. Now he read even the "extraordinaries" pasted up outside the *Champion* office, and had become a political expert, though nobody pressed him to say exactly where these suddenly luminous European places were.

"With Austria and Serbia at each other's throats it's just a matter of time. We'll be in it."

Between courses Mr Gilchrist and Billy rehearsed a sequence of events using salt cellar, butter dish, knife, fork, spoon and plate. Austria struck Serbia chimed Russia gonged Germany rang France roused Britain.

"*See?*"

Alan Gilchrist threatened the table with a knife (Germany). It shifted from his wife to Walter, who nodded.

But until this minute, when the knife flashed under his chin, the goings-on in the papers hadn't touched Walter at all. One fact followed the other all year, but remotely, dry as a time chart in a history lesson. Now it occured to Walter that his own standpoint was closest to Billy's. He'd wanted change — here it came! Mountains in the northern hemisphere were already rising, falling, clashing. Shock waves bowled through the oceans, struck the coastal cities and cracked the glass calm of the everyday, shooting up-country to craze towns and remote homesteads all in a matter of minutes. Incredible that a distant quarrel between foreigners could wreak such an astonishing transformation, yet leave a person feeling expectant!

Billy described how a hundred costumed skaters had rumbled and squeaked their way round the hall, which was so full that couples even used the stage. Eddie Harkness had skated right off the edge. At nine thirty they had squeezed against the walls to watch Mr Harley Davidson, the world champ, leap over three chairs. Mr Farlow won the best costume with "Aboriginal Chief", and the comic prize went to Mr Deal's "Dark Town Barber". But who got the loudest cheers? Miss Finity as "Britannia" and Jack McGee as "The Admiral".

After the meal the men sat in front of the fire. Mr Gilchrist studied Billy's *Herald* in the yellow lamplight while Billy and Walter sprawled at his feet smoking their pipes.

"It looks a certainty. If England goes in we'll be in it too."

"*If*," reflected Billy. "It'd be just our luck if she don't."

"I say she will," said Walter. "If distant places like Australia are ready, why should the old country hesitate?"

They toyed with differing opinions, not because they held them, but because the facts were so few.

"What the pommies want is to call Australia in and sit back."

"One in, all in."

"I reckon we're gamer."

"They've got the army. We'd just be extra. Wouldn't we?"

"We've got the *fight*," concluded Billy. He heaved a log to the centre of the fire and admired a tower of sparks.

For a while, in the intensified firelight, all talk ceased. Alan Gilchrist dropped the paper to his lap — the flames chopped his face with hard shadows. He barely knew why, but war would be welcome.

Silent before the fire, he thought of his land as a bastion — nothing less — from which he would willingly send forth magnificent confirmations of title. Yet earlier, questioned by his wife, he had turned red in an effort to explain: "The thing is to get on with it!"

Billy watched miniature cliffs of red-hot wood collapsing. Fire absorbed him. It was strange that war had never occured to him before. He was made for it! If all the excitement fizzled out he'd be desperate.

Other more practical needs drove him. If war came, he could escape. Away from his father, stone-hearted now, and a drunk. Away from the silent churchyard that haunted him, yet was not itself haunted. Away from the consequences of news from Wellington which lay in a crumpled letter in his pocket. Trouble was brewing there, though not with his name attached to it. Not yet.

"Yes, sir!" said Billy into the silence.

"Would you be scared?" asked Walter.

"Not me."

"Now wait a minute," said Mr Gilchrist, denying his own intensity of thought, "we're talking about a national event, not a jaunt for youngsters." He made a show of hunting though the paper for farm news, struggling with himself over the thought that if Walter was to go off to war he would be glad. Six months or more had been enough to show that he and his son were strangers. To be honest, he disliked the boy — who was half the time locked in hostile broodiness, and the other half gushing with green ideas.

"I'm sure I'd be scared," Walter continued, "because of a dream I had about Blacky. When was it?"

"Get on with the show," said his father, rolling the paper tight and prodding Billy.

"It was in the cadets — only it wasn't. There we were marching through scrub. You too," he said to Billy, who liked to figure in such phantom lives as other people's dreams gave him. "On we went through wattle and saplings and suchlike. It was a sandy sort of place. We advanced in line with our rifles at the ready looking for something."

"Rabbits?" The suggestion came from his father.

"We arrived at a ship's gun. A barbiette."

"What's that in English?" asked Billy.

"I couldn't see what was going on but something told me to watch out. Then I realized that the — blighters — wanted to put me in the gun and fire me through the barrel. I've never been so scared. Now this is the funny part. The bloke in charge was Blacky Reid."

"That'd be him all right."

Mr Gilchrist stood and stretched. "Blacky's always had you bluffed. He's all wind."

"Don't be so sure," said Billy, out of a mixture of friendship for Blacky and hard knowledge: "But it'd be him all right, he'd be there, telling all and sundry what to do."

"A windbag."

"I woke up then. I remember — it was last Christmas."

His father tapped his pipe on the edge of the fireplace: "I'm for bed."

From the kitchen they heard him talking in undertones to his wife, who after a minute came through to say goodnight.

"I want no more hysterical war talk," she ordered. Then footsteps knocked on the bare boards of the hall; they heard the click of a door, the whimper of a dog, and a mopoke calling across the cold ocean of trees.

In front of the fire Walter and Billy shook hands and swore that "if the worst came" they would join up together.

The pact surprised both of them, and decided Billy on a confession.

"Are you and the Reilly girl still writing?"

"I wrote once, but she never replied. Good riddance, eh?" He managed a grin, but thought: How does Billy know? If that Scott woman's been fiddling with the mails —

"I seen her. It was after Mum died," said Billy, "when I was in Sydney. I bumped into her." He told no lie. "We talked. She told me the two of you were corresponding." Because of Walter's uncomprehending look he added: "Writing letters to each other."

"She to me? You've been bloody quiet about it. When I met her at the railway at Christmas she asked me to write, so I put down the news and sent it off. But she never replied."

"To hear her talk you'd have thought the two of you were scratching away like mad. Women! Who can fathom 'em?"

"*You,*" Walter spoke with sudden vehemence: "Why do you think she said she'd written when she hadn't? Come on — " His tone swung between scorn and helpless submission. Clumsily he lifted the poker and jammed it among logs.

Billy spoke calmly. "She was putting me off for one thing. She couldn't spare the time of day. Anyone'd think I was a pig — fresh from the trough — the way she kept her distance."

It sounded wrong. What about Billy's siding with the Reids at harvest time, the way he'd never talked straight about his trip away, especially concerning Wellington — now Sydney too —

"Come off it!" Walter snapped, and the poker was in the air, its tip glowing cherry-white. He could have, he really wanted to, Billy ought to —

Down came the poker with a smack on the sooty bricks.

"That's a dangerous instrument," said Billy coolly.

"So are you." Either it was belt him with the poker, or do it with words.

Billy reclined without speaking, and who could tell if it was cunning or innocence that held his tongue? Besides, the burst of anger had stripped Walter of hostility. And Billy's silence, though it wasn't forgiving — impregnable rather — somehow took a share of the blame.

Billy played on this. Dumb guilt, he knew, lent him an air of integrity. In silence practically anything could be shammed.

"She likes you, Wally. I used to say, didn't I? that

you've got a real chance there. She asked all about you." Billy reclined on a cushion and nestled his head on his arms. "A hero! That'd be the way to win 'em over." He rolled to his side and looked at Walter. "You could just march in and take her. No messing about. No knocking on the door. The direct approach. Nothing like it."

"It's not me."

Billy spat into the heart of the fire. "If this war comes off we'll be well out of that kind of trouble. What do you say?"

At midnight Billy set off for home. At the start he rode slowly, smoking the tail end of a pipe, coat collar turned high, hat rammed low to keep the icy air from his ears. He held the reins in one hand and let the horse follow the track of her own accord. She was an ex-polo pony from Narromine called Novelty, for which he'd paid a fortune two months before; she had good Arab from somewhere, and a touch of draught as well.

Soon after leaving the yards Billy muttered to himself: "Wally's a mug." A little later he shouted: "*A mug!*"

Back at the house, standing at the far end of the veranda — taking a leak into the bushes — Walter heard the phrase but failed to identify it as human. It seemed one of those shifts of matter peculiar to the bush at night, as unfathomable to diurnal creatures as blackness itself.

When Billy reached the crest of the ridge he looked back. A tiny yellow light swayed and went out. Then he and Novelty moved alone through the universe.

He thought about galloping and they galloped. He thought about going faster, dangerously fast, and Novelty fairly devoured the track. Billy bellowed, and the horse answered by leaping forward into flight. And weren't the stars also hissing and tumbling ahead? The night was a vast future into which they hurled, man and beast with bared teeth, bone and muscle flung against the passionless depth of things.

When they came to the high clearing, which was now a disc of frosted grass, Billy dismounted. He set the horse free and squatted for a minute to catch his breath. His face burned. Then he lay full length on the ground and rolled over and over. Novelty tracked him, head down. Billy might have been happy, like a horse taking a dust bath, or in agony, like a man who has been poisoned but does not know it. Novelty's reins, loose on the ground, rustled alongside.

"A mug," Billy said once more, but the judgment no longer mattered, for now, his mind fixed on war, his senses feasted on a host of new sensations.

It was Tom Larsen the young schoolteacher who brought the news of the outbreak of war to Walter, pointedly playing it down. He wouldn't be in it — not for quids.

"Why not?" Excitement raised odd peaks in Walter's voice.

"Because I'm not bored," the teacher consented to answer. By then Walter had collected Peapod and found himself fumbling wildly with buckles. He was mad to be off, but not sure where. Billy's!

The teacher had not kept his head: it only seemed

that way. With school finished early he had grabbed his bike and pedalled furiously out of town to be alone, finding himself at the gate of "Whispering Pines" an hour or so before sunset.

He mumbled something about the conflict between England and Germany having to do with money — who was to get the upper hand in a market. Walter had no patience with such a viewpoint. It was too dry to express the quality of what was happening, too narrow for its magnitude. If Larsen's beliefs were measured up to fit people, as he said they were, then how come he missed seeing the opportunity that the war's adventure offered to the human frame?

The teacher continued: Why shake yourself free of superstition only to attach yourself to a new set of delusions? Another thing — but Walter was in the saddle now, and Peapod, sensing a chase, had to be held hard. He circled excitedly while Tom withdrew a couple of yards, clutching the fragile frame of his bike.

Right-oh, what *was* the other thing?

In retreat, and cooled off from his ride, the mottled purple of Larsen's face had sunk to its usual grey.

"Forget it!" he shouted.

They now saw Billy thundering down the track brandishing a kind of sword, a length of silvery sapling. The two boys on horseback circled the isolated teacher who despite his serious outlook was the same age. Only he wouldn't join in, except to bellow, "On to death and glory!"

There — the "other thing" was out.

In return he brandished a sardonic fist to make his meaning plain, but Billy took up the cry and meant it. Then he drew alongside Walter and said, "Let's tell the girls", and with a careless whoop in the direction of the teacher they set off.

Larsen watched their disappearing canter through the trees rocking and tilting through a series of frames in the late afternoon.

At Bindogundra the cousins hadn't heard.

"It's not so wonderful," shrugged Ethel. But when Aunty Bea started hugging the boys she perked up, and thrust Walter against a veranda post to give him a kiss. Long-faced Uncle Len shook hands: "I'm too old." At this Aunty Bea put an arm around his shoulders, and the moment hung in memory for that reason as much as any other.

Then they were off again, working their horses into a steaming sweat along the Parkes road, finally arriving long after dark. On the way in they had stopped, solemnly shaken hands, and repeated the oath of the Sunday before.

Nothing else seemed worth doing.

While the outlying streets of the town were wide and empty as ever, those near its heart ran with a kind of fever. Figures dashed from door to door. Knots of talkers raised their hats and cried "Hurrah!" as the horses shifted past. The hotels — once they reached the asphalt clatter of the main street — streamed with light and excited voices and the drumming of boots on wooden floorboards. Four men marched down the centre of the road singing "Rule Britannia", arms hooked around shoulders, stolid as working bullocks. A platoon of boys followed bearing sticks and pick handles; a Union Jack hung from the balcony of the Royal.

New ways of behaviour had descended as if by revelation.

Blacky and the rest would be there, but for once Walter didn't mind. Tonight the clash of persons was dead. One nation stood, swayed, roared, shoulder to shoulder. In the bar, beers were passed head-high in chains of dozens. Pound notes were slapped to the wet counter and no-one seemed concerned about change.

Sure enough, Blacky's gang held a corner. As the latecomers surged towards them a splash of beer fell on Walter's forehead and trickled down his face.

"I've been baptized," he said stupidly. A slopping glass from somewhere was thrust into his hand. There was Billy already gulping.

"Drink up, boys!" shouted Blacky. "Here's to the stoush!"

"We'll knock their heads together till their brains run out," giggled Ned.

"I ain't going to wait," crowed Eddie, "I'm off to Sydney tonight. I'm taking the car."

"Me too!" Ned squeaked.

The whole room was drunk.

Suddenly Blacky held a pistol — a lustreless cattle-killing Colt. In a second his arm jerked stiff in the air, two shots barked, and the hand dropped. Then Ned held the pistol and another shot rang into the cloud of descending dust and peppery plaster.

Sergeant Gregory materialized with the publican, and Ned was marched off. The policeman entrusted Blacky with the pistol — he'd brazenly asked for it back — and a wag even proposed three cheers for King and Blacky Reid.

"Ned'll take his time now," pronounced Blacky.

Meanwhile Eddie, propped on the wall, seemed to have dropped out of things. During the excitement he'd hardly reacted. Now he swayed red-eyed, with hair pasted to his forehead. His lips appeared thicker than usual, as if he'd bitten them earlier in an agony of indecision. He turned to Walter and Billy.

"What about you two?'

"We're going. Too right!"

Walter's first beers had elated him. Now with his third half-emptied he felt sober. This rush to join up, once he'd seen its force in the town, deadened the cold swill in his stomach and made it impossible to get drunk, though the excitement thundered on. A dog went wild among three hundred legs until it was kicked clear. Martha Bryant responded to the toast "Our Women" —

"I like that," murmured Blacky —

But Walter had caught the same mood as Eddie. He took a fourth beer, a fifth, before the excitement was readmitted. A minute ago he'd fallen to saying, "I'll have to see how things stand with Dad," when his dad was part of the scheme, but now . . . *Now!* the whole world was ablaze. Tipping his head back for a final drink, surging out to the cold yard, he was at last on fire as he headed for home.

Billy decided to stay.

Alone without distractions Walter's senses crackled through the past or raced forward in electric dashes. He tried to add himself up, to make something of his past self to thrust into the future whole and unbreakable. Because the idea of going to the war was a simple one, with its mix of abandonment and submission, of colour, noise, pride, he really did conclude, under a sky of almost deserted imponderables — once upon a time he could have named half a hundred stars — that the clash of history whose noise beckoned had done him a favour. He noted the smudged Magellanic clouds over to the south, and caught at his back three stars setting in the west — names out of reach, but without mystery now, because all cavities that once had tantalized, the gulfs of How Big? How Old? Where Does It Go? When Will It End? somehow presented themselves for answer in the span of his own actions. To go! His life pulsed forward in this active phrase, which would solve all, and was itself everything.

His ears ached from the cold, his cheeks lacked feeling. He experimented with a word to Peapod, but through wooden lips it issued merely as a chunk of noise. Cold nights, train smells, warm horse smells, pain in August — his life was marked by the events of late winter and early spring. This was the time when wattles in bloom almost squatted under their own yellow weight, tree after tree aligned through the ranges. It was a year since he'd first clapped eyes on Frances — what if he hadn't? No — even with his letter posted, and then the dwindling summer of no-reply, he felt more alive than he would have otherwise. Was it a trick of the season, to make something go wrong (his fall from Coalheap had started it), then have it fill his thoughts till he was grateful? The months after Christmas he'd felt thwarted and shamed. Well, the rules had changed. The world had changed.

He would write again.

His parents were still up, sitting close to the stove. The iron kettle hummed in waiting. There was no reproach for his wild exit. He described the unrestrained scenes in town, biting alternately a thickly buttered crust and a lump of cheese.

"There's time for thought," said Mrs Gilchrist on hearing of the urge some felt to rush off immediately.

"War," said her husband. "It's a fact." He took a piece of red gum for the stove and turned it over in his lumpy hands.

Walter rephrased all he'd read in the papers, talked on and on, and his parents hung on the words as if he'd coined them. He pictured himself as a far-flung son of the empire called to shield the heart of the mother country. His halting accents gave the platitudes rough force.

"So," he concluded, "I'll be in it."

But his mother was unmoved. "We need you here, Wally. You've never mentioned the army in your life."

"We can manage," said her husband.

"Not so long ago we couldn't." She bunched a tea-cloth into a ball and abandoned it on the table, where it uncoiled hopelessly. "Alan, you were all for stopping Wally from going to the university — now he's to be killed."

"Not a chance, Mum"

"You'll kill him!" she hurled at the father.

"It's up to Wally. I can't say no. Douggie can come home early."

Why at this moment did Walter wish to condemn his father as irreclaimably weak?

At last she appealed to him. "If only you could give me *reasons*. I don't hate the Germans. None of us do. Why, Mrs Schuler is a German! I do not want my son to kill his fellow creatures."

"It won't be like that!" But how did he know? Then to grant his mother something, not liking to see her so isolated, he said: "Tom Larsen claims it's all cooked up."

"He's a ratbag," said his father.

At the end Mrs Gilchrist's voice lost all trace of supplication. She stated, "Nobody can tell me why," and there the conversation finished.

On Sunday the district poured into the three o'clock service to hear Mr Fox preach on "Germany's policy, the Long Arm and the Mailed Fist". The national anthem was sung afterwards, and at the door the minister held Walter by the shoulders — the pose almost threatened a kiss — and said, "Half your luck."

"It's bound to be finished before I get away," replied Walter deprecatingly. One minute he really hoped it would, the next he was mad to go. Eddie had already. Billy was to set off the following Friday. The Reid boys decided to put the Peppers on the farm forthwith and try their luck. Duncan Grieve and the unmarried Scott brothers rode to Forbes one day looking for work and never came back.

Everything Walter looked at now was sharp-outlined. Tin roofs seemed sliced from crystal, while sprouts of spring grass on the damp creekbanks were brilliant yet sombre, like green velvet. When low clouds parted to let through the sun, patches of the countryside would suddenly illuminate. It was a post-quaternary landscape, the soft heaven of a new epoch. The usual agents of change, erosion and weathering, were replaced by light and emotion. From here Walter was to step he knew not where — except that if he once gave up, and said, as he was still able to, *no*, then this pastel erasure of the ordinary past would cease, never again to tip forward into a million new colours, nor soften — ever — the infinity of hard rocks, stubborn hills, and motionless plains that threatened to hold him.

Mr Gilchrist purchased "seat of war" maps which were stuck to the dining room wall. He placed a red tag in the North Sea, where, it was said, guns had been heard.

Off they went to the big open air patriotic meeting held the night before Billy's departure: Walter and Billy with their fathers — though Mr Mackenzie was sour about Billy's plans.

"He'll do what he wants. He's done it before."

"You can rely on me for a hand," said Alan Gilchrist, whacking his unsteady neighbour on the back.

"I've got a big club handy for the next man who greets me with, 'anything fresh about the war?' " complained Billy. But in the next breath he added: "What's the news?" and was as anxious as anyone to taste the meeting's excitement.

The theme, announced by the mayor, was that every man who owned stock or had the right of citizenship should help to protect those rights. Though his face formed the hub for spokes of the British flag hung at his back, he said they were not assembled in any spirit of jingoism, but to deal with the most serious question in the history of Europe since the days of the Spanish Armada.

Tom Larsen arrived at Walter's elbow. "Jingoism," he stated, pointing to the platform as if at a blackboard.

"Didn't you hear him say it wasn't?"

The mayor now roused the crowd with his auctioneer's voice, asking for donations in cash and kind for the comfort of those who went to the front, and to make sure that the wants of their dependents were provided for.

"That's the stuff," said Mr Gilchrist.

First Mr Smallcombe sprinted up. Right away he and his brother were donating a rail truck of fat sheep. The chief thing was to feed the men.

"I'll send a truckload of scholars," muttered Tom, though only Walter heard.

Skinny Jones then danced aloft. He said the occasion was one for special efforts. They had one of the finest countries in the world. There was no place where a man could get better returns for his investments. Jones Brothers would donate half a truck of sheep.

"He's my man," said Tom, elbowing Walter and releasing a grim hee-haw. "You see? Money's at the core."

A drunk arrived on the stairs of the podium, balanced like a jelly as he tried to speak, but was captured by Constable Arkwright to cries of: "Put him in the army!"

One farmer shouted, "I'll give twenty-five." Others: "Put me down for ten . . . fifteen . . . a draught mare . . . oats." Promises flowed forward in a wild flooding of property into battle: if weapons had been to hand, and an enemy sighted, even the stiffest among them would have given chase. With a voice like a drum and perspiration sprouting from forehead and cheeks, Alan Gilchrist promised the proceeds from his next thirty ewes, and Mr J. Westcott donated a sulky to be disposed of as the committee thought fit.

Too loud this time, Tom said: "I'll drive it to England."

"Shut up," said Billy.

"When's the 'chalky' going?" asked a voice two

rows back. Another voice ferociously struck: "We oughter help him." After that Tom held his tongue. The gas lamps run up for the occasion barely reached this far — when Walter turned to identify the callers he saw only a log jam of brown hat brims.

The band struck up and the crowd milled round, unwilling to be prised from its discovered one voice. "Rule Britannia", "La Marseillaise", the Russian national anthem, and "God Save the King" were played before the meeting broke up.

"Don't that music stir you?" asked Billy as they parted. "*Whoompf!*" he gestured, curving an imaginary bayonet upwards.

Then, as simply as stepping through a doorway, Billy caught the next day's train to Sydney. A week later a letter arrived from Trooper Mackenzie, Australian Light Horse, enclosing money for Novelty to be railed to Liverpool.

At the Agricultural Bureau picnic, held two days before Walter left, four hundred picnickers gave three explosive cheers for Walter and the other six who were soon to go, and sang "Auld Lang Syne". After the formalities Ethel asked if he'd walk down to the creek with her. She wore a loose calico tunic for the sports. Whenever a fold of the material swayed against him he felt the weight of a friendly limb, or hip, and once, he was certain, a breast.

Under a canopy of wattle she suddenly said: "You can kiss me if you like."

"But we're not going together."

"It doesn't matter."

"You'd expect me to write — I couldn't."

He listened to the frogs in the bristly reeds. She removed her sandshoes and he saw an X-ray picture of toes in dirt-stained socks.

"Don't be a dill. Haven't you kissed a girl before?"

"Too right I have."

At first she was all bone, and smelt in patches of sawdust from the Ladies' Nail Drive, which she'd won. And of sweat. Then her lips seemed all consideration. He discovered himself flat on his back in the shade, almost a baby, while Ethel manipulated his adult responses from heaven. She took his hand and guided it to the now-taut fabric at her chest. "Move it," she mumbled. Here he discovered a cushioned, un-Ethel-like part, as wonderfully boneless as her lips. Experimentally he shifted to his side and embraced her. She said, "Oh, yes, hug me," and guided his shy hand through an armhole where under her singlet it encountered, like a soft toy, the small handful of her breast and its button of nipple. Then he felt her hand fumbling at his fly, which by then was so upraised that part of his concentration had been spent on wondering if she'd noticed. Broad daylight or not, he and Ethel were personally linked — he'd never felt so closely in contact with anyone. His hand plied ceaselessly from one loose-hanging breast to the other, while she did the same between his legs, making him gasp when she released two buttons and slipped cool fingers inside.

Then it ended.

Ethel was on her feet screeching at two shapes lurking in the paperbarks, barely ten yards away. "You stinking Spicers, you bloody little spies!" She grabbed a stick and advanced on the now-standing boy and girl. The moment they blew raspberries and ran, Walter remembered his buttons, fixed them, and was on his feet by the time Ethel turned around.

As they walked back to the picnic she said, "You can't say you've never been kissed."

He was about to object, but said: "Thanks."

"I'll still be here after the war," she went on matter-of-factly, "Why not visit me then?"

"I will, definitely." Looking at her side-on he discerned a different profile from before. Not sharp and hungry at all, but soft and sad. He ought to have been shocked by what had just happened, but wasn't. He had no curiosity about her — just a liking.

"Those things we did back there. I liked them."

"Of course you did."

Above the bank they could see the hats of the long jump judges. A balloon drifted past then burst on a thorn bush leaving scrappy green rags. They circumnavigated the sportsfield staying clear of the crowd.

"When a girl says 'come and visit', does she always mean it?"

"Anyone's welcome who's nice."

"Would you say it just out of politeness?"

"Not me!"

"Would someone else?"

"Someone?"

She gave him a look which showed she understood. Billy was certain to have mugged her up on Frances — though in probing, Walter hadn't meant her to realize. He said, "I didn't mean a special person," intending to say "no-one in particular." But it was too late.

"Oh, sure. *She* would have meant it."

The sharp profile returned. A peculiar white knuckle showed on the tip of her nose. Could she possibly be jealous? But it didn't last.

"Here's why," she said, good humouredly stiffening her right index finger on the palm of her left hand. "One: the Gilchrist money."

"That's a myth." But as the district could see, Alan Gilchrist sailed through the bad seasons — this year had been bad so far — and still sent his sons away to school.

"Two: you tickle a girl's interest." She laughed, he blushed.

"Three: you're leaving."

"Just that?"

"A girl hates to lose things."

"But I wasn't leaving when the invitation was issued."

"Was she?"

They had almost reached their families.

"Does a girl hate to lose even those things she hasn't got?"

"Some do. Especially what they haven't got."

"What's number four?"

"There isn't one."

"I saw — you were about to count off another."

He bumped her shoulder accidently and she glanced at him unguardedly, taking the contact as a gesture of affection.

"I can't answer."

"Come on. We're not playing riddles!"

But she galloped off, asking who won tilting-the-ring and the Old Buffers' race. When her name came up for a prize she ran backwards past Walter and called, "Honest, I can't say."

The bump, a mere chance intimacy, in the meantime must have made her wonder. For when the picnic boiled itself out, and the sun sank low and cold, and a string of sulkies and drays set off for the road junction with knots of walkers following, she very cosily took his arm.

"I know all about the girl in Sydney. Billy told me."

"She's just someone I met. We've hardly ever spoken." He wanted her to see how little there was to it. And there really wasn't. Who was Frances now? A hum thinning out along dark rails.

She sought his hand and held it among the folds of her tunic where no-one could see.

"I wish we'd — got to be friends — before," Walter managed. He felt a kind of drunkenness with this angular girl beside him. Across the paddocks, under cut-out hills, a mist had developed. Above, the first star glared through a pinprick in the stretched blue. In a hollow they entered a band of cold air, then rose out of it into an atmosphere of dust and pollen stirred by the passing crowd. Ethel sneezed. Walter said: "Everyone's suddenly taken to me because I'm going. You'd hardly believe the change in my father — all year he's been rotten, but when the war business got going he did a double somersault."

"I suppose he knows what he's missing."

"No — he hates me."

"When you and Billy came with the news I felt awful. Sometimes I get feelings about things. F'rinstance I knew Aunt Elsie Mackenzie was going to die."

"So did we all."

"I knew before anyone. I watched her once in church: she seemed to disappear. Uncle Hugh put his arm right through her when he reached for his hymn book."

Ethel's practical sports-shoes trudged on beside Walter's boots.

"She might have just ducked outside for a tick."

"You think I'm mad. Do you want to hear something else?"

"It depends."

"After the war you and Billy will be safe. I had a dream where the two of you lived in houses with wives and babies."

"Is that a promise? I think I'd rather die."

"You mustn't joke. Your wife was awfully pretty."

She released his hand, and leaned on his elbow for support while fishing for a pebble. The last picnickers had long since passed them and gathered fifty yards farther on, where the T-junction sent its arms north and south.

"Any more dreams?"

"The both of you were unhappy. Billy just stared at me. I *know* this war's going to change people."

"It'll be a lark."

But Ethel's dream unsettled him. The fate she pictured — that of the unhappy returnee — tossed him far ahead of anything he'd thought up for himself. War was a game involving picketed horses grazing under a bank while their riders in bush jackets and bandoliers crawled through rocks and grass on elbows and stomachs and popped their rifles at other distant figures, shabbily clad. The trouble with Ethel's scalp-creeping predictions was the way they planted him right here, at home, the very spurning of which was an act the war itself enabled.

"What about the final thing you wouldn't tell me. Was it good news or bad?"

"I'll have to think."

"Was it about Frances Reilly?"

"*Who?*" She scuffed the gravel angrily. He'd broken

a rule by mentioning her name.

While he waited for an answer he discovered he understood a secret about the war. About his going.

It was this: every place, every person, had come to him bearing love. That was the reason why the country glowed specially yellow and green; why his mother had cried the other day when Douggie, home for the holidays, played drums on the pudding plates while their father watched cheerily; why flags draped every poor settlement hall; why Ethel had kissed him at the sports, why now she once more took his arm and steered him towards the junction. Love, love — only it didn't mean charity or comfort, nor even kindness. It was a torch of passion hurled from the darkness of a million small lives, which Walter was expected to catch and keep alight for others. Out of these thoughts he blurted:

"What if I didn't go?"

But Ethel passed no comment. She smiled a farewell and said, "You're right — it *was* about her. I'm sure she's —"

"Well?"

"I'm sure she's not like me — soft hearted. Oh, that doesn't mean bad luck for you. She'll take what she wants, and keep it. But do you think I'll ever amount to anything? The district's got me, and I'm stuck fast. Imagine, I've never been more than thirty miles from home. I can't see my life changing."

"You'll marry."

But Walter was dull when it came to predictions. And so dull in relation to Ethel that he couldn't picture her beyond the moment of their parting. Not one ounce of her.

"Marry? Even Duncan's done a bunk."

She pecked him on the cheek in front of everyone. "Come back," she whispered, and he knew that she meant to her, to their tangle by the creek, and not just "alive". The spirit of this command cancelled the gloom of their parting exchanges, and for the first time Walter grasped her prediction of his survival as a formula for breezing through the months ahead.

"I'd be a mug not to," he whispered in reply. With a sharp finger she poked him in the stomach.

The next day, an hour before the evening meal, Walter sat at the desk in the room called The Office. It was really a long bench, with invoices, letters, account books and catalogues stacked by his meticulous father in neat piles under the window. The chair was swivel-based, with fat leather padding on the seat. He took a clean sheet of paper, uncapped the inkwell, dipped the pen, let the blue liquid drain down, wiped the nib on the inkwell's glass lip, examined it, rattled the bone shaft of the pen on his teeth, and stared out the window.

What should he say?

His view extended down the home valley, a mere depression, to the blobs of trees on the low basking hills at the far side of the road. The last sunlight searching at ground level illuminated humped tree-roots and caused the grass to shine.

He stared, chewing the pen.

His mind leapt to impossible conclusions — there he was after the war with Frances, only she wasn't "awfully pretty". When he saw a lump of child on her knee the scene went blank. All he wanted was a word with her. Then she squirmed in his arms under the wattle at the sports; ah — he travelled on the train again, this time without Mrs Stinson, and when the lights went out he chased her for a kiss, but free of a tunnel she sat staring enigmatically out the window . . . But he too sat staring out a window, attached to this moment, these circumstances, this ignorance, lack of will, habit. One second ago the sun had been everywhere, lying in the grass gullies, unfocused at the edges but strong as gold at the centre. The next second it had gone, and the green undulations turned grey as cardboard. And in the room he was aware of hearing the last tick, but one, of the clock.

Again he dipped the nib and this time wrote the letter. He wrote slowly. He said he was glad at last to hear news of her from Billy. The war had caused a lot of excitement in Parkes. How were they taking it in the city? Quite a number had left already including Billy and others not known to her. He supposed many she knew must be going from Forbes. He was leaving soon himself. Time permitting, he would like to call on her in Sydney . . .

The light almost gone, Walter found himself leaning low over the paper as he wrote. When he reached the bottom of the page his face almost touched it. So in the near-darkness he bent a half-inch lower and deposited a kiss, feeling nothing at all like the way he'd felt with Ethel. His fresh-shaven face rustled across the dry surface. Then he signed his name, addressed and sealed an envelope, and sat awaiting the call to dinner.

10
The World of Men and Women

"You'd better come with us," offered Frank Barton after they left the train at Central.

They made their way up Pitt Street, soon entering a narrow-fronted hotel where Frank and Nugget Arthur were known, and where the woman in charge, fishing in a drawer for keys, did what Frank asked when he said: "Best give the young chap a room to his self."

The two older soldiers left Walter at the first floor landing. A red-carpeted corridor ended at small windows in far distant walls. It was as if the narrow hotel had widened behind the facade, becoming greater than it seemed. Cane chairs and lounges relaxed in the gloom.

Then up Walter climbed to his room under the roof, placing two feet on each step as a child climbs.

Today was his twenty-first day in the army. Climbing the steps he counted them all, remembering each for its novelty, including the oath that had put an end to so much unfinished business, propelling him from one world to another: ". . . I will in all matters appertaining to my service discharge my duty according to the law. So help me God."

His room was narrow, with a single iron bed against the wall and just enough space for the door to open. Part of the ceiling was occupied by the underside of the continuing stair, a white-painted box that he could reach without stretching and creak with the palm of his hand. He liked the feeling of just this timbery stair leading to the sky, and his hand supporting it. A small casement window, chest high with stiff lace curtains, admitted chunks of last minute sunlight. He lay on the bed, boots on, and watched the magnified patterns of flowers move in and out of focus as the curtain shifted in a light breeze. Hairs of sunlit cotton threw shadows of microscopic life on the plastered wall. If he lay with his shoulder blades flat on the bed he could breathe deeply without feeling pain.

Was that why Frank and Nugget had invited him to tag along on this, their first weekend leave? Because of the fight with Pig Nolan?

Pig was a light horse recruit who had brought his nickname down from Gunnedah where his father owned a clothing store. He was Gunnedah's Eddie Harkness, the son of a town dignitary, only neater, with sandy brushed hair, a mouth of expensively maintained teeth and well-kept nails brought up to the touch of twill and banknotes. Also he was sharper than Eddie, smart and knowing, quick with figures. In a trice he became the regimental bookie, and that was how the trouble between them started.

Walter had put sixpence on Nugget Arthur the day of the horsebreaking. He stood a head taller than Pig and craned to see how the stake was recorded.

"Eyes off."

"I was just looking."

"Pay more, see more."

They stood outside the mess hut. An orderly wiped his hands ready to clatter the iron triangle for breakfast. Men were draped everywhere in blue early morning shadows.

When Walter innocently looked even closer Pig said, "Shit, I'm going to have to smack your little fingers," all the while inscribing neat figures with a slim blue pencil.

"It's my money."

"It's mine till settlement." Then Pig added exasperatedly: "This must be baby's first bet."

"What'd you say?"

But Pig snapped the book shut and joined the others: Nugget Arthur squatting in grass at the base of a flagpole with knees bent up to his chin, his face after years of horsebreaking like a brown knobbly pear; Frank Barton with a shoulder propped on the same pole while his words uncoiled downwards; Bluey Clarke with elbows resting on the ledge of a tankstand (rump protruding) and with crossed feet swinging almost free of the ground; Boof Lucas also with an elbow on the tankstand, his face cupped in the palm of a hand so that his tallow-pale fleshy cheek bulged under his left eye. Frank Barton was the neatest person Walter had ever met. He searched continually for balls of fluff and flecks of cotton, finding snagged seeds on his trousers, and now, without distaste, diverting a wee white grub in mid-hoop from its journey towards a shirt pocket. With his head bent down it was difficult, always, to hear what he said.

He started to speak to Walter. Then the breakfast gong rang anyway, and they moved in. Bluey Clarke landed at a walk. Boof unstuck his hand but the bulge persisted, a farcical feature. Nugget Arthur limped for a couple of paces before his circulation got moving again. And on his toes Frank Barton climbed the steps of the mess hut with the smooth motion of a kangaroo dog. Somewhere among the others Pig Nolan had slithered inside unnoticed.

149

Mustered from the resting paddocks after breakfast the horses moved in tight, frantic circles, heads held high in panic and manes flying as gates were opened and mounts selected one by one for breaking; "Warrigals" from Narromine, but soon to be tamed and their sturdy Waler temperaments exploited. It was a long day. At noon Billy had turned up, flash in full dress uniform having ridden across from the other camp in a headquarters detachment. They talked in the privileged shade of a marquee, then following lunch Walter perched on the rails with a hundred others, a raucous spectator among many.

Afterwards he found Pig sitting cross-legged in the mouth of his tent counting money.

"I understand you owe me two bob."

" 'Understand'? Either I owe it or I don't."

"Sixpence at four to one. Nugget Arthur."

Nolan made a pained show of consulting his book, dotting this, crossing that, licking a finger in feigned self-absorption.

"Well?"

A florin butterflied through the late afternoon light. "Now be a good boy and keep half for your mum and don't get drunk on the change."

After locating the coin Walter hauled on a guy rope to straighten himself.

"Sorry?"

"Sorry?" returned Pig in the same tone.

"What are you getting at?"

"Always seeing things that aren't there." Nolan clicked his tongue mock-parentally as he slithered the remaining coins into a small canvas bag and buttoned the notes into a shirt pocket. "I'm blessed if you're not."

Walter found himself blocking the entrance.

"Out of my way, *boy*." Pig used two fingers reversed in the up-you position insolently to stroke rather than push his way past. Walter replied by ramming the shorter man palm-flat on the sternum. Pig surprisingly fell backwards and landed unbalanced in a percussive heap.

"*Struth* —"

Perhaps a second or two passed while he pawed his way up from the boards, perhaps no time at all. For Pig flew, plummetting horizontally at stomach height to butt Walter in the solar plexus with his deft hard head.

A toppling Walter asked, *"Hook? Hook?"* wheezing the throat-high word a body makes when it requires air. He doubled over and nature co-operated by allowing a mouthful. But not Pig. Down came a rabbit punch.

Walter tried to point out, as if to a jury, *"Dirty fighter."* It was an impotent appeal. A black curtain dropped and as suddenly climbed clear. Now he was lying on the ground and could see the toes of Nolan's boots a couple of feet away. But how unfair: one boot flew towards his chest and winded him once more with an oddly painless blow (here it was to hurt most later). The other lifted from the turf, dithered experimentally until it swung opposite his mouth, then hard leather deposited an exact and painful kiss on his upper lip.

Two feet took pity and left. Two feet unaccountably hostile picked their way across the patchy grass and disappeared. It seemed appropriate that a sharp-edged stone should materialize in the salty red stream which poured from Walter's mouth. But when he spat the object clear it turned into a tooth. Who was the kneeling stranger asking, "Mate?"

And this other who came running down the tent lines to stop with hands on hips: "Well, I'll be buggered. The quietest fight I've ever heard."

Go away. I'm ashamed.

A bugle call climbed into the air above the camp and curled there, hanging like a question mark.

His mind struggled to ask why. Why the fight? Groggily it seemed to have been over sixpence. Later he tried to explain things to Ollie Melrose who said, "Get back at him. But wait your chance and make it stick."

Pig lacked charm, his power was charm's opposite, but the end result was the same. Everyone deferred to him. When Walter saw Pig surrounded by a bunch of cronies he felt like the lone enemy of evil. Some of those cronies were also Walter's new friends.

Even Frank and Nugget, these two wet heads of slicked down hair crossing the street to the Regal Café because the hotel did not serve an evening meal. Walter had dozed: now he hung from the window and watched the free show forty feet beneath, where the two known heads glistened, conferred, and bumped through swing doors. From high up the street revealed its hidden purposes. No movement appeared random, as it would from ground level. It was easy for Walter to envisage for himself a serene track of fate leading from upper Pitt Street to the Quay, and across the harbour to Cremorne.

He was too excited to feel hungry.

Too happy.

Five days ago a note had arrived from Frances

saying *Come next Saturday. We'll be keeping watch on all
ferries* (the last phrase twice underlined, so that it flew
from the surface of the blue notepaper). And she had
finished *How Exciting!* in a burst of rocketry that
glowed even now.

Certainly throwing Pig Nolan into a heap of
shadows.

Walter had been given light duties in the officers'
stables when who should poke his nose through the
railings but Pig. It was the day of the letter, though:
nothing could touch the idiotically smiling trooper
with his bucket, shovel, broom, and inclination to
whistle (except it hurt).

"Look who's drawn the easy life."

Wait, warned an inner voice. Another side of him
wanted to rush the gap, rattle the bucket, and
childishly snarl. A third party was busy groping for a
smart crack. A fourth fumed wordless.

By good luck Captain Ashworth's "Daisy"
(hindquarters square-on to Pig) lifted her tail. The
perfect oval that formed when muscles drew back filled
with a half sphere of shit which enlarged, swelled like a
green eye, rolled clear and slapped to the floor. It was
followed by several more, a sequence of rapid
dissolving drumbeats. Walter clownishly shrugged:

What can I add?

Pig slung an economical pellet of spit at the
slithering mound, and departed.

He could wait. Happiness had that effect:
everything, it seemed, could wait. Paying back Pig,
food, sleep, even the journey to Cremorne could be
infinitely delayed. Happiness took care of time with a
golden promise: *now and forever . . .*

The room had turned almost completely dark. Walter stared at the ceiling and thought about home. Suddenly he was back on the place, swishing a stick through grass behind the house, eating dinner from a white plate rimmed with silver (a hated combination), listening to Douggie's chatter while thinking of something else. But this Walter-at-home experienced an elating effect of fulfilment: he was able to view himself in the future. It was like looking into the facing mirrors of a barber's shop and seeing not only the identical reflected images demanded by the laws of light but also varying images of himself as he must appear to others. The Walter who after his fight with Pig had angrily demanded a splash of water from a nearby firebucket and could not understand why his helpers refused (the bucket had been filled with sand) was, it had to be admitted, a bit of a prig. Introspective youth is always priggish —

Don't look. I'm ashamed. Ashamed of my blood, ashamed of my tooth lying in the grass (here come the ants). Ashamed of this humiliated body.

Why?

Because I love it. I love its name. I love my self and my self is broken (broken in the mirror). The prig in the mirror preceded by his physical template — about eighth down, sharp-outlined but one dimensional, not yet misty pale in the cube of glass. The army's purchase: Weight, ten stone eight. Height, five feet ten. Chest thirty-seven, expanded, forty-one. Age, twenty. Moles and identification marks, one under left nipple. Eyes, blue. Hair, brown. Religion, Presbyterian.

Pig had seen deeper than this.

And deeper too than —

Name?

Walter Edward Gilchrist.
Age?
Twenty.
Give date of birth.
Third of April, 1894.
Occupation?
I help my father.
Father's occupation? (tap of pencil)
Farmer.
That makes you *Farmer*.
(A pause)
Next of kin?
My mum or my dad?
Father.
Alan Gilchrist, "Whispering Pines", Mt Cookapoi, via Parkes, New South Wales —

Pig had brushed aside the outline fitted by these labels, impatiently thrust past any explanation, and socked the prig they sheltered, socked him hard and fair.

Fair? Here was an odd number in the line of barber's shop selves deferring to Pig's judgment as readily as the next man, accepting not just the punishment he dealt, but his right to hand it out. What nonsense. I am the calm bloke of good fortune, the calm good bloke of fortune, the fortunate good of calm bloke . . . . Frank? Nugget? Ollie? They all appeared as witnesses, and when the barber in a judge's wig asked if such was the case they replied:

"Yeah, it's like he says."

The many selves settled to one, the mirror faded,

155

and he woke: the room had sailed some way into the night; the ceiling was grey and low-hung like a cloud. Then out of the cloud came the sound of an unoiled hinge being slowly opened. No, the creak of wood. The roof. Someone was creeping up the stairway to the roof. A female giggle came wrapped in a deep-voiced murmur. Walter crossed to the window feeling ill from waking too early, from falling asleep in his clothes. From below came the *clap-clep-clup* of a slowing carthorse, and the grate of iron-rimmed wheels.

"Don't," said the female voice over Walter's head. But the protest was followed by an unrestrained version of the stairbound giggle. Then again the male murmur, still muffled. Walter perched on the window-ledge and leaned out till he saw the underside of curved rails, and just visible through the iron an army trouser lapped in folds of dark skirt.

Now the man's voice came through clearly. "You're hard, Marge." It was Frank Barton.

The woman spoke at length, but now it was her turn to bury the words in cloth, or have them sucked away by the drop, or whatever it was that took them out of understanding: possibly just lack of context on Walter's part, because clusters of enigmatic phrasing remained (had he heard everything, but none of it sense?):

" . . . walk instead of dancing . . . "

" . . . That's what I think. After that — a comrade . . . "

" . . . My kind of promise . . . "

Voices you might hear when passing a theatre on a hot summer's night . . .

"Bill."

Then thunder on the narrow stairs (Frank) followed by a buffeting descent of wind (her): confusion that swirled on the landing outside Walter's door. Unhesitatingly he knelt at the keyhole. Skirt, waist, back and dark head descended in hurried steps, but then side-on sped back. Yanked upwards? For a second the woman's midriff filled the view, a blue woollen jacket with a thick belt of the same material, and in place of the buckle a large button. Lit from below in the stairwell's pale electric light, the button stared at Walter like a large eye containing a single yellow spiricle.

Then she sank, and although the standing form of Frank momentarily intruded, Walter found himself staring directly into her face. She was actually embracing Frank's legs after an apparent drop to her knees, and guiltily Walter whipped his head aside. But she was oblivious to his spying. Young, with full lips and a broad chin, her repose might have been submissive, but no. It was both determined and surrendering, revealing the feminine gift of control in the midst of a sensual crisis. On her head sat a round black dish of hat with a rim as stiff as metal. When she intensified the embrace by hugging Frank's knees the rim carelessly dented.

With uncharacteristic force Frank said: "My room. Now." Her eyes, such smoky glass, closed, rested, and she stood.

They left, but Walter stayed on his knees, wondering. A minute later doors rattled in the still corridor below and with short steps and stocky Nugget Arthur climbed the stairs to the roof.

In semi-darkness Walter poured water from the jug

on the bedside table and splashed his face. He damped a corner of the towel and wiped chest and underarms. Then he undressed and climbed into bed. He lay between cool sheets and shifted his hands (wincing) behind his head. Should he feel cheap for spying? He realized now why the powdered dame at the downstairs desk had engaged in mysterious eye-play with Frank, and why the youthful companion had been consigned to an attic. The hotel obviously was a place for assignations.

But he admired Frank and the woman. Suddenly Frank's whole life spread out for inspection, not in its details but in character. Occupation, drover; age, thirty-two; place of abode, Moree. Walter knew no more facts than these, yet a sense of dignity and drama, of adult passion, now attached to the couple. And Nugget aloft, smoking his pipe as the night slipped away, he too attained stature in the world of men and women.

Although the hotel served no evening meal its tiny dining room managed breakfast. Frank and Nugget arrived together, and lo! the manageress ushered in the smokey-eyed woman (no disapproval there). Frank leaned across:

"Wally, I'd like you to meet my fiancée, Marjorie Hicks."

The breakfast passed like a convivial family gathering, with no hint of the night's secrets.

By eight thirty Walter had navigated Pitt Street as far as Martin Place. Along the way old men had shaken his hand, a greengrocer had given him an apple, and a woman in a doorway had winked invitingly: the world loved his uniform. In Martin Place a newspaper seller ran across and waved a *Herald* under his nose, and he stumbled to the Quay immersed in war news.

"Hey soldier!" — another apple, which he noisily munched.

France — that's where they'd be in no time flat. He rolled the paper into a tight scroll and slapped it against the seam of his trousers. France: the satanic face of Robespierre, the fierce *Sans Culottes* and months with names like exotic fruit. Liberty, equality, fraternity . . . vaguely he glued together old injustices and this war, where the British forces were on the side of progress. He supposed the Germans were an *Ancien Regime* that must be struck down: only more vicious, more determined, rotten but not rotted. Not yet! Ha!

He reached the Quay in a fighting mood. The ferry was not due for another twenty minutes so he promenaded, using the *Herald* as a swagger stick.

"Who reaps the profit? *I'll tell you.*"

A man on a fruit box had gathered a crowd of a dozen or so where a street ran down from the Rocks.

"Nobody," came a lame interjection from an onlooker in a canvas apron.

"Nobody? Do you believe that? Do you believe that?" cried the speaker in what seemed genuine alarm. Short, prominent-jawed, wearing thick spectacles and speaking in lisping but resonant accents, middle aged, a foreigner, he stepped down from the box which skidded and crashed behind him. "I'll tell you. It's the bosses who reap the profit. They build the guns, they make the ships, they fill brass shells with powder and put lead noses on them, but they aren't the one to stand up and shoot them off. Oh no. It's —" here he pointed to Walter, "it's mother's sons like this lad."

The man in the canvas apron clapped mockingly with cupped hands.

The speaker stepped down and threaded left and right to confront Walter while the spectators formed a ring.

"Who do you think you're fighting for?"

"It's *what,* not who." The words came easily: the argument had been rehearsed with Tom Larsen. Walter struck a pose with hands on hips, towering above the speaker. "Liberty," he extemporized, "equality, and fraternity. All that stuff." The crowd laughed: he laughed with them.

"Look at the wealthy classes, the munitions makers, the clothing manufacturers, the food companies, even the boot polish and brass polish makers. How many of them are serving in your company?"

"Never counted 'em." The crowd was his. "Wait a sec — we've got Arnotts' Biscuits. Colonel Arnott," he informed the watchers.

"The boy's got bite."

"What does it matter?" The speaker turned on them, the clowns: "I'll support this war," he struck his own chest with an audible knock, "when *all* the people who own Australia are prepared to fight for Australia. Then I'll don the khaki."

"They wouldn't have you, you're undersized."

Three wheezing breaths and the man was off again. "The wealthiest should be put in the front ranks, the middle class next, and then the politicians, lawyers, sky pilots, and judges in that order. When that happens I'll be with you, brother."

"Good on you," said Walter. He had intended the comment to sound derisive, but it came out differently,

160

as if he believed the man had said something worthwhile. Damn. It was the wrong time to be serious, the wrong place, here by the water where the salt tang came loaded with fish smells, and on nearby ships flapped the toy flags of half a dozen nations.

As they talked the warm sun brightly intruded, and Walter found himself edged around until it struck him in the eyes. The crowd lost interest and sauntered off. Then Walter heard the man say: *"Don't go to hell."*

They were alone: the moon-faced orator and the uniformed youth. And a strange thing happened.

It was exactly as if one of his childhood "staring attacks" had recurred, not engulfing him this time in a blank absence but creating two worlds, one of the street where brick and wood and water shone bright as crockery, the other of metaphor rushing vividly into reality. For it was all *as if:* as if he stood at the end of a chute down which four heavy weights, tombstones? yet also just the four words of the man trundled towards him, though so little time had passed that the two stood eye to eye: the fellow's finger still upraised, the rasping *hell* yet flying from his throat. As the weights waddled closer the sunlit morning darkened, the life of the city never paused but certainly it slowed . . . as it slows for a drunk man and enables his body to weave through complication. And it was with a drunk's happiness that Walter witnessed the deadly weights rumble harmlessly by, as he knew they would.

Nothing could touch him. He was charmed and blessed. His eye caught a placard where a fat John Bull's braces flew off as he carved a turkey called Labour. In the midst of foolish joy Walter grabbed the man by the shoulder, a padded hand-grip to retain his balance, and giggled. The speaker's flow had barely

161

been interrupted, but in puzzlement he slowed, losing his shrill conviction as the rehearsed words slid to a halt:

"Because if you go to hell you'll have gone there to give piratical, plutocratic parasites a bigger slice of heaven." Then he said, "Oh dear," and guided Walter to a seat on the upset fruit box. "Did I bother you?"

"Sorry, I wasn't listening." The same words serving now as years before they had served as apology to the kindly Mr Dougherty at Mt Cookapoi school, when time and again the teacher had guided him back to the world of globes and atlases after a "little absence".

"Take this," the sweating man said. It seemed to be a biscuit or wafer (it was a business card). "I've a son in the army," he sorrowfully admitted. There *were* crumbs on his sleeve. He munched a biscuit produced from the same pocket. "Keep an eye out for him. Pliz?" The thick yellow card read: "Miles Milojevic, teacher of languages", and gave a Paddington address. "In the midst of difference," lisped the foreigner, "we find affinity. I love my son and he loves me. We share the same ideals. He's not young, nor active. Why did he go?" Walter drew himself to his feet with the old man shaking his hand and clinging to his elbow. "I'm a Serbian, but all my life I've been against national frontiers. The whole muddle started with my country." He seemed curiously proud of the fact. Then he brushed the front of Walter's tunic where crumbs could not possibly have flown. "Good luck, and trust to God for your safety." He gave a sigh and began to gather his gear, ignoring Walter completely as if the particular case had no contribution to make to the general task resumed, nor ever had.

Walter wanted to grab the man and say, What does

it matter? What does any of it matter, all this to and fro when I'm about to dance across the water? But he only mumbled, "Oh, well . . . ", straightened his hat and set off.

On the ferry he stood near the bows where nobody else came, for balance holding the chugging craft's forward flagpole. He wondered when Frances would see him (or if), and whether the statue's pose he struck was what she might want of him, or whether he ought to loll in the shade, one leg nonchalantly on the rail prior to leaping ashore (forgetfully) at the last minute. Or else hide himself inside where the ladies sat, and disembark as a surprise. The tiled roofs of houses slid closer, dabs of smouldering paint on a hazy blue canvas. He concentrated his gaze on the bushy heights, not once consulting the wharf. He determined to find something of all-consuming interest up there, just an inch short of the skyline. His attention stayed aloft while the engine slowed, the boat bumped the piles, and the gangplank slapped palm-down demanding his springboard leap.

Even as he sped clear of the shed and slowed to a saunter he refused to be diverted from the long-distance objective. He would not turn, he told himself, before that waving fleck of blue off to the left actually spoke (sprinting closer, sweeps of white gesticulating). He mounted steps to a park and their paths intersected.

"Hey you!" — so different from the ladylike coo he expected that he dropped his guard as she landed at his side puffing, "Gosh didn't you see me?"

In the midst of his muttered hellos she pronounced:

"You *are* the handsomest man in uniform I've seen," and without hesitation took his arm ... took the uniform's arm. But a living limb was inside it, flexing, steadying, hard from work, driving itself to make her feel his strength, even though as they set off she was the one in charge. His tongue felt dry and wooden, drilled through the base and glued, like a toy cockatoo's.

"You're so much older," she observed, and for fifty yards did all the talking.

"See the cat there under the oleanders ...

"Guess which place is ours?" She slowed, hung back, and pointed so that her sleeve fell clear to leave an arm bare for his eye to align itself along. The pure fogged crystal of a fingernail wavered across three of four identical double-storied facades until, engrossed in an encounter of cheek against forearm Walter happened to make a movement something like a nod, and the arm fell away.

"Kitty kitty kitty?" Frances half-knelt to attract the cat but still with four fingers retained a hold on his arm. She had changed too, though he dared not say so. Her hair released from its schoolgirl's pigtail swayed across her back, and when she craned forward to softly snick her fingers the dark stream rushed over her shoulders parting left and right, leaving a glimpse of white neck.

"Pussy puss. Ah, you sweet careless darling. You don't like your mummy do you. You don't —" The cat arched its neck against a calf swathed in blue folds of dress. Tiny white flowers circled the hem, diving in and out. The nonsense she talked at first offended Walter because it seemed to exclude him. Then it thrilled him, because the pressure of her fingers remained to show she had not, as it seemed, gone drifting away at the first sight of a ginger tom. Therefore the stock phrases of endearment, new to ears from a male-dominated household, quickly took on an edge of intimacy.

She was staring up at him: dark concerned eyes.

"Well?"

"Well what?"

"Aren't you going to give him a pat?"

The cat snaked between his legs, doubled back, arched greedily against his knee and purred in a long series of serrated burps.

"Walter, he loves you."

He scooped the cat into a crook of his left arm while Frances reached across stroking the striped tail. Thus they spent the next twenty-five yards, a lifetime of near-embrace which ended abruptly when the cat clawed its way clear at sight of a bird. "Stupid cat!" said Frances with excessive vehemence, and released his arm.

"You hoo!" called a voice from an upper window.

"Hurry on down!" Frances yelled back. Did she need something or someone else, now that the cat had gone, to occupy the space between them?

A flushed, slightly overweight, intensely round-eyed girl appeared at the door to greet them.

"This is Walter Gilchrist at last. Meet my best friend Diana Benedetto. Please shake hands."

They obeyed, Diana bursting out with: "Are you the only one so far?"

"Only one?"

Then they told him about the party. Someone called Harry Crowell was coming (unavoidably), and did he know Robert Gillen from away out the other side of

Condobolin? Also such a wonderfully good friend, an *actress* named Sharon Keeley. And surely he'd heard from Billy — because as well Billy Mackenzie was due any minute.

Glumly Walter said no. But in the dark hall he gripped Frances fiercely by the elbow (brazen it out!) and swung her to face him: "I was hoping to have you all to myself", approximately the fourth sentence he had dared since the ferry.

"Oh, you shall," she caught a breath, giving him a grateful look. "I promise." And again she took his arm, this time with a fervour, he swore, equal to his own.

11
Secrets

Billy loved his uniform, but in certain situations would dirty it without thinking. Thus before a full dress parade on the Wednesday after a stray dog had gone wild in the horse lines he chased the colonel's saddled but riderless hunter through saplings and brought the mare safely back to camp the long way round, down through the swirling creek and up. Scratched and grinning he breasted the mockery of the headquarters detachment (his mates) and threw a mud-splattered salute at the chief:

"She's calm as a baby . . . They shot the dog."

Billy loved the light horse and its business with animals; the leather and brass, the confectionary odour of saddle soap, and the unfamiliar tasks of grooming — no longer after a hard ride was a horse given merely a quick wipe down and a feed of oats before being turned out into a paddock. But also he loved the strictly military side: the sweet Armourine oil which seemed pure enough to heal the sick, the glimmery but dull-drying Bisley Dead Black the crack shots used to blacken their rifle sights, and the ammunition in its heavy boxes, the cartridges themselves, the way each was identical with the next, and their seeming endlessness. He found himself whistling for hours on end as he groomed Novelty up to the shine of the equestrian painting that had been hastily hung in the otherwise rough and open-sided mess hut. And although it was no part of the light horse's function (being mounted infantry) he and the riproaring Tip Markworthy had secretly practised firing from the saddle like Frontier tribesmen.

The army loved Billy in return. He was selected for a special demonstration in the Domain, where before embarkation they were to mount a tournament involving tent-pegging, tilting at the ring, lemon cutting — the display to be brought to an end with an exhibition of wrestling on horseback, a Balaclava *Melee,* and a massed charge towards the crowd.

He intended inviting the Reillys to come and see him. By God he did, right off.

But his uniform had been dirtied on the ferry. In getting it clean before showing himself he ended up lurking out of sight down near the water, fumbling about, furious, like a man with something to hide, or to discover — climbing back peeping through parted shrubs, peering over the crowns of bald rocks and now from the shaded side of a thick-boled gum: approaching clumsily from the rear of the house which he now realized was not the rear at all, but the proper front, showing a grand facade of triangled timber and pillowed stone to the bush-clad shore of Mosman Bay, an aspect which most arrivals never saw because it was the wrong way round from the ferry path.

To his amazement a cowboy emerged from the back door and with a wild cry leapt onto the grass. A stream of other figures followed, some of whom Billy recognized: Frances, her mother, then a plump giggling dark-haired girl pursued by a thin blonde one followed by Helen the maid wiping her eyes, and last an aloof character in a striped blazer — it was the Harry-someone Billy knew by sight.

He calculated the range: fifty yards, no allowance needed for wind — bag first "whomsoever occupies the centre of attention whatever his badges of rank or lack of them". Pot the fair-headed cowboy! who in his South American costume now whistled, summoning a fox terrier that hurtled down the side path. In a flash three balls on a length of cord blurred through the air, and the little dog whined as it tumbled.

The onlookers clapped.

Harry Crow (Crowell!) alone took an interest in the outside world. For a second his gaze glided towards the point where Billy stood, then jerkily took up the flight of a seagull and flapped away. Billy supposed he had better make himself public, but still hestitated. The letter had said twelve, it was now one. He would not have been in this muddle except for a conversation with a deckhand on the ferry that had led to a dirty belowdecks meeting with the Scottish engineer. A trip through the engineroom was followed by steam-heated tea that burnt his lips, and an interminable shouted conversation about the size, weight, coaling capacity, number of rivets, name of captain (*och!* he'd missed his stop), age of youngest boy sailor, ports of call, ports not called — of a dreadnought, *H.M.S. Dreadnought* herself, in the bowels of which this Glaswegian had once served. Billy would have gladly put his feet up and talked horses and rifles for the two rounds of the harbour he spent out of sight before disembarking: but he had not been able to get a word in. The man carried a pellet of lint in his left nostril, lodged there from blowing his nose on a fistful of cotton waste. When he drew breath preparatory to laughing the fluffy pod disappeared, then peeped out again to signal more talk, more tea, more wasted time that Billy out of perplexity and politeness could not bring to a stop. Perplexed because he had elected himself to the world's centre: polished leggings, supple straps, gleaming emu feathers in his hat — what was he doing tongue-tied in a thumping hell? When at last he climbed from the oily heat and leapt ashore the deckhand called after him that there had been another light horseman on deck the previous time round — he'd looked in to tell him, but (swift glance over his shoulder) Haggis Head did not appreciate interruptions.

So there was Walter standing off to one side of Frances making cow eyes, and it was clear the mother disapproved. Did he think no-one could see? Mrs Reilly steered her daughter closer to the figure in fancy-dress who now uncoiled a long leather whip — the lash broad as the tail of a banner — and sent the thing hovering kite-fashion over their heads. Walter jumped out of the way when Frances almost collided providentially into his arms. Like most overanxious men he needed a lesson in what a woman meant by the word "gallantry". But did it matter? Although a hook was firmly in his mouth it was a million to one she would want to reel him in. How confoundedly ill-equipped he looked, having chosen himself a uniform (no-one else could have picked it) just a fraction too short in the legs, ditto at the sleeves, and tight across the shoulders. Or had he grown in the weeks since enlistment? It was not out of the question. His bray of laughter carried across the grass as awkwardly he leapt for the fluttering thong to bring it down, missed, and toppled over.

Billy had no such trouble with the world's diversions. These days he donned his rough grace as easily as his uniform, knowing what he wanted from his fellow creatures by way of consolation and reward, how to reach for it, how to *take*. It was his polish that men envied and women admired: and under it his cheek. He was about to choose this moment to reveal himself, but the group went into a thong-fingering huddle, and he stepped back, an excluded soul in shadow.

Here lay a problem. While Billy's grace made Walter feel raw, there was another kind of grace that Billy felt had been withheld from him. Why had he been first to swing a leg over the already-sprinting Novelty and daringly, dangerously pelt after the colonel's maddened mare? It had nothing to do with winning the approval of the man. The truth was that Billy's entire person made a demand of something beyond the world, but the world (as this something's mouthpiece) sent back no answer. Was it God he still wanted to talk to? Although it looked otherwise, the world for Billy was a prison from within whose walls others could be seen enjoying free and unmerited favour from ... somewhere. It wasn't worldly grace, so it must have been the other.

Bugger him — there was Walter, ungainly, unworldly, now trailing indoors with the rest, enjoying a last glance round at the green and sunlit world that for him was no prison at all — more like a chapel, where he blundered, knelt, and was given — given what?

The cowboy was Robert Gillen. *Gaucho*, more properly. The balls and twine were a toy version of the

171

Argentinian *bolas* collected on the trip with his father. They had been absent from Australia nearly all year inspecting properties held by the family. Though he and Billy had never met, the moment they were introduced they discovered a host of common acquaintances upstream from Condobolin. Minutes after showing himself and stepping inside the house Billy was calling him "Rob", refilling his glass, quizzing him about distant places. Gillen showed Billy a postcard of a gaucho wayside shrine, a memorial to the heroic stand of one man against a recruiting sergeant. The gauchos fought in armies, he said, but on their own terms. Billy inspected the photograph in the brown light of the front parlour where Mrs Reilly had herded them for sherry.

"To them it's a sacred spot?"

"They're just station workers, but they've got their own way of looking at things. They're fiercely proud."

"That's what I'd like to see here,"said Billy, tapping the picture. "Little flags on long poles where you could rein in and think about things. Don't you reckon?"

Gillen laughed, and after a second Billy laughed too.

From overhead came the knock of heels and once the pounding of stockinged feet as someone ran the full length of a corridor. (The women had excused themselves for a minute to clean up.) Harry said to Walter:

"You look unhappy. Doesn't army life suit?"

"Why don't you try it yourself?" He was about to smile at the man and make a joke of it, but Frances descended. Could she join them? Walter opened his mouth to say yes but she sidled between Gillen and Billy and contributed to a round of laughter. Then she turned to Billy and admired his uniform. A voice beside Walter hissed:

"Jealous?"

Walter flared: "No, you silly poof."

It was the wrong word.

Harry's reaction was remarkable. Walter had used an expression of contemptuous though not hostile rejection: a "poof" at school was someone who dressed smartly, a thoroughgoing dandy.

The man's face coloured through the range of a ripe peach, sunset red rising through yellow, and then came a determined fit of coughing. Frances reached over and banged him heartily on the back.

"Get it up, Harry. What's wrong?"

"I just called him a —"

"Er," said Harry.

"I threw away a match and it started a bushfire," said Walter. "How was I to know?"

"Look," warned the man. But he was powerless.

Frances had other fish to fry:

"I keep meaning to ask," she switched to Walter's side, took his elbow. "Why didn't you ever reply to my letter?"

"Which one?" Stupid question. For months he had waited.

"January? February?" She turned to Harry. "I gave it to you to post. Remember?"

"I can't exactly say."

"But Harry!"

"Of course I sent it. Just teasing."

"It never arrived up home," said Walter. "But Billy mentioned a letter when he told me he'd run into you. I blamed the local postmistress."

"I *posted* it."

"I wonder what really happened?" Her candour unmistakably blamed Harry. She held his eye.

"This is rich."

But for the moment Harry was safe from further cross-examination. All were diverted by one of Billy's guffaws: *hoop, Hoop, HOOP!*

"They're shaped like pumpkins," Robert Gillen could be heard saying *sotto voce,* "and dance to the concertina. You'll find the odd beauty among them — the type the men kill each other for, with knives."

"Then why marry one?" asked Billy.

"Oh, no. *She's* pure Spanish. Dark hair, flashing eyes. She went to school in England."

"Go on, England."

Frances whispered to Walter: "Billy turned mother's head. Did he tell you?"

Walter saw a skeleton's fading handprint when Harry removed his clammy palm from the cedar sideboard.

"When, just now?"

"No, silly, when he called that time."

Something was building up, *had* built since that distant February — a cloud whose anvil head still towered high above them. What was Billy's game? What was hers?

After further polite chat concerning the future Mrs Gillen, Billy left the room saying, "Give me a minute", and Robert stared out the window.

"Billy came *here?*" asked Walter.

"Where else — we haven't moved."

"You're making fun of me."

"No, honest . . . As usual he tried to kiss me."

Harry sipped his sherry with a noise that could have meant anything.

"Do be quiet," snapped Frances. Harry allowed himself to take this — he was almost family. But when Walter said: "Why don't you mind your own business?" he left the room.

" *Walter!*" But Frances stifled a giggle and added, "You're as bold as I am. Anyway, Harry deserves what he gets."

In a rush Walter asked: "Frances, I want you to come for a walk with me later on. Just you and me. Will you?" Another record broken: he had never before spoken her name aloud.

Before she could answer Billy re-entered the room wearing the silver spurs and chaps of cowhide. He clasped the black gaucho hat across his heart and sang, "Be mine for everr, Ros-*marr*-eeta". Gillen grabbed the hat and led him into a monotonous dance which he accompanied by buzzing through his teeth in imitation of a concertina. The others crowded the doorway — Sharon Keeley itching to be in the act, Mrs Reilly attacking the keys of the piano, randomly pounding as if she had never played the instrument in her life, and Diana red-faced taking the opportunity to stare at Walter and Frances. The dancers seemed prepared to circle the room endlessly — sleepwalkers with lolling tongues.

"Please, let's join in," urged Frances. She tugged at Walter's sleeve, but he refused. Gillen swooped on Sharon and caused her to squeal co-operatively, and Billy — bloody Billy — took no time at all to note what was going on between Walter and Frances. He bowed low and was extending his hand when a bell rang, a loud hard clang in the hall followed by the maid's croaking, "Lunch is served".

"What's all this?" asked Billy when they were seated. He had been steered by Mrs Reilly to a place opposite Diana. There had been savouries in the front room, a variety of "angels on horseback" which Billy munched hungrily in case things ran short at dinner. Now this; the tabletop resembling a bay crowded with many-coloured yachts nudged by glass barges, in every direction a horizon of china, clouds of flowers, and a scented breeze hanging over all. Billy called loudly to Walter: "What do you recognize, eh?" Sharon sat between then. Clockwise from Billy's left the round table was arranged thus: Sharon, Walter, Mrs Reilly, Frances, Harry, Diana and Robert.

Hoarsely Frances whispered: "Mum, *why* did you put me next to him?" and Harry heard. Even as he conversed with Diana, asking if the captain her father had yet packed his bags ready for the war, he shot Mrs Reilly a look — *control your bitch.*

"Was the dance — I know you were making fun — but was the dance in the native manner?" asked Sharon.

"No-o," Robert reflected. "They do it slower."

"Furryfood," said Billy, pointing a tiny fork at Robert's joke. He swallowed painfully. "I mean, very good." Then he laughed at himself, dangling the fork between two fingers like a cigarette.

"There's tons to eat," said Frances. "This is only the start."

"We wanted to say how proud we were of Walter and Billy. But I'm not proposing a toast. We'll save that for the champagne."

Harry asked about army food: "It's all right," said Billy, "bearing in mind the time it takes to flavour a rock and boil a horse."

Mrs Reilly struck a spoon against a silver dish: *"Boys."* Then she shifted herself slightly forward to dominate the table, giving the impression of floating above the seat of her chair. Frances touched her on the wrist, signalling *we're together.* Her mother was enjoying the occasion. Somehow she was able to moderate the responses of others until they reached her level of expectation, which did not exclude a lot of fun: so the coarseness settled but not the hilarity.

But were mother and daughter truly "together" on this occasion?

"Good, rough old Pat," Mrs Reilly had confessed of their absent provider the night she and her daughter talked about the marriage: "He has all the daintiness ascribed to woman when it comes to certain aspects of matrimony." Then Frances asked: "Do you?" and her mother had laughed showing the insides of her mouth with all back teeth missing, upper and lower. She laughed the same way now, except with dentures restored. It was still rather ugly. Frances wondered if her own laugh was the same, and resolved to cultivate a different one. On looking to the end of the table she caught Walter gazing longingly in her direction, so in return she flashed a quick, sealed-lip smile (the new style) at which he switched his attention shyly to Sharon.

Frances felt Harry's touch: "Franny, could you pass the salt?"

"I'm not *Franny.*"

"He's rude," whispered Harry of Walter, "but I think he's a nice boy." He dusted his plate of already salty oysters. She heard one descend. Then he turned to her and winked a reddish eye, proposing a truce.

"Bosh," she responded.

Soon, Frances decided, she would tell her mother what she had learnt yesterday about Harry. The conversation around the table increased in intensity. Everyone except Harry and Frances seemed to be conducting two exchanges at once, with sentences flying across the table like streamers. Harry therefore took the opportunity to grab Frances by the wrist and command her suddenly frightened attention: "I know Sharon's been feeding you a pack of lies about my private life," he whispered hoarsely. "She's trying to ruin me. Don't *you* start, do you understand? Now your boy from the bush is treating me like a leper. It's no fun, drop it."

His fingers left a taut bracelet of burning skin.

"You *hurt* me."

When the soup started arriving Frances waved Helen to serve in the other direction, so that she herself would be last. She smiled and even feigned the giggles as the others progressively sniffed their plates and made noises of approval. Robert took his, Diana hers. Then as Helen advanced towards Harry there occurred one of those polite dining table pauses when with spoons grasped awaiting a signal from the hostess no-one speaks, and into the gap that occurs someone — who first? — needs must rush.

It was Sharon. And the phrase she uttered just as Harry's fluttering hand escorted (but did not touch) the plate toward its point of destination was enough to cause the hand to rebel. As Sharon spoke Frances saw what Sharon but no-one else seemed to notice, that with his thumb Harry tilted the plate causing it to flood the edge of the tablecloth and drip shimmeringly between himself and Diana, spotting a dress on one side, a trouser-leg on the other, before the amber tide ebbed.

Sharon had said, quite casually, "Have you heard

from Alf Taylor lately?" It was a public declaration of their private battle.

Everyone laughed over the "accident" and resumed their soup, including Harry after performing an exaggerated acceptance of a fresh plate from the mortified Helen (who blamed herself).

"Aren't you going to say 'sorry'?" Frances asked him.

"It wasn't my fault."

"Pooh," she whispered.

The name was just a name, but to Harry it must have been like a placard held aloft baring in crude letters the innermost secret of his soul. In the circumstances he made an admirable recovery: but it was Sharon, not Frances, who assisted by a brief but compassionate recoil from malice. She brushed a curtain of straight blonde hair back from an ear, looked at Harry with her peculiarly damp, blue-eyed stare (unfocused like a baby's) and changed the subject.

Frances condemned Harry more than ever, because in a way she hardly wished to understand he was now a force in shaping her life. She seemed unable to develop an idea or a feeling without relating it to pressure from somewhere, and the process, when it came to a head, as maddeningly it did now, made her wonder if her whole life was to be composed of these hectic and despairing dashes from one enforced commitment to another while glancing at monsters that bellowed and clawed from the pit below. No, it was not Harry so much as the story about him which threatened her composure. She *mustn't* blame him: but she did. She could not help herself. She hated him for what Sharon had told her.

Harry was not what he seemed. No-one was what they seemed. The whole world was building towards nothing but chaos — the war playing its erosive part as well, whereas till now she had thought of it as nothing but an entertaining occasion for males to dress up and go abroad. In Harry's tale she witnessed not just the betrayal of affection, but its failure.

The war, Sharon had giggled when embarking on her story, was having its effect on Harry. Not that he would or even could join the army. It was something almost too unbelievable, really quite sensational. Could Frances take it? They sat (it was only yesterday) in the sunroom at the rear of Sharon's parents' house, a projecting glass box hanging on spidery legs over a green gully thick with ferns and lantana, with an emerald glimpse of the harbour far below. Sharon smoked her cigarette from an enamelled holder. Frances smoked too, almost expertly. Already Harry was in line for a very senior position at the woolstores, but his friend, his dear friend whose place in Harry's affections only Sharon knew about — whose name rarely sounded on Harry's lips except when alone — had gone into uniform and cruelly disdained even to look in. Harry himself "fain would follow" (Sharon's mocking words): but dangling below his trim-muscled torso one leg was shorter than the other. This was evident to his clubmates when they saw him at rest between swooping dives on the monkey bars, but it hardly ever showed at any other time because Harry buried his limp in an ornate set of affectations in which blazer, pipe and cane played their part, as did his theatrical training. When all else failed Harry would pull a personality from his thespian's bag of tricks and make himself whole by dissimulation.

"But that's not so bad. Sharon, you're evil," said Frances blowing smoke. "I feel sorry for him. It's touching. Poor Harry — lame all this time and putting a brave face on it."

Sharon raised her eyebrows and looked at Frances, making a vain attempt to cover her protuberant front teeth — which she said were her worst feature and had caused her to dislike herself to the extent that now, at the age of twenty-six, she had become "shameless". ("All the stories you hear about me are true, my darling.")

Now she said, "Oh, you haven't understood! I'm going to have to spell it out."

Could she not see that Harry liked men? *Loved* men? He was — the word sounded blind with sterile vowels — a homosexual.

"What does that mean?" Frances had asked in shock, knowing full well.

Then: "Does he . . . *do* anything?"

"Of course he does. Yes, with his pals. Not Alf Taylor, though it was Alf who opened my eyes to him. Alf's a scamp. There's a story about Alf and me going the rounds. You'd better be warned — every word of it's true." Sharon circled the room, picking a fleck of tobacco from her tongue and affixing it to the window glass, which was like still water from where Frances sat (now collapsed on a cushion), blue deep and pure water encircling a world whose continents had disappeared and would have to be made all over again, because the previous ones had been only an illusion of wholeness.

Sharon said with a malice Frances was as yet too green to detect: "*Your* place . . . He boasted to Alf about hanging around your place and pulling the wool over the eyes of your mother. Though he's frightened, just a touch, that she might get ideas about him. Romantic ideas."

Frances felt ill.

Sharon talked on, sticking pins in Harry, laughing about Alf Taylor, confessing to several affairs with leading men in the dramatic society (boasting about them, rather: and Frances in a deep cool part of herself thought, If I ever need to, I shall come to Sharon for advice). For at least an hour as she talked Frances slowly realized that her conveniently fatherless family was for Harry a form of cover. His preference for his own sex, being socially unacceptable, forced on Harry an adroitness, even an expertise in many arts including that of courting women. This art now threatened his cover: it was the very mystery of its termination short of a palpable objective (in a shower of roses, say) that had already aroused Frances's hostility.

In Sharon's opinion such pressures on Harry had caused him to go slightly ga-ga.

Even so, Frances could not pity him. She was furious at being used. She recalled dozens of occasions when Harry had dismissed her heedless teasing with cruel ferocity. Somehow she demanded of him the impossible: that he should have told them about himself from the start.

After Sharon's revelations Frances had had dreams in which right and wrong, male and female, truth and lies lay tangled, as on a sickbed, under the cloudy eye of an indifferent creator. In the morning Helen had brought a pot of tea, and from under the loose-fitting lid, when she poured, crept an amber tear. She lacked the will to stand alone, she told herself. She feared failure. She was no longer at an age when it was possible to do absolutely nothing about an ambition yet still dream of it securely. What had she *done?* Dreamed through an entire year, gossiped, read books, gone to the theatre, gazed at herself in a mirror. Would it not be wonderful, for relief, to surrender to something new?

Now, at the table, Frances found herself looking at Robert Gillen, who with news of his foreign engagement had killed dead her mother's match-making. He had hardly glanced at her, not that she cared. Frances most definitely was not property. (Though when the time came, and he looked, her wish was that he would be touched with chagrin at her unexpected beauty). Anyway, his face was too pale, and his ears stuck out at angles like stable doors, and he was too at ease. She wondered if he despised the whole lot of them. Sharon was making a fool of herself by playing up to him, but he seemed unable to make her out, giving her mildly puzzled, appraising looks in the brief moments when she was not fawning. Perhaps he was wondering about her age. Twenty-six? "Believe every rumour you hear about me," Sharon had said. Well, one ran that she was actually a decade older, and had appeared as leading lady in a play at Orange before the turn of the century.

Then Frances found herself listening to the curly-headed youth making melancholy jokes at the far end of the table. In a moment her reverie matched his earlier one — she nipped a fingernail — *So it is to be Walter!* and the thought surprised her. Did it matter that she did not love him? Her thoughts ran on, contradictory and anxious, yet also somehow calculating. They came in a rush as spaces were cleared for the fish. Oh, but she *did* love him . . . or could. He was now voluble but lonely at the end of the table. How stupid it would be to fall in love with someone so young: but how impudent! Also, how brave. She alone would prove affection, with her it would survive.

"I don't think he's funny at all," hissed her mother.

"I was thinking of something else."

"It's rude not to join in. You're a thousand miles away."

So she started a bowl of preserved grapes on a journey around the table. "My apologies."

But then: what would they find to say to each other? She seemed to know more about — things — than he did. Though he was tanned and healthy and strong there was something unfinished about him. Robert Gillen on the other hand, sallow from his winter in the Argentine, even with a touch of jaundice in his looks, gained, no doubt, from the poker game that had continued non-stop if you believed him from the River Plate to Woolloomooloo, was a man. But Frances decided she needed at this moment, had needed always? a degree of helplessness in the object of her affections. Not utter helplessness — Walter had character — but certainly someone without plans for her, or secret usages, who would like her for as long as she wished (a fatal phrase, which she allowed to glide past unquestioned), who was not clever enough to outwit her, nor diabolical enough to win her abject devotion.

Walter, even if he had chanced to study Frances's face during these minutes, would not have dared to read in it the intentions that were forming. They

184

matched too closely his own desires. And Frances would have been offended if someone, her mother, say, or the observant Diana, somehow had peered into her head and declared, "Why Franny, those thoughts you're having. They only prove your cruel streak." Instead she pictured one or the other performing such an action, but with the declaration ending differently: "Why, Franny, see? You can be happy after all."

Walter had never eaten a meal like it. Nor had Billy, yet he navigated his way through the two different kinds of fish, adroitly plonked crab mayonnaise in the right place, never once dipped an elbow in the bowl of mysterious sauce, and through it all fired conversational rounds to gents and ladies alike, keeping the whole table hopping until, with the distribution of champagne glasses but before the appearance of the wine, they all felt tipsy, and the lightning bolt that had caused Harry to upset his soup seemed to sizzle harmlessly away. Frances was back in circulation, smiling at everyone. Walter had decided that her withdrawal from the chatter was somehow related to him. Was she working out how to say No to his suggested walk?

Mrs Reilly was on her feet, her fizzing glass upraised. "Here's to dear friends." Walter struggled to join the rest but Billy grunted: "It's for us."

"Harry?" His job was to circle the table filling glasses for the toast. At Billy's shoulder he said, "I envy you your great opportunity," but at Walter's said nothing.

"Let us pledge our thoughts to those in uniform."

185

"Walter and Billy," they mumbled, "Billy and Walter."

"To your safe return."

"Shouldn't we do 'the King'?" asked Sharon.

When that was done Billy said, "All right, Wal, say something."

"Me?" He stood. The glass trembled in his hand. He placed it carefully on the table, then shifted it slightly to match the damp ring of its previous resting place. When he looked up, there was Frances, her dark eyes encouraging him, and her smile. "When we decided to have a try for the war, Billy and I, we didn't expect a spread like this . . . I think it is the greatest opportunity for a chap to make a man of himself, those that come back from this war will be men of the right sort that anyone would be proud of. And we'll be back. I didn't tell you," he said in an aside to Billy to which they all listened in silence, "but Ethel had a vision where we came back safe and sound."

"That's my cousin,"Billy announced. "She's got the gift of seeing into the future."

Walter resumed his seat. Speeches were not supposed to peter out like that, but what could he say? Frances's encouragement had started him off, but then the same warmth made him tongue-tied. Mrs Reilly looked furious.

"Billy, would you like to say a few words?"

"I couldn't add to what Wally said."

"I'd like you to."

Billy drained his glass, took a bottle from Harry, then waved bottle and glass together in invitation: "All right, on your feet Wally, let's toast 'em." He delivered a rambling "thank you" which finished with a large wet kiss for Mrs Reilly, and made her happy.

"Franny?"

Frances left the room and returned with two neatly wrapped brown-paper parcels tied in blue string and topped by a plain white card.

"Goodness me," said Billy.

Frances set the presents before them and gave each a kiss. Walter's was perfunctory, he thought, whereas when she dipped to peck Billy's cheek he grabbed her arm and she lingered a second longer, not seeming to mind at all.

They had been given Vest Pocket Kodaks — "As small as a diary and tells the story better," said Harry.

"Hey, Diana, boo!" said Billy, pretending to take a snap. Diana covered her face with a napkin.

"Take my picture later?" Frances asked Walter.

"Too right!" She had said it: never a doubt — she had agreed to step out with him, alone.

As they drained their glasses, each happily, mockingly toasting the rest, it was plain to Frances that Diana had fallen for someone at the table. After Billy's joke her cheeks stayed flushed, and she concentrated on the tabletop as her fingers tilted knives and spoons one way and another to catch the light. It cheered Frances to wonder who. Not Billy (absurd thought). Robert? Throughout the meal she had hardly eaten, and when the soup spilled to freckle her lap she had seemed not to notice, although obedient to instinct she had stood, stared, and cleaned up.

Of course — Walter was Diana's type. He knew all about science, he was sensitive and charmingly withdrawn. Frances imagined them bursting with things to say to each other. There — with a kind of hot defiance Diana conquered her hesitation and stared at him. He was engrossed in side-talk with Robert — about the highest peak in the Andes, the acreage of the pampas, the width of the *Rio Plata* at the mouth: all the dull facts Diana loved. Robert let drop that his fiancée Rosa had a fierce serve at tennis, a slight but beguiling cast in one eye, a low laugh, and liked to drink rum and water. Walter as he listened displayed a profile which Frances herself found heart-catching, so why shouldn't her friend? It was etched in bronze, having the self-contained seriousness of a medallion. Diana could feast herself on such involvement with impunity. He would never look up. Not for minutes. Nor did Frances mind. It focused her feelings to have a rival: it even helped create them. She felt as if she really had made a choice, and it was the correct one.

Diana said, "Golly, such a lot of water."

"You can't see the other side."

"What about the Australians who went?"

"That was to Paraguay, up-river."

"I don't know why anyone would want to leave Australia, not for there. You make it sound so empty and fierce."

Diana was going well. She and Walter were exchanging nods. Diana had not even blushed. Then with a shock Frances saw the truth.

Billy said: "We're going, we're leaving Australia. I'm glad. I'm sick of it. Anything for a change, what do you say . . . Diana?"

Poor Diana. She would not look at him, but coloured to the roots of hair which showed black against an unfading rush of mercurochrome red. So it was Billy. Poor Diana — Billy himself saw it happen. He saw the pretty, plump face reveal its secret. He turned to Sharon: "I can't say I'll be at all sorry to see the last of these shores."

"Not the 'last', I hope."

Then Billy peeped back at Diana. She fumbled with her untouched plate and muttered:

"I'll give Helen a hand." A fishknife wallowed to the floor.

"No —" Mrs Reilly would help.

Diana shot a mute appeal to Frances: *What should I do now? Save me!* She had burned beyond redness and was dried of colour, staring at her friend from a face with the dusty pallor of a rockmelon, craning down to retrieve her knife, thus keeping childishly hidden from Billy's sight.

"Nobody's said a word about the army," said Frances in a loud voice. "Excuse me Billy, but we're all dying to hear about it. Walter? Don't you feel like heroes already, so splendidly outfitted? You'll have Robert on your tail in no time."

Sharon wickedly flicked her eyebrows: "And Harry."

"No," said Mrs Reilly in all seriousness. "Harry's doing important work."

"The Wool Clip," Harry announced with gravity, and it seemed he had already shorn, baled, pressed, railed and shipped the nation's wealth with his own bare lanoline-shiny hands. Or was about to.

"Walter?" His attention was still with Robert, who was answering an earlier question about the mode of constructing tennis courts in Santa Fe province.

"Packed earth," Robert informed the expectant silence.

Walter sipped his champagne before speaking. If he

looked not quite in touch, if he looked as gummy and dazed as he felt, he did not care. He had been correct after all to feel that yesterday and all today he had been travelling towards the centre of a vast wheel: here he was only a breath away from the nucleus. If he were to reach out, and if Frances from her end reached too, they would touch. And there it would be, the point from which all directions radiate.

"Army life is a killing bore," said Diana, having been brought up in barracks. She was now recovered. She turned to Frances (her oblique way of saying *Thanks*): "Believe me."

Walter rolled a piece of bread into a ball as he spoke: "Nobody talks about the war at camp, not the war proper. We don't know where we're going, or when."

"We just want to be in it," Billy told them, "for the hell of it."

Sharon at his elbow wailed in mock distress: "I was born the wrong sex."

"You're at the camp all day and you feel you've never been anywhere else," said Walter, flicking the pellet of bread at Billy.

"It's like he says."

"There's a chap there who cleans horses' teeth with powder." The others were eating again. Helen brought on plates the size of oval windows around which bright painted flowers struggled to escape from slabs of cold beef, turkey, ham and veal. "I've never seen horses so pampered."

"Hear that?" Billy stropped the hairs of his arm with a flattened hand. Under the regular slap ran a continuous whisper: "Grooming."

"It's the Indian Army influence," said Robert, whose family fortune was partly based on the remount trade.

"Things are — the other way around — at the top end of the world," said Billy. He had almost said *arse over tit*. "They put the horses under cover at night. In France," he addressed Sharon, "there's snow and ice."

"Who's the officer with the red face and white moustache?" asked Mrs Reilly. "I once met your commanders at the Benedettos'. I couldn't talk — nor could he. Would anyone like mustard?"

Mrs Reilly was sure the war would soon be over. Harry had said so.

"Correct?" She passed him the mustard pot.

"Tah, yes." Harry foresaw an armistice with territorial concessions to follow, and rather thought the Germans might come off best. He'd known some German woolbuyers — very go-ahead — and had a high opinion of German steel, ships, business methods. The nation abounded in *ad infinitums*. He was sure that German efficiency, their hatred of waste, their love of tying loose ends would not allow things to drag on.

"They're very thick on the ground in South America", said Robert, and went on to describe a scheme involving dirigibles mooted by a neighbour of his future father-in-law, a "Herr Schreiner". Robert thought the scheme would be ideal for Australia — he enthusiastically described a time when ships of the air would carry station wool to Sydney in time for the sales, irrespective of floods, or carry fodder in drought time to starving flocks . . . he went further, predicting that by 1930 the large outback stations would each have their own garage for 'planes and dirigibles, and the ladies' hack would have given place to the monoplane, and the horse, "our dear old friend," would have been relegated to the pasture to be fattened for beef, in the same way as the bullock of today.

Mrs Reilly wistfully observed: "And you could bring this about all on your own, couldn't you."

"He's got his father's head for business," said Harry, and asked: "Did you like them, the Germans over there?"

"Schreiner couldn't stomach British superiority. I wanted him to teach me how to fly his plane, but he wouldn't. He used to come over Rosa's *estancia* at sunset, clattering away like some kind of insect."

"Don't mistake *me*," said Harry, "I'm British to the bootstraps." And certainly his defence of Germans was unlike him. Only a few months ago he had constantly run them down. Frances said:

"Why the change?"

"No change."

"Fibber."

"Now look!"

"Mum, Harry didn't post my letter to Walter," (a vengeful whisper). Harry tipped back on his chair and said to Robert: "I don't like them, honest, as a race they're a bunch of upstarts. One individual, perhaps two. That's all I meant."

"As a race they sound all right," said Walter, "but we're going to have to handle the individuals."

"They're such sticklers for what they want. I wouldn't take them lightly," said Robert.

Sharon said: "Remember when the Archduke came out here? We went to the station to see his train coming through from Narromine, and an officer with the party — such a handsome boy — was disgusted

192

because the Duke wouldn't eat anything he'd shot, but insisted that the whole lot be stuffed."

"But you would have been only a child then, Sharon," said Mrs Reilly. She mouthed some rapid arithmetic. "You would have been only three — four? It was in '93."

They all looked at Sharon, who unblushingly replied: "They — held me up — my parents. It was when we lived in Orange."

"But it's good that you have some German friends," said Mrs Reilly to Harry. "I think it's awful just to hate on principle, otherwise we'll end up like the Irish." Though her husband had once shared her bed, he had never shared her background.

"Oh *friends*," echoed Frances, still keeping her voice low, by that means attempting to hold the dispute, like a twisted napkin, out of sight at their end of the table. Still in an undertone she said to her mother, "I think Harry wants the war to end quickly so he won't have to go."

"Unfair!"

Low voices or not, everyone heard. Billy said, "The army's not desperate. They're turning men away. Even if *you* wanted to go," he threw a pitying glance at the golden-haired heir to the Gillen acres, "they'd have to think twice."

"I'll go if they give me an aeroplane, but on the ground I've had all the excitement I can take. Did I tell you? I was shot at in mistake for an infamous half-breed." He re-created the incident: there he was with the crumbling brick of a ladies' dress shop spitting fragments at him while he sheltered in the lee of a rapidly percolating limousine. Rosa, it appeared, was not unused to gun-play, and calmly took a dress into the changing room and locked the door, emerging in a smashing gown after the show was over. They shot the man. He turned his head when the *policia* whistled low, and Robert whistled softly, to show the deadly ease with which a life may be despatched.

"Do you think, perhaps, that Ro — *her* — she didn't care one way or the other?" asked Sharon.

"Heavens no. She's just plucky."

"What colour was the dress?" asked Frances, who envied Rosa's pluck. Robert gave a picture of something they could tell was the smartest thing that side of London, or this. It was quite deflating. When was he "bringing her over"? Would it be a Sydney wedding? Could they come? Wouldn't he be lonely?

Then the meal was over, and time passed with a green golden swiftness thanks to the heady wine through which they all swam, loud-voiced, leaving their appointed seats and moving in contrary circles around the table, here a palm flattened between an abandoned serving of Charlotte Rousse and one of apple pie while someone leaned and talked, their cigarette ash in a coffee cup, here Helen levering elbows aside as she attempted to clear things, there — everywhere — the chance to linger one's gaze on the dark damp eye, the unique eyebrows, and the promised lips of a loved one in the verdant light of mid-afternoon.

"Why did you look at Harry so funnily, before?"

"He winked at me."

Walter found himself pumping Mrs Reilly's hand: "Wonderful! Wonderful!"

"I'm glad," but she plucked the half-full glass from his hand and placed it on Helen's passing tray, and said sternly to Frances, "He's had quite enough." But why should he resent it? Though she would not dare interfere with Robert Gillen like that, or even Billy, suddenly he loved her too and she could have done anything.

"What about our walk? Now?"

"Yes. I do promise. But not now. Mum?" She disappeared to help.

At his elbow Sharon leaned close to Robert. Complaining about delays with the wool cheque he said, "It's damned frustrating, I must talk to Harry about it," and Harry instantly hove up. Then Sharon in the full hearing of anyone who cared to listen made a raw confession: "I'm frustrated too."

Frances re-entered the room and started to make her way towards Walter. But this tete-a-tete stood between. She opened her mouth to say "excuse me" but the pair was engrossed. Robert had drunk too much and was now red-faced and puffy around his in-appropriately boyish eyes with their reluctant creases. "I'm staying at the Australia all this week."

"Really? But I'm meeting a friend there on Monday evening."

"Look me up. Ask for me any time after four."

"All right. I shall."

"This person you're meeting —"

"Do *you* have a friend?"

"Indeed I do."

"Then — shall we? — I mean, can we say five, definitely?"

Walter and Frances found themselves looking into each other's eyes — as if in a game of dares they held on: eye dissolving into eye, their eavesdropping providing a chorus both urgent and plain as it demanded, if they were to touch, an end to sentiment for him and for her an end to hesitation.

"About the walk?"

"Can you stay? Mum says stay to tea if you like. Yes? Then let's go later, when it's cool." She took his arm and guided him to the window, then turned to look at him because the light fell full on his face, whereas to Walter hers was darkened by the brilliance of the outside world.

．

Before the light failed Billy took more than two dozen photographs, but no grouping, he found, ever arranged itself to show just what it was about the day that he wished to hold, stare at, then tear to pieces. When the film was developed and printed — perhaps he would find it then. He needed time to think, having concluded as the afternoon lengthened that it was not just Walter who irritated him like a rash, but nearly everyone there except Diana.

Not that he gave anything away. Instead he had laughed, waving them together and apart like a professional, then scuttling forward to arrange a fold of dress and pinch a leg (Diana's), and they had laughed, and the kookaburras cackled as the low sun saluted tawny branches, and Walter put his arm around his shoulders at one stage, and he in return put an arm around Walter's and they had sung sentimental songs down by the water, bare footed, bare stockinged, until the stars came out and Mrs Reilly coo-eed from the heights to call them up for sandwiches and ginger beer.

Then he had shaken Robert Gillen's hand, thanked the hostess and her daughter, giving an extra squeeze to Diana's proffered hand because he knew she liked him, and finally he had set off, buttoning his jacket, for the ferry.

Diana and the maid were the only people at the lunch he had felt any liking for at all. Earlier on, when he had blundered into the kitchen for a glass of water and heard Helen saying matter-of-factly to Mrs Reilly while her hands glistened with soapsuds, "They're not my type. The war is going to be such fun for them. Nor's Mr Gillen my type — Lord, no — he'll sit at home like many but bet your boots *he* won't be grieving. Oh! Can I help you, Mr Mackenzie?" he had liked her. She had resembled his mother standing there, bravely complaining, though she was young. She was embarrassed and bold. And for a second Billy did not feel alone in the world.

Also a truth struck him while talking with Walter and Robert Gillen after the party had spilled onto the lawn, finishing a last bottle of champagne and making their minds up about the expedition down to the rocks. What had they been talking about? Gillen expressed the hope that the "dingo" he had left in charge of his polo ponies had been keeping them up to the mark during his absence. Now it happened that Billy fancied himself at polo. He had played in scratch matches around the district, where the game had no meaning other than itself (the local butcher was captain), and since joining up had trained with the major who was an enthusiast and liked Billy's determination and Novelty's experience. So when Gillen said to Walter, "Come up home some time and take a look at them. You might even like a game, eh?" Billy waited for an invitation too, but did not get one, nor did Walter drop a hint.

So the jolly smiles that had been flashed at Billy, the questions and the playing up to him, the easygoing tales of South America that Gillen had seemed to tell for Billy's sake as much as anyone else's, just went for nothing.

Then something happened when he almost reached the wharf that made him change his mind. Frances came running along the path and invited him back. Walter was staying — please, for Diana's sake — would he stay too?

So he did, but lived to regret the decision, and for different reasons so did Walter.

Part Three

12
Midnight Welcome

Even when burning strands of tobacco soared to the ground, when the dead match joined them and the chamber once again went black, the officer's curious face insisted on yielding up its details: silvered lips, an old parrot's hook of dusty nose, forehead squarely frowning, and yet — he'd laughed. All the way up the hill, guiding the newly-arrived light horsemen to a high trench in the terrifying darkness, the few times he'd spoken, there'd been a quack of laughter: "You'll come under fire, so don't wet your jodhpurs — drift left — talk and you'll lose your teeth." The mouth that issued the warnings itself spluttered toothlessly, counting each man with a thump on his pack: "This way. Follow the string. The heathen can't reach us now . . ."

At last someone found a candle. Its flame curved through the air behind the smoking man and puttered into a nook of hollowed-out earth, where it grew enormous. "Small chaps are as good as giants," he drawled reassuringly to Carl Peters, whose nickname was Lizzie. Then he stood upright, the only man in the chamber able to do so without banging his head. "It's not the constitution," he observed, "but Mr Colt makes all men equal." The closest face was still Lizzie's, a nodding freckled thistle. "I've seen big men crumble," the officer's laughter became a nose-cleaning operation,

"I'm not one myself."

They waited for him to spit, but heard a creaking liquid swallow. The place where they sat was a rough and dusty chamber joined to the forward trench line by a narrow tunnel-like communication trench. Similar chambers, roofed with logs and tin sheets, stretched away on either side.

"You, you and you," the officer pointed, "doss here with my chaps. The rest take the next bend round." It took only seconds for his exhausted infantrymen to drape themselves on sacking and expire like over-worked sheepdogs, while Lizzie and the rest of the new arrivals slipped around the corner leaving the three men picked by the officer too excited to sleep. Two found adjoining ledges, while the other, dark-bodied and cream-haired, perched himself between strangers. Morosely he raised a buttock and farted. "Boof —" hissed Frank Barton, who was smoothing a handkerchief on his pack for a pillowcase. His younger neighbour, head between his knees, tore at slimed knots in bootlaces.

Boof shuffled between them. "Who did the half-pint think he was — him and his bloody niggers."

The exhausted sooty-faced soldiers slept on.

Boof squatted: "Wal?"

"How about finding the ventilation."

"I called him 'Shorty' in the dark. That's what done it."

Walter ploughed a hand through greasy coils of hair. "He was trying to make Lizzie feel better. Couldn't you tell?"

Boof was the same age — twenty or so — but Walter was a puzzle. Tall, pale-faced with prominent eyebrows, he characteristically sat with elbows balanced on bony knees, hands clasped tight, giving out the unfocused look he offered Boof now.

"Bullshit," Boof insisted.

From his ledge Frank purred: "Wally's right. The major picked Lizzie for a nerve case. But I've seen Lizzie bounce back — he's a tiger ... Cool off, Boof. You're all worked up over nothing ... have a smoke ... Lizzie ought to be grateful ... it's stuffy like a mine in here, ain't it?"

A peaceful influence, Frank talked on. Boof succumbed, rocked on his haunches, hummed a soft and tuneful *Lonesome Pine*. It was then that Walter making a last attempt to loosen his bootlaces discovered his wound, an inch-long scratch along a crease on the palm of his right hand: hardly more obvious than a snip of pink thread. An inoculation against the worst. It had happened that night during their climb through the dark, when a spray of gravel had been flung up by a sniper's random bullet. The projectile hissed, stones slithered. Walter had fanned a hand across his eyes deflecting a trickle of spiked earth while Lizzie caught a fragment in the web of flesh between thumb and forefinger: "A snake," he had squeaked. Only then had the special *tock* of low-aimed rifle fire separated itself from the rest to indicate a sniper. "Suck it," the major had wheezed, then urged the file upwards.

Now Boof said cheerily, "They'd better watch out."

With everyone settled, the sound of the guns leaked through hidden crevices: half a hundred dust pans and brushes knocking and clattering.

"What happened to Bluey?"

Frank smoothed his moustache: "I never saw. He waited. No, he was with us at dark."

"Hear that one —" Shrapnel scattered overhead like

a handful of gravel, troublemaker's gravel in a side street of town.

"I could do with a laugh."

"It's closing in."

On their arrival from the bivouac down near the beach, where they had spent two nervous days under the stars after sailing from Egypt, the dugout had seemed wonderfully safe, with its entrance sandbagged like an impregnable stack of wheat, the depths supported by props of newly barked wood — a deep burrow, unlike the surface funk-holes of the past few days.

The chill spring air crept in, Frank snored.

Someone — a giant — moved heavy sideboards from side to side in a bare room overhead. A dead weight dropped and struck a spine deep in the earth. Walter's booted heels rattled on the tin support at the end of his ledge: his head trembled, bounced. "Frank — what the hell!" Light from a slush lamp cast sweeping shadows that collided and drew apart like huge eyelids in a metal sky. How long had he slept under their scrutiny — "Frank?" There'd been another heavy explosion. Propped on an elbow, Walter saw Frank cross himself, then unsnap the leather lid of his watch.

"It's just gone one."

On the far side of the chamber their lieutenant appeared trailing a rifle, peering at the face of one draped form after another.

"*Sss*, over here."

Later, one of the infantrymen vomited into a tin.

Another, lying awake smoking, waved to Walter through the gloom as if from a silent drifting dinghy on a subterranean lake.

Was it a dream — the major returning, exchanging words with those of his men awake, pausing a moment right here to say, "I'm Major Mason. Where are you from, sonny?"

Two stretcher bearers moved through the chamber carrying a limp body. Opposite Walter's ledge one of them bumped his head and the man they were carrying rolled to the floor, a log of stained bandages.

"Fix him good," said the first bearer, while the second knelt, spun loops of rope, and viciously tugged them tight.

"I knew him," croaked Walter, with horror recognizing a face he had not seen for years. It was Andy Pettigrew, the head prefect of 1910. As the bearers moved off, Pettigrew seemed lost in contemplation of sour duty. Then the lower half of his right leg flopped loose, swinging from the knee — resulting in a change of mood: the dangling leg belonged to a carefree spectator at the boat races. Frank spoke a name in his sleep: "Mossie," and Andy Pettigrew's straw boater sailed into the harbour. All Walter could think was: "I've outlived him."

"Tea?"

It was dawn. Their first day in the forward line of trenches was beginning. At Walter's elbow, a fist proffering a quart pot. Frank already up, rifle on knees, the bolt sliding back and forth as he listened for the scrape of grit. Frank dipping his ear, the metal rapidly slicking. Frank fastidiously wiping an invisible mote with the ball of his thumb.

The tea-pouring soldier took a mug for himself and joined them. He was unshaven, with a drunkard's yellow eyes and moist laugh. But he spoke his name firmly. No, not a drunkard — a man who had never slept. "Get ready to hold your breath," said this George Mullens, "when the morning breeze springs up you'll need to." He aimed a finger at the bulkhead of earth that separated the support trench from the firing line: "They'll come wafting through with the early sun." He meant the thousands of decomposing Turks who had died in the attack of several nights before — the night Walter and Frank and Boof and the rest of the Second Brigade of Light Horse had grated ashore on the Peninsula and ignorantly stared about. They had arrived on the beach incredulous, unable to imagine that the chaos on the heights overhead was caused by one group of humans in battle with another. Lizzie had said: "They're just skiting. The old hands are showing off to put the wind up us." Because of a peculiarity in the atmosphere they had been able to follow the course of artillery shells across the sky: red hot delights. Then the regiment had been urged along single-file paths to a mysterious knoll, where they scraped holes and were told to wait for an enemy who at that instant was attacking the upper positions in his thousands. But he never streamed down the gullies as expected, because of this — the slaughter described by George Mullens.

"It was pathetic," he said, "like a rabbit drive."

A while later, when Frank in embarrassment started cleaning his rifle all over again — Mullens's eyes balanced on a glass brink of tears — the exhausted soldier said: "They asked for it, but we've all got blood on our hands now." A dirty mitt swiped at his neck bristles, then hovered in front of his face as if beseeching his own silence. "Their officers drove them towards us while we sent 'em back — to hell. Do their lot have a hell? Some of the rifles overheated and seized up." He told about a well known cricketer who'd perched on the parapet taking pot-shots until he toppled backwards.

As Mullens talked in his crazed voice men cracked biscuits, sipped tea, licked apricot jam from fingers. "Some offered money for a chance. There were queues — and fights when one wouldn't give over to let the next take his place. They ran up and down with blood in their boots." The fatherly Frank reached out: "Spare us the details, eh?" But Mullens brushed his hand clear and continued, a thick-lipped boxer lurching through his last round. "The lance-corporal came back with an ammo box under each arm singing 'Rose of Tralee'. The wounded helped, ripping lids off. Meantime the Turks crept up again, and we fired with those great — flopping — *men* — falling dead on the sandbags."

A diffident interruption from Major Mason — "Mullens, the tale's got whiskers" — only stirred the man further. He stood, banging his head on a rafter, the factual *donk* failing to bring him to his senses, and shouted, "Hurrah! The hounds are on the run!"

Ah, but then he squatted, smiled, shrugged, and the spectators exchanged bashful looks. Not everyone was made in the stamp of —

"Mullens!" barked the major as the sly madman scooped up his rifle and set off, sidestepping men seated, men half kneeling, men with biscuits partway jammed in bulging mouths: a frieze of astonishment.

"That's just Mullens," the major paused, breathing

hard, "you mustn't mind him." He straightened his hat and streaked off in pursuit.

"Baa! Baa!" bleated Lizzie Peters, employing a much favoured expression.

Mullens had headed straight for the front line.

Boof Lucas turned white, but taking a cue from Lizzie rotated a finger round a scone-fat ear. Then they heard a familiar voice:

"Oi!"

Handshakes and unfathomable explanations from Bluey Clarke, who had materialized in their midst sitting on an upturned Fray Bentos crate. "I slept in a hole," he blithely announced. "When I woke up I was here." They pressed him for details of his disappearance and he talked blithely of taking a wrong turn in the dark and ending up in a gully filled with corpses.

As Bluey spoke the major and another officer returned with the unresisting form of George Mullens slumped between. They settled him to the ground and tried to explain:

"He was all right a second ago, wasn't he?"

"He laughed," complained the tubby captain. "He came to his senses."

Around the uninjured-seeming form they laced the air with worry. Any moment now, please Christ, it seemed that Mullens would spring to his feet and once again fly. But when the major raised a wing of khaki a flash of red was revealed. As he slid a wallet from the left breast pocket the place flooded with wet colour. "Someone mind this," he appealed, and the smudged memento passed to Walter who examined it while the officer continued his fretful task of tapping, thrusting, retrieving across the entire person.

Because of the wallet's chance arrival in his hands Walter found himself wondering about the dead man's nerves. It was ordinary — the usual stiff rectangle of muscat-coloured leather opening to display stitched pockets for banknotes, a miniature leather belt and paybook, elastic brace and tiny notebook, and a leather pencil cylinder, its occupant wearing a .22 calibre brass hat. Walter flipped the notebook open and consumed the entries:

October 20:	Left Sydney on "Euripedes" (A14)
October 26:	Arrived Albany
October 31:	Left Albany
November 9:	"Emden" sunk
November 17:	At Colombo
November 25:	Aden
December 2:	Port Said
December 3:	Alexandria
December 4:	Mena Camp
April 4:	Left Mena
April 12:	Arrived Lemnos
April 25:	The day

Not even a thumbprint marked the white silence of the remaining pages. Walter pocketed the pencil because down near the beach he had lost his own.

"Tah," the filthy hand of Major Mason intruded, "Mullens was a fine soldier." But a second later he murmured in an aside: "Another dull dog gone."

The words, a gummy mumble, had been addressed to the captain, who now called for attention by striking a mess tin with a spoon. "Okay?" he sang in the wake of the bearers as they departed with Mullens, "Right-oh?"

Walter squeezed between Bluey and Frank on the ledge and picked at a crust of snot. "Don't do that," said Bluey, who was moralistic as well as cheery, "it's a filthy habit." Walter's fingers still held the smell of grubby leather, which was like the smell of potatoes — all that was left of the dead man's living thoughts.

After announcing his name — Captain Veegan — the speaker said: "The fellow who died was Private George Mullens. We mustn't blame him."

"No," ruminated Major Mason at his elbow.

"He took his rifle just now and tried to climb the parapet but was stopped by a bullet. A chance shot, it caught him *here"* — he raised an arm and cupped a ghostly blowfly. "Now look, the idea at present is to hang on without stirring things up too much. That's the word from the heads."

This consignment of Mullens's actions to the realm of tactical error was accompanied by a look in the eye for each newcomer. "Do you understand?"

A real fly now entered the chamber, fumbling in front of the captain's belly, then weaving dozily out of reach. He handed over to the major, who said "Um, er" cleared his throat and poked his hat a half-inch higher. The fly's yellow stomach bumped along at dirt level, pursued through powdery dust by Captain Veegan's whacking bootleather.

The major at last found his voice. "Until very recently it was the vogue round here to hold your rifle above your head and fire from the 'surrender' position. That method doesn't work any more. We lost a man called Broome at lunch time yesterday. You'll get your chance . . . " He went on for some time telling them what to do about water, ammunition, when to duck off to the subsiding slit of earth at the back of the trench

— a place of weeping stains he called the regimental latrine — how overcrowding in the front line was to be avoided by a few men at a time going forward with guides, how bayonets were to be kept at hand, voices kept low, wits about them.

At the end of this speech their lieutenant slid alongside Frank. "I had a bash at the dirty arseholes," he boasted. The major had just then consulted his watch, tapped it to show he'd be right back, and disappeared. Frank sniffed the black nostril of Charlie Bushel's rifle. "I threw it in the air and fired — like he said not to."

"Good for you." The two had joined up together at Moree and Frank showed no regard for his mate's lately acquired commission.

"I'll stick with you, eh?" proposed Walter to Bluey. Frank combed his hair using the pocket-polished underside of a tobacco tin as a mirror: "Count me in." Nervously they shifted the dull rhomboidal weights of full magazines from one hand to the other, then with a clatter fitted them. Back and forth went a dozen bolts.

Across Walter's knees Bluey said, "I wonder what they're doing at home?" and Frank replied: "It'll be cooler." The two were not especially friendly, therefore it gave Walter a calming sense of importance to exist for a while as the transmitter of one's inconsequence to the other.

"I joined the army to get away from the wife and boy," said Bluey, giving his ginger locks a rapid scratch. "Now I can't stop worrying about them."

Across the way Boof Lucas sat stolidly awaiting the fateful order. Long ago, at Rosebery on the first day, no-one had been able to guess what use a heavyweight clod like Boof would be to a troop of mobile horse. He ambled around butting into arguments, then as quickly settled himself into bland reverie. He weighed over sixteen stone, almost as much as Colonel Ryrie, the brigade's heaviest, and complained when confronted by any task requiring effort. But in the riding test they had given him a malicious stallion and watched amazed as he glided over the jumps and pivoted at the turns with the contour-line steadiness of a ballet dancer. Another surprise: he played the violin . . . But at rest these fiddler's hands were bunches of sausage, their meat boiled near to splitting inside lustreless grey tissue. Once, half a year ago, Boof had stirred and ventured a thought out loud to Walter. It had come during their endless wallow through the Indian Ocean, when both had agreed that war meant somebody had to die, but not us. Privately Walter had added *not me,* and then and there had killed Boof off to save his own skin while they gasped in the canvas shade of "B" deck. But why did it have to be Boof? Thick-armed, thick-chested, thick-legged, thick-headed: yet with something that ensured his value as a hostage — a soul like a tidy red fish drifting against a bloated lens of aquarium glass.

Pinned to a corner by Charlie Bushel the captain yawned: "Is that so? Ah — hmm? The devil! Yep-yep, yair, yep. Oh? Hawp!"

Boof raised his hat and rustled a bull's-crown of fibrous hair.

Bluey. Listen to Bluey. *Listen.*

Lazily Bluey's nasal voice drifted through sheets of mountain haze: "When the holes were dug this Marcus Dent character said, 'If you ever needed to get rid of a body you could chop it up and put it under the fence posts'. And that's what he done."

"There was a similar case at Pokataroo," drawled

Frank. "Only this fellow, he ... he ... Christ bugger me."

Frank, who never swore, fell silent, for with a grin and a cocked thumb the major had appeared in the doorway and issued his order:

"Ready?"

13
Opening Bat

It was simple. You grasped your rifle and shuffled forward. It was a dance to the beat of water bottles banged on dry clay, feet shuffling — yours among them: a dance to your own dance, to the loudening frogs' chorus of small arms fire, the jab of elbows, and slithering nervous yawns. While the entire line halted in a damp neck of tunnel, Lizzie, next in front, tugged at the coiled plasticine of his ears.

Walter busied himself by gnawing hairless knuckles, licking them as once he had Frances's. By this means he experienced a feeling of lifting away . . . to Cremorne. Time was so short — life was so short, halting halfway down a finger, midway through an oarstroke — he leapt to a rock and sprinted uphill to the Reillys' house where he smacked the flimsy letter and demanded an explanation. Why had she written:

Not a moment passes when I fail to think of you in your great struggle . . .

And so on; whereas before she'd enclosed black sprigs of secret hair, and babbled wildly for pages.

Why?

From grey darkness they inched to lighter shadows of smoky blue, then ascended toe-stubbing steps until far ahead a box of sunlight appeared, so bright that one half seemed to detach itself and oscillate against the other. Here the order was passed down to wait, so they clung to their gear for yet another alarmed minute: cockroaches in the murky recesses of a cupboard.

Then a fresh order flushed them out, and they entered the front line.

A whistled waltz (Lizzie's) hung in mid-bar, the sunlight hurt, one man was directed to the left, another to the right; Walter's arm was gripped and pushed by a paw dotted with bristling warts. Part of the rear wall of the trench had collapsed, the white sun flitted harshly between sandbagged horizons, the stench, the dust's arid penetration. Later Walter would coolly re-examine a dead man's face that suddenly loomed left of his knee, a face dug clear from the broken wall of trench where during the night the Turks had blown a mine and the man had suffocated. He would recall a fist pathetically bared next to an ear, and study the rigid record of feeling thus imprinted — the shock of a mouth crammed with dirt, the resentment of dented eyelids, the desperation of fingernails black and split from suffocated scrabbling.

Somewhere Major Mason had hailed them from a recessed shelter, the kind used by fettlers in railway tunnels, then slipped out to follow, but that was one, two, three bends back: now Walter's companion butted him to a halt with a bony shoulder, said "Reg Hurst" bartering for a name in return, withdrawing from their handshake with a definite wiping action, adding in a controlled educated voice, "This was my spot, now it's to be yours. You're welcome to it," between times rubbing eyes translucent as sliced veal. The others, also halted, peeked from the wings. Walter saw the major with the grinning heads of Frank and Bluey sprouting from each shoulder, and in the upward direction, just short of where the trench climbed and turned a corner to nowhere, he saw Lieutenant Bushel and Sergeant Madox conferring humourlessly with Captain Veegan.

Walter immediately felt calm. He waved right and left. The feeling strengthened. Ordinary details met his eye: a feather-tucking bird, a file of black ants, capillary shrub roots in cross-section, and Reg Hurst, the placid organizer, domestically occupied.

Idiotically Walter smiled: "What's all this for?"

Hurst had been rummaging through a pile of blankets. "They're in case of bombs. When one comes over we use 'em and hope for the best." The blanket he passed to Walter held a clear marble of condensation dropped from his nose, through which a nest of safe silvery hairs was magnified. "If there's time I'll demonstrate." Then, spine against the forward wall, he folded his hands around his shins, rested the bristled planes of his face on his kneecaps, and snoozed.

"All set?" called Madox.

"All set?" Walter mimicked along to Frank and Bluey.

After a while Hurst stirred from his doze: "Have you heard of the third of May?"

"Who hasn't?" No, that was the wrong tone: "Not much," and located a match to clean his teeth. The place still seemed to have exaggerated its effects. Even the sun had softened, the stink had wandered away, and gosh! it really had been a bird hopping around in the open, a little scrub bird no bigger than a sparrow holding still on the parapet, peering at him, working a delicate note out of its tweezer-like beak.

"We lost half our men," said Hurst. He studied

Walter's face. "It all happened in a dream, beyond recall." He sighed, a young man, then shifted on his haunches, glassy eyes searching for a window on sanity with the slick desperation of air bubbles in a spirit level.

Abruptly the scrub bird shrieked again. Then it fluttered from rear trench to front, describing a half circle over their heads: and a Turkish bullet smashed noisily along the curve's diameter. At this Walter leapt for his blankets, but after attentively cocking an ear Hurst reassured him. He loosened a grey silk handkerchief from his neck and draped it over his face: "Watch for the black cricket balls. Then you'll know the game's hotting up."

Other trenches attended to the routine discharge of firearms, but here the task was simply to wait, and now that the breeze had swung once more around to the Australian line, to try not to gag on the renewed stench. Walter set his pipe frenziedly crackling and sought a return to the orderly illusions of a minute ago: "Do the birds come round all the time?"

No answer.

He wished Hurst would buckle down to an explanation of the trench system. He worried also that the prematurely balding soldier might be too tired and slow even to shift himself should a bomb suddenly flop over. Walter sat there. Fear nibbled and gnawed. That's all it did — fear had no intelligence, it never explained, nor asked, nor understood. It nibbled and gnawed, took a breather, then started all over again.

The silken mouth articulated: "What did you do before the war?"

"I helped my father on the farm. What about you?"

"I was a teacher. Can you imagine? When the war came I decided I was all books and no life. I don't subscribe to that theory now."

Away went the handkerchief, out came his pipe. They exchanged tobacco.

Hurst made a peremptory announcement: "I'm twenty-eight and I've got the clap. The old school would be shocked." He named an eminent college in Adelaide. "Surprised?"

"No, plenty have it," Walter managed. But the idea affronted him — Hurst's confession. A teacher.

"My case is not so bad. I got off lightly — for a Christian. I'd never kissed a girl. Never been drunk. Should I be sorry? Look at me, I caned boys who swore."

Walter looked as instructed, and sure enough found himself frozen under the gaze of a schoolmaster. "I'll bet you taught science."

"Maths and divinity. I wasn't a minister exactly, but near enough. What do you think — God or no God?"

"There's ... something," muttered Walter. He wanted to put it more strongly: but most of all he wanted Hurst to shut up.

"A cock and bull tale! The body is absolutely the end."

This was no minister talking. "You must have believed something. Once."

"I was an expert," Hurst concluded doubtfully. "Then I looked behind the bloody scenes."

The sky made new noises. Thunder curved up from the sea and spikes of rushing air descended on hidden gullies to twang horrendously. Walter in a panic said: "Don't you think we ought to be getting ready?"

"We are." But even so Hurst sharpened his alertness, crouching and knocking his pipe, glancing left and right, and once even pressing an ear to the floor of the

218

trench. "Quiet as the grave." The new noises he dismissed as "the Royal Navy's technique for transporting brass into Turkey."

"*Listen*," the man grabbed his arm: "All that I just told you — it's bull."

"You're still a Christian," Walter dumbly informed him.

"The whole business. I was never a . . . minister. It was someone else."

"Oh." This was shadow-boxing — shadow-wrestling — the way Hurst switched from silence to sincerity to a malicious twist of identity on the edge of a vast drop. Making a fool of Walter. Then raving ceaselessly.

"Do you read books?"

All right, if Hurst wanted to play games so would he, but seriously, and only to keep his balance. He feigned a recent self, the one he had donned in Egypt but feared he had already left behind like a change of skin. "Lately I've read *Beauchamp's Career* and half of Shakespeare, and lots of 'light-weights'" (Ollie Melrose's phrase). He exhausted his new-found acquaintance with literature, but waved an arm in the air as if dozens more circulated where he had tossed them.

But who was Hurst now? He ranted as though from a platform.

"Books contain too many ideas. They're bad. A man has an idea, but on its own it's useless. Good for a laugh. So he sets it down in a book and before long there's Germany, here's Britain, great nations founded on great ideals. Have you ever seen a great ideal raise its head except in conflict with another?" He stabbed a finger on the open page of history: "Bang!" and after a pause sniffed theatrically in the direction of no-man's land: "Books created that mess. Ideas on the move meet bodies that resist them — the poor saps."

"I don't follow."

"The end of thought — ideas in uniform. That's why we're here, books. The trouble is that books don't have bodies in them. That's the essence, young fella. Books haven't caught up to the modern world as yet. Put a body in a book. There's a twist. *Ideas* could then stroll round hand in hand." His picture of a world where books did not exist became more and more fanciful. He dropped in bits from *Alice Through the Looking Glass* as if they were his own. Only nothing he said was funny.

Walter resolved that next time he would smother the sly swervings of the mad before they got started. He lost his patience, tried not to show it, but everything came out: "Hurst, we've been here for two hours. Christ, and all you can do, *you* —" he deleted an insult, "is rave. Put a sock in it!"

The major hopped past.

"Hurst, you magger. Do what the boy says."

Hurst smiled: "It doesn't pay to lose your block. No sir." He shared his water bottle, and the surprisingly rum-scented liquid did its work, forcing from Walter a shamed apology. Close up the man's face stank. His lips twitched when smiling as if strung from rubber bands. At the roots of his whiskers dirt lay in small clumps like scabs.

Suddenly a double crack of Australian rifle fire leapt from the upper bend of the trench. Straightaway the

Turks responded, sending maddened golfers to whip arid divots from the lip of the parapet. Where was fear? This was its antidote! Dust and splinters of gravel rattled downwards. Hurst explained that the shots had been fired by a light horse sharpshooter who after only a day spent ranging this part of the line was known as "The Murderer". "Bugger him," said Hurst, cupping his hands and shouting at the unseen sniper: "Stick your head up your arse!" In an aside he said: "No room for Methodists here." From the supple enunciation Walter could tell he'd long since learned to swear.

"Blankets!" He was in control.

Out on the never-to-be-sighted surface of the earth a sound like the *woof* of petrol fires gave way to the terse ripping of tinfoil. "The major's motto is never hold back. I won't be the odd man out." Action, it seemed, was the one test he had passed long ago. The strange tricks of his contemplative self were nowhere in sight.

"Hurst?" called the major, "You're opening bat."

The first bomb dribbled in. A globe, black and absolute, with a smoking wick.

Hurst leapt and retreated, leaving a magical square of blanket on the ground. For a second the sphere huddled under it, a dangerous lump, while Hurst considered his timing. Then he jumped again to hold the blanket down and the end was announced in a defeated gush of wind and a suppressed sunset.

Though Walter was safe, his fright at the damped explosion caused him to leap and take refuge, foolishly erect, on the nearby fire-step. For an instant his hat appeared above the parapet, presenting to the world a surfacing khaki duck which Turkish snipers spotted from two directions and invisibly printed with X, horizontally across, as it rose and dipped. The bullets as they scored past found an echo in Reg Hurst's darting whispers: *"Christ"* in one ear, *"Almighty"* in the other.

Then more bombs each. Black fruit greedily collected. Limbs in a tangle — once he and Hurst embraced, heads knocking, while fuses gloated.

A rule of physics: bombs roll towards, never away.

A photograph: Major Mason crouched like a circus monkey, blanket at the ready. And at the other swing of the lens, Madox and Bushel with anxious faces.

Hurst's insanity: "Eggs-a-cook. Hoop, la!"

And at last the trench setting sail: moorings slipped, the wharf sliding backwards. The farewelling bombers holding their length, yet the projectiles striking farther along, near the major's cubbyhole.

Now Bluey was in the thick of it, a ginger and tan scuffle. Where was Frank? Then Bluey scurried out of sight and the major waddled into view alone.

For a minute nothing happened. The officer found time to fiddle with a stub of cigarette and joke for all to hear that he'd light it from the next bomb. The bomb came, he snuffed it. But it was followed too quickly by a second one which thudded at his heels, then stropped itself out of reach. The major lunged, tripped, spun lengthwise, and sprawled beside the projectile which instantly exploded.

The walls of the trench lit up for a final photograph.

Walter and Hurst huddled unharmed as the fizz of lightning gave way to dust. They spat grit, then spotted a heap of discarded clothing thrown against the rear wall: it was the major. His hat blown clear had flown to the parapet where it sat uncertainly. And on looking closer, his head — bald, unbloodied, sickeningly smooth — balanced on a pulped chest.

Carelessly Hurst ran to him: "Can you hear me?"

"Yes," bubbled a voice, "do shut up." A pool of blood lay still and deep in a fold of his trousers.

"I'll see you through, Alec," murmured Hurst.

The fateful bomb appeared to have been the last. Now the Turks concentrated on shooting the hat, which shortly slipped to rejoin the man — the corpse — in an absurd trajectory of reconciliation.

"It's never me," said Hurst wonderingly.

Except for the tut-tut-tut of distant machinegun fire, all was silence. Then, from the other lines, Walter heard shouted orders in an unknown language. He looked around with a query for Hurst, but something occurred suddenly to smear the man into invisibility. The words rattled against each other as if seeking the right partners ... Of course! From the outside of an echoing bucket he understood their malicious intent —

Hands thrust his shoulders down. A stretcher bearer hung over him. He decided to sleep but the man said: "Here's an aspirin," and a pannikin striking his teeth woke him properly. "You and Hurst are gluttons for luck." The man spoke in a Welsh accent: *glue-tones.*

Where were they?

Blood, smears and slabs of it, covered Walter's unbuttoned shirt and stomach. The orderly gave him a rag and a dish of eucalyptus-smelling water. While he wiped himself clean he learned the explanation. A final bomb had lodged unnoticed between the dying major's legs and exploded while he and Reg Hurst knelt on either side. It had knocked them out, painted them with blood, but otherwise left them unhurt.

"This here's the late major's pozzie," said the orderly. "You're to kip here till you come properly round." He spoke resentfully. It hadn't been his idea. But he handed over a packet of papers and a generous pinch of tobacco. As soon as he left, a sealed cauldron in Walter's stomach blew its lid — he vomited hot amber-coloured liquid onto the hardpacked floor, where it wandered acridly close to his face (there was no ledge: he sprawled on the ground itself).

Only then did Walter take note of his surroundings. At first the place seemed vast as a shed, but detail after detail shrank it in, until a hastily-piled heap of sandbags, the "door", nudged his elbow, the roof sagged dangerously low, and the back wall, an oblong gallery of harried pick marks, seemed close to collapse.

The gully outside echoed with wind, loose canvas snapping to a curve, a distant explosion. But echoes are never all sounded. Something fluttered at his elbow, someone, a face in a photograph — the major's wife — her picture propped on a shrine-like shelf where a stub of candle and three folded white handkerchiefs exuded the odour of beeswax and lavender. Dark hair (rang the echo) hooded eyes.

The same as Frances's.

The person who now spoke a lost girl's name in this cramped place was surely mad. The relic curled in his hand; he straightened it against the wall where light fell softly. He apologized to — nothingness — for the pride that had coolly siezed him when the dead prefect appeared, for the way he had gloated over being alive. The selfsame pride that had surveyed the crazed George Mullens, dispassionately scanned his notebook, and later raged at Reg Hurst . . . *Sorry.*

Gone was his competence for the simplest task of

224

hope, the placement of one thought forward of another. Frances rustled alongside — lavender, lavender and white — she took his finger as might a child and stifled a giggle at the enormity of their bumping climb upstairs to a hotel room hardly bigger than this one.

14
A Black Sheep

"Son?"

"Bugger off!"

"Sonny, I'm on my way."

A bout of shoulder-shaking set in, when all Walter wanted was to lie nibbling the grass stalks of a dream. But reluctantly he threaded through trees at the base of a cliff, arm over arm climbed broken granite blocks, then emerged on a dark heath where Reg Hurst, a giant in khaki, reached out for his hand: "Good luck."

His palms were powder dry. "Who's that?" Walter pointed to a pale officer paring his nails in the gloom.

"He's a toff from HQ," Hurst whispered. "My second cousin, the aunty's boy. Well, keep your head down. Don't brood." He handed Walter a piece of chocolate and a wrinkled orange.

"Is he a tanksinker?" A ridiculous shred of dream —

"Oh Christ! He's a barrister. How's your head tonight? *He's a silly arse.*"

"I'm tired."

"Save the chocolate. 'Bye!"

Hurst was determined to take a swim down at the beach. All day through their sandbag-filling and lugging he had talked about the cooling green pressure of the Aegean, where soon he would plunge.

After waking and being declared fit for duty, all that day Walter and Hurst had stuck together. At least

Hurst had stuck to Walter, bothering at something that only at the very end did Walter understand, or seem to, for perhaps not until now, at this fatigued moment, with Hurst gone (certainly for ever) did Walter properly grasp what had happened, what Hurst, gabbling, had spent the day trying to say. Trying to achieve —

"It's my last day," he began. "I can teach you a thing or two that might save your skin, if you care to listen."

"Well, no bullshit like before."

The bomb blast had changed him. After their narrow escape he must have decided that impersonation, the least enriching of vanities, could no longer sustain him. At mealtimes he nudged Walter aside and spoke with nervous nonchalance, tugging his lower lip downwards with a loose-skinned finger to reveal melancholy teeth like those of a horse in extreme old age. He seemed to fear that whatever he wished to convey would be snatched from him and destroyed if eavesdroppers guessed at its intensity.

Bluey and Frank muttered about Hurst's being plucky but wriggly: and he overheard them. Later he slipped to Frank: "I've heard of drovers taking consolation with their flocks. Can you confirm it?"

Alone with Walter he clamped him by the upper arm in culmination of a tale or a confession, and threatening the pungent foreign embrace of the unwashed demanded a reaction . . . for at last Hurst had a true story to tell.

He had been praying, he said, when the war news came. Not alone (that he never did) but to an audience of three hundred. Each morning from nine till half-past the school hall fell to the charge of his father, who was both chaplain and deputy headmaster. Reg was required to assist with readings from the gospels and to sincerely gripe his way through the endless sheets of typewritten entreaty concocted by his father. His real job was assistant groundkeeper. The closest he came to the teaching of maths and divinity was when he clattered a mower to and fro beneath the windows of his father's strict classroom.

"I was a failure," Hurst confided to his toecaps. "Mind you, I had my hour. Believe it or not I was once school captain, and dux as well. What else could I do," he asked wonderingly, "afterwards?"

His little brother Roy had been killed on April the twenty-fifth.

"He had a mind of his own— a good brain— he rowed in the eight for the varsity and was three parts through his articles with a dud-arse firm owned by a kind of uncle. He stood up to the old man on my behalf more than once. It was the old story. The worse I became, the better he liked me. But he didn't need me. Just once — once he got a girl in trouble and came to me for tactical advice. He used to call me a 'thorough-going rogue', but I was just an idea of the nipper's, really . . . By Christ I was bored! If it hadn't been for the war I would have been in prison by now.

"I used to faze people. I'd mag, like the major said, mag, mag, mag, and then when I'd got them properly fooled I'd poke my tongue out and watch their hair frizzle. Just for the sport. Dad used to say that little Roy had all the will and pride. The two things I lacked. And did I kick to hear him tell it! But he was right . . . The war was made for the likes of us, Gilchrist, not for bloody Roy."

At a dozen angles of that dust-filled day, as if sighting down the spokes of an intricate compass,

Hurst pointed to features that he and Walter in his view shared. At some late hour he ran them all together and rattled through the list in his surrogate preacher's voice. Only now the text was his own, and delivered without hypocrisy. And of course it was all wrong. Not a pack of lies exactly — the queer opposite, rather — a truth willed into being by Hurst that had naught to do with the facts. Both were young, he claimed, and shared a lack of religious belief. Hadn't Walter mentioned trouble with a girl? Hurst had had his share, by golly. What about their daring, eh? The two bomb stoppers. And their luck —

But then Walter stopped objecting and wearily closed his eyes. When it came to awareness of other people, Hurst's air of having slithered around on the one level since leaving school made him seem younger, somehow, than Walter himself.

Hunched away from his mates pursuing a stubborn mission of unity, it was as though Hurst had flung his arms around the shoulders of two ghostly figures, one with his own name, the other bearing Walter's, and drawn them together to shape an indivisible third. "We both had nothing to lose by coming here. So why should fate pick on us?"

Then came the whisper and chat of cards being shuffled by a bored quartet of infantrymen awaiting the order to leave. Which card was to be dealt cold onto wood? Which to stay warm in the dealer's fist? Chance conversed with itself in the language of the card pack, the language of the whetstone, a rhythmical stroke and strop.

"Hurst, when did Roy die?"

Hurst did not know. At least not exactly. Possibly even before the sun came up on that first day, because one of his mates reported seeing him in the half light dash off after a fat Turk and fail to come back. Another said Roy had been sighted "taking a snack" in a gully. Yet the biscuit-munching Roy at that moment might have been already dead, the hand supposedly seen in the act of conveying food to his mouth already frozen with lucky youth's astonishment at the betrayal of its gifts. When the body was identified three days later who needed to ask such questions? He was dead like the rest. Arriving later on that first day Hurst remembered thinking how queer it was that small bodies should be sent to attack such steep slopes. Some were draped on bushes where they had tumbled after being shot. He knew then that Roy must have been among them. He was so damnably *keen.* Trust Roy to rush forever upwards — only this time, for once, he ran not into the arms of a prizegiving committee but over hurdles of pointed steel and through criss-crossed tapes of invisible lead, and was slung into a yawning hole for his pains.

"Poor bloody Roy."

Hurst claimed to have captured a Turkish soldier who could easily have been his brother's killer.

"My mate Stubbings had his bayonet fixed — when up jumped the Jacko like a rabbit and threw his rifle away. He tried to go all ways at once: he shitted his pants. Stubbings went at him like a steam train, bayonet flying, and do you know I actually closed my eyes?"

Hurst paused for effect.

"I thought he was done. But Stubbings's blade had only gone into his haversack. When I opened my eyes we had a prisoner. If I'd known for sure about Roy I would have shot him as a last favour. I did worse later."

Hurst tapped his teeth tunelessly while Boof spaded gravel into the drooping mouth of Walter's sandbag. Frank knelt wiping sweat from under his chin after a bout of listless shovelling. The time swirled somewhere in mid-afternoon.

"Roy was religious," Hurst said as they plodded again from A to B.

So am I, Walter wanted to say. Rebellion stirred at the daylong imposition of one person on another. "So'm," was as far as he reached, because in the next breath Hurst livened things up with some news:

"I didn't suffer myself because of Roy's pious streak, but he gave hell to a school chaplain who went off the rails. They discovered him naked one night in the Founders' Fountain — poor old 'Potty'."

Potty Fox, he explained.

"Fox was the name of our minister at home."

"David Anthony Fox? He's the one."

The sincere bone in a cassock. Potty? The glinting specs. *Potty.*

"He moved to New South Wales after S.A. His little boy was trampled to death by a horse. Rolled on and then trampled. But listen, he's here with the army. He buried Roy. They swear by him in the tenth."

"It can't be. He's all nerves." But it could have been him. It *was.* For in the month after Walter left home his mother had written with news of the Foxes' abrupt departure.

"When Potty lost his head I'll never forget how Roy

snubbed the both of them. Our Roy was dainty in patches. Potty gave up being a Christian and went in for the Greek gods. But of course it all straightened out in time. They were good to me. And now Potty has buried Roy . . . "

They had arrived at the rear of the trench where an empty sniper's post provided sanctuary for a hurried cigarette. In silence they filled the furtive dome with fumes. After a minute Reg twisted around cautiously to align his face with a slit of grey light from the outside.

"Take a look."

A rumpled view unfolded upwards in the sun's glare like a long strip of rag. Then the rag fluttered away (eyes adjusting to the glare) to show the landscape as if in a dirty mirror, the kind one might find domestically surviving in a rubbish tip, its flaked and dusty frosting still working insanely to prove the wholeness of the world: here crusted, rough, and hopeless, but there lucidly deep.

"What do you see?"

"A mess."

"Look to the right."

"Nothing."

"There's a Turkish trench somewhere. Higher . . . "

Hurst described a glimpse of this lofty enemy trench before the last Turkish attack, when dozens of bayonets like the sharpened points of pencils had rattled into view before being tipped out.

"See?"

"Nope."

Hurst advanced a stiff finger along which Walter sighted. Charred blots on the glassy vista bloomed into three dimensions. The illusion of a mirror faded, but its frame (the dark slit) held, daringly balanced on the rim of the ascending ridge and then giddily sliding over the invisible heads of converging gullies, advancing itself higher to a treacherous gash ("*There,* by the sprouty hump") where for weeks the Turks had been able to look down on the rear of several Australian trenches and on the human sheep tracks staggering up from the sea. Hurst spoke of rudimentary sandbagged shelters whose names sounded already ageless as those of medieval towns: Russell's Top, Pope's Hill, The Chessboard, Bloody Angle, Quinn's Post. And their denizens were men hurled onto those various elevated points where they dangled as if under a giant's chin, and could not drop free neither could they worm deeper in . . .

Soon Hurst announced that the place was dangerous, and they ducked out, catching up with the detail in its new workplace, a chamber of wordless half-naked forms toiling in the queer dusty light of a ruined gymnasium.

More of the same malodorous food at dusk.

"What do you know?" said a full mouth, "I haven't heard a gun all day."

And it was true that the mind had taught the body to behave as if each nerve were not straining constantly towards the sound of battle like a field of brittle sunflowers locked to the passage of the sun. As if.

"I ran into Potty down at the beach. He was with my cousin Chuck and the headquarters crowd, but he's nothing like Chuck. The word I'd use is game. He goes everywhere with the men. Did you ever notice his wild streak?"

Walter recalled the minister standing in the varnished prow of his pulpit, a weirdly garbed fisherman gesturing to God or the tide. But when he transferred him to a longboat with oars creaking like church timbers as it glided down an aisle of polished water, a congregation of blank-faced soldiers on either side, the picture would not fit. Whenever danger loomed the minister panicked.

Captain Veegan grabbed them for an emergency. They filled a dozen sandbags and lugged them to the mouth of a communication trench, then passed them forward to the front line where Hurst and his unhappy mates as their last detested duty supervised the hefting aloft of these gravelly pods. Back in the bombproof chamber they submitted to a lecture from the captain on the art of modern earthworks before Hurst found the chance to go on.

It emerged that he believed in some sort of religion after all. Only it was not religion exactly, but a kind of psychology that came to lose all the cold notations of science and branched into a fantastic series of tunnels, most of which were walled off with solid dead-ends. Then it became clear that for all his talk Hurst was expressing nothing more than the battered realism of the survivor. Dead ends were part of the game: you had to throw yourself at them, said Hurst, and take your luck. At one point he said, "All survivors are entitled to a belief in miracles". At another, "I'm the only member of my section left alive. Snowy and Bert and Cedric Pearson, they're all—" And he tapped his forehead. "*In there.*"

There was more of this, but eventually Hurst's philosophy reduced itself to a simple appeal:

"When I shove off," he said, "spare me a thought, eh?"

Walls. Later Walter was to recall nearly everything Hurst said, and chant it to himself at the edge of madness. He was to restructure Reg Hurst, replace his wart-blighted hands on punished knees, build again the crossbeam of his shoulders, drape from them his grimy shirt, and set above all the whiskered stain of his skull with its bright living eyes. When Walter came to throw himself at a solid wall and through it and lie on the other side listening to his heart with its worn piston restarting, stroking up — he spoke to the image of Hurst again, and again took in that meagre thing that Hurst had imparted to him: Hurst's brief life to store with his own. By then there would be others. A ghostly troop: arms and legs of them, hollowed chests, gaping backs, and blue faces.

15
Muhammedan Tile

At the wharf on the day of their departure Frances had thrown Walter her silk scarf, flinging this last token of contact in among strangers. Nugget Arthur took the catch, passing it to Walter who waved it from the railing as the iron cliff of the *Suevic* enacted their ultimate rift while they mourned it unknowingly. In Egypt he carried the scarf everywhere, but in the weeks after the arrival of her cold letter left it alone. Now he ran his lips through its folds, those echoes of her creased clothing in the night, and sought the trace of perfume that clung to its hem, the warmth of her enclosed body released by the scarf's unknotting, the thermal waves of her kiss. Now he wanted to sleep, wanted to dream, and did so with his knees drawn up on the stone-corrugated groundsheet. But it was not Frances who came to him out of the smooth veil of the scarf, but a girl resembling her, the one he had walked past in Alexandria, and walked past again, and again before stopping and daring to go in. The dark-eyed girl of indeterminate nationality who had clicked the door behind them, served coffee from a silver pot, and invited his hands to search among scented robes for this — a tumbling outwards into cool air, a graceful triple somersault with an exquisite tuck, and a curving under-water glide to a silvery surface where she smiled down at him from a small sad mouth, then disappeared, shimmering, her short straight nose, her low broad forehead thatched with glossy black hair, her dream self dissolving into damp coins and leaves of light.

Bugger and blast. He woke and cursed the still-pulsing pungent semen as it stickily dammed in his trousers. Frank on one side, Mick Aitcheson on the other: would they notice?

That day in Alexandria when he reached the street a newspaper seller had chased him, a man smaller than anyone in Australia with a black apricot for a face and one skewed leg absurdly trying to run off to the side:

"Very goot news, English 'vancin."

"Bully for the English."

"Very goot news: strike in Glas*gow*."

"P.O.Q."

"Very goot news: Lord Roberts dead."

"About time."

The tanned dwarf produced a rag: "Mister, clean 'im boots?" Wherever he went, "merchants" followed. In the end he reached the *Athens* cafe bearing an armload of oranges and figs. Five loose cigarettes, two behind each ear, one wet in his mouth, had been thrust impudently at him so that now, collapsed at a table cascading bounty, he foolishly tossed a handful of coins at his pursuers (a spray of brazen confetti through the cafe's wide open front) forcing a waiter beat off the more determined.

It had been typical of Ollie Melrose to arrange a meeting place, set a time, insist on that time with a flickerless stare of ocean-blue eyes under brows like thunder, and then not turn up. But after thirty-seven minutes by the pearl clockface, and six cold glasses of beer, when Walter began to think about gathering his parcels and counting *paisa* for the Greek, there arrived without apology the supercilious Englishman in his Australian uniform. First he had been required to deliver a chit for the horses to an elusive officer at the docks, and then, then? Another habit of Ollie's was to lug his chair forward giving the legs a fascinated squawk and with a snap of fingers ("Lager!") donate all his attention to his interlocutor. Or seem to. One needed experience of such occasions to comprehend the rudeness of the motion. Deep down he was saying, Stuff your little world, chum. If I was to go into details about mine you'd never understand.

Walter told a tipsy set of lies about a cushioned and carpeted room. Here his bought love at the height of their professional entanglement had actually raised a haunch and scratched herself. But this and other details he skipped. After the heart-stopping revelation in the street all had been drab: the picked nose, the yellow nails like old ivory spoons (inverted). For Ollie he draped a Persian carpet on the wall where only the ruined hulls of mosquitoes had clung, and he patched and then multiplied a scatter of ruptured cushions. His description of the girl was to recur in the dream of weeks later, but in the waking world perfection had not been purchasable.

One thing he told Ollie was true. The girl had beckoned him with her resemblance to Frances. (It hadn't survived the stairs, but why say so?) Because he knew all about the letter from home with its indifferent formal phrases, Ollie said:

"You could have taken it worse."

"How?"

"A wronged man feels better for a smack of revenge . . . Welcome to the wide world."

Then it seemed that Ollie had indeed admitted Walter to full membership of his club, a worldly enclosure where the rough and tough blended appealingly with culture.

But after more beers the impression weakened. Walter strained forward stupidly to wag a finger at his mentor, asserting that to square things with Frances would demand a different sort of accounting. Something much closer to home. Wouldn't it?

Outside, the pavement tilted. Walter surged off in the wrong direction. Bloody Ollie with his way of lording it over a bloke, then whacking his shoulder, as he just had, proposing a sightseeing tour on the way to the station —

Yet —

"You could be right," Walter grunted after five minutes' plodding in the proper direction followed by a head-clearing halt to pelt half the oranges at a persistent merchant.

"Why so?"

They pissed against a wall in an alley. Foam surged at their feet while an urchin watched earnestly.

"Oh *Christ*, Ollie, you just told me. I wanted to get back at her I s'pose. But it didn't work. The other was —"

"Overripe? I've never yet met one who wasn't moulting. You have to go out to the villages to find 'em fresh."

He addressed the ragged boy.

"From all the deceits of the world, the flesh, and the devil, Good Lord, deliver us."

He advised Walter:

"The aesthetic solution, that's what you need."

Ollie's habit was to demand a certain formula, but on winning its recital demand something more. Or seem to: as if the truth, the moment he pounced on it, turned pathetically unappetizing. And it was typical of him to pour cold water on what had been, after all, exactly the experience he himself had several times recommended.

Angry at finding himself childishly, tearfully, endlessly awake, Walter clenched and unclenched his fists seeking control. Where was Ollie at this very moment? Somewhere in a gully back from the beach where half the squadron had been left digging a hole to China while the rest had been delivered up and abandoned here at the price of a dead major, a suicided madman, and a long-winded failure named Hurst who had preached (magged) cut and run. The floor of the bombproof chamber pitched at such an angle that fingernails clawed the earth and clung to it as if to a stormy clifftop. A giddy stupor was the cause, and only three hours left before the pre-dawn stand-to, when he and his section, their stint of fatigues exchanged for something less exhausting but more dangerous, would once again step giddily out into nothingness. Though his eyes were closed Walter experienced none of the thankfully collapsed concentration of the sleeping man. He was — well, Reg Hurst had thrown him a (not unkind) parting look which plainly said: I thought you were the type who'd listen. I think I was wrong. You're such a stunned, wooden type, really. At the beginning you wanted to make sense of me, but you're lost. I kept talking, we all

˙like to shout down an empty well — but —

Lost.

The place where they slept was a new chamber, smaller than before, still half-formed with temporary props and a soon-to-be-abandoned look, though the plan was to make it permanent. It had an air of inviting a direct hit. The men were cramped in two rows, most with their blankets drawn over their heads as if already dead and awaiting a burial party.

Asleep? Awake? A third state existed where sheet after sheet of fire-blackened galvanized iron peeled from a shadowed stack and slithered almost noiselessly here, there, alarming the ears with its sly and terrifying guillotine-rasp, then bounding off to flutter over the abyss in recriminating flocks, whispering of fate as debris whispers in a willy willy.

But memory if it took care could still re-enact those last ever-echoing hours of freedom, which had begun at two pm on the Thursday in Alexandria after the disembarked horses, a shipload of remounts from Queensland, had been safely hup-hooed to their train for Cairo, and Ollie Melrose and Walter found themselves among the elated six who drew short straws for an afternoon's leave. Walter saw himself alight from the "Circular" tram after plying a route taking in the Quays, and

— but look (memory demanded) excuse me, you dazed Australian trooper, why do you hold your hands protectively over your head? The future has not yet made its claim. In a minute you'll freely dawdle down that street of bleached awnings, and among ravaged faces glimpse a form, and a face, to tantalize unbearably.

Thus passed the hour from two to three.

241

From three to three thirty-seven exactly passed the wait for Ollie. And between four and five the afternoon bloomed with colour and life. In the city of Alexandria, where ageless brick and stone volunteered their outlines as sanctuary for wandering thoughts, the evanescent seemed not as usual to have shimmered and gone, but to have defied the world's hardest rule and been rendered solid. This happened when Walter, sobered on their sightseeing tour, was steered by Ollie into the tiled portico of a church.

Not a church exactly: a mosque.

They clutched their parcels but kicked off their boots as was the custom and dribbled tiny coins into the lap of an old man at the door whose hidden mouth, wreathed in silver whiskers, made smacking noises over the valueless currency. Outside, the place was nothing — a hole in a wall framed by black- and red-painted bricks — but past a heavy leather curtain the most astonishing sight met them: coloured tiles mounting up and up with light pouring from everywhere as if through the glazed belly of an enormous jar.

Ollie said nothing but padded softly in a circle with his neck tipped rearwards and his hands folded un-militarily behind his back. On his third or fourth circuit he cruised alongside and said pedantically in travel-dented upperclass English: "The door of the pulpit, see? has duplicated Cufic inscriptions, which on the right read from right to left, as is usual, and on the left are reversed for the sake of symmetry: a good instance of the decorative tendency of Arab art." Then he whispered away in his smelly socks.

Something . . . something had descended from that wonderful dome of old geometry, where sprang to life a pot of flowers, deep cornflower-blue, so beautiful that it went on duplicating itself all the way down to a finite horizon of rucked sawdust. Up went the flowers again, and ever-down, weaving their way through a fretwork that here was white, there yellow, here china-blue, there green, until the finite horizon deflecting the flowers again upwards bounded an infinity of motion.

Walter now paraded in the track of Ollie like an assistant school inspector. In their protestant wonder both might have been engaged in an assessment of the place of wall tiles in public instruction.

In unhurried contemplation Walter felt himself absorb the dome's lesson, but it was difficult to shift whole from Egypt, that cloudless land of ever-snoozing monuments with eroded paws on monumental knees, to *here*, after a day of Hurst and constricting burrows, where at noon had come a sudden thunderstorm, and afterwards, briefly, drizzle: then, overhead, a stemmed rivulet in the rotten earth had burst, confirming the pallor of the unsightable sky — and a dun stream had vomited through to scour clear a dead man's leg built into the earthworks.

Stopping even the mouth of Hurst.

What was it about "lessons" that made them elusive? Were they lessons only for the duration of their precipitation in words, later to evaporate, like the storm, and leave things as arid and unknowable as ever? Did nothing stick? Were they just sayings which the body, that alternately ruthless and pathetic companion of the soul, sneered at, rejected, or most terribly, with deadly acceptance, permitted — just to have the lesson reveal in greatest extremity the washed-clean deadness of the body's lack of understanding?

Far down a silvery corridor of ocean, cold wet leaf

heads of eucalypt in a gust of wind burst open to show the grey home-paddock bones of granite. Here Coalheap had clattered Walter to earth and then whizz bang in hospital Miss Edie Davis — here, gone — had challenged his sixteen-year-old equanimity. Spinning from the effort he had met the challenge.

Again Walter caught at the discovery made in the mosque. And an absurd, fanciful thing it was, at the gangling age of twenty-one to have grasped this idea of art and his destiny being intertwined. In the mosque it had expressed itself as a wish to walk obliquely away from all past selves, and yet to retain them. To play with their patterns, to organize, fragment, and reconstruct — otherwise all heartburning and anguish, and bliss as well, might seem nothing but ashes in the wind. And such a thought could not be borne.

He felt a fool and dared not breathe a word of this to Ollie.

At last Walter dozed, and not only did the force and certainty of the feeling return, but it buoyed him up, carried him along to a point where fate picked him out from the thousands of others similarly sleeping on those racked slopes and promised to deliver him into a magnificent vocation far from here and safe from harm.

But (awake again) it did not seem so.

What a bastard fate was to pluck him from Australia, set him on the rails to war, then give him a vivid glimpse of the what-might-be before tossing him wastefully into the realm of never-shall. He was in no way unique. Had not Hurst said that on the battlefield the mass of men were not so very different from . . . this special person whose billion cells and self-regarding sensations told him he would never die? Whose path to a cruel glimpse of destiny was for military youth a much-frequented one through the room of a whore? Who, an innocent, had been surprised by the way the bought girl's manner alluded to the sincere tremors of two other girls he had kissed, Ethel and Frances, one fleetingly, the other (he had thought) to the depths of her soul. Who had left the room as if more than a scant hour of experience had been gained, steadied by a ritually heartfelt farewell — the emission of a trans-national sigh. But who found that the satisfaction thus obtained had the force of a lie believed by no-one. Who was so recently born into his true self that it must show like the guileless gleam of a baby, for Hurst the bad listener after all day talking about himself had in a parting phrase caught Walter to perfection:

"Don't brood. Brooding's no good. The sensitive type and the clod end up the same."

So what did all these hot heaped-on thoughts matter? Ceiling-starer or snorer, they were all 100-1 leapers whose cogitations had not the slightest effect on their fate. Still the sheets of corrugated iron slid, rasped, fluttered over the chasm without cease.

Behind the pulpit of the mosque a propped-open door led to a portico that resembled a narrow and low hayshed, satisfying to walk under because of the excessive number of columns supporting its light roof. They strolled to the end and sprawled on a cool marble bench. Walter remarked on the resemblance to "things at home", and Ollie, the approver, disapprover, and educator of his listeners, deigned to approve. "Ah yes, Gibbon maintains that it was from the portico the

Romans learned to live, reason, and to die."

"Like our verandas," offered Walter.

A persistent tapping could be heard from a nearby lane. After leaving the mosque they investigated, finding a road mender sitting on a one-legged stool, a brief spike topped by a wooden disc, levering fractured paving stones from the narrow thoroughfare. The smell of wood fires gave the place the air of having been stumbled across in a gully in the midst of weeks-long stump burning, so much a part of the earth did this tang seem. But not so the sweaty spices, nor the effortlessly foreign way the workman slid an entire piece of stone one-handedly through the air and bedded it at his toes, all the while gazing about with a half-smile and maintaining a questioning wail of conversation with half a hundred passers-by. A tar-chinned cauldron smoked within reach, and nearby stood a horse and dray, the dray almost shattering under its load, the horse repeatedly nodding as if stunned but swimming to stay upright.

"Excuse me," Ollie pointed from horse to man as he advanced, "that's no way to treat an animal."

Walter thought so too, but worse was the threat of a scene. Ollie made them by habit.

The road mender stood. "Scusame?" His un-supported stool dropped dead like a top at the end of its spin. He was no music hall Gyppo, but the gap-toothed smile had many times been snitched from such eastern alleys to be guffawed at on the stage.

"The nag! The nag!" shouted Ollie.

"Ter Nog?" the man seemed to ask. He had thrust a miniature crowbar through a knotted rope supporting baggy trousers.

"Cruel. Crew-all. *Crool*!"

246

"Cruel?" An exact replica of Ollie's sour British exasperation. The crowd pressed close for this burst of inadvertent theatre.

"All right all *right*," Ollie barked. He shouldered his way to the near-side shaft, where he hammered a confusion of knots and buckles on the horse's flank. The road mender now understood the situation. Ollie wanted his horse. Ollie was taking his horse!

Transformed, he appealed to the crowd, using his midget crowbar as a demagogue's rod of office. It was also a weapon —

A deadly weapon, raised, advancing on Ollie, bobbing high on a wave of moans, Ollie-killing moans, a chorus of offended Muhammedans.

The way out of the situation suddenly unfolded like a set of picture postcards, a concertina of Alexandria streetscenes wobbling free of their stiff envelope. A happy, silly, blotched brown sequence of escape.

First, the horse showed its dislike of Ollie by attempting to bite and kick. The road man brandished his iron bar: and this was the opening souvenir scene, captioned *Baksheesh?* in honour of the word uttered by the man in the midst of his dangerous hesitation.

He was willing to sell.

Walter pressed a fist-wet ball of notes into the fellow's hand. When the crowd saw this its hostility dropped to a curious hum. So Ollie was clear with Walter bracing his elbow before any one of the fifty locals raised his eyes from the money. Curved awnings, a glimpse of melancholy horse, and a huddle of merchants crammed the frame of this second remembrance. Only the brown eyes of urchins in fancy dress stared away from the centre of interest. *Pyjamas worn in street (daytime)* Walter's indelibly arrowed message to the family would say.

Ollie permitted himself to be shunted to safety, but threw obscenities down the generations at the nameless names of the quadruped's forbears — a curse on the "fucking four-footed elongated brains of their sottish species".

Still, they were well-away. Number three's composition, bare of locals, showed two military figures sauntering down a weirdly empty street. *An afternoon of leave.*

What a circus!

But where were the parcels? Whisked away through the thieving crowd . . . At this realization Ollie let fly with his most obscene string of curses: a complicated and blasphemous proposal involving the bared and willing hindquarters of Christ and Allah. Few Australians were as inventive as Ollie when it came to swearing, and none offended so carelessly. And between them how much had they paid? Adding it all up, translating it into Australian money, all of one and ninepence halfpenny.

"Come on Ollie, it was only fruit." And in an aside: "People will hear." Ollie really ought to be more careful — but too late: a pulse of the gritty desert *khamsin* had collected the foul-mouthed load and slapped it against the ears of two English nurses who were advancing, heads down, hands on hats to battle the wind.

"Oops," said Ollie, fingering a tooth. When the nurses drew close he saluted.

"Hello Australians," snapped the brisk unpretty one, while the other searched ahead.

Ollie swivelled and tried to tag along. "I'm from home, y'know."

The older one's face said: So it was *you*. Their pace quickened, and they rattled up the station steps with the precision of wound-up toys.

There in the final wind-slapped *View from the Bab el Gedid Station* was fixed Walter's last look at Alexandria. Without Ollie his experience of the place would have been flat. No tiled spectacle to dream about, no brothel he supposed, and no fun of the chase, which was why the difficult Ollie stayed his friend, and why Alexandria when he thought about it glowed beneath the horizon.

When they returned to the camp on the outskirts of Cairo the world turned upside down. Did they want to go *now,* bellowed the brigadier at a mass assembly of regiments, did they want to leave their horses in Egypt and sail as infantry to the Dardanelles, did they want to join the *fight*?

From their thousand apprehensions they had replied, and heard an echo clap between the desert's endless nothing and the green world of the Nile.

Even though he lent his own raw-throated yell to the rest, and indeed was mad to go because of a pounding expectant heart and an animal's hunger to wheel and run and savage the imponderable future, the living voice that was now Walter's whole self muttered a helpless condemnation. Now, with dawn soon to sicken with its grey soapsud light, his lips once more moved to frame the dry exclamation: "What a damn fool I was to get into this!"

He must have slept after all, because Mick Aitcheson instead of lying on the ground next to him shifted to the wall and hung there, an immortally alarmed example of the taxidermist's art. This same Mick who in Egypt had punched a dozen biceps and prodded a score of stomachs in delighted endorsement of the brigade's fate, who had leapt like a spider monkey (bright glass eyes) into the arms of Boof, dropped from there and flung himself at — of all people — Blacky Reid.

And Blacky and Walter had talked.

"How's Ned?"

"How's your dad?"

"Good enough."

In the same regiment but assigned to a different squadron, Walter had long since been relieved to discover that even so narrowly separated he and Blacky hardly ever saw each other.

"Old Pepper put an axe in his foot."

"Bad?"

They searched the horizon standing side by side, hunting blinding hillocks of sand for a sight of the stone haystacks of the pharaohs . . . or anything.

"Douggie finishes school this year. For good."

"The devil."

"It's the war."

Blacky chewed a match. Who was going to yawn first?

"I hear you've been on a jaunt."

"There and back. What a place!"

"Alexandria." (A statement.)

"Alexandria." (An echo.)

And so on, the sentences exchanged with the polite tap-pock of a game of French cricket, neither needing nor wishing to run for the ball because if they did there might just be a wrangle.

"Things won't seem the same at home after this."

"There'll be a lot of changes. When we get back."

Had Blacky been about to say "if"?

Never.

"Do you know Pig Nolan?" The question signalled a change of pace. Blacky disposed of a flayed wet match and selected a fresh one. "A good bloke, Pig."

"I don't see a great deal of him." Yet he did: Walter saw the bastard all the time, plotting, insinuating. "Pig and I — we don't get along all that well."

"No?"

The soaring slowness of the question meant that Blacky had adjusted the angle of his bat ever so slightly to deal the ball a subtle hook.

Are we about to get stuck into it? Should I let fly with a sizzling return?

In the event Walter just plucked the question from the air and pocketed it briskly.

"I'd better be off."

They shook hands as if one or the other meant it.

As Walter ploughed through the crowd to find his friends he took comfort from the thought that the clash of nations would do away with the contest of individuals. But he was wrong; for as early as their second evening on the peninsula he caught Blacky and Pig with their heads together. Or rather they caught him, because crouched in a plot of three or four around the belly of a cooking stove Blacky had seen him pass, and flung a long looping whistle, as to a sheep dog.

"Hey, boy!"

And in the shadow of danger to all could plainly be seen a venomous ulterior struggle more lasting, more ingenious than that of armies. Hatred, less capricious than friendship, survived. Friendship needed warmth and light, also protection and containment, which was why the city glowing at the butt of the Mediterranean had seemed a proper vessel for life — not this shattered lidless hive where men flew off one by one into darkness.

He had been among friends when after the handshake with Blacky he and Ollie recounted their experiences to those who had missed out on the trip to Alexandria. Walter affected a knowledge of the water-front life engaging in a contest with Ollie's. Then Ollie announced that he had inside knowledge of the city, mentioning for the first time that he had visited it twice before, once in 1909 and again three years later.

"Wally big-mouth," observed Boof. But what did it matter? Ollie for ten years had kicked around the world (including a war in Mexico). He was odd, well-read, and at thirty-one older, tough and moody. He struck out at an angle from all that was was expected of an Englishman. He and the half dozen others strolling against the tight blue scrim of the desert morning formed a confederation of souls (Walter thought) each to the rest — when all was said and done — clear as polished glass. They were friends, marked off from characters like Pig and Blacky, from all whose souls blocked light with the sullen black-windowed secretiveness of a funeral parlour. Friends who kicked sand chiacking their way to hypothetical glory, Frank, Nugget, Bluey, Boof, Ollie, all of them, at that moment of dispersal, hearing the regimental bugler in the palms down by the horse lines poop-poop two blurry notes from proud cavalry brass preparatory to uttering the long and pure morning call.

Lying in the bombproof chamber in the grimly whizzing hours of early morning Walter waited for a burst of meaning to flow at this memory of the bugler in Egypt about to sound his serious music.

He remembered the men breaking off and heading for the horse lines, each wrapped in his own response to the sad tones of "Stables", the most beautiful and domestic of all bugle calls: "Come to the stables all men that are able and give your poor horses some hay and some corn . . ."

They had vaulted heels-down on sanded slopes or crunched across wind-scoured stones. Passing through the tent lines they twanged guy ropes and ran whining fingers along taut canvas. They walked away from the purpose that had brought them half way around the world and the decision just taken to go into battle without their horses; away from the human, the raw-tongued, the alarm and misapprehension that was their unseen but true uniform, and were forgiven — better, transported from — the sulking weight of their bodies by the brass rails of the bugle as they set off to do their grooming for the last time, gracefully absolved and released from all they had done and were about to do, draped by the wandering ribbons of intricate bugling, which began now somehow to echo among its own earlier notes, entire phrases leaving for the silken distances of the sand-ocean only to return thin but re-charged to wander above the men as might glass rods (deep tinted blue) in a serene experiment of fate, creating a faint electricity to which the men thoughtfully submitted, scraps of hair rising under its power to attract the light and the harmless, scraps of wool, silk, feathers, paper, bran, gold leaf, and then all this movement joined by the sad brown heads of hundreds of horses in their picket-lines, heads shaking and bobbing with elastic polyphonic rhythm up up down as the men arrived and were greeted, nuzzled, ushered in to a last ritual embrace with the living things they had been called to care for.

16
Remembering Why

Reg Hurst died at dawn.

Poised for his dip at the wharf he had been clowning when shrapnel flurried across purple water and then cruelly lifted, slicing his legs off. His trunk, according to a witness, entered the sea with arms outflung in the manner of a man delighting in a headfirst dive. A minute later he surfaced, and when the shelling stopped they fished him out with a pole.

"Did you know him?" asked the stretcher bearer who brought the news, the freak dive being his only reason for mentioning yet another death.

"Wally did."

They kept on with their breakfast. It was easy to put this mangled Hurst out of mind. An image persisted of a living person who, so it happened, by commonplace dictate of chance would never again be seen.

He had been a cow to Boof. He had bothered the fair-minded Frank Barton, who now tried to put a finger on what it was about him. Mick Aitcheson in deprived but reasonable tones said, "He *owes* me a shilling" (debris of a bet). But forces other than economic ones kept Hurst alive. They all seemed to agree that he had been up to something. Was it exhaustion or bravado? He had seemed to *want* to go . . . he and the Mullens character — they were all of a piece. Amid the scrape of mess tins a circle of faces looked to Hurst's mate for an answer:

"Wally?"

But as he groped for a phrase, clearing his throat, spoons clattered and living currents tugged out to sea the pale, paler, palest blood of Hurst, and curiosity rippled to indifference. One mentioned a racehorse, another a boxer, a third wondered about a girl who had sworn not to be his for ever.

Walter alone was left to contemplate the structures devised by Hurst for his own survival. Something else Hurst had said, Walter recalled, turned out to be true: "After the third or fourth man goes you will be amazed how easily you accept the idea of death without a pang, and feel delight at the sense of power this acceptance gives you." And though he lacked Reg Hurst's zest for extremes, definitely a supple plating that had not been there before dented and returned when he touched it with memory. It was the first layer of nature's tougher grey after an eternity of rubbed and weeping thought. He said to Bluey: "The others think Hurst had reached breaking point. Not Hurst."

"During the bombing, wasn't he the bloke who shouted, 'Box on. They can't beat us!'?" Desultorily they chipped a memorial to the black sheep from Adelaide.

"He was a loser at home."

"I could see a trace of the whip-shy cur in his manner."

"What do you think you are, Bluey, one of Hurst's 'hawk people' or one of his 'rabbit people'?"

Bluey wielded a trowel of biscuit with craftsmanlike care, collecting bacon fat from each corner of his dish, then sucking it through thin lips. Walter leaned forward in a typical knot of puzzlement, allowing

256

Bluey to complete his meal in silence. Then he let fly with an explosion:

"My mind seems all speeded up!"

Bluey had turned to filing the point from a bullet . . . and why shouldn't he? The word was out that the shocking injuries inflicted on dead Australians could only have been caused by dumdums and exploding bullets. Walter blundered on while Bluey's face said: *Oh, put a lid on it.*

"We seemed to understand each other, though it was funny. Hurst did all the talking. He had the oddest ideas —" How could the business of walls be put to Bluey?

"For fuck's sake!" muttered Bluey, exaggerating a nicked finger.

Lizzie Peters suddenly turned every head by appearing in the doorway, skinny and taut, bleating, "They're gonna stop the bloody fighting."

Lizzie had something important to tell them. The truth. Why else would he stamp his foot? *Listen.* Why else was he motioning leftwise with a becking arm like the neck of a mud-spattered swan, thus indicating a new presence? And why else would a queerly uniformed officer appear and nod casually to the men after shaking the hand of red-nosed Captain Naylor? British, he was, a naval commander. Followed by a gaggle of heads from HQ.

After they passed through, Lizzie repeated the news and Walter felt the settling into himself of a pleasant weight. The future! He had not properly understood that the future had gone. Now it was back. His agitated nerves sank down and fed on a rich fare framed and sealed like honey, the orderly combs of time and circumstance. An inner hum mounted to a —

"Yippee!" which accompanied his spinning hat as it flew towards Lizzie.

"Don't you realize," said Frank Barton, "that once they've cleaned up the mess out there the whole shebang will start all over again?"

Walter and Lizzie, the fools, had been about to waltz.

Twenty minutes later a glum file waited in the throat of the communication trench. Where darkness ended the British officer crouched and shouted in Turkish with his left cheek almost touching the sunlit wall. Head tilted back, he was a man demanding entry into a house occupied by a maniac: shouting, imploring, listening, wary. Confused responses could be heard from the other lines, a reminder that here the two sides were closer than anywhere else. All round, the firing seemed to drain away.

The Briton smoked tailor-made cigarettes from a tin, and at times the silence was so complete that the men heard the silken paper rustle. What was a sailor doing so far from the sea? No, he was not a sailor, said someone, but an agent: one day navy, the next a footslogger. He crosses back and forth to Turkey disguised as a beggar. Whenever he wishes he crawls on his belly to the other lines and walks around picking up information. He passes for one of their own. His name is Aubrey. Aub. He brings trouble with him when he comes to the front line, though, because if the Jackos don't like what he says they always try and wipe him out. So stand by for bullets and bombs. The Turks invariably take Aub for a deserter in the service of their enemy.

Under their feet, the Australians knew, miners, men from Kalgoorlie, Broken Hill, Ballarat, were busy digging secret tunnels. So were the Turks. In one place opposing shafts had come face to face forming a line of communication between the two sides. A forbidden line. Sandbags had been erected, guards posted: a kind of peace reigned — so what was Aub doing up here, when he could go down into the earth if he liked and shake hands with the opposition?

A kind of game was being played, that was the trouble, while below, where dwelt the breathless miners and the breathless dead, was completed the potential true arc of a handshake . . . Simple enough to make it real: We do apologize for bothering you. We just don't know what came over us. Removal of hats and caps, scratching of heads. Here, have a cup of tea, and (fingers in mouth to whistle up the cook) a brace of hot buttered scones. There's only one thing. Keep your mouth shut about all this, will you? We'll camp up here, you and us, till things quieten down in the old country. A game of poker? Are you partial to a little swy? Now tell us about this harem business up in the city.

But Aubrey persisted, his palm glued to the wet clay wall which overnight drizzle had converted to the consistency of "greased egg". He spoke so that all could hear:

"We'll give the blighters a minute or two to think things over, then I'll have another go." With his accomplices he shifted back into the mouth of the communication trench where again they made polite noises in the direction of the men, lit up, waited.

"Electricity is the queerest stuff imaginable," ran Boof's conversation with Mick. "It's kind of nothing."

Captain Naylor tried to intrude on the HQ group, who in turn attempted a word with the poms, who in their turn, like all officers of their race, seemed perpetually on holidays.

"Last night Kyriakides heard a nightingale. And I swear the cuckoo had changed his note, worried by the shrapnel."

"Ellis took delivery of more champagne yesterday. But do you think the bounder will share? There ought to be a rule in the mess." The speaker was definitely unpleasant. He had none of Aub's air of quick interest in things.

Frank chose this moment to give a recipe for damper to Sergeant Madox: "The secret is to use a scant cup of milk instead of water, then add two handfuls of chopped sage and one of onions. I always carry a tin of Glaxo on the road."

"The secret to brownie is dripping," contributed Madox.

"By June you'll find the Balkan flies a treat," Aub told his mate. He then swivelled round to the men and raised his voice a half-octave, endowing it with an almost feminine sinewy strength: "I hope you boys are keeping your shit covered, otherwise in the hot weather we'll all be sick."

"What's the game?" asked Bluey.

The rumour had been right: both sides were finding the stench of dead bodies unbearable. Worse, they were a health hazard. After several false starts with white flags flying on sticks and both sides firing on emissaries from farther up or down the line, he, a commander of RN Intelligence, was attempting to make proper arrangements. One day of No Shooting would be enough.

They asked him the Turkish for Good day, How are you? and Do you have a sister? Also they politely wished to know where he had picked up the language.

"This is my old stamping ground. I'm a journalist by trade. Don't underestimate the Turk. He's a stubborn fighter."

Bluey started on a cigarette, the slow balletic ritual involving papered lip, hands working like silent millstones, an elbow turned in, prehensile wrist curved out — the process occupying the attention of the English as might a native custom in a remote annexation. "We don't have nightingales at home," said Bluey between licks, "nor your kind of cuckoo either, except in clocks." The cigarette remained unlit, swinging like a lazy pendulum: "Ours is the pallid type." He then unclipped the cigarette and whistled two haze-coloured notes, perfect steps on a scale never completed because they started again, *ah-sip, ah-sip,* imitating the cuckoo's eternally blunted attempt at a regular series.

"Very beautiful, don't you think?" said the second Englishman to his boss without reference to Bluey, who seemed to serve as an inanimate colonial phonograph.

"You hear him at his best in the wheat, towards evening."

At the commander's request Bluey then imitated other birds — a plover, then a currawong, filling the crowded pipe where they hunched with abrupt sad sounds. Then he began on the wonga pigeon, *wonk-wonk-wonk,* a call he said could be heard up to half a mile away and was often repeated more than a hundred times in succession. Bluey started repeating it but Frank interrupted, saying how delicious the bird was stuffed with minced veal, covered with buttered paper, and —

The officer raised a hand. The firing had stopped altogether and in the distance a Turk was shouting. The Britisher listened, scuttled forward, listened again and made an entry in his notebook, echoed the phrases in his piercing alto and declared the job done: "They want to parley."

As he left, Walter hurriedly asked in a voice not his own (the voice of reason): "Is there any chance they might decide to stop for good?"

"You mean stop the war? Not without a diplomatic motive. And there's none to hand. This is a strictly military moment. Do you undestand?"

He did. And it was crueller, crueller by far, than just barging on, bloated bodies and all.

The officer left the way he had come, with a nod to each and a handshake for Bluey, heading for the beach where soon a Turk would take a lonely blindfold walk along a strip of shingle and the arrangements would be properly made.

But when Walter reached his post things were so unexpectedly peaceful that he relaxed in the Reg Hurst position with his back to the enemy. So easy and quiet was it with only the odd dutiful bullet swiping overhead that he let go, lulled by a shore breeze that lifted the pong and rolled it out to sea. Lulled also by the sunlight, still not so very hot, he removed his shirt and began "chatting", picking tiny lice from the folds. When a trail of escapers set off in a dotted line for his trousers, dispassionately with blades of fingernail he killed every one.

An instant later he heard a peculiar dull clang which seemed to rise in the air before rooting itself in the earth. Then drowsily he selected another job: cleaning the sights of his rifle.

But the clang turned out to be no passing oddity.

Farther up the line Frank and Bluey had been digging with short-handled shovels and picks when Frank forgetfully raised his shovel too high and collected on its curved face one of those desultory bullets (desultory in a crowd, fiercely vengeful on its own). It deflected downwards, harmlessly grazed his forehead but ploughed a wild furrow across chest and stomach.

It was this gash that Walter stared at ten minutes later when the bearers carried Frank past, and found horror compounded by greedy curiosity: the phenomenon he witnessed was that of a friend unmasked to show an inhuman geography of peaks and hollows where arêtes of upright torn shirt were hung with ruby snow.

Frank, you are one of us . . .

"Wally?" The eyes black and shiny, mouth dry, lips streaked with little frayed strings of dough . . . a hand exploring outwards like the searching tendril of a still-growing plant. "Where's Nugget?"

"He's around."

Boof appeared and tactlessly blurted, "Nugget's down at the beach or somewhere, with the others." But Frank seemed to have passed out again though still he gripped Walter by the wrist. The bearers resumed their waddling progress. The front line was too narrow for stretchers.

Six more steps and Frank moaned, "How's my dial?"

"Clean as a whistle."

263

"Good. I wouldn't want Marge or Mossy to see me with a busted dial." At the mouth of the communication trench they loaded him onto a stretcher. Blood seeped through the canvas and hung beaded there, rusty and wet, like something vile from an abandoned waterbag. Frank's right hand crawled across his stomach to search amid the mess in a vain attempt to smother the pain.

"Why ain't Nugget here?"

"He's coming."

"For Christ's sake, he's down at the beach!"

"Aw, Frank."

As they negotiated the turn into safety and shade Frank's moans intensified. He let go and bellowed, "They've butchered me!" Between blubbering intakes of breath and intervening gusts of loud surprise he said, "Fucking shit, fucking shit, fucking shit."

Walter thought: I know it must hurt, but why doesn't he shut his teeth on it? He's letting himself down. Frank . . . Our father aged thirty-two who wields a silent spindle. It's not like this is it? For you are brave, Frank, your soul is a flame of silence and you will snuff it by bawling.

Charlie Bushel, white-faced, knelt eye to eye with Walter and issued an order: "Back to your post."

"I can't, he won't let me."

"Frank?" said Charlie. "It's me, Charles. Let him go. I'm sorry you're hurt."

"Get me a priest."

The grip tightened.

"How do you feel now?" They all waited for an answer to Charlie's stupid question.

"Help!" Frank tugged Walter's arm like a bellrope.

"There's no priest up here," said Charlie. Then

cruelly he repeated it, shouting. *"There's — no — priest!"*

Along the communication trench Frank's voice cleared. "I had a good horse," he intoned, "and I sold it." With every lurch of the stretcher he repeated himself. "I had a good horse, had a good horse, and I sold it."

They carried him through places turning darker and darker until it seemed the nursery rhyme intonation would stop and with a cry, enveloped in a red egg of nothing-but-pain, he would shrink to a baby and die.

But in the support trench that served as a casualty clearing station he came to himself. The bearers found a ledge and bandaged him as best they could.

"I'm sorry for letting go. It's like I was kicked in the guts by a bullock. It's like there's cods in there that won't stop hurting." With horror Walter saw a silk-sheened tube of intestine shining through.

"We can't take him any further like this," said the leading bearer. Charlie drew him aside.

"A priest or a doctor?"

"Flip a coin. There's a doctor around, but only the angel Gabriel could rouse him now."

"Well fetch a priest. And hurry." He justified his concern: "We're from the same town."

"Any bastard'll do, won't he? Any religion?" The orderly picked dry snot from a black toothbrush of nose-hair, ignoring the extrusion of fingernail dirt (blood?) that travelled up a nostril, wiggled crankily, and emerged for examination. Then he gave Frank a morphine injection and entered the dose in his pay book.

"He's a Mick. Take care you fetch the right brand."

Officers came and went before the orderly

eventually departed. Captain Naylor sent Charlie off on a job (he went willingly) but asked Walter to stay.

"I can't do anything."

"Aren't you his mate?"

"Yes. But Nugget Arthur's his closest mate."

"Arthur's with the other mob, and look, son, it'll make no difference. The truth is he's not going to live. He won't even come round again." Together they checked Frank's face for signs of life in case he made a liar out of him, a face so pale that dark shades flickered underneath as if a smoky dusk had come at the end of a cloudless day.

The dying man said: "Is that you?"

"It's Walter Gilchrist." So ravenous is self-pity that he wanted Frank to see his tears. "Nugget's around," he added despairingly.

"Nug, remember Wally at the Cri?"

"This *is* Wally." But he drew back when Frank's eyes opened. What if the intact brain in its torn container condemned him for his shameless self-regard? So in order to appear honest he was required to lie, and play along at being Nugget. He stared at the wall where someone had glued a newspaper clipping, all ribbed and still wet — an advocacy of the six golden rules of outdoor hygiene. Frank said, "Let's have a last drink, a rum, after the girls go. What do you say?"

"All right."

"The only trouble is, I can't remember why we came to town. Was it the horses?"

"The war."

Because of the diminished firing, noises from the

farther distance thundered long and dramatically. An exchange of artillery on the lower slopes boomed with the sound of two trains noisily approaching each other on a railway bridge. The wash of their impact came later, less importantly. All vigour and threat was contained in their passage across the lower sky, a journey that commenced over and over. Frank's eyes alertly traced the source of the sound. Though fate was writing a conclusion and signing it personally his, he seemed unconcerned. Or felt no fear. Or was a sick man who a minute before had been hale, who understood only that pain was drawing him aside from his old self, but nonetheless fought that belief. With eyes closed he said:

"You never did like Marge, did you."

"That's not true. She's — lovely," Walter breathed. He took a draught of breath and spun Frank's life out. "She's a lovely girl, Frank, with such a serene face. As soon as I clapped eyes on her I knew she was happy. Not many girls are calm like she is. I liked that button on her dress. She's got a nice laugh."

"She's not to know how I copped it."

"Come on, Frank, you're just knocked around a bit."

"Tell Mossy, though. Write to her uncle."

"Whatever you want."

"Tell Marge I died fighting."

"Sure".

"There's a gate . . . a gate . . . " Frank's eyes opened greasily as he peered at Walter and tried to speak more forcefully. For a second it seemed as if he was trying to sit up, to look at something. A gate? The gate of heaven? Was this how death crept over a man, one world fading out while the next showed up ahead? This time Walter really did lean close, close enough for

Frank's sour milk breath and blood-filmed spittle to reach him, close enough for a stubbled cheek audibly to scrape Walter's sleeve, and for the inert lizard skin of the nine parts dead to state its condition with cold factuality. "There's a gape . . . a gaping hole in me, ain't there?"

"They're fetching a doctor. The ambulance chap went. I've been in a hospital, Frank. They can do wonders."

"I met my brother in Perth," said Frank. "He's got no kids. Do you know how to mend a watch? He's a grocer."

Then Frank began to wheeze as prelude to another bout of pain, but before the agony gathered force he passed out. Was he dead? Perhaps it was just the morphine taking effect. Walter had to know. He scuttled to one end of the chamber, then the other. Someone had been here a minute ago when Frank was issuing his instructions. All right, I'll find out myself . . . but Frank's pulse was smeared with blood. His eyes — Walter raised a lid and a blind but living pupil met his. The lid settled back slowly like finger-printed tar on a hot day.

It was no longer true that everything seemed speeded up. Things were the other way round, sick and slow at the world's tired end, a million years AD, when Walter smoked a pipe at the bedside of the last generation but one. Was it true that Frank had suddenly struck a wall as Hurst had fancied, falling back while Walter glided through? In Frank's dying was. visible a microscopic progress, as if clusters of memory were sliding clear of nutritive experience and gathering somewhere grey and cold for the final starvation.

Still nobody came, and Walter allowed this disagreeable thought to age in smoke until his pipe reduced to an acrid dottle. For the living there would be no more surprises. All tended down into the same vortex, with consolation nothing but word-play. So when Frank spoke yet again, Walter regarded him as already dead, and responded monotonously. Frank asked:

"Father?"

"Can you hear me, Frank? It's only Wally."

"Yes, Father."

Oh, Christ. What now? The Catholic dead needed oil and Latin hocus pocus.

"Is it done?"

"Yes." Walter gabbled a conclusion: "In the name of our Lord Jesus Christ, Amen." It fooled Frank (he decided) but Christ was dead a million years past.

"Frank, may the Lord Jesus Christ give you — a decent place in heaven, Frank Barton."

And a voice behind him said, "Amen." A voice from the past.

Potty Fox!

"You're too late," (the world had ended).

"I'm not a Catholic priest, but —"

Walter reached out a hand to the khaki-clad minister, who (stupid man) failed to recognize him. A tired conventional smile played around thin lips. His handshake for Walter came straight from the chaplains' rule-book: sincere but inhuman, meant for the agony of the multitude, ill attuned to the throes of one. But his eyes were remarkable. No longer the intense marble of home, they had softened. Yet it was a discomforting change. For the alteration appeared to have come about by the constant release of an inner heat, so that hot and restless the eyes begged for sponging in cold water.

"What have we here? Oh, how terribly sad."

But who did he think he was, just glancing at the nearly-dead and then applying all this false charity to someone he took for a perfect stranger. No, the hand grasped by Potty was not meant for shaking —

Oh no.

It was meant for striking the minister down. Hit him! this incarnation of bullshit.

But no blow came. Instead, a suppressed whimper, a string of sobs, for dizzy at relief in any form, the next few minutes for Walter passed in a kind of faint.

Somehow Potty guided him to a ledge away from Frank leaving the dying man faintly gurgling like a waterpipe, and from a creased paper bag took a glassy heap of barley sugar from which he levered a sticky lozenge and placed it on Walter's tongue.

"I'm Chaplain Fox." Still oblivious.

Slumped with curved spine beside the minister, staring with the dazed air of an apprehended miscreant, Walter cracked the lolly and heard it crunch with a dozen fractures. The sound flung him in imagination through a landscape of breaking nerves: grass made of iron pickets, a stubble of nails, vines of barbed wire, flowers of bursting steel, the shocking sunlight of signal lights and their successive waves of ghastly moonlight.

Here was the breaking point. Not one, but many, an endless run with no bucolic gasping on the far side of a wall. A maze, rather, beyond human capacity to solve, because it required the human for its building blocks.

Helplessly Walter accepted a pat on the back as

270

Potty (how futile) strove to raise him up with practical comforts and cheering phrases. But what about Frank? Did he no longer matter because he was just bones now and a bag of blood, and a heartbeat (perhaps) performing its last weird somersaults? Walter found himself condemning the minister for taking the same view of the nearly-dead Frank that he had a minute before taken himself: that he was beyond comfort, already gone.

"How about him?"

"He's quiet," said Potty after taking a look. "Shall we pray?"

Walter shrugged, and stared at the floor to avoid the man's poached egg eyes. "Our Father . . ."

There was something collusive about the way Potty administered his treatment for the pangs of war. It was equally military in purpose to the sounding of the retreat at sunset, those moments when the bugle offered with its melodious *Come Home! Come Home! Come Home!* an illusion of wholeness at the end, when all along the motive was to restore and fling lives back into the fray.

"I'll go to him," said Mr Fox when Frank gave a sudden cry. He placed a restraining hand on Walter's knee, and smiled, quizzical this time on the brink of recognition. Then it struck Walter that the oddness in the minister's eyes was nothing more than the bewildered and nervous look of a man who had mislaid his glasses. Could it be that simple? Walter cursed what he saw as a limitation that prevented him from adhering to the surface of things, which had him bounding always from the cosmic to the underground. He cursed this as unsteadiness, but an overactive imagination has its rewards. Watching the minister at work Walter developed a sense of being a spectator at the play of his own fate. This was horrible, but also absorbing. It was as if his life had become a three dimensional performance wherein feeling as well as action were available to himself-as-onlooker: the carved, flesh-coloured figures part of a fascinating, enigmatic drama of the world that illumined, inevitably, the enigmas of the self.

Thus curiosity calmed him, and with its callous power, healed.

Mr Fox unrolled a stained white surplice and knelt at Frank's side. Like an ineptly slaughtered animal Frank refused to die, but gasped and tensed.

"Our Lord Jesus Christ, who hath left power to His church to absolve all sinners who truly repent and believe in Him, of His great mercy forgive thee thine offences," — Frank's moans had earned him this sermon — "and by the authority committed unto me, I absolve thee from all thy sins in the name of the father and of the Son and of the Holy Ghost amen."

A conversation ensued, declining sounds and searching fingertips on one side, words on the other. Frank was being attended to by the real article now and he must have realized, for Potty signalled Walter to come closer.

"He wants you to give a message to someone called Nugget."

"Wally?" The name dribbled from Frank's lips. Inch by inch he once again forced out the instructions relating to Marge and Mossie.

"I'll tell him."

At least there, at the bitter end, Mr Fox's role appeared substantial. Not just a military appendage, but a manifestation of love. "Lo, I am with you always," he murmured, "even unto the end of the world."

Wide-eyed now, Frank faced the two of them and groped (it seemed) through the loneliness of pain and shock for sympathy and confidence. Frank the lover . . . If only this straining in the gloom led to a hotel rooftop, and the hand in yours, Frank, belonged to the girl with the impassive face and lustrous eyes. "The eternal arms of God's love are about you," said Mr Fox, and repeated the assurance many times as if performing an act of mesmerism. "Don't you feel the grip of Christ's pierced hands? The Christ who has been through it all Himself." He leaned forward and blocked Walter's view. When he shifted back Frank's eyes were still. Mr. Fox hestitantly made the sign of the cross, then recited loudly and firmly: "Unto God's gracious mercy and protection we commit you. The Lord bless you and keep you, the Lord make His face to shine upon you and be gracious unto you, and give you His peace, now and for evermore."

When Walter stood (still wearing his hat) he found others around him— Potty had known they were there, and these final words were meant for their ears, an impromptu service to which they muttered a rough "Amen": Boof, Walter Madox, Bluey. Potty took Walter by the elbow and said: "I'll write to your dear parents and tell them you're safe and well."

"If you like."

Walter had been moved at the end, but no longer by

the drawn out death of Frank. The warm and huge tear that tickled his cheek and dipped to leak saltily across his lips had been for the words, for the emotion sentimentally stirred by language, and for his own lost selves flaking away and away into the past (brief panicked lives: mice fleeing the harvester). The latest self had become on the instant indifferent to the sight of death, but not to ceremonies for the dead.

"What is it, then?" The minister poised a pencil over his notebook. He had asked Bluey as well:

"Mrs A.T. Clarke, Full Moon Flat, via Mookerawa — but I ain't religious. Does it matter that I'm not christened?" Bluey twisted a handkerchief, shy and defiant.

When Mr Fox turned to Walter it was clear that even now he did not recognize him. The offer to write to his parents was another of those quick charitable duties that a chaplain held ready to fit anyone, like a field dressing.

"You know who I am," prompted Walter sheepishly.

"From the college?"

"From Mt Cookapoi." Walter removed his hat and ran a hand through old bedsprings of hair.

After the "of-courses" and "how-could-I's" Mr Fox confessed that he needed sleep, rubbed his eyes (Bluey fetched a pint of tea), smacked his palms and asked was it not with feelings of strange and fearsome delight that they at last found themselves "up against it"?

All Walter's phantoms of survival ran away and hid their faces. "Yes," he said, gripping his mug, "It's like starting the 'hundred'."

"I'm fully alive here," confided the minister. Musingly he said: " 'He steadfastly set his face to go to

Jerusalem' . . . I suppose I joined up as a kind of personal test. Even ministers have their personal crises, you know . . . "

There was something of the old madness in the way he stared across the rim of his mug — as once he had stared toward a Sunday horizon of glare and stubble. This effect became marked when he found his glasses and wedged them onto the bony bridge of his nose.

"Ah," he exclaimed, and examined their faces.

Walter Madox handed across a piece of paper containing his name and address.

"What about you?" the minister asked Boof.

"There's no-one. Just me."

"My great regret is leaving the wife and little daughter behind," said the minister, addressing the words to Boof who looked sour.

Suddenly an idea was in the air. "I wonder if you two could help me. Wait here." The chaplain dashed off to find Captain Naylor.

"If there's one type I can't stand it's the parson," said Boof. "I've never met one who wasn't out to make a bloke feel a fool just for being alive."

"When they act like one of us," agreed Bluey, "you feel they've no right. And when they're all fired up with God and Christ, what's that to do with a bloke?"

The chaplain returned with Charlie Bushel to say it was all arranged. Walter and Bluey had been detailed to help him in some hard but rewarding work. They were to go with a bearer at dusk to a point called Waterfall Gully where two tracks met below the trench, and there rendezvous at a sort of tent flap. After Potty left, Charlie with a grin told them that the tent flap was the morgue. He said he hoped they had their undertaker's tickets.

17
Chloride of Lime

It was dark when they set off. The stars were blurred as though smeared on thick oiled glass, and they crouched, making their guide impatient, fearing a shattering hammer blow. But as they slithered deeper down they realized that the snipers of a few nights before had ceased operating, and excitedly they tasted freedom by standing upright. On a sharp corner, plunging into a herb bush, Bluey filled his pockets with crushed stalks.

They found Potty at work with an electric torch, his fingers partly enclosing the glass, causing light to fan in pink blades across the faces of the dead. Six corpses lay in a row awaiting Indian bearers who would hoist them on stretchers down to the less steep part of the valley, and from there convey them in mule carts to the cemetery.

"Which is Frank?" The light picked him out.

"The dead are expressionless, aren't they," said Potty. "They've exhausted the range of feeling."

Decomposition had not yet set in. Under low canvas in the furtive light the faces were like stone knights in a makeshift tomb.

"They don't look rested," said Bluey. "What is it about them faces?"

"Here come the Sikhs," said Potty. A garbled phrase rose from below, followed by a ripple of dislodged gravel, and then silence. Bluey swung his rifle to the side and then to the front in case of a Turkish patrol. Potty laughed at the thought: "Our men are all round."

Suddenly a huge figure loomed from the darkness above. Bluey's rifle, in another charge of nerves, banged Walter's kneecap.

"Jesus!"

"It's Doherty," said Potty. The announcement, though edged with exasperation, was also a greeting. A giant materialized holding one end of a stretcher from which he tipped, cruelly, a badly wounded man.

"We found this here Injun up in the scrub. I think he's just about to kick the bucket, he's been shot clean through the guts. You'd better tell him about God."

The Sikh seemed indifferent to Potty's close study of his face, and with good reason: "He's dead already."

"Let's push on down," Doherty said to his mate.

Walter and Bluey stacked the dead man beside the rest. Neither spoke. The corpse was lighter than a wheat bag by far, but clumsily balanced, which made it hard for Walter to think of the task as part of a day's work, which was the mental trick he had determined to perform to overcome revulsion at touching dead bodies. At school the juniors had once staged a rebellion in the locker room, throwing themselves in a pile and refusing to move. The seniors had been given the job of peeling the inert forms clear and lugging them outside. But these boots in his hands never kicked, and the turbanless head of greasy hair dangling between Bluey's shins neither twisted nor butted.

They were catching their breath when Doherty's voice flew up through the darkness. "Hey, Rev! There's another Injun down here keeps asking for wine. Have you got anything to drink?"

They scrambled down the path and found a bearer doubled over holding his stomach. He had slipped from the track and hauled himself up again. The wound was black, perhaps a day old.

"You damn fool," said Potty, "he's trying to tell you to wind a bandage around his wound." The Sikh burial party arrived as Potty pulled a clean dressing from his pocket. He applied it with steady hands while Walter cupped the torch. Then he sent the Sikhs on up the hill while Walter and Bluey hitched the wounded man between them and dropped into the black pool of the valley, lurching like competitors in a three-legged race.

Down at the carts they found themselves in a place resembling a mining camp. Here were ammunition boxes, planks, rolls of wire, empty water containers, and men, hollow-eyed clumps of wounded, some wedged into the hillside where eroded slits had been chipped wider, others carelessly dumped in the open. A few slept, but most stared with the wide eyes of nocturnal creatures. The healthy laboured. Everything — men, materials, even the dead — seemed destined for service in an underworld where a nameless ore of frantic value was to be found, and the mine was hereabouts, testified the haunted labourers, though no-one knew exactly where.

Potty took a breather after finding a doctor for the Sikh, and sprawled with Walter in the dust exchanging impressions of home. Mr Fox had not liked Parkes, it was too open after his South Australian hill country. An argument developed with Bluey umpiring. All that Walter loved the minister hated: frozen puddles in winter, low clouds of guncotton blue bowling up from the south, and the summer furnace that glaringly struck distant vistas out of existence. He would mention no names, but also the people, the congregation, had not been kind to him. "Your parents are fine folk," he said politely. But Walter knew that they too had given the minister only the average regard.

Coming down the hill Walter had changed his mind about Mr Fox. His desperate care to manoeuvre the Sikh without needless hurt, the way he poured kindly phrases into the dark man's ear and drawled "Of course you are" when the fellow, stung by pain, had cried "Bill cool tucker-ah, Sahib" (or something) which Potty said meant "Quite fit" — add to this the memory of Frank clawing at his precipice of life while Potty worked to hold him there — indeed everything Potty had done this day (when Walter put it in a new light) seemed bravely set against the values of these few square miles of butchery. Even his position as a brace to hold men ready for military death, while very real, was an accidental side effect of his gift of love. And his directness and simplicity, like everything else about him, showed he was no longer the subtle madman.

So Walter blurted a complaint to the new man about the old:

"I always had trouble with your sermons."

"As I did myself."

"No — my fault — they were above my head."

"And often above mine. It was a confused time. If only I could go back now, back to a pulpit. I don't think I was a Christian then."

"Are you now?" asked Bluey.

"The Christian truth is bedrock. Such a simple lesson to come from pain." Tiredly accepting a suck

279

from Walter's pipe he repositioned himself on a stack of empty sandbags and confessed: "Mind you, I was no stranger to pain before. It's just that I failed when I tried to apply faith to the intellect, rather than to the world . . . *You've* changed!" he suddenly switched his attention and poked Walter in the ribs.

"Have I?"

"I couldn't see the thinker. Haven't you rid yourself of more than a touch of self-satisfaction?"

"He's always brooding about something," pronounced Bluey.

"The outer man must be cultivated. Can I have some more of that pipe? Poetry is a deceit."

"How come you didn't recognize me before?"

The minister launched into a sermon. But here the dusty words were lapped around by objects that gave them force. "Change has altered us all. Don't you care more about others now? The army demonstrates that all of us are linked, even enemies. But so does Christ."

"I can't tell," muttered Walter. But something heartening had been said. Potty had gone as it were ahead of him, taunting with analysis an as yet undeveloped cast of character, and by such a means . . . creating it. The cloud of self was desperate for highlights.

Bluey was bored. "When do we get started?" He struck matches, lighting up the minister's face between them.

"Soon. I need a rest. They don't train men of the cloth for the outdoors." Mr Fox outlined his usual night's routine: a round of the hospital tents near the beach, then back to the gully for funerals. He called them "funerals" as if everyone turned up, when in truth for the past few nights he had been the only one in attendance, an unseen, unheard figure rolling bodies into a trench, intoning a few ancient words, looping identity discs on the necks of crosses, then back to his dugout on the heights at two or three in the morning.

Bluey strolled to a donkey and felt over it from teeth to tail for quality. Walter found the inactivity wonderfully refreshing. His agonized self-questioning did not seem so wasteful after all. The past few days of fear and panic had been half in alarm at the imminent destruction of an incomplete self. Now here was Potty Fox telling him that the self was never incomplete: never quite. It even seemed possible that he would escape into the future, for here was a man of faith blithely assuming that a future existed.

"What will you do after the war?"

"I don't know."

"The farm?"

"No."

"Won't your father expect you back?"

"I wanted to be a geologist. Now I don't know." Walter scanned his prospects and saw something unseen before. "I might have a go at becoming a journalist. I've got a friend, Ollie Melrose, who sends things off to the papers. They never publish them." He then ventured an innocently vain opinion that later was to cause trouble: "I think I could do better."

"You should keep a diary."

"Here? I've done nothing important."

"Have you considered the church?"

"Cut it out!"

"You should give it some thought. Especially now you've been as deep as a man can go."

Potty had not understood him after all. Suddenly it all seemed bullshit again. But Walter found something to add, a blatant unfurling of ambition:

"Art." The word flew straight from Egypt, from the mosque. So somehow his dreams *were* mixed up in religion, and perhaps that was what Potty saw . . . Potty who now glanced peculiarly at him:

"Paints?"

But he could not explain, suddenly wouldn't, because with shock he realized that it was not Egypt after all that lay at the root of his budding ideas, but Frances. She had talked on and on about art and he had only half listened. The words since then had been percolating insidiously upwards until, needing to build a new soul to oust her, he had spilled her ideas out in a stream coloured as his own. He was nothing but a drab skull of echoes. And worse, he was still bonded insanely to *her.*

"Doesn't it sicken you? How can you go on?" And then with vehemence, taking it out on the Reverend Potty Fox, slapping him with bitterness and a prescience of his own widening failure to grasp anything: "Reg Hurst's dead!"

He watched the minister's face while the announcement clanged around this furtively lamplit compound. His face (Walter now realized) was younger than Bluey's who was twenty-seven. It was too unweathered to bear its burden of personal history. "I'm sorry," Walter muttered, "sorry for doing my block."

Plainly the news was no surprise, though he said (and Walter believed him), "I hadn't heard." He made no attempt to ask how Walter knew about Hurst, alive or dead, but calmly accepted that both should know him.

This was unsettling. It seemed cold.

"The most difficult virtue to acquire is fortitude. Reg had it in abundance."

Bluey drifted back and said: "There are some jokers brewing up that I know from Dubbo. Have I got time to join them?"

"We're off in ten minutes."

Walter tried to mend he knew not what. "For Reg's part he was full of praise for the job you did burying his brother."

"That took fortitude, all my store of it. I'm inclined to think that the Christian virtues are a gift, but fortitude must be hard won. Their father will be a broken man. He loved Reg best, you know."

"Hurst told me otherwise."

"No, he loved him. But loved him badly, which was something Reg could never understand. Reg had numerous blind spots. I wish I could get them all together, I'd make them understand, by Christ! Such a gifted family."

Walter shrank from the blaspheming parson but was compelled by the emotion in his voice to seek his eyes. They were in shadow. He was bent over his lap making an adjustment to the torch that would enable the bulb, shielded by its conical reflector, to be attached to his belt while a wire ran to the batteries in his shirt pocket. Hour by hour he had become younger. Now, crouched over the smothered bulb, he was a strained equal, tough as a pale thong, all his theology scraped away to leave a vital servant of the kind and the sane. "When all this is finished," he looked up, "I'll refresh myself with the things I cast away. Plain speech for one! I think I'll work with the poor." The light flickered on and off. "Reg was remarkable.

"He broke into the school and wrote slogans on the

blackboards. His father called the police. It was an awfully childish thing for a man in his twenties to do. But there you are. That was Reg. A father's love can face both ways. It can be all-accepting and cruel at the same time. Doctor Hurst was saddled with the cruel kind in his relations with Reg, whereas anything went as far as Roy was concerned."

"He said he'd found himself here."

Potty asked for Walter's impressions and despite his criticisms of Reg's limitations seemed pleased to hear them. But something puzzled Walter about a minister of religion's praise for a miscreant's character: "His philosophy seemed unchristian. Not unkind, but atheistic. He said he believed everything stopped with the body."

Potty pointed out that the last place one should expect to find spiritual illumination was in the "gross corruption" of battle. He objected to ministers at home talking about war as a character-building device. He had done so himself, and was sorry though not entirely wrong: it was just that the conventional and the expected did not happen, e.g. Reg. But afterwards, ah, when time for reflection would be found, then a man would be able to discover the window in his soul that looked on to eternity, and then it would be the chaplain's duty to "catch his scattered senses".

Again the minister used the word "bedrock". If Reg took the materialist line then it was not all that different from the line taken by Potty himself. The universe of the spirit dwelt a hand's breadth away from the universe of chaos. The merest rent in the fabric between the world and —

But the chaplain remembered himself, just when most lively and interesting. He donned his specs and they showed again the secretive opaque lenses remembered from home, only now the effect was dim and smoky. He stood and swirled into darkness, hailing the Sikhs who had at last materialized with the dead from Waterfall Gully. He fetched Bluey, returned for Walter, and they set off in a file towards the cemetery.

As they shuffled along Bluey told Walter that while poking around during the wait he had found a neat stack of rifles and bandoliers beside apparently unused though properly packed haversacks. On asking an officer who they were for he was told "it would be tragical to enquire". He stopped Walter at one point and said, "That sky pilot friend of yours gives me the creeps."

"He's all right. He's better here than he was there."

Bluey had few dislikes. But when he fixed on one, that was it. His cheerfulness never faded, it just became blithe hostility. When the line halted at a wider part of the gully he clamped Walter by the shoulder: "Haven't you noticed? He don't give a fuck about exposing us. Listen!" Along the length of track just traversed they heard the clatter of a spent bullet denting and sliding through boxes and tins abandoned on either side. "I don't trust him. He's like bloody Reg Hurst. Hang around him too long and we'll be smeared all over the place like a mad woman's shit."

They came to a shelf of land behind the beach near the exit of Shrapnel Gully, a spot the chaplains had started calling "God's Acre". After the Sikhs had set the bodies down in rows and departed, Potty gave the night's work a preliminary scan. Other dead were here from earlier. They stretched off into the dark, a tangled skein increasingly decomposed. Among them Bluey found someone he knew: he pointed, uttered a drowning syllable, and vomited. Bluey had reached his breaking point. Walter feebly placed a hand on his back:

"What's up?"

"Piss off."

He strode to a gravelly depression, a hole the size of a bathtub, squatted and refused to move. "This is not human work," he complained when the chaplain remonstrated. Then he said: "Aw, shit. Give me a minute. I knew Wiley Banks and I've got to think." It was not just that he knew the man and grieved. Banks's face had been half torn away and was infected with maggots. "Wiley often used to sing for us. You should have heard his voice."

"I have," said Potty. "I knew all these men. Don't tell me about Wiley Banks. His favourite song was *The Trumpeter*. I can hear him singing now." He took Bluey's elbow and helped him to his feet, the thin torchlight at his waist contracting for a second to a faint moon that wandered back and forth across Bluey's stomach.

" 'Tread light o'er the dead of the valley'. Isn't that the one?"

After wiping his mouth Bluey set to work in the stinking graveyard.

Then it was Walter's turn to vomit. For this was not like the stink of a dead animal in the bush with its furry, coppery stench easily breasted. Nor even like the smell of the dead on the heights, which fell back now and then before a breeze. Here one was compelled to walk to the mucked heart of matter, reach out a hand, plunge it into the black pulp and grasp for a slimy bone which itself was only the outer casing of something deeper, darker, more horrible and endless. And all the while to go on, deep breath after breath, breathing as in a nightmare a medium fit only for another species.

Yet thankfully not only the body emptied itself of pure scruple here, but also the mind. After taking a mouth-clearing swill from his water bottle Walter set fiercely to work. Bluey grabbed the leg of a recent somebody and Walter an arm. Could the grazing of lately immobilized backsides possibly matter? At first with respect they manoeuvred the bodies from their lines, and then roughly. Bluey remembered the broken stalks of herb — it was thyme — a pungent green stain that showed on their handkerchiefs in the dark and restrained the clinging odour until, like poison, the stench rebuffed sweetness and entered the blood.

After each two or three bodies had been lain in the ditch they raided a bag of chloride of lime and frantically powdered the corpses until the air became sharp with a smell like laundry bleach, and the dusted shapes of men revealed themselves as in a photographic negative. Then they sprayed earth from alternating shovels, paused, and were lulled by Potty's words: "I am the resurrection and the life . . . Man that is born of woman hath but a short time to live and is full of misery. He cometh up and is cut down like a flower." Once he threw in a text for his helpers: "Be not weary in well-doing, for in due season ye shall reap, if ye faint not." This was when Frank, his stomach wound smelling like bad meat, was covered as quickly as any other. The thrill of holiness in these pauses overcame revulsion, or else it was the thrill of ghostliness . . . "What if one of these poor saps is still alive?" asked

Bluey. Walter swore that a cold hand had moved in his: but Potty checked and found that the man had been shot through the heart.

At the end of the last row ten Turks were lumped together for interment after the forty-two Australians. Bluey told a joke about a cave in no-man's-land at Cape Helles that had been abandoned by the English on arrival of a goat. But when a Turk looked in the goat had departed in disgust. "These here smell better than our chaps," said Walter, "because they're smellier alive than dead." Bluey said: "Return to sender — hey, mother! *Chop-chop!*" But Potty shut them up.

Then they set the crosses upright, hammered them in, and were told by Potty of a place at the beach where they could find a cup of tea and sleep for the night. By then it was one thirty, and they were beginning to see strange shapes — a bush became General Hamilton and strode forward with a hand extended for shaking before its whitish tips settled; a group of wounded lying on a vast and lumpy tarpaulin awaiting their shift to a hospital tent was transformed: real men, right enough, but the way their blood-soaked lint glistened under the sweep of Potty's torch made it seem, for an alarmed second, that a chest of jewels had been tipped over them, and they had no knowledge of it, except that the colours weighed them down in rubiate slabs, and they knew they would never again rise with the power that had been so easily and recently theirs. As the three filed closer to the sea they heard a frog croaking in the intervals between bullets. Its voice came from another world again, where nature, not man with his hatred and cruelty, ruled the earth.

The scene at the chaplain's dugout also had its hallucinatory aspect. They were greeted by a colleague of Potty's, a tall wakeful man wearing a clerical collar and a brown neck-protector suspended from his cap. He produced fresh tea as promised and served it from a china teapot. "Uncracked," he proudly pointed. Then he showed the sleeping place to Walter and Bluey, a roomy, clean-swept hutch, iron-roofed, with sandbagged walls half-set into the hillside. Along the rear wall of earth ran a bowed wooden shelf where wildflowers, purple and white, luminous as felt in the candlelight, were bunched in empty jam tins. Between each lot of flowers were stacked Bibles, hymn sheets, communion cups and wine. It would be like sleeping in the vestry of a church. Outside, a giant kettle dangled above red coals, and there were sweet biscuits as well as the usual dry. "This sea," said the other chaplain, a Reverend Ray, indicating darkness from which could be heard, faintly, the slap of wavelets, "is where St Paul passed by ship from Troas to Neapolis. Plainly in sight of this spot."

Bluey and Walter kept swaying forward from exhaustion, but Potty eagerly spouted the text: "Therefore loosing from Troas, we came with a straight course to Samothracia, and the next day to Neapolis."

"Can't you readily picture the little boat?" asked the tall minister of Potty.

"Oh, yes," said the wide-awake other, as if this was what made everything cheap at the price, these glimpses of Christian contiguity. You could tell they had been though this ridiculous but not stupid conversation many times, these men, who of all those stranded on the peninsula were doomed to moral agony whatever the physical comforts they snatched for themselves or thrust, brave palliatives, on others — cocoa, magazines, writing paper, or a night's rest in safety. Even Bluey, on the point of wading in, could see that.

"I'm for dreamland," he said, and the ministers, wanting to talk a while longer, smiled a motherly goodnight. As Walter tipped his tealeaves to the ground he heard Chaplain Ray mutter, not without bitterness, "There stood a man of Macedonia, and prayed him, saying, come over into Macedonia, and help us."

Bluey called back: "Should we snuff the candle?"

Then, when they were settled, he said to Walter, "We could have done better by Frank. How can we tell the boys we just — dumped him."

"His funeral was as good as the rest's."

"Still —" He reached out and pinched the candleflame.

Men tramped up and down outside, and from the beach came muffled shouts, the whinny of donkeys, the bang of iron on wood, the flop of tin. Earlier, a brief glimpse of the beach in the faint grey mist of distant searchlights propped between battleships and shore had revealed a kind of confused bayside goods yard, long and narrow, with soldiers instead of stevedores milling around purposelessly. But by now their tasks must have been sorted out because either side of the dugout resounded as thoroughfares must have . . . where? . . . in ancient Cairo . . . before the invention of the wheel. Nothing was older than Cairo. Nothing . . . and Walter pursued the thought, age melting into age down echoing archways of weathered stone on which the generations registered as shadows, if at all, and the individual was naught but the sound of a footstep fading before the space of life was done.

Bluey was still awake. "I couldn't wash properly," he complained.

"Nor me."

"They ought to let us off after all we've done . . . *Wally?*" Bluey was crying. To cover himself he gulped, "Christ, what a joke."

Walter tried to find a word to encompass the day just finished, something to throw to Bluey in expiation of its terrors. But if the right word existed it was wandering white-faced in shocked circles far from memory. Before Walter finally fell asleep he piled up extra blankets and burrowed in, also wanting to cry but unable to do so. If ever there was a night when nightmares would rack his mind, this was it — but he slept dreamlessly and woke refreshed.

In the morning Bluey was gone, and Potty's palliasse in the corner lay neat as an unused hospital bed. Why were things so quiet? The hour was late (he sat up in alarm: *past stand-to),* already sunlight pressed into the gully and with its beachside intensity brightened the cave where he lay. From far away came the lazy pop of rifle fire, and was it just his mood that made him decide that the shooting lacked heart? For seconds at a time nothing at all could be heard. Then it started again . . . the rattle of a switch of peppercorn absentmindedly flicking leather. Settling back on his blankets, making a pile under his head for a pillow, he filled a pipe and resolved not to move until ordered. After a minute he heard footsteps and then the voices of Bluey and Mr Fox at the fire.

"Oh, I know what you're driving at, padre. At home I used to go to church and all that, but this bloody war has knocked it all out of me. How can you believe in a God of love? He don't *love* no-one. Look what happened to Wiley Banks. And what about young Wally? One bloke dropping dead after another, practically in his arms. He's had the shit knocked out of him."

Then the voice of Chaplain Ray cut in, raised in objection to the swearing, and was pounced upon by Bluey's reply: "*Shit* to bad language."

Potty's response was unclear, but his tone scolding, and Bluey's words then fearfully angry: "Go and complain to your God about the buggered bodies," (he was yelling now, moving farther off). "Don't mamby-pamby me about my lip." Through a gap in the blankets that served as a door Walter saw Bluey seat himself on a knoll and face the sea.

This defence of his feelings by Bluey surprised him. He looked again — Bluey the guard. True friends sprang up when least expected, and from the foulest muddles.

Mr Fox brought Walter a cup of tea and Walter shrugged, smiling feebly. "Bluey's not himself."

"Another hard day ahead." Yet the minister spoke almost gleefully: *"Listen."*

"They don't seem too keen on it. What's up?"

"The armistice is agreed to. At seven thirty everything stops."

Walter sat upright and splashed tea: "Go on!"

"There'll be lots to do, I'll need you and Blue again." The way he said "Blue" was wrong, in the manner of someone overfamiliar to mask dislike.

"I don't think so," said Walter. "I mean, hadn't we

better get back to our mob?"

"It's all fixed. I had an inkling of this yesterday."

"Oh."

"Don't get up. There's ages before we start."

Potty's hand strayed along the shelf and plucked a fat little Bible. He riffled the pages and became absorbed. The morning had clouded over and a drizzle began.

Well, why should Bluey be left undefended?

"I heard some of what Bluey said."

The minister left a finger marking his place and looked up slowly, uttering an "Mmmm?" of irritation.

"There doesn't seem much to be said for the other side. *Your* side. Not after what we saw last night."

"I thought we'd talked this through yesterday," said Potty, abandoning his text. "But never mind." The snug Bible went *phut* as he slapped it down.

"If He's all around, how can He let this go on? He could have easily stopped it before things got bad."

"God limited His own power when He made man free. There's no freedom to do right without a freedom to do wrong. See what I mean?"

Walter took a loud sip of his tea. God sounded like a foolish headmaster. And cruel.

"He works by appealing to free men. His whole life, Christ's, was an appeal for the absolutely free loyalty and love of people like you and me. He showed us what it might cost — there was no making things attractive and easy. Where good and evil meet, inside or outside, there must and should be war. This eternal fight, inside and out, isn't that the moral equivalent of war?"

"Are 'they' all bad and are 'we' all good?"

For a minute the minister had no answer. He threw

back the blanket at the door to show the drizzle lifting its dull curtain. Bluey now sat in a shaft of sunlight, pricked with glistening mist. He tossed the dregs of his tea away, but stayed seated, tossed pebbles at a tin, smoked.

"*En masse,*" said Potty at last, "I've heard it claimed that this is almost the first time Christian principles have been applied to international relations."

It seemed they were all to be Christs at Gallipoli, devoting their lives to the enactment of a moral drama. But it didn't fit. Mankind was more a writhing garbage heap, dead or alive — feasting, competing, stealing one from the other. The rank discharges of the dead showed it last night, as did the living on the heights as they sought out the living of another race, and increased their self-esteem by killing them.

Yet there was one person who fitted the picture: Potty himself. But not now — last night when he played the healer on the hill, and later as the pilgrim breathing sane consolation on the track to the charnel pit.

Now? Bugger him.

Anything, any point to be proven, Walter believed, had to be done with few words and lots of action, otherwise it was conjecture. So now Potty was just a preacher again, dragging others up his own mental Calvary, potty all over again, all clarity obscured, a man who had lost the self-proclaimed honour of plain speech.

"There, does that clear things up?" And he left Walter feeling suddenly exhausted, desperate for a code of his own to put up against those who ran the world.

The track was busy again with tramping soldiers, one of whom asked Walter, now sunning himself at the entrance, if he had seen Doherty.

"You mean a big vulgar bloke?"

"Vulgar? He'd kill you for less."

"Then it must have been him I saw last night, tipping darkies off stretchers."

"What are you? Some kind of clown?" The speaker (Walter stood, extended a hand) was Ozzie Deep, last seen punching tickets at the Forbes Mail. After mutual recognition set in Ozzie grew confidential, and grinning said, "Always, you never missed," when Walter flashed out a hand and tipped Ozzie's hat over his eyes. It appeared that Private Doherty was one who never rested from money-getting. In the midst of battle he was rumoured to have knelt on the chest of a debtor and squeezed him for ten shillings. Ozzie knew for a fact that the chaplains had sacked Doherty from a burial detail because he was caught knocking gold fillings from the mouth of a Turkish officer. "I'm on his list," said Ozzie, "Christ knows why. He's a savage. Well, if I keep moving . . ."

Bluey had been joined by another figure, a medical orderly with prominent red armbands. Walter was reluctant to close the gap and make it a threesome — he would have to thank Bluey for his words, and that would be awkward, for though it was a relief suddenly to find himself unsentimentally pitied and thus be-friended, Walter was more at home with the edginess that prevails between those who are not quite mates. On friendship's other shore the true individualist sees a mire of disillusion. Bluey and the stranger were clapping each other on the back and shaking hands. The chap reminded Walter of Billy Mackenzie — his cap off-square in jaunty truculence, the stocky stance which even when relaxed and conversational carried an air of resistance. A slightly frontwards-leaning man he was, with the habit of chopping a toe in the dirt to make a hole, and then wedging a toecap in it while the other foot employed itself on a similar project, as if to state, *This man will not be budged one inch. Try me.*

So when Walter snoozed in the sunlight wih his chin on his hands it was natural that his childhood friend should appear in the garb of the medical orderly. Walter tried to tell him about the burial detail, but memory insisted that his most recent experience was when his dog Ajax had hurt his nearside rear paw while following him to school. A blissful moment; though when he turned to look Billy was no longer part of it. Cream Puff, his school pony, a horse with a passion for Scotch thistles which usually she picked with her lips drawn delicately back to avoid the prickles, now munched them hungrily, spikes and all, while Ajax whimpered unseen. All this took place in a room, he now saw, whose walls (blink) suddenly fell back to reveal the real world and its confounded enclosures: a corridor of gully, a bar of shingle, a thin catwalk of horizon — and something else, a shoulder and a red cross, then a face bobbing across to confront his own.

"I'll be blowed."

"*I'll* be blowed."

"I just had a dream about you and me and Cream Puff. Only — I'll be damned — you weren't in it."

"You had a dream about me and I wasn't in it ? Typical," Billy turned to Bluey Clarke, "typical Walter Gilchrist material."

The transformed Billy drew up a crate, planted himself on it, and beamed. "What do you think of my outfit?"

Walter scratched his head.

"I'm an ambulance-wallah. Not a bad sort of life."

"What made you change?"

"Wipe that look from your face. It's the real me. Say, when will the reverend be back? Him and me don't see eye to eye."

"Stay for a cup of tea," said Bluey, and busied himself out of earshot.

"If Foxy sees me I'm done," whispered Billy. "Keep it under your hat, but this ambulance stunt is just for today. The bloody chaplains won't have a bar of it."

"Too late. Here he is."

Mr Fox strode around the corner of the gully. But he found a stone in his boot and stooped to release it.

"I've always got the old place on my mind, haven't you? Cook-a-poi," he pronounced nostalgically, and edged off a couple of paces, gauging the minister's next move. "Let's have a yarn sometime later."

"Where can I find you?"

Billy smartly surveyed a line of escape through the slum of sandbagged dugouts on the hillside. "Ask for Lieutenant— I'm one of his — haven't you heard?" He took a deep breath and braced himself for a standing start, waving cheekily to the lumbering Potty. After a second he lowered the arm and aimed it like a rifle. "I'm one of Lieutenant 'Skipper' Fagan's snipers, I was in your vicinity the other day — where were you?" He triggered a "click" with his tongue, said "Cheerio", then sprinted across the pitted hillside and disappeared.

Potty pursued him for fifty yards, stumbled twice, and returned examining grazed palms. "I don't know why I bother. He's the devil for taunting a man. They want him at headquarters, a Captain Benedetto there has been seeking him for days. I've a suspicion its news to his advantage, but the young fool won't stop for me." On a silk handkerchief bearing an embroidered *D* the minister dabbed his hands, blew his nose, then stuffed a pocket until it bulged like an outsized carbuncle, which he stroked.

"Have you seen much of him?"

"Not till today."

"The few times we've had words I must say he never mentioned you, though you must have heard of his doings, surely."

"Nothing."

"But he's the one who killed the Turkish sniper in the pine tree the day after General Bridges was shot. It made him instantly famous. He's killed many since."

"That can't be right. It's not *Billy* they're talking about . . ."

"Billy and 'The Murderer' are one and the same," announced the minister.

18
Views from Home

After the unceasing din of battle the silence of the armistice seemed to whisper. It was like being in a cave, only a cave with a painted roof where clouds hung motionless over modelled gullies and a plaster beach. The faces of men as they climbed to vantage points and dumbly stared gave the impression that this inexplicably intact landscape was no illusion, but that everything that had passed before had been. Only an hour or two ago the horizon had hovered just above a man's scalp and to gaze at it however briefly had meant death. The enemy appeared to feel the same — that bewhiskered peasant working without bitterness alongside the stringy invader of his motherland.

But the world they now saw was not the one they had stepped from brief weeks before. On finding themselves free for the first time to take a good look round they felt uneasy. Untroubled haze and immense glassy vistas — what world was it? They wore the uniform of custodians, and by forthright exercise of responsibility had won the right to a vision — but when it came it was a vision of a world that ignored their presence. Heartbreak and sacrifice revealed nothing but a beauty disdainful of effort.

From ruptured earth clambered Turkish officers in pale blue uniforms who raised braided arms to direct their burial parties or salute Australian counterparts. At intervals they too gazed across unruffled water to the islands of Imbros and distant Samothrace. Hitherto sunken horizons had been cranked up to show vistas undreamt of in a night where morality had one outcome only — a result so vile and narrow with its bloated and decomposing judgments that surely it would not be permitted to recur. Among stripped and shattered twigs lay a torn face, a knee, a haversack with tatters of canvas streaming oddly out, as if in a stiff breeze. Bushes sparkled from an early shower, and a bird flew up demanding that the eye return to locate another, such ordinary events being miracles.

Billy reached the heights untouched by the elation of the stopped battle. Not for him the rectangle of cardboard stuck to his hat with the name of his home town printed on it in large letters, nor the fretful hunt for conversation up and down a line warily released on an unexpected holiday. After escaping the chaplain he had climbed with his camera folded flat in a pocket where it was no more conspicuous than a tin of herrings. Others were out for souvenir snapshots, but not Billy. Box Brownies and Vest Pocket Kodaks appeared from nowhere to memorialize the true preoccupation of the soldier at rest — shutters gaped wide on ham actors straining under the weight of empty canisters, on grim-faced frauds lining up unseen targets of clowning mate or blank wall . . . And in one such group Billy found Walter, now freed from his jobs with the minister. They arranged a meeting place for later on, then Billy asked:

"Which way did Foxy go?"

"North."

"Then I'll go south."

Because of the smell Walter smoked his pipe until his tongue burnt. Otherwise he tried to give no thought to tomorrow. But not so Billy, who continued working his way along the lip of the parapet wearing a white armistice armband in addition to his red crosses. He saw dead Turks with wounds just as gaping as those deplored on dead Australians, and decided therefore that the enemy had not been using exploding bullets as many had thought. He was neither shocked nor stirred by the inhuman scenes, though he gagged at the stench. His sense of purpose was a remedy for mental disruption. When he found a useful landmark that gave a line on a vulnerable Turkish position he dropped into the trench, marked the spot on his map, and noted down the details in his large hand ("there reinforcemants might be got at from humpleft of X"). Where possible he unfolded his camera, scrupulously calculated the exposure, and framed a shot through a loophole. Photography was banned — so what?

Towards two o'clock he was adjusting the camera when a shadow fell across his view and then a pair of legs blocked it. He shouted to no effect, so climbed up to find an officer standing there. The man had been staring down gullies to the sea. He waved aside Billy's apologies and accepted a cigarette. He was tall and olive skinned with round dark eyes and a brown bald head. He mopped under his hat with a faded purple handkerchief. Did he also dab at a tear? He was a South Africa veteran, he told Billy, and was hardened to all sorts of sights, though he had never witnessed anything like the scene before him, where the battlefield, all save a few unfinished burials, had become a graveyard, and in a few hours would become a battlefield again.

"Where are you from?" the officer asked vaguely. At that instant Billy read the name stamped in gold on the leather of his binocular case: *Benedetto*.

"The Hunter Valley," Billy hastily lied, then changed his mind. The man took him for a stretcher bearer; it would have been easy to walk away unrecognized — but bugger that.

Billy was about to introduce himself when Captain Benedetto said: "I have a daughter at home in trouble." He spoke softly: "I've been thinking about her."

"Trouble?"

The officer climbed into the trench and invited Billy to follow. They lowered themselves from ruptured sandbags onto a firestep amid a torrent of dislodged gravel, and then stood at the mouth of a communication trench like chance acquaintances at the corner of a city street while crowds swirled by.

"I can't talk about it."

"No?" Billy thrust his pay book into the man's hands. "I'm not who you think. I'm on a stunt for Mr Fagan."

The captain licked a finger and turned a page. "So you're Mackenzie. I've been looking for you. They said you were a rough diamond with little respect for the niceties. Well, you've done yourself proud this time. My daughter is to have a baby in August."

"Diana?"

"I've been wanting to meet you, Mackenzie. I've sent messages everywhere." He handed Billy a slip of paper on which was lettered: *Wm. Mackenzie trooper ALH please contact Capt. C. Benedetto HQ Beach*. "Do you know what I've had in mind? A thrashing."

"I wouldn't have come," Billy smiled at the message, "not for a thrashing."

"You're a caution, lad."

"I'm not ashamed." Billy threw in a *sir*. "We're planning to get married."

Suddenly Captain Benedetto's hand darted out and Billy feinted, raising a bared forearm. Then it was the captain's turn to smile: "I'm not a violent man. A thrashing? No, but I like to sum a fellow up. You're not my choice for a son in law." He made the movement again, this time more slowly, picking at Billy's armbands. "What's all this? It looks like shabby tricks."

"Orders," Billy mumbled.

"I've always let my wife and daughter go their own way. And whyever not? Women's world and all that. This is the last trouble I expected." Billy could have told him that there was no such thing as a woman's world that did not include men. "Look, call on me at Headquarters. We'll have to talk. Marriage? I've never understood my daughter."

"She's made me happy."

"I've always got something — rum, tobacco — you chaps take so many risks."

"Thank you, sir."

Billy waved as he turned the corner. It was intended as a salute but changed halfway through to a farewell between equals.

A father! thought Billy. All right, that's good, I'm to be a pa. He made one of his songs out of it, feeling happy. Yep, he'd go to the captain as invited. But not yet. He'd wait for the crowning touch. He'd wait until he was a hero. To think a captain could be such a mug.

"The last thing he expected, etcetera." But he was a likeable cove, without any bullshit. A father! All right, that's good, I'm to be a pa — and he was still humming this ditty several hours later when he reached the rest area where he and Walter had agreed to meet. The first person he saw was Blacky Reid. All right, that's good:

"Hey! Blacky! I'm to be a —"

"How's things?"

"What a day!"

"Do you think so? It's the first time I ever saw so many dead. It's knocked the shit out of me." Blacky was standing in a peculiarly stiff pose, legs apart and knees slightly bent reminding Billy of an inexperienced rider after a long day in the saddle. "To cap it all I've got the ringer's complaint. Piles. They're real humdingers."

"If you get shot in the arsehole you'll be right. Ha, Ha! Clean you out."

"It's not funny!" This was the old snarling Blacky, but amazingly drained of his power to push people into line. "Why does everyone laugh?"

"Sore bums are funny," shrugged Billy, sitting on a sheet of tin and taking out tobacco, "I don't know why." He decided not to tell Blacky his news.

A man claimed the tin and Billy was forced to stand again.

"Anyway you shouldn't sit on hard surfaces. That's how I got them."

"You're worse than someone's mother. What's got into you?"

"I bloody told you."

"It's not the end of the world."

"You wait till you get them, bugger it."

"Then I'll wait. Have you seen Wally?"

"No, but wasn't he hit? I heard a rumour."

"We're supposed to meet here."

"It must have been someone else who got it," said Blacky in a don't-care tone.

"Wally was there when Frank Barton got killed. The bomb knocked him cold."

"Frank Barton? I never knew him." Blacky winced, concerned only for himself. He always had been, Billy realized, who with two lives in his care wondered how he could ever have been taken in by the selfishness of Blacky's bluster. It was just as Walter's father had said — Blacky was all wind.

Billy caught sight of Walter lining up for a wad of tea from a dixie, and hurriedly excused himself. As he strode across the open area which was about half the size of a football field, dodging cooking fires and sprawled sleeping men, he heard a sound so unexpected it seemed a trick of some kind: the bleating of sheep.

"Ease up, I'm scalded," said Walter as Billy grabbed his arm.

"Come over here where no-one can listen."

"Did you hear the sheep?"

The serene evening air, cleared of battle smoke and stench, mocked and teased human susceptibility. The armistice was due to end any minute.

"What if we all held our fire," said Walter, stopping and cocking his head: sheep, definitely sheep. Therefore anything was possible.

"Come *on*," urged Billy, steering him to a spot under a bank. It was a safe position even when the guns were operating, but farther into the open, where Blacky limped among desultory fires, shells had been known to land. Though Billy desperately wanted to tell Walter his news he spent a minute explaining how the ridge above "shadowed" them from Turkish artillery. Then he asked:

"What's the last thing you'd expect me to be?"

"I don't have to guess, Mr Fox told me. You're nicknamed 'The Murderer'."

"Not that. That's a joke."

"Is it?"

"I just do my job. It doesn't feel like anything. The *last* thing you'd expect me to be. Come on —"

"I can't guess."

"A father."

Walter, bugger him, showed no surprise. He reacted slowly, reflectively: "It was bound to happen to one or the other of us, after the hotel. But have you only just heard?" He did some mental arithmetic.

"August," said Billy. "It's due in August. What if we were home by then? She cares about me. *Me.*"

Walter stared at his boots feeling envious. Envy — one or the other never seemed free of its petty disgrace.

"You're lucky," he managed. It was not that he envied Billy the circumstances — he hardly considered them — it was Billy's pure happiness that stung.

"Remember what Ethel told you? A wife and child. Now I *know* I'll be getting out of this place alive."

From high in the gullies came a lone rifle shot. They stopped talking and listened. Those tending fires straightened themselves and looked apprehensive. An infantryman with a dish of stew allowed it to dribble and stain his trousers as he stared upwards. In a few seconds the first shot was joined by others — the popping of kindling at the start of a blaze. Blacky limped across and was the first to speak:

"That's torn it."

"Were you like me," asked Walter, "wondering if nothing would happen?"

"I was," said Blacky, "I surely was."

They shook hands.

"We heard you might have been hit. Even dead," Blacky said, striving to look concerned. He nodded at the low hill beyond which lay the beach. "Did you hear the sheep?"

"It was just imagination. Someone playing the fool," said Walter. It had been a common practice among the Australians in Egypt to bleat when a well-liked officer made an unpopular announcement.

"Like hell it was. Pig Nolan's down there now, requisitioning a hogget. He never lets up."

"I couldn't give a *fuck* about Pig any more," said Walter with vehemence. He rarely swore like this: to do so was a mark of his ascendance over Blacky, over Pig, over all his acquaintance except Billy. Also a sign of his irritation at the fear that hummed through his body at the first shot: fear mournful and ominous like wind groaning through trees.

"All right. Don't lose a feather."

This talk of Pig did not touch him as it used to. Enemies were everywhere now, and brutally impersonal. Somewhere in the past week Walter had woken from a nightmare in which people were turned inside out. Pink glistening bodies with corded veins and pearl rib bones jostled and crowded together, their skulls gristle-hard, eyeless, but somehow alive. What did personality matter in a movement where the individual had no place? Where was Pig in that horde with his rumoured threat of keeping "one up the funnel" for those he disliked, Walter prime among them? Pig no longer mattered.

When Blacky left Billy said: "I met her father. He didn't know me from Adam. Look —" he took a much folded letter from his pocket, "she's said she'll marry me."

"Because of the baby?"

"She's never mentioned the baby. It was the father that told me. Do you know one of the chief rules for sniping? Take on the background. If a man is somewhere he shouldn't be, the observer hardly ever sees him unless the man overdoes it. Nature is natural — so I could have got away without letting on who I was. But I told him." Billy was triumphant. "I can't get over the way she never said a word. Didn't Frances never say nothing?"

"Nothing."

Billy was too inexperienced a triumphant to resist the vindictiveness that often goes with that state. He handed Walter a much folded letter:

"You can read it — all of it. It's where she says she'll marry me. There's other news there about Frances."

"I can't help thinking she's gone cool on me."

"Frances? Cool? That's a laugh. She's taken up with Robert Gillen, that's what she's done."

As Billy watched Walter concentrating over the letter, sorting the loose pages into order, his lower lip trembling and his adam's apple sliding up and down like the uncoupled shaft of a windmill in a hopeless attempt to stem tears, and then the letter rattling in his hands as he shifted each page under to read the next, he was sorry, and for the first time wished himself back in Australia, with Walter on the land somewhere nearby, and the two of them safe, as predicted by Ethel.

When Walter finished the letter he said: "I knew it." But his face showed that he had just received the surprise of his life.

Nervously Billy said, "I've got you to thank for everything. Do you know what? I'm happy. I'm a changed man. I'll bet it was you who got me invited back that night, eh? Frances wouldn't have done it on her own. Right?" Billy did not believe that a human person had bestowed this gift of happiness that was so astonishingly his, but he wanted to make up for being the bearer of bad news.

But Billy was right, it had been Walter that long ago night who persuaded Frances to dash for the ferry and bring Billy back. She would not have done it if Diana herself had not added her entreaty — an anxious nod. Then the four of them had strolled to the point to watch the moon hovering above distant Vaucluse, plunging a million white blades into the harbour. After a while they drifted to different benches, and Frances, twisting around, muttered with a giggle: "I think Billy and Diana are kissing." Walter then snaked an arm around her shoulders and vigorously drew her towards him.

"You're a surprise packet," she murmured.

That was when the downward slide had started, the unfathomable delight she bestowed on him and its reverse, the bitter history of betrayal, the first detailed in action and long in memory, the second muddy with doubt until he found this sharp stone bedded in Diana's letter:

Franny talks of no-one but Robert, I suppose it's a disgrace.

He had winced with pain as they kissed because of his sore ribs. But his sudden discomfort released from her a kiss on his cheek that soon changed to the warm application of mouth upon mouth which astonished him, and the pain melted, releasing a sensation that he needed to describe as soon as they separated to catch breath and listen to the racing of hearts: but she spoke first —

"I could do this for ever."

He believed her. She too, he thought, had discovered the golden ecstasy at the centre of what was — he saw it now — his pilgrimage alone.

"It's like —" they kissed again before he could say: "A golden arrow! Electrified!"

"Tell me more. Is that nice? That?" This was the very Frances who, Diana's letter said, had been "finding her way" with Walter, who "had always known she would hurt him."

He remembered her curiosity.

"Where does it hurt?"

Delicate fingers climbed his sore ribs.

"Ouch!"

Then with swift intimacy her hand was inside his shirt. This was different from being touched by Ethel. It was as if he had eaten something in a dream — her fingers fluttered on his stomach — an impossible dish composed of substance, sensation, emotion.

She spoke naked words, "You poor darling", and allowed herself to be touched as he pleased.

But after all they had been two strangers on a seat overlooking rocks and water. A yellow lamp swung from tram wires at the terminus and the insects of early summer surrounded it, sending enlarged shadows to swoop over the foliage. Soon they would stand, straighten creased clothing, and yawn from unresolved emotion.

He told her about the hotel, daring to say "lovers go there", and about the feeling he had had since leaving camp the day before that something good was bound to happen between them.

"These lovers — do they give their names?"

The question planted itself like a shoot of willow. How could a fool like Walter have guessed that an experimental mood was upon this girl — soft, undangerous! — who ran sharp fingernails up and down his ribs, who took his hand and scored the fleshy palm as if inscribing a claim, who kissed him clumsily and aggressively, drawing a knee across his lap, a knee hidden in the folds of her dress that rested on the uncomfortable fact of his erection.

Billy and Diana were similarly entwined.

"Billy was seen with a black girl in the yard of the hotel. I'm not supposed to know. Don't you feel that Billy's mysteries are all a bit like that?"

"Like what?"

At the time he had thought of her profile as dreamy and speculative, but now it struck him how anxious she must have been. Anxious for what? Here was the phrase in Diana's letter: "She's happy now but will it last? Franny's bad nerves spoil so much. Whatever she finds in one place needs something from somewhere else, something unobtainable, before it satisfies her. So nothing satisfies her."

"Dad says Billy is sly," said Frances. "Neat as a pin, polite, and then — doing *that*."

According to Diana's letter Billy at that moment on the other bench had been honourably occupied: "Remember when you kissed me in the park? And said something foolish? I thought you were making fun of me and for a whole minute I disliked you." She had starred "rather foolish" and written "our secret" in the margin at right angles to the rest of the letter.

Frances had asked for a cigarette.

"Are you supposed to smoke?"

"Oh *give* it to me," and she plucked from Walter's lips the drooping cigarette he had just rolled. Then she composed herself with a hand cupped on her knee, and said: "How would I look in a moonlight photograph?"

"Mysterious."

It was no longer the mystery of personality that intrigued him (if only it had been) but the mystery of flesh.

"Do you think I'm mysterious? Really? It's a nice thing to say."

"I was thinking about when we came down together on the train. I wanted to kiss you then. Would you have minded? But I couldn't work you out."

"Pretend I'm on the train now," she answered. "Kiss me." She looked out a play-acted window to where the ferry, having slipped its moorings and headed around the point, was gliding past on the opposite side. "Oh look! What town is that? Aren't they pretty lights!"

He stood over her as he had long ago when raising her fallen blanket, and she stared up at him as before. He bent, tasting her tobacco-pungent breath, but before he could plant his kiss she said: "I didn't think of you in that way at all. Not for a minute. Do you think that strange?"

He kissed her anyway, not at all disquieted that she was again wearing the self-contained look that had been hers on the train — at this most intimate of moments when all (so he thought) had been revealed.

Walter handed the letter back to Billy, who stuffed it together with his armbands into a trouser pocket. Side by side they sat, each wanting a signal from the other. Then both spoke at once: "Why didn't she tell me?" The phrasing matched perfectly, but only Billy laughed. For once he felt superior in all ways to Walter, convinced he was free of the poison of resentment. In a rush of feeling he scrutinized his own least slip, and took up the burdens of others in his joy: "It's not bloody fair is it, Christ I'd like to show bloody Gillen around the bloody trenches."

Walter said nothing.

A characteristic of the place where they sat was its patch of green grass. A well had been dug here after the landing but now it was dry. Trampled but still juicy tufts bore witness to a soak where clean water trickled through the earth a hundred feet or more below the trenches. Still there was nothing either could say. Both nibbled and sucked at green stalks. Not words but time was needed, thought Walter, to correct the imbalance of fortune between them, time that ruthlessly narrowed their future as the walls of the gully narrowed — that climbed, threshed and spat around the dark scrub on the skyline where a whirlpool of venomous geography existed to entrap it. Complaining, enraged, but inevitably condemned.

"Take these," said Billy, handing Walter a small package. "I've been waiting for the chance to show them to you." Walter peeled back much-folded tarpaper to find a dozen smaller packages within, each enclosing a photograph. The wrapping was of fine but tough tissue paper, the kind used to protect frontispieces in books. The photo inside showed a white disc — a straw hat on a knee — and a wedge of sky bearing down like the outline of South America.

"The exposure was all right," said Billy. "They buggered it up in the printing."

It had been taken the Saturday they had gone to the Botanical Gardens, when Billy went mad with his camera using up three rolls of film and finally breaking Diana's reserve — so that when the ever willing Frances at last persuaded her to join in a "spring dance" against the backdrop of a Moreton Bay fig she threw a leg almost as high as her friend's and Billy caught the motion forever. It was more like a highland fling — there they were, hand in hand, two left legs flying, smiling into each other's eyes. Frances's left arm was fully extended, her palm upturned to catch (should chance permit) all she considered her due, while Diana's stayed closer in, fingers modestly enclosing a sprig of gum nuts. They smiled, they were happy, and afterwards when they sat fanning themselves with their vast wheels of hats Walter had knelt beside Billy while he attempted a more reflective picture. "Look over here. Now look away. Whoa! Bugger, they moved. Hey Frances! Now tell them to hold it."

"Hold still!" And as if in emphasis a clap of thunder had echoed across the city.

"Do you know my trouble?" asked Billy as he squatted on the grass and folded the camera away.

"Have you finished?" called Frances.

"*F. 16* at one fiftieth," muttered Billy, and scribbled the number on a slip of paper which he slid inside his wallet. Walter waited for the answer — Billy seemed about to make a confession. But all he said was: "I don't know how to develop and print my own pictures. I'd like to do everything myself."

"Hurry up, we'll get wet!"

They set off for a hall in Elizabeth Street where the explorer Mawson was to give a lecture at three.

"Do we have to?" said Frances.

"I don't care one way or the other," said Billy, but he became enthusiastic when Diana said she wanted to go.

The idea had been Walter's but when he brought it up Frances had just drifted away from him. The secret he thought he had learned by kissing her was no use after a week of separation. He felt too shy to offer his arm in public, and when he went up to her at a shop window and leaned a palm on the glass to enclose her, she ducked out. Yet the Saturday outing had been her plan. About the following weekend too, when she would be staying with Diana, she was full of plans.

Finding themselves at a corner waiting for Billy and Diana (arm in arm) to catch up, Frances said: "Do you wonder what they talk about?" Then, slipping behind to listen, they discovered them absorbed like children in a string of comparisons — "I likes" and "don't likes" about food, modes of transport, even the raindrops that chased them into the nave of an insurance office. When they made a dash for it Diana shrieked "Don't!", but Billy lifted her off the ground anyway, and she sped along with heels locked in a glide of pleasure.

In the hall Walter ran his fingers along the shining runners of a sled. He felt clumsy and half made. Wordlessly he followed Frances as she marvelled at the smoothness of the wood despite its scratch marks. When he mumbled that the scratches were exactly like photographs he had seen of glaciated stone, no-one bothered to listen.

"Come on, look at these."

A spirit stove, a wireless transmitter, a fur suit and a pair of snow goggles were arranged on a table for inspection. Billy tried the goggles on, and groped about like a blind man while Diana blushed and told him to stop.

But when they sat down things changed. Many other soldiers were in the hall, and suddenly it was clear that the attraction of the Antarctic explorer's adventures had brought them here not merely because of the wet afternoon, but out of fellow feeling. Like Mawson, they felt themselves embarked on an adventure with a true Australian flavour. "I was privileged to rally the 'sons of the younger son' ", said the explorer in his opening remarks. They knew what he meant. He surveyed the audience with clear eyes and a proud jaw that were themselves a reward for effort. Walter felt less removed from a meaningful existence, and found the strength to tell himself that in such an arena Frances did not matter . . .

In planning his trip, said Mawson, he had found an opportunity to prove that the young men of this young country could rise to those traditions that had made the history of British polar exploration one of triumphant endeavour as well as of tragic sacrifice.

At this remark Frances took Walter's hand.

An attendant with a long hooked pole tugged at black curtains high on the wall to block out the light in readiness for the moving pictures. Without warning, before the hall was properly dark, the flickering scenes of toil began. For a while it was impossible to see anything except a blob that might have been anything

— a balaclava helmet, the head of a seal, the prow of a ship. Then the strange world of ice sprang into being, and as Walter leaned forward, absorbed, to catch the explorer's commentary, Frances whispered: "You look so romantic in the cold light."

After that it seemed nothing could ever go wrong — not with Frances, not with the world. Walter told himself he was made of the stuff of heroes, and for as long as Frances fed him with admiration, he was.

Two of Billy's photographs were left, but before Walter could study them other members of his troop filed into the gully. Some started cooking. others engaged in horseplay in the fading light. "Hey," Charlie Bushel informed Walter when he caught sight of him, "You're back with us now. No more slacking."

Lizzie and Boof played leapfrog. Bluey slow bowled a stone to Mick Aitcheson, who struck it with a plank. They saw Walter engrossed and left him alone, except that Bluey trotted over juggling the stone from hand to hand: "We're feeding here," he informed Walter, "then heading south."

"Where's the Rev?" asked Billy.

"Gone to buggery," said Bluey, indicating with a thrust of his thumb the top of the gully where the light was grey, already heavy with the murk of renewed battle. But then, almost at the very moment of Bluey's gesture, the place lit up as the setting sun shifted from under a cloud. A rubble-filled crook of the gully's inverted V glowed as if picked out by a spotlight. In mock alarm Bluey cried, "I didn't mean it, Lord, I love thy servant."

Walter was pleased to see his companions again. His worst terrors seemed to have settled. When the sunlight faded from the heights he returned to the last two photographs, barely able to see them.

Both had been taken on the morning of the last Saturday within minutes of each other, and from the same position. Billy and Walter had changed at the hotel and travelled to Cremorne in ordinary clothes. Billy had found a patch of grass on the slope above the water, someone's private garden with a pile of torso sized rocks on coarse grass that gradually slipped from focus as it swept up towards the lens. Nearly all Billy's photographs were taken from a low angle, and all showed his eye for symmetry. One picture was of Walter, the other of Frances. Billy had placed Walter across on the right hand edge, so that in a seated pose, "reading" a magazine, he had the full weight of the rocks behind him.

"You've caught me," said Walter. "You ought to take up photography as a job." But he did not really think so, for Billy's approach, though deft, was monotonous — he looked at nearly all his subjects in the same way.

Frances had been taken more squarely on, the effect being one of lightness. Even though the other components of the scene almost crowded in on her it was as if she floated, strung invisibly to the shrub at one shoulder, the rocks at the other — and was just tethered to the curvature of grass. She too was reading, only with the pages of the magazine scrolled anyhow under the spine. The fine bones of her hands were visible, and also the veins under her skin. She looked accepting — doing what she wanted — not actually reading, but seeming to. Not enjoying a quiet moment in the corner of a garden, but observed and memorialized at it.

Had she always been acting out a role?

With their departure date irreversibly fixed Frances had become wildly affectionate. Before and after the photographs she clung to Walter's side, and back in the house asked him up to her room to "see something", and there with the door closed behind him, among odours of powder and perfume, with a cupboard door hanging wide to show her petticoats, they had kissed. First while standing, and then while she sat on his knee, and finally dropping to embrace full length on the bed. She had removed her wide-lapelled jacket, but when things reached their intensest pitch and Walter's blind fingers searched her high collar to release cold white buttons she abruptly kicked herself to her feet and thrust one arm and then another back into the rumpled jacket. She was flushed, her eyes shone, her teeth were white and her tongue red.

She pinned back a loose strand of hair while standing at the window and said in a light voice, "Don't go, there's so much to talk about." Then she tugged at her cuffs and looked at him enquiringly.

"I'm not about to go anywhere. Does your mother know we're here?"

"No, I mean don't go away to the war." She knelt beside the bed where Walter reclined full length, his heels propped on the ornate iron railing.

"I can't stop home now."

"What if," Frances hesitated. She nodded at a book on her bedside table while clasping his hand. "Have you read *Anna Karenina*? She did what she wanted."

"What if, what?"

"Oh, what if you didn't go." But that was not what

319

she had been about to say. *What if we were lovers* — that was the unasked question.

"I can't give it up now. It's too late," and his heart thumped because he knew that this resolute answer was the one she wanted.

"Still, I wish you could."

Later that night after the theatre, following a change of plan that took Walter by surprise but not the other three, Frances had so abandoned herself to this wish that he knew he must stay — what else could be more important than the union that had so abruptly and miraculously become possible? But by then they were naked together on a narrow hotel bed.

And a week later, when she had farewelled him at the wharves, the plea seemed a mixture of joy and hysteria. First she had held him tightly, sobbing, "I'll be alone. What shall I do? There's only me." And he had never thought it strange that when he awkwardly said, "I'll marry you the minute I get back," she had not replied, but had dried her eyes with her mother's handkerchief and with curiosity asked, "What happens next?" The band had stopped playing, an order rang out. Then as they marched away she ran alongside and tossed her scarf among the wheeling soldiers, and he had caught a glimpse of her smile when someone whistled low.

But he had always been stupid in relation to Francis, he decided. At the theatre it had taken him a minute to realize, as he stood on a stairway with Billy during an interval, just what was going on. "The girls want to take a look at the hotel, after," said Billy. Male forms jostled as they pushed past on their way to the crowded, urine-stinking cellar. Then Billy breathed the

320

secret: "Actually they'll stop the night with us. It's fixed."

When Walter handed the photographs back to Billy it was without expectation of ever seeing them again or indeed of ever seeing Billy again. And the feeling, far from being momentous, seemed everyday. There was nothing unusual about a fate meted out wilfully, but in the end inexorably, as the evidence on the heights showed. One thing was certain — they were parting friends.

"It all seems nonsense, what we done before," said Billy. He meant everything — his life, Walter's. In a few words he did something Walter never expected. He reached past the adult control of their friendship to the stormier days of truce and quarrel that seemed to have spanned all their lives, stretching back to when they were seated by their mothers on a rug, swaddled in capes and frocks, eyeing each other like members of hostile species.

"We got it all wrong, didn't we?"

"I suppose we did."

Having signalled his departure with this gust of generosity Billy seemed reluctant to leave. If love could do this to Billy, thought Walter, what might it not achieve? Billy told Walter that just before the night at the hotel with Diana he had been half inclined to chuck it in, and take up with a girl from St Peters who appeared one day at the camp looking for her brother, leaving Billy with an address and more than half a promise . . . But Walter mustn't get him wrong, he would not have done anything, it was just that Diana woke him up to himself, she "threw him". With Diana he knew he would have to become a bigger person, not just now and again but all his life. And at moments he thought he wasn't equal to it.

Billy, who never cracked.

Did Frances do this to Walter? No, she wouldn't have. The night at the hotel, Billy abruptly went on, had been Frances's idea.

"Frances's?"

"She put it up to Diana, who put it to me."

"I would have been game," Walter asserted, knowing that the others had picked his character exactly. He would have dithered, of course, and wasted time and asked everyone to think twice. He needed a *fait accompli,* which they gave him.

Was that why Billy had appealed to his sense of fair play, exploited it, rather, when at the theatre that night he had gone on to say: "Diana and me have talked about marriage."

"Well, that's good." Walter had tried to shake Billy's hand, but congratulations apparently were not in order.

"It's only vague at the moment. An idea."

They had finished at the urinal and again found themselves on the stairs. It was only right that Billy should have the opportunity to enjoy what would doubtless be his if there had been no war . . . This was the night Frances was expected to stay at the Benedettos', but Diana had informed her mother of a last minute reversal of plan. With each mother believing her daughter to be in the care of the other, what else could be done?

"When you say 'the night'," Walter caught Billy's sleeve to delay him, "do you mean —" and the sentence drifted into silence, completing itself in Walter's raised eyebrows and in Billy's confirming wink.

During the second half of the programme Frances hardly spoke, but held Walter's hand or let hers rest on his knee as she leaned forward and laughed, or followed the action with sober absorption. During a scene change she said, "I was sitting here, and you were over there. You looked so intense. Are you still the same person?"

"No. Frances —" The lights died and they kissed in the sudden blackness.

"Wal?"

They had shifted farther under the bank because someone had come by and pointed to a heap of rubble just out from the grasspatch, telling them that it had not been there this time yesterday, but of course they knew, didn't they, that a Turkish shell wasted no time, though it whistled a mournful warning on its way. When they were safe Billy took his boots off.

"I thought you were going."

"I am."

He dropped the boots at arm's length and sighed. The boots were his no longer: in the gloom they seemed to belong to a third, invisible person who had shuffled up to pose a question and now awaited a response. Billy peeled flakes of grey skin from his heels and rubbed between his toes to remove pellets of darker dirt. "Wal? Do you think we could make a proper go of it, me and Diana?"

Never before had he asked Walter's advice.

"I think we could," he went on, not waiting for an answer. "I'd like to start out somewhere on my own. She'd be in it." He emphasized her vigour by patting the pocket where Diana's sensible but impassioned epistle lay hidden. "You ought to take a trip up to Wellington some time. Somewhere near the river," he mused, "round Bluey Clarke country. It'd do me. A few horses, hay — I worked there for a bloke called —", his voice trailed off.

Walter prompted him: "Bluey told me about a murder."

"He did? He don't know a thing."

"Do you?"

Billy grunted and reached for his boots. "What's one body after all this? I found the wife of the farmer I worked for buried in a paddock. He gave me a hundred quid to shut up."

"If you go back there, will you tell?"

"Dent hanged himself at Christmas."

Charlie Bushel passed among the men with a message: "Off in five minutes," and told Walter to collect his kit and to make sure he thanked Boof for lugging it down.

"As if you're not well mannered," said Billy, offering Walter another sign of esteem. But the very fact of his doing so was a measure of the rapid alteration in their fortunes.

Captain Naylor emerged from darkness and congratulated Walter on the good work he had done for Chaplain Fox.

"And who are you?" he asked, peering at Billy.

"I'm 'The Murderer' ", Billy sardonically answered.

"Ah hah. You look kind enough. Keep it up, eh?" In the dark he touched his nose in habitual emphasis of its ugliness. "The Murderer?" And again he laughed.

"Well?" asked Billy, at last slinging his rifle across his back and collecting the leather telescope case. "If it all comes right at the end, what about it? She's not my type, but that's the secret. Y'know, I haven't felt better in years. I feel — hell — what do I feel?" He laughed in the darkness and shook Walter's hand, forgetting that he had asked yet another question and not waited for an answer. "You'll be right," he called over his shoulder to Walter as he plodded off. "Remember Ethel and what she said? She's always spot on."

Then in file Walter's squadron stumbled past empty crates with planks like mammoth ribcages, and heard donkeys braying but no trace of the bleating sheep, and were pleased to see in these gullies near the beach that the wounded had been shifted with none replacing them in the vacant bloodstained places. Then they found themselves tending south where the steep-sided gullies widened as if spreading their arms, and the enemy lines obliged by curving farther off across flatter ground, and a wider expanse of the sea, they knew, would in the morning become visible, though now it was just an awareness of a greater blackness rucked against the land like an immense bedspread.

Miraculously there was straw to sleep on. They burrowed in, and without talking turned over to stare at a sky full of stars. At home on mild nights Walter liked to lie in the grass and force himself to view the night sky not as a dimensionless scattering of points of light but as a deep and dark crystal wherein near and far were related, with the earth and the patch of it he occupied bonded to the farthest reach of space. Could it be so here, among these odd northern constellations?

After the tears and frantic questioning of why she was here, what were they *doing,* and how it was wrong, so terribly wrong, Frances had stared into the moonlit yard of the hotel with fingers covering her mouth while Walter sat on the bed with his hands dangling between his knees thinking the same thoughts. Neither spoke.

Earlier, on their arrival from the theatre, Billy and Diana had gone up first, and after a wait Walter and Frances followed. When they found the foyer deserted, and unglimpsed entered the shadowy stairwell, she had giggled, hurrying him along from behind with nervously playful pushes. But in the room her mood changed. A step had been taken from which there was no turning back. What could Diana have been thinking to talk her into it? She wished she had not agreed. Then she named Billy as the force behind this shameful adventure. Billy did not know right from wrong and did not care. She blamed the war. Why was Walter going? Did he have to? He must believe that without the war she would not have agreed to come. Did he believe her?

"Walter?"

She drew a breath and waited for him to snip the thread of her performance. She wanted to feel arms closing tightly around her, she wanted to sink into the room's darkness which was without morality, without obligation — unless, as she half feared, morality consisted wholly of reaction to practical consequence. And such a concern, to be truthful, had forcefully overcome her upon entering the unlit room with its moonwhite square of window, its virginal bedspread, and the pale tiles surrounding a tiny grate. For her childhood had been spent being chased in and out of such rooms with their tidewrack of partnerings guilty and otherwise. She heard footsteps in the corridor and irrationally wondered if it was her father, or someone who knew him and would tell, or a drunken guest or merely a strange one — the kind who opened doors by mistake, and stared.

To sweep her clear of such fears she was dependent on a person whose strength was no greater than hers — who was himself a victim of prevarication and awe. An absurd feat confronted him. He was incapable of imagining how the fully-clothed Frances with her turned back would become the undressed Frances in his arms. How comically ignorant he was, not of the practical motions that must follow (the stallion and the mare hid no secrets) but of the human etiquette involved. There must be words to accompany that abrupt union: how ridiculous not to know them.

Frances felt a mixture of curiosity and impatience. She rubbed the glass and it squeaked, so she turned and smiled. But Walter was staring at the floor. Would her life never begin?

"You mustn't think I won't come back," he said, looking up. "Ethel saw it clear as anything."

"What is it about this Ethel? Is she nice?"

"We went walking at the picnic. After a while she kissed me."

"Did you kiss her in return?"

"You'll have to guess."

"I'll bet you did."

"Why?"

Frances crossed the floor and balanced herself on the edge of the bed. "You couldn't resist her. She's prettier than me."

"But you've never met her. She's not."

"Not prettier?"

"She knows who you are. She's watched you at the station."

They kissed, bumping foreheads. Frances twisted herself closer. Her mouth was dry. Then she lost balance, and a second later they found themselves side by side on the bed.

"Did you touch her?"

"Yes."

"Where?"

Frances seemed lashed into starched layers that nowhere gave access to anything soft. He could feel heat rising from her cheeks and then, in a gust, a closer heat released from her loosened bodice.

"She touched me."

"Where?"

So it went on, until piece by piece clothing was negotiated to the floor.

She said, "I'm cold," and as he drew up the cover she became someone else entirely — not the sociable person of irresolute and tempting gestures, nor the soul he sometimes thought of as deep and at other times as vaporous, nor the figure in time on whose past and future he made tentative claim. She existed, in that moment, as nothing more than a body. And it was with the intelligence of one body seeking entrance into another, and with the foolish and human practicalities also involved, that these two finally met.

"May I," Walter murmured politely, "put my . . . self . . . in there?" He placed a hand between her legs and felt her respond with a bolt of sensation to his wondering exploration of a rustling dry and then suddenly humid place. The question was needless but she whispered "Yes," her head turned sideways into

328

the pillow. There was a moment of blindness then as Walter's searching engaged in a baffled encounter, but all at once clumsiness ended and an embrace became possible that placed the body of Frances closer to him even than his own, with fragments of perfumed ear and hair, nipple and buttock, bone and pulsing artery rising through him, then all swirling, as in a whirlpool, softly enclosing both in one or the other's amazed sigh before spilling from walls down to a centre, an endlessly promising descent of sensation in which Frances showed she was one with Walter, unreservedly one, by uttering a delighted, drowning cry.

Lying in straw, with the stars refusing to deepen overhead but maintaining a frosted flatness, Walter slowly became aware of a closer horizon than the one actually marking earth from sky. It was a nearby hill, a hump of darkness with two low ridges flowing out to enclose the sleeping men like the walls of an unlit amphitheatre. Half awake, half dreaming Walter thought: it's as though we're on stage and out there is an audience seated on dark tiers.

In the past twenty-four hours Walter had definitely changed. On this day of no shooting, he realized, he had narrowed his hopes for himself and dulled his nervous excesses — and he resolved to cling to this dullness. The speculations of the likes of Reg Hurst were trapped between walls formed by pickets of crosses. Even here in this herb-scented hollow Walter had seen efficient stacks of crosses ready to mark the remains of those who surrounded him, still dreaming or praying, calling out in their sleep, hungry, or thirsty, or sleeplessly rising to poke at sad embers with a stick.

When at last he slept he found himself hard at work, still facing the amphitheatre of hills but seated now at the centre of a ramshackle machine made of wood and galvanized iron. "I'm going now," said Walter. But as he tried to pull his legs out he discovered them fixed to the floor. He heard a moaning chorus cry *"Hang on!"* With shock he saw an expectant audience packed tightly into the amphitheatre, the curious and dull reddened faces of home staring back at his own sweating features.

19
The River Flowing

"Did you hear Mrs Gillen shouting at Rob last night? She doesn't like us being here," said Frances.

It was almost time for breakfast. She and Diana wore shawls and faced each other drinking tea across a low table. Two grey cats crept along a dark line of damp at the edge of the veranda boards.

"I wonder what she thinks," Frances continued. "She stared right through me. Did you notice her careful speech? You shouldn't worry, it's me she disapproves of, a publican's daughter. I'm sure she drinks. I *know* she does."

"Didn't we resolve not to care?" said Diana, mockingly quoting Frances's words back at her.

"She couldn't wait to say hello and goodbye. I'll bet her tipple's gin, or something fancier," Frances mused, recalling Mrs Gillen's pungent scent during the obligatory kiss, and trying to remember the name of a bottle of exotic spirits in the private bar of the Albion that no-one ever ordered. "I don't care," she concluded. "Cross my heart. But I'm interested to know what people think."

"*I* worry about things all the time. I've never said any different. I was just reminding you of your own resolution."

"Remind away," said Frances, leaving the table and standing as close to the edge of the veranda as she could go without getting wet. From here she could see the creek and its fringe of trees a half-mile distant in the misty rain: a frayed green doorsnake with dark twists of stuffing poking up. In clear weather the roofs of the settlement on the ridge four miles away were visible, but now everything in that direction was shrouded.

"It's true you've got nothing to worry about. Nothing that shows," muttered Diana. Frances made no reply but moved farther away. Last night after unpacking they had stepped from their adjoining rooms to stand here shivering. A wall of lightning-illuminated cloud had surged towards them bringing cold gusts of wind and a wild storm that overnight had become this obliterating change of season. By morning things were sodden enough for hoofprints on the road beside the garden fence instantly to become flooded half moons, and when a dray crept past bearing a sack-covered sheep's carcass to the kitchen it left twin trails that for a moment ran clean and shiny before filling with fawn sludge.

"She even got our names mixed up," said Frances on rejoining her friend.

"Anyway, I liked her."

"You would."

"Are we going to argue here as well?"

"I didn't start it."

"She's interested in the war, really, quite interested."

"Then you're bound to have lots to talk about. But if you keep twisting your ring like that someone's going to get suspicious. Leave it alone."

Diana rested her hands on the edge of the table but after a few seconds started again.

"What if they guessed? I'd be so embarrassed."

"What you're suffering from is funk," said Frances,

who lately had found a philosophy to match her instincts. It had to do with having no regrets.

"You're so sure of yourself," said Diana, who privately regarded Frances's newfound belief in herself as nothing but amorality. Then with trepidation, because there was now something awesome about her friend, she added: "As if you'd never done anything wrong."

"Pride is something different." But then Frances laughed: "Oh, come on, this is too funny to be serious." And she considered again the amusing spot they were in, with Diana supposedly married to a Mr Benedetto (thus able to use her own surname) and acting as Frances's chaperon.

But there was nothing funny in the situation for Diana, who had been dragged to the Gillens against her will and unnecessarily exposed to possible shame, whereas Frances, she felt, had not a shred of shame left. So Diana sat there biting her lower lip and twisting her ring in fear of what might go wrong. At the sound of footsteps coming along the veranda they put their cups down and tried to look composed.

"May I?" Mr Gillen drew up a chair. The tea tray had all along carried an extra cup. "Rob's gone chasing sheep but he made me promise to look after you. What a night! I've sent a man into town for the mail, and who knows, if the river rises, someone," he sneaked a look at Diana, "may just have the honour of a 'Westbury' birthplace."

"A flood?" asked Frances, while Diana, blushing, folded her hands in her lap.

"I'd say August," said Mr Gillen, still addressing the mother-to-be.

"Or September," Diana nodded.

"That wretched creek," he went on. "If it backs up to billy-oh, then we're done. Do you mind? You can stay as long as you like, you know." He rested his hand with its sprouting hairs and weathered liver spots on Frances's knee and gave a squeeze. It was an old man's hand but stronger and more certain of itself than any youth's. Frances felt suddenly trapped — floods, Rob gone off, the sprawling house like a raft sailing nowhere. Mr Gillen slid his thumb with exploratory pressure along the edge of her kneecap. Could all the family now know Diana's secret? Rob had sworn not to tell.

But then with grave fatherliness and without a trace of opportunism Mr Gillen led them, one on each arm, along the veranda of the guest wing and down to the dining room, where soon Mrs Gillen joined them for breakfast. And she too was friendly, full of plans for filling what would certainly be the wet days ahead — not at all the person who had shrieked at her son the previous midnight. She recalled the visit of the Archduke Ferdinand to Narromine, when they had all gone shooting with the Macks, and pretended to remember Frances's parents from that time. Imagine! The man whose death had touched off the war had actually shaken her hand. She had wondered for twenty years about the arrogance of someone who had never bothered to learn English. So recovered was Mrs Gillen from her night-time self that Diana immediately decided that a housemaid had done the unladylike screaming, or else it had been a fight in the married quarters across "the avenue" or even the black cockatoo screeching to be removed from the garden where its wire cage hung squeaking in the path of the storm.

Frances was not deceived by the heavy drinker's

morning brightness. She had seen it too many times. Yet to discover it here among such wealth and secure ownership was disturbing. Only Rob held her interest and he had gone galloping off in the mud without so much as a "good morning".

The plan had been Mrs Reilly's, hatched in March when Diana was still at home with her mother and her condition still an easily kept secret (but only just). The two girls were to go to Forbes and stay with Pat Reilly. Frances was to look after her father and Diana as her companion would be safely removed from society. She was unknown in the district and would raise no eyebrows by being introduced as "Mrs" — there were plenty of young wives whose husbands with the finest of motives had upped and gone. In the meantime an attempt would be made to arrange a marriage with the farflung Billy — heaven alone knew how, but it was the only way. At the start they thought he might be back in time, but when the first lists of killed appeared in the papers and a gloomy appraisal of the position by Captain Benedetto followed, it seemed more likely that Billy would never be back.

Diana had faced her mother and undertaken to write to Billy immediately with news of "her state". But she delayed, not wanting to risk a dream in which Billy was always as he had been in those weeks before departure: weeks that promised a lifetime of calm acceptance. So she told her mother yes, she *had* written: but arrived at the Gillens in mid-June with the task still undone.

Frances had happily declared that she would go to

Forbes, the closest town of any size to the Gillens'
place, fifty miles distant. She stopped thinking about
England and the stage and as early as March swore that
she was in love "for the first time ever" and would do
anything to be near him. If necessary, she told Diana,
she would live in rags and cook hot dinners in that tin
hut beloved of her mother, though with the Gillens,
everyone knew, such a fate was unthinkable. Robert
Gillen called regularly in the New Year and after two
months Mrs Reilly noticed how Frances posted fewer
and fewer letter overseas — the sombre Walter
Gilchrist had passed from her life like a bout of fever.
But when Mrs Reilly began to express her thoughts
aloud and worry seriously about the South American
fiancée Frances told her never to bring the subject up
again, *never*. So, because Mrs Reilly had the next day
peered through the trees and seen Robert and Frances
kissing in a rowing boat as they bobbed along the inner
side of the point, she decided to let events similarly
take their course, and drift.

The truth was that Frances still did not care about
marriage. This annoyed Diana, whose advanced views
were in retreat. She argued that Frances could easily be
left out in the cold. What about Robert's flirtation with
Sharon Keeley at the luncheon last November? Frances
made no excuses. It was what he was like with her that
mattered. He made her forget everything, she was
happy. That was as much as she ever said, except to
confess that all they had ever done was kiss. What did
they talk about? Sheep, motor cars, polo, the theatre.
Had he ever made any "improper" suggestions? None.
She liked his strong steady hands, his blue eyes, the
way he doubted nothing and seemed to know exactly
why he had been placed on the earth.

So a strain had developed between the two friends. Each felt that the other was putting on something false — slipping into the disguises of adulthood. Diana saw a Frances no less spirited, but one who spent herself on a doubtful cause. If expressed, they would each have flung the same accusation at the other, the word would have been "uninteresting". Neither Mrs Reilly nor Frances had blinked an eye the night when Frances played "Claire de Lune" and Robert had asked, as an encore, for "something jolly". Money and position blinded the mother, but what had deflected Frances? She said: "He started noticing me. I suppose I wanted him to from the start, and didn't know it."

"Poor Walter."

"I don't even think about him."

"Never?"

"You want me to say I'm sorry. I won't."

"I never stop thinking about Billy in his great struggle. Aren't you sorry at least for that?"

"Just listen to yourself!"

But long ago for want of something to write Frances had adopted Diana's stuffy phrase in her last letter to Walter. It was true that she hardly thought about the war, whereas Diana had purchased the very latest "Seat of War" maps showing the Dardanelles, and even brought them with her to the Gillens, so that when Mrs Gillen at the breakfast table asked the distance from the battleground to Constantinople, she was able to look it up.

"What a shame I'm an old man," said Mr Gillen, taking Frances's hand while Diana and his wife went into conference at the far end of the table. "You make me wish I was twenty-five again." But to Frances he belonged to the room, its spirit was his, dark and chilly, full of heavy furniture and silver plate. Prizewinning cups lined the sideboard and overflowed into glass-fronted cupboards. In summer this room might just possibly form a deep refuge from the heat. Now it was a cold heart. On the walls hung framed photographs of beribboned bulls and historic wheat stacks. There were thin ancestors, fat babies, and whole fleets of sailing ships. Flocks of sheep posed with their bulbous-necked sires. Over the fireplace hung an oil painting of a defiant stag captured among geometric rocks by three grimacing dogs. Suddenly Frances thought: *There's no place for me here,* and in the ponderous gloom she was surprised to feel lighthearted at the discovery.

The rain eased and they set off for a tour of the yards wearing oversized Wellingtons and heavy oilskins. Diana asked questions while Frances trailed behind. When Mr Gillen slipped away to find his manager Diana said: "We'll have pigs, they eat all the scraps. And wheat and Merino sheep."

"We?"

"Me and Billy."

On his return Mr Gillen asked: "Aren't your husband's people on the land? Rob said something about a place in Victoria."

"He was in New South Wales when we met," said Diana cheerily. She enjoyed lying about her supposed marriage only if the answers, like this one, came out as a kind of truth. Frances on the other hand had taken to lying expansively even when it did not matter.

"What's their place called?" asked Mr Gillen, shouldering open the door of a shed to reveal peacocks pecking among the dusty wheat. A name had not occurred to them. Then from the grey rafters came a peacock's melodious shriek: "How beautiful!" said Frances, taking the old man by the arm and diverting him from enquiry. The birds clambered on taut wheat sacks and clasped uncertain claws on the iron parts of machines. Mr Gillen pointed out a seed drill, a harrow, innumerable implements stretching the dry length of the shed in orderly files. "Keith Fryer looked after all this, but now that he's joined the army, the devil, it's to be Rob's concern."

They turned to discover a peacock standing just inside the propped-open doorway, fanning its tail in full display.

"Would you like a feather?" asked Mr Gillen. As he advanced towards the bird it folded away its tail and stalked aside.

"*From* the bird?" Frances protested. "Oh, no!" But Mr Gillen suddenly dropped to his knees and gathered it up. "Please don't" — then after a scuffle and a squawk he turned to hold the central eye out to her.

"Take it."

"I can't." Blood was visible at the point of the quill as if it had been dipped in watery red ink. The other peacocks posted themselves on struts. Mr Gillen was annoyed. He seemed about to snap the feather in two. Instead he thrust it at Diana and brusquely asked if they wished to see the pigs. "Yes, *please*," (from Diana as she brushed her lips with the feather).

The few hundred yards they tramped through revealed a place more like a small town than a farm. It boasted a crossroads, a butchery, a blacksmith's shop, several weatherboard houses set at angles to each other with their own fences and gardens, huts for shearers

and stockmen, and way down near the creek a blacks'
camp identifiable by wisps of smoke rising from among
the trees.

After the pigs the rain intensified, and Mr Gillen
consulted his watch. "Morning tea time," he
announced. Since the peacocks he had not addressed a
word to Frances nor even looked at her. Now he
abandoned them to the care of a freckled yardboy who
led the way back to the house while keeping his head
down.

"He's an old brute," Frances muttered as they
sloshed along.

One of the wives appeared on her veranda ostensibly
to wring out a mop, and a lean stockman riding past
wheeled to ask their guide a question, then tipped his
had pointedly at Frances. She was relieved to see
Robert's horse tied to the garden gate. Pleased too that
he was the only one to appear at morning tea, which
they took in a room with plenty of windows, rugs on
the floor, and deep chairs.

"How was mother at breakfast?" Robert asked. "She
thinks of nothing but the war."

"Was that her last night?"

"Oh, Frances," cautioned Diana while breaking open
a scone that puffed steam.

"We argued about the war."

"Really? What about it?"

"Whether I should go." He reached for Frances's
hand and held it the way he always did, without a hint
of undue pressure. "Should I?"

"No, please don't."

"You don't know which way I argued," Robert
continued, "for or against. Come on, guess."

"What about Rosa? Wouldn't it be mean to go off
before she gets here?"

340

"You tell me when she's arriving," shrugged Robert, buttering scones and passing them round on a thin plate. His reddened hands looked enlarged after a morning's work in the wet.

"When *is* she?"

But he only laughed and said, "Do you like the room?"

She nodded. It made her feel welcome. Although it was a male room with trophies like the other it had cushions and a pile of magazines. The silver and bronze cups were not prizes for gross animals but displayed small models of horses vigorously galloping while tiny men on their backs brandished silver mallets. The fire, held in an iron cradle, was made up ready.

"It's my room. Mine alone," Robert boasted. "No-one comes in here unless I invite them."

In the afternoon Frances rode with Robert down to the woolshed while Diana stayed in her room to write the long-postponed letter to Billy. The rain fell heavily, but without a breath of wind. Frances held Robert tight around the waist while the horse picked its way through the roaring, silvery gloom. She had dreamed of doing this, and tried to recapture something of her reverie while watching leaves and sticks, damp and black, glide underneath. When he lifted her down they kissed, their oilskins coupling with wet sliding sounds, and rain blurring her vision. But like all his kisses this one had none of the passion she hoped for. Instead Robert seemed lost in consideration of experiences that did not touch her. Now, almost for the last time, she stood in awe of this preoccupation.

Although as Diana said she took liberties with Robert it had never been at moments like this.

Inside he set to work pulling samples of wool from assorted bales. At first Frances sat on a dark and slippery rail, balancing herself by holding to a nail in an upright. When a cold current of air knifed through the slats he arranged a seat for her in a gap between curved warm bales, covered her legs with clean sacking, and then got on with his work.

After a while he began talking about South America. He sang in Spanish a familiar tuneless ditty that she applauded (he had sung it before). They talked about the war, and again Frances protested: was it necessary for *everyone* to go? Robert was curious about Billy and Walter. He was beginning to wonder if there was not something in war that he needed to discover for himself. This surprised Frances — it had never occurred to her that he might be envious. He had always seemed to have so much more to his makeup than Billy and Walter, as if he was richer in himself and more glorious, and had no need of the dubious prizes of battle.

At intervals Robert washed his hands in a soapy basin and dried each finger on a towel hanging from a wire hook. Then he wrote details in a notebook. Rain sounded continuously on the iron roof, and again Frances had the feeling that the place she was in was on the move, the woolshed and its outbuildings sailing the plains towards some vague and disappointing destination.

"Tell me the truth," she suddenly asked. "When is Rosa coming?" She knew he had received fresh news, because at lunchtime when the man brought the mail Robert had retired with a fat envelope.

Until this very minute Frances had felt in Robert's company none of the discontent nor the impulsiveness that had characterized her feelings for Walter. It was as though Robert with a power that Walter lacked had reached across and put that discordant part of her life into tune. When they kissed, it was not a matter of seeking sensation but of accepting it. She had never stopped to think about him, his thoughts, his future — except that now, seeing him engrossed in examination of the crimp that was the heart of the Gillens' empire, she felt an urge to disrupt.

"I don't think you really love her."

Robert looked up. "She's in England with her father." His face under its pad of blond hair was bright with an idea. "By golly! I could join an English regiment."

"How seriously do you take me?" Frances asked. And then she demanded of him in a voice that almost broke: *"How seriously?"*

"You're a delight," he said, advancing and kissing her on the cheek, then tugging at one of the plaits she had twisted her hair into to save it from the rain. He had said that kind of thing before. It was the code of their friendship. Yet now when he turned aside Frances started to cry.

It wasn't fair. The world was determined to go about its business without regard to her. Half the males she knew had sailed off the edge of the map, and there was Robert with his back turned tidying the classing table, and he was about to go too. Didn't he realize that here among the towering bales under a drumming roof he could have lain down beside her and done whatever he wished? But not now — not from now on — because now a deeper power than the body's stirred and demanded his notice. He would have to acknowledge her pride. He would have to acknowledge the uniqueness she had once chosen for herself and had this minute recovered in a spate of hastily dabbed tears on burning cheeks. What had she been thinking all these months? Into what backwater had her ulterior motives led?

After a final scrupulous wash Robert said: "Come and I'll show you the view from the tower." They climbed a greasy ladder into the rafters, Robert going first, reaching down for her hand and hoisting her onto a landing of springy slats. The tower consisted of a rectangle of tin with louvred ventilation windows. Crouched on a platform beside a nest of ropes and pulleys they were able to peer outside.

The road was visible. It emerged from the drive, crossed the home paddocks, then dipped into a hollow near the creek. But it no longer re-emerged to wander up the bank on the opposite side. Instead a green-grey tongue of water protruded through the trees from the direction of the river. Then Frances saw a file of women and children making their way to high ground from the blacks' camp. Some held sheets of tin over their heads and others bark. A few carried bundles and were unprotected, giving them the appearance of large-thoraxed ants heading for higher ground after the destruction of their nest.

"They'll camp at the old shearers' quarters till this is over."

"Where are the men?"

Robert shrugged. "Some are out looking for sheep. Who knows where the rest are? They'll turn up."

With Frances sitting behind he rode down to the sheds and asked the women if they were right for flour and tea. Frances tried not to look at them, for here she was, dry and privileged, while girls her own age existed on bare sufferance. Did the girl Billy had attacked in the back yard of her father's hotel belong to these "Westbury" blacks? A naked boy of seven or so ran out into the rain and then back to his mother who hugged him while he laughed and shivered.

It was raining worse than ever when Frances knocked on Diana's door, and on hearing no answer entered. She was asleep, sprawled with mouth open and fine hands protectively splayed on her belly. Frances stared out into the garden. Gutters overflowed in anguished sheets, leaves on the grass struggled to raise themselves against the strident pressure of the rain. The only breeze came from water shifting the air around as it fell. Then, turning to leave, Frances knocked a tin of pins off the dressing table where they had been weighing down several sheets of writing paper. After a glance at Diana, half-stooped as if to collect the scattered pins, she started reading at the top of the page. It was a letter to Billy:

" . . . punishment. The minister should talk to me first! I could persuade him in no time that you are a good person and I know you are religious. The churches do not understand the religion of a person who is not a churchgoer. I had resolved to say nothing once again about what has been uppermost in my mind these many months, but your 'us in our house' etc. with its picture of a third person whose true existence you had no inkling of made me sing with joy. But write to me soon about your feelings because until then, I can't help it! I will be atremble. We came to Forbes because of the baby and I am known as 'Mrs Benedetto'. Though it shames me, I shall be known as such until I can proudly take your name. Nobody suspects and I am treated royally, but always nervous. Not even F's father knows. I should faint if *your* father appeared as he is known at the hotel.

"Do you see Walter? I feel so dreadfully sorry for him. F has behaved carelessly. I do hold this against her as a weakness. Harry Crowell a scandal in himself told me that in his opinion F was deceiving and selfish and knew her own mind better than she let on. Robert has his Rosa and I doubt if F is anything more than a child to him. I cry when I think of your troubles, deaths etc. and danger, and the torment added for Walter who sends F a torrent of letters that stay unanswered. Stupidest of all now that I have seen more of R he is not worth it. What am I doing writing like this in the house of my host! I must tell you —"

Frances turned the page to find a huge cross scrawled through the following paragraphs. The nib had dug into the paper and thrown an angry black spray:

" — everything. I am sure R despises me. He addressed too many remarks in my direction, making up for a wish not to speak to me at all. When he agreed to this visit I asked if he could take us in his car past your father's farm but when the time came he apologetically said he feared a change of weather. When events proved him right he was as smug as the cat that swallowed the canary. As we left town he pointed to the scrub and said, 'It's country like this where Billy comes from, not worth the "candle".' I said it could be desert, I didn't care. But from a ridge F showed me the blue range miles away and it looked magical. Last year she would have laughed with Mr Gillen who is struck by her but she responds oddly. She flirted with him at breakfast but was hideously rude on our walk this morning when he offered her a peacock's feather. Her rebuff stung, it was as if she had slapped him and I had to pretend not to notice. I suppose it would be easy to blame her 'nerves' but when they consist of everything she does it makes things difficult for her friends. As I am her only friend and fast losing patience I suppose I ought to feel sorry for her but I can't. In my heart now there is room for no-one but you.

"In R's favour he is talking of going to the war. The latest lists in the papers show the seriousness of things. I have found how important it is to *care,* I know you have too. If you knew how I set you above these people! How proud I would be to relate your exploits under your own name. We were late last night and had a 'scratch' tea but even so were served by the maids one Irish the other Aboriginal who were got up specially. You can guess the scale of things. The floors are polished daily. We are given imported preserves, then there are the outbuildings like barracks. I am . . ."

Diana mumbled in her sleep and Frances scooped up the pins and escaped to the veranda, closing the doors clumsily with a bang. A sudden gust of wind bowled hoops of rain under the eaves and she got wet, letting go the doors which rattled as she sped away. What a fool Diana was! Hoisting her petty triumph with Billy over everyone. She had poured all her science and clear thinking down the drain, and settled for what? The tin shed.

At dinner that night Diana started to sniffle and had to leave the room for a handkerchief. She explained that her door had blown open during her sleep and she had woken soaked. Her letter to Billy was ruined, she would have to write again. By the time the men were taking their port (Fleming the manager had joined them) Diana was launched into an endless string of sneezes. Just as well — Fleming knew Western Victoria like the back of his hand but was blowed if he had ever come across any Benedettos.

In the middle of the night Frances woke with a start to hear someone trying her door. The handle rattled one way, then the other. She reached for the greenstone ashtray Robert had procured for her bedtime cigarette, and raised it ready. The rain still pelted down and it was so dark that even the faint light leaking from the hall lamp that burned around a bend of the corridor was of no use. Then the door hinges squeaked and she thought: It's Robert, or else his father. If so she would strike the old man on the shins. But a ghost entered — Diana.

"I can't sleep. I'm so hot. My hands slipped and slid on the door."

"You're on fire!"

"Can I sleep in your bed? I'm having nightmares but I'm still awake."

"I'll fetch Mrs Gillen."

"No. All right. No, it's too much of a bother. The white cabinet in the kitchen has medicines in it. Could you get something from there?"

Illness acted as a galvanizer of friendship. Suddenly it seemed important to act as one. Frances fumbled her way to the lamp and bore it through the long silent passageways of the house. She returned with a tray of bottles and powders, and dosed Diana until she turned benign and drowsy.

"I've been a fool."

"Why?"

"I wrote horrible things about you in the letter to Billy. The letter that was ruined."

"If it's ruined it doesn't matter, does it?"

"Why are you being nice to me?"

"Why shouldn't I be?"

"I was awake. I saw you reading my letter. I couldn't move. When you left the door blew open and I just lay there letting everything get soaked."

Diana yawned and curled up like a spaniel. The bed was a wide one but after a time she radiated so much heat that Frances shifted to a chair and wrapped herself in a quilt. A kind of phosphorescence now hung in the clouds, showing that a bright moon had risen somewhere above the turbulence. Then, miles away, the clouds must have parted because illumined land was suddenly revealed — clots of trees at the edge of a silver blade of floodwater. The river was testing the strength of its tributaries, slicing out islands and lagoons in the night.

Towards morning Diana awoke complaining of pain in the chest. She had difficulty breathing. At first daylight when she coughed into a handkerchief they were alarmed to see a jellied gob of rusty sputum. Frances placed an arm around her shoulders and held a towel while she coughed again. The basis of their friendship had always rested in one or both feeling helpless or alone. Until the war this complementary need had masked their differences. But war had swung everyone's life into the measure of its waltz, breaking up old loyalties and serenely betraying new ones.

This was how Frances saw things as wholeheartedly she nursed Diana, picturing herself no longer as the impulsive lover known to Walter, nor as the ready sacrifice for Robert, but as precursor to a new self over-riding both, fast-developing in response to the war whose currents tugged at the shores of every living heart. Why else did they find themselves ringed by floodwaters? Why else was Diana in peril, wincing as she breathed, her forehead lined with sweat like tiny pearls. "The baby," she muttered, "will it be all right?" They were children again, but the war forbade them so to act, this same war that had urged them to step through the mirage of morality and had delivered them to their doubtful haven in the central west.

Though Frances had spent hours staring into the night it was Diana who truly faced nothingness. Neither uttered the word "pneumonia" but when Frances left to rouse Mrs Gillen there was panic in Diana's voice.

A man was sent to town to fetch the doctor. There was no question of Dr Starkie not coming straight away. When the Gillens summoned, he came. Robert tried to persuade Frances to ride down to the creek with him and wait for the rowing boat that would bring the doctor across, but she refused to leave Diana: and saw the doctor coming anyway — a faraway speck among the drowned branches of eucalypts.

She described his coming to Diana whose pain was worse by mid-afternoon and her fever high. Was it the perception of fever that made Diana turn the picture of the small boat coming through the tops of the trees into a heartening rescue for herself? The doctor in her imagination entered the branching vessels of her lungs and drifted on the fluid there, effecting a cure.

He was a young man, portly and sandy haired. He had tried to enlist, he said over a whisky in the parlour, but too many doctors had the same idea. But he would be off soon — it was the only thing to do. He said all sorts of reassuring things about Diana, but Frances in a rush of guilt wanted to know the worst.

"What if she doesn't pull through?" She sat on the arm of a chair wearing a dark blue apron. As she spoke Mrs Gillen downed her second glass of whisky.

"Not recover suddenly? These fevers often just ease off. It could be a slower process, there's no way of telling. Feed her up when you can and keep her comfortable. Soup?" He addressed Mrs Gillen, who nodded.

"But what if things go wrong," Frances insisted, "badly wrong."

"We mustn't have gloom," said the doctor impatiently. "Run along now and see that she's happy, and I'll look in again before I go."

"After the week — could she die?"

The doctor held up two fingers while Mrs Gillen poured from the decanter. "What have we here, a Jeremiah?"

"Please, I'm not a child," said Frances, a protest that elicited such a look of horrified disapproval from Mrs Gillen that Frances immediately left the room.

She fled to her bedroom where she cried until no tears were left, then hurried in to be with her friend. The word "crisis" had alarmed her. They both knew the signs. Girls at school had died of pneumonia. The disease came like a silent arrow to lodge painfully in the breast. When the invisible shaft dissolved, a few days of hectic fever followed when the patient felt better. Then a sudden gust of extinction. Or else recovery thanks to what might just as well have been the roll of dice, and the girls were back at wooden desks instead of in wooden boxes.

"If I die," asked Diana after two days, "promise me you'll be nice to Billy?"

"No, because you won't die."

"Write to him and tell him I love him. He probably doesn't believe me." Diana lay back wearily in the pillows.

"He believes you."

On Friday a letter arrived with the boat bringing the doctor for his second visit.

"Franny, listen! He already knows: 'Now I can truly see us on the farm, me and you and the nipper, like my c-u-s-e-n says. Don't take notice of people, they don't know right from wrong. I'll be back when I can.' Isn't he an awful letter writer? I love every word. He ran into Dad. Dad knows — I'll kill my mother for telling him — no, why should I? I'm so happy! I'll die happy!"

But the doctor was pleased, and did not predict her death.

Then after seven days she faltered. The fever intensified and one night she hardly knew who she was. All week Frances had done for Diana whatever was needed, staying at her side, sponging her down, trying to calm her panic when breathing became so difficult that she seemed to be drowning.

Frances herself suffered a kind of delirium. She hardly noticed the help being given by Mrs Gillen, who supervised the food, or the help that came from the housemaids who supplied stacks of clean dry sheets from the clothesline where they flapped between intermittent showers like the flags of a besieged citadel. The black boy died, the shivering seven year old Frances had seen at the old shearers' huts. It was as if small glowing points of life were being extinguished and only the most strenuous act of will could shield them from fate. The news of the boy's death from pneumonia was brought by his aunt, a maid named Isabel, who reported it unemotionally, as if the name belonged to a list of unknown dead in a battle even more remote than the one at the Dardanelles.

Though Frances was near to exhaustion she discovered in work of this kind an ability to forget herself. If Diana had died at that moment she too would have been as dispassionate as Isabel in making the announcement. Life came and went in the darkness — her own among others. But to attend to the extremity of its passage — there was something exhilarating in the desperate novelty of it all. Thus when Robert caught her in the corridor late in the night of this, Diana's worst day, she allowed herself to listen to what he had been telling her all week: that she was a saint. He hurried it through with an urgent invitation for her to take a walk for five minutes in the night air. She broke free and went to look at Diana, who miraculously slept. So Frances gave Robert ten minutes that stretched to twenty, at the end of which she was astonished to find herself in his room which they had approached through a circuit of the damp garden: it had its own private entrance off the far veranda. She lay on a leather couch, eyes closed, her head tipped back while Robert ran his fingers through her hair. Then she leapt up and ran through the night, and he followed.

Diana's crisis had passed. She was cool to the touch. Her breath no longer caught but was peacefully deep. Robert left to tell his mother the good news: it was past one o'clock. When he returned Frances was asleep in the chair. He carried her to her room and whispered, "I'll put you to bed. All right?"

The events that followed alarmed her, but not until the morning. She awoke remembering Robert climbing in with her, his hands roving her body while despite herself she posed a whispery question: "Do you love me?" And his saying, "Yes, I love you." So the uncaring body had as if in a dream allowed itself to succumb. She had no memory of pleasure, only of a deep but interrupted sleep. But now in daylight she was ashamed. What had she been thinking after her resolution of the week before? There had been no doubt to resolve in action, as with Walter. No longer, she knew, did she have the excuse of infatuation. He was dull, he told the same stories over and over: and if he ever again mentioned South America and the day he had sheltered from a bandit outside a dress shop she would tell him off.

Frances told herself that her moral sense had been drugged by lack of sleep: but it had been something more shocking than that. In the letter to Billy, Diana had accused her of knowing her own mind better than she let on, and it was true. For in the night she had admitted Robert to her bed and now was cold to him for the most wilful of reasons — she had wished to punish his long indifference. And having done so, she allowed herself to despise him.

At breakfast Diana sat up in bed and drank a cup of tea. "I feel that your whole week has been wasted," she sighed. Her gratitude expressed itself in grotesque phrasing: "Baby and I say thank you."

"As soon as you're well enough we'll leave." Frances leant close and whispered: "I can't take another minute of Robert. I've gone off him, God help me."

"Oh, Franny."

"Last night when I was too tired to care — he took advantage of me."

Diana could not look Frances in the eye.

"He seemed to take lots for granted. I wonder if he heard about me and Walter? The Hotel. Did you tell him?"

"Me? Don't be mad."

"I suppose his mother worked me out. She's evil enough herself to be expert on the sins of others."

"Franny, who are you fooling?" Diana suddenly could take no more: "You threw yourself at him and now you must take the consequences. I don't like you when you try to pretend."

Suddenly they were back in one of their breathless exchanges from the days of innocence. Only now the speculative had descended and was acting itself out in their own lives. Friend appraised friend; except both knew they were true friends no longer.

"Neither of us has any sense," Diana said dully.

"Bother the rules. *Their* rules," asserted Frances.

"It's so comfortable here." Sunlight touched the edge of the bed. The floodwaters were still up, but around the house everything was drying out after two days of sunshine. Diana's wedding ring glowed as she held it up to the light.

"What's ahead of us? asked Frances despondently.

"Everything!" Diana announced.

When Robert realized that Frances no longer felt the same he was puzzled then indignant. He accused her of leading him on. She could see that his sudden infatuation was real enough. Over the next few days he constantly tried to touch her. "Would you marry me instead of Rosa?" she asked.

"Yes."

But now he seemed so humourless and solid. His liking for dressing up which had made him seem so much fun (the *gaucho* outfit, and his insistence on dressing for dinner) she now saw as advertisement for a soul without depth. He liked best to talk about his travels and his success with money and stock. He had never been any different! She remembered February days when she had done nothing but sit in the window at home and watch for the ferries arriving in case he should come. And now? Rosa could have him.

When he lost his temper and called her names she became angry and used, insult as an excuse to leave. Diana was now well enough. Would he please arrange things? Or she would tell his mother how he crept into guests' bedrooms.

Mr Gillen took them down to the water in a sulky. He stamped around in the sour mud shifting bags to the boat and lifting Diana into the stern. Then Frances found both father and son looking at her. Who would carry her across? Quickly Frances turned to Henry Fleming who had come for the rowing: "Could you help me in?" But before acting Fleming asked, "Boss?"

in recognition of others' property: and was given the nod. As they pulled away from the shore Mr Gillen lifted his hat, and was still standing there when the boat, a hundred yards off, was caught by an unexpected current and disappeared through the trees.

"This bloody river!" Fleming shouted. As light as a leaf the boat spun in circles while he wrestled with the oars. Though they were well away from the usual course of the river they had struck it in an aberrant mood. During the night it had surged across a string of drowned billabongs and now directed the force of its flow through what had yesterday been a peaceful lake. But what fun! There was suddenly no need to make conversation with Robert, who sat facing them. He took out a paddle and helped hold the boat steady while Fleming strained.

"Go with the current."

"Can you hold her?"

"We're away!"

They skimmed along without any need for oars, but in the wrong direction.

Diana and Frances trailed their fingers in the water. Then there was a bump. The bows had struck a submerged branch protruding from a tree. Frances reached up and crushed a leaf in her hand, inhaling the sharp fresh smell of eucalyptus.

"Bugger. Sorry ladies. Bugger!" grunted the red-faced Fleming. They giggled. Diana reached for a spray of leaves but missed, then tried again. The bows resting on the branch rose slightly with the force of the current pushing at the stern, then suddenly they lifted steeply — it was as if the branch formed a greasy slipway and the boat was being winched aloft — and though Frances managed to reach forward and grip Robert's outstretched hand Diana missed and plopped into the water. Miraculously she stood only waist deep, her feet by chance having found another part of the log. She balanced herself by at last grasping a fistful of grey gumleaves, and giggled. Robert clambered down to haul her in, but she said: "Wait a second, my foot's caught. In for a penny, here we go!" and took a deep breath before ducking to release whatever it was that held her.

At that moment the branch where the boat rested made an ominous shearing sound and sank, and the boat floated free, propelled for a few feet backwards against the current by the force of the branch's sinking.

"Diana!" screamed Frances, while the lightened craft drifted sideways across an unbroken surface. Fleming wildly lashed a rope to the tree while Robert dived. "It's deep!" he gasped.

Diana had disappeared.

Then Fleming was in the water too, and Frances found herself alone in the boat hearing a crow flap and caw feet above her head, seeing Robert's boots float away escorted by swirling thumbprints of current in the mustard-coloured flood.

"Diana, Diana can you hear me?" Frances called, in the hope that she had drifted downstream and somewhere lay gasping within earshot.

Then a terrible half hour passed during which the searchers broke the surface countless times, one after the other, but always with the same report:

"Nothing."

"Nothing."

20
The Balkan Gun Pits

Before anything, when God was considering how the world might be brought into existence, when the earth was without form, and void; when darkness was upon the deep and only the spirit of God moved upon the face of the waters, before the words formed themselves and the Creator spoke, saying, "Let there be light", a different word must have been in his mind.

Surely the word was "perhaps", thought Walter.

Otherwise why did thousands lie dead whom life had selected for three score years and ten? The rattle of dice and the hum of a gambler's glee answered every prayer. Why else had Boof made it back to the lines one morning after a night patrol, bellowing with pride for the doctor after inching up and down gullies for seven hours, a human sled with the inert form of Lizzie Peters gripped to his chest, Boof creeping upon the earth, believing he had won a reprieve for his mate who at some time in that struggle had silently died.

Otherwise how had it come to pass that Walter, having sprinted four hundred yards this day intermittently within sight of men with rifles who tried to kill him, now found himself exhausted but still alive, face-down breathing painfully but unscathed in a foul smelling pit?

Then came a shock of realization: he was in the wrong place.

He had reached there by going on all fours after leaving the main trench, but at the brigadier's shout had stood as ordered and sprinted, recklessly leaping the ducked head of the foremost man of the foremost covering party, almost booting him in the ear, sprinting blindly at first and then for this blur of trench and at last making it — to find it empty, stinking of urine, a cigarette butt still smouldering, a dented light horse sun helmet lying where it had fallen.

Then he sat up and fitted the helmet because it was his own, knocked there as he had dived. So the men he was carrying a message to had already gone. They had retreated anyway, without waiting to be told. Somehow he had missed them in that frantic run over tangling heath when he had thought only of himself, watching his boots dance across blurred ground as he reeled into his lungs coil after coil of unexpected air. But now his lungs hurt. His pants were wet! He loosened them and squatted like an animal, watching a yellow puddle enlarge.

He thought he heard his own name being called from the low ridge just visible in the direction of the sea, and swore he had seen a flash of fabric there like the rump of a small creature slipping into the scrub. Then he bit his thumb, tugged it clear and sobbed, because he wanted to stand and shout *Hang on, this is no wasted body writhing.*

But machine guns with their long wandering streams of reprimand began firing, and bitterly Walter realized that it was because of his presence in the trench, in these old earthworks and brick-shored hiding holes from some forgotten Turkish war, that the gunners were sending their wavering banners over. And after a while he calculated that not just the Turks, but the

Australian gunners too were keeping an eye on this spot and every minute or so chattering their fire across the rim of the brick-edged hole in case he forgot himself. The most disheartening predicament for a soldier to find himself in had befallen Walter: he was under fire from his own side as well as the other.

How stupid he was to have thought that someone out there on the surface of the doomed earth had called his name. The men he had been sent to contact were from a different regiment, Queenslanders who even if they had turned to witness his leap as they scrambled to safety would not have known him from Adam. Then he realized that he faced a brick wall, one he had actually dived through: real, not imagined in the dim departed fertile brain of a Reg Hurst. But there was no dusting himself now and picking up where things had left off. A lid of blue sky fitted over the top of the trench as surely as a slab of stone secures a grave.

Then came the voice again, with no "perhaps" about it. Someone out there was calling his name.

A month before, after the one day armistice, in late May and those early weeks of June while flies multiplied daily in the rising heat and the first men started falling sick, Walter had taken to hard work as to a narcotic. He went-to fiercely as he had at his last harvest, when Billy's mother lay dying and every living thing had seemed to carry a sentence of death. In the new lines near the sea, where daily they dug, a dusty bubble of safety existed in the steadily deepened ground. But every bite of the pick, each chew of the shovel kept him alive just for the day when his fate would at last be fixed. He had known it all along: there was no forgetting rubbed skin even though it formed a lump of callous. The tools of war permitted no relinquishment. Long ago death had ceased to be a matter of speculation. In these weeks of labour, and in the tense period of waiting that followed, nothing happened that did not signal the inching closer of the incident that would so spectacularly mark him off from the living: his wild run to the Balkan Gun Pits in full view of friend and enemy; which marked him off as others had been marked off, sometimes with a heartening flash of magnificence as when Boof hauled Lizzie home against all odds, but mostly not.

Death had become a fact of geography. Here and there a twig was bent, then it snapped. Blood could be sighted on the rim of the hills not just at sunset and dawn but at any time: midnight struck, and by light of star or candle the black shine of departing life unceasingly flowed.

Movement was suffocatingly limited. In many places death came from standing upright, for the sky was invisibly deadly even when holiday blue or inhabited by gliding spinnakers of cloud. The sky varied in height, sometimes unpredictably — at certain spots lifting with a sudden rush of freedom to show mile after mile of idly wind-ruffled sea; but mostly hugging the whipped scrub that in patches was nothing more than charred earth where low brushfires had raced up dry gullies and expired. Here earth and sky were composed of the same deadly mix.

As they trudged back to Rest Gully at evening, or broke off for a swim at the beach, odd funnels of mortality would suddenly ram down from nowhere and a peppery maelstrom leave a streak of blood in the water, or a man collapsed on the track clutching a shattered arm, or just limp, as happened with Captain Filbert the regimental vet, who had no business with animals at Gallipoli but had desperately wanted to see what it was all about. In death the large nose and delicate white hands of his quizzical modesty were so apparently alive that those who paused to look expected his lips to part and the officer to speak to them in his very proper Melbourne manner.

With the hot weather, half the men found themselves squatting innumerable times a day at the fly-infested latrines. Here Mick Aitcheson had been found one morning having fainted the night before, his stained trousers wet and stinking from diarrhoea. But thus far Walter's health held. It had to do with the condensed milk he got from Ollie, though Boof claimed that all three were fit because they dipped into his supply of homeopathic pills, a leached and crumbly collection he kept in a baking powder tin.

Those who were sick did their work, tried to eat, and slept. None had the will for argument, let alone fights: so one day when Ollie and Walter suddenly fought there was no audience, except for Boof intervening to break it up, the three friends grappling foolishly on a gloomy hot evening before the worst of the digging was done.

Ollie started quietly, and in a friendly tone, his danger sign: "I've just been talking to that parson of yours, and he tells me you've got ideas."

"About what?" Walter had scrounged a white biscuit, the favoured kind that did not dry the mouth and break the teeth, and was about to take a bite. But Ollie astonishingly dashed the food into the dust.

"He didn't know you were bullshitting."

363

"You've ruined my bloody tucker." That was all Walter could think of, the biscuit lying where fat iridescent flies descended from above, and from below writhed maggots in their ribbed dustcoats.

"My books," Ollie sneered. "Christ, you wouldn't have known what they meant without me. Beauchamp's bloody Career!"

"I just said I'd read them."

"You had to tell him you were 'going in for the writing game' when all this was over."

"That's not what I said."

"No," and here Ollie tried to grab Walter's collar in his white fist: "You had to go one better. You crippling well told the preacher I was no good at it and you planned to beat me at my own game. Well let me tell you, chum, you couldn't hold a candle to the pucker of my arsehole."

It was then that Boof broke things up, when Walter was casting frantically around for a weapon because Ollie had already grasped a shovel and was waving its flat face dangerously close.

Boof . . . who later that night produced his violin from God knew where, and roused an astounded crowd.

"What's your pick, Ollie?" asked Boof after running through a string of others' choices.

"Ask Wally first," said Ollie jerking his thumb, with this gesture possibly apologizing for his outburst, though he was never to say "sorry".

But then nor was Walter.

"Jerusalem," Walter at last requested. He had been thinking of home and church and a thousand details of existence far from here. "The hymn," he added, in case Boof had not understood, "And did those feet": but

364

Boof was already playing, sawing the first sonorous bars into an Arabic wail before settling into the glorious notes that were nothing now but sensation devoid of any object, because the promise contained in the hymn had already been cruelly curtailed.

Yet there was something pure in the despair they all shared. It was the very opposite of hope and fruition yet it was palpably part of the world as God had made it. Suddenly Walter saw, and so must have Ollie, that the things they held in common were more real to them now than their differences. It was not any one of their shared difficulties that achieved this, but their sum: the way all movement through time had been cancelled, and in the perpetual present moment the reliance of others on one's own strength and quickness became the lone hostage each possessed against the utter extinction that might come even before the heart truly stopped beating and the eye seeing. So this was the mystery of armies, the secret of glory, and the trick of personality that transformed querulous youth into creatures of self-sacrifice.

It was why Mick Aitcheson, after his awesome collapse, refused to see the doctor but cleaned up and limped back to the lines.

It was why, when Captain Naylor said, "Ah, here's our man," Walter, crouching at his post, had unfolded himself.

And because the brigadier happened to be there among "C" Squadron when he needed a runner, it was why Walter after a moment of heartstopping hesitation had gone.

"He's tall enough, and fleet of foot are you son?"

The last words Walter remembered saying before

setting off were: "I was damn awkward on my feet at school."

For much of the month of June, hidden in prickly scrub not far from the Second Brigade positions, Billy in his way gave thought to the same mystery: the puzzle of man's adhesion to what he hated. On this point it was not his own case that bothered him, but that of the rest, the haggard unshaven host flop-bellied among the low seaside ridges or clinging to the giddy ravines above, those who hatèd the circumstance of their daily life as Billy loved his.

By contrast his job was a privileged one, though he shirked no privation. His pattern was to creep out at night and settle himself. Then during the morning hour he would observe shrubs divesting themselves of blankets, and see rocks kneel and stretch. Though tempted he dared not shoot. Once he found himself within yards of a Turkish patrol but they moved off without seeing him. In late May it was a different kind of war down there, open, a matter of watch and tell as each side extended new trench lines. There was none of the close bruising horror that continued on the heights. Throughout early June it was Billy's territory, shared with a handful of other scouts and snipers. For a while it was a boys' war. At full daylight he would wriggle his way back, or, more often, stay out all day, drowsing, taking sips of heated stale water, not daring to smoke his pipe except on hazy days when scrub fires leapt up the dry gullies and threatened to make a leaping wallaby out of him for the sport of his opposite numbers.

On his own Billy had time to think. He had never believed in change for himself but now it was happening. He discovered a new kind of straining within that was partner to the wondrous nerve strain he experienced as a sniper. Aspiration flowered in Billy as it had never hinted of doing in his earlier life: he saw happy days ahead and realized how badly he needed them, for while his task in the war did not disturb him, lately he had started to worry about another part of himself. Diana provided the contrast that brought it out, otherwise the thing that disturbed him might still lie unexamined in the darkness of his mind. It went further back than her, to a night long ago and the following morning when Pat Reilly had taken his money at the Albion Hotel, and told him never to show his face there again.

It was not until Billy was on the ocean after leaving Australia that he experienced again the feeling of grinding fury that had gripped him at night behind the Albion. It was not until then that he even recognized it in himself, and remembered. But this time it was different, for there was no cause. He had simply woken one morning in a state of mental anguish, taken a panicked look around the crowded sleeping deck, then rushed up the oily ladder to the open air. But the feeling remained: it was as if all sensation had sunk to a leaden sheet upon which his life was stretched.

Billy's ship was a horse transport, a craft given over to animals and the men who tended them. The steel hatches between decks on their upper sides formed flat areas for fights and card games. Here men squatted for a quick smoke between duties. That morning in the midst of drawled speculation someone had suggested a buckjumping contest, and within minutes a crowd gathered and an unbroken remount was led out:

"Who's game?"

Billy stepped forward and scrambled atop the clattering mare and found himself digging his heels in her flanks hardly knowing where he was or what was happening. A distant voice shouted a warning:

"Watch your head!" and Billy realized that each jolting arch of the animal took him to within inches of thick steel plate, and threatened to crack his oppressive skull like an egg.

He was better after that, as if something had been drained clear.

Then what about the Cairo dealer in silverware who had cheated Tip Markworthy? Billy had beaten him around the face until the others were forced to drag him clear, still swinging punches.

Upon their arrival at the Dardanelles Billy had given no thought to these interior attacks of malice. The high point had been learning of Diana's expectant motherhood, which made him feel as if he had been lifted out of himself entirely and another and better self was in the making.

But now that he was isolated, away from the main trenches and their hectic trouble, he wondered. He had allowed himself to think that God was taking a direct part in his life. But the voice that hovered around his most secretive inner person prompted nothing but evil.

All Billy's concentration now worked at holding on to the happiness he needed. If only he could lift it to a spot in his mind where it would never fade! For the first time in his life Billy approached a conscious philosophy. How was he to live?

Imperfect parts of these thoughts he attempted to set down in letters to Diana. Now, his hat sprouting leaves and his face caked with mud to make him indistinguishable from the surface of the earth, he took out his stub of pencil and grubby notebook and tried again.

And all the while the news of Diana's death having left Australia a week before lurched across half the world before striking a shore where its voice almost drowned in the reverse traffic of other such fates. But still it persisted, lying for a while in a grey mail pouch, disappearing under a sheet of official forms, then at last leaping into the hand of someone who knew where Billy might be found.

Billy drowsed on through this hot noon in a thorny thicket surrounded by pungent wild thyme. The way to safety lay across the bared shoulder of one of the ridges that ran like buckled cardboard parallel to the sea. He would have to wait for darkness before crawling in.

In despite of his nickname Billy had not yet killed a fellow creature face to face. They called him "The Murderer" because of the zealously flushed shadow of General Bridges's supposed assassin fluttering from the pine tree on Russell's Top, and for the dozen or more glimpses vouchsafed him of unwary headshapes fatally exposing their mortality to his snap shooting along the upper part of the line. But Billy did not feel as he knew a killer must. Nothing but a practical equation arranged itself in his mind: the death of the enemy equalled the security of his place in the world.

This common enough solution to the soldier's predicament meant more to Billy than just his own survival. To the army, righteously flung on the shores of a foreign land but not seeing itself as an invader, closing with a foe produced the supreme justifying platitude of its existence: we are not whole until sundered. But Billy as an individual had arrived on the peninsula still in pieces (though he hardly knew it) and was now earnestly engaged in making himself whole. Billy's rarity as a soldier came from this atypical union of private thoughts and military function. If such inner conjunctions were visible he would have been declared a prized oddity even in this most individualistic of armies.

Now as he shook himself awake and scanned the baking gorse for anything unusual, the two streams of purpose ran inseparably. There was no doubting that the aimless diversions of youth were done. Billy unsheathed his telescope while lying on his side and fitted it to a makeshift tripod of stones. He was on the edge of things here, lying out in unclaimed ground where daily he had watched the opposing lines extend their fragile hold, each seemingly in response to the other. Nourished by death, only the inanimate was truly alive.

Suddenly on the heights a terrible row erupted. Machine guns seemed to be attempting to stitch together a ball of chaotic noise — rifle fire, bombs, what might have been the subterranean thump of a mine. It was a concentrated event, with loose ends of noise being whipped back into the heart of the blaze by the invisible tongs of an enraged blacksmith. Something panicked in the bushes over Billy's head. It was not a bird but an "over" from Lone Pine. Wild firing ran up and down the line, but with this one exhausted exception nothing further came his way.

Because Billy was remote from the fight he felt

something of the power of a creator. He heard the contained chaos rise and fall to a pattern, whereas to those clambering to face its storm for a brief moment of bewildered glory it was something else entirely: and nothing would ever be able to convince them otherwise.

Under ordinary circumstances the average soldier sees or knows little of what goes on around him. But Billy gained the feeling that the turmoil of those individuals battling aloft was but a minute detail in the unfolding of a great pattern. It could not be otherwise. Even to contemplate the thought brought him close to a glimpse of the darkness he feared. So Billy settled himself into a mood where he presided over the invisible importance of the battle like a hen protecting an egg.

"Steady . . . Freddy," he breathed as he held the telescope to his eye. The blue and silver of the lens filled with underwater light, a round window of blurred shapes. Then as he twisted the instrument into a moment of focus he thought he glimpsed the face of a man. A vegetable man, or a clay one embedded in the soil. It was no illusion. When he relocated focus the man was still there. By an extraordinary chance the telescope had fixed on the face of another sniper, like Billy lying far out on the flank commanding a wide view of the new Australian trenches threading their way down Harris Ridge.

At first Billy peered at him as might a scientist viewing a threatening microbe under a microscope. But he was also overcome by admiration. The Turkish sniper was perfectly still. A curlew frozen to the earth could not have been more invisible, nor a mopoke in a tree. "Bad luck," Billy told the other. Fragments of character shimmered through the condensed air — the steady eyes, the finger raised with steely slowness to cautiously seek out an itch, an action that made Billy's ear itchy also. He stared for ages at his enemy until the bond of unknowing that divided them disappeared.

Later, when his shot had been fired and he was making his way back to the lines, he would begin to consider again the million to one chance that had enabled him in all those acres of nothing to unveil the hidden threat. Then he would see the discovery as a sign, and choose to set himself apart from ordinary men because of the swift token of recognition granted to the aspiration of his soul. The thought would buoy him up for hours — until that moment, not so very far into the future, when Potty Fox would thrust into his hands the telegraph message with its news of Diana's death.

Then Billy would make another discovery. He would learn how the reversal of morality need not alter behaviour. After eruptive news people often go on doing what they did before, only with new and more terrible sets of reasons.

In the dawn light he had already marked various ranges: a discolouration in the scrub to the left of his target set it just short of five hundred yards. When he slid his eye from the telescope a mere dent of shade showed the hidden place where another human breathed and plotted in blissful ignorance. He took a deep breath and listened to his heartbeat. A steady mind means a steady body, as "Skipper" Fagan put it. Your rifle and Mother Earth will be your two closest friends when the whips begin to crack.

Billy angled his body a little to the left of the line of fire, clasping the weapon loosely in his hands, allowing the ground to take the weight. He imagined a taut wire stretching along his line of sight to the mark opposite. At this moment of preparation Billy was always able to look away, and again look back to find the wire still there. He slowly worked the bolt. The faint metallic slide and click blended with the noise of insects. The insides of his feet gripped firmly against the hospitable ground. He wriggled for ease and comfort and firmness, and for the pleasure of what he was about to do. Now came the moment for absolute steadiness when he would become vulnerable to any unseen watcher who might happen to stare at his hide and see the unnatural straight line of the rifle lift against the scalloped curves of nature, and the man-shape declare itself like a figure in a picture puzzle book.

As he raised the rifle his chest, head and arms rose in obedience. His entire being moved to the imperatives of the rifle. As always he was held by the magic of its weighted but manoeuvrable length, its invisible power over nearby horizons. He jutted his left arm slightly outwards so that his elbows formed stays, as in timber work. He was ready, alert in that state where the devoted marksman knows the whole visible world subservient to his next move. As Billy felt the first pressure of the trigger he took a deep slow breath and held it. It was a moment for tasting the perfect stillness of death as he had never tasted it before. Excitement like the tickle from a low voltage battery sat at the tip of his tongue. He wiped it away with a quick pointed lick. What other name but "murderer" was there for a person who in the eternity before the second pull found satisfaction for a deep appetite?

But there still seemed a chance for the distant Turk to shift an inch one way or the other and save his own life. Billy could never predict the crucial moment. That was where the other man's chance lay. Split fractions of fractions of seconds were available, and it was then that Billy imagined another person's finger reaching down and flicking the pin forward — igniting the powder, jolting the braced shell, sending the spiralling projectile on its way.

The word "murderer" would never fit. It was as if Billy were the instrument of a greater power, the force that made the rifle and put a man behind it.

After firing he held the rifle steady, "following through" while an alarming echo lashed the still valley. Then it weakened against the constant battle rumble from higher up. Only then did Billy let out his breath. Everything had been done right and he knew, as always, that someone at the end of the taut wire lay dead. The trick now was to find the spot with the naked eye, but the wire had twanged towards the target along with the bullet, forming part of the destructive force now spent.

He lowered the rifle and set his eye to the telescope. He was now able to take a leisurely look at the target, an indulgence that the deadly fire on the heights during previous weeks had not permitted.

The man's head protruded only a few inches forward of its previous position. The face, having struck the earth, seemed to have ploughed outwards into a patch of sunlight. Just this detail of humiliation touched Billy. Blood gathered on a temple, black as the hair surrounding it, but catching the light.

It took Billy some time to realize that his killing of the Turkish sniper had taken place in one of those moods of personal obliteration he had sworn to be rid of. But the mood had changed its character. It now brought great elation instead of anger, a sense of timelessness in the midst of necessity. The killer, having erased the object of his passion, thinks he will then be free from the burden of the passion for ever.

Walter had been tricked. The voice calling his name had been an illusion. He would never leave this hole alive.

He knew it was wrong to feel bitterness, but nothing else served. He huddled against the forward part of the trench saying to himself: *It's all been a waste.*

There had always been something further up ahead. Always. Since his first steps taken from one parent to the other the world had been calling out with its promise. Even as he had sprinted through bullets just minutes before there had been something. *Get there, get there,* prompted the inner voice. *Then you will see.* Well now he was there, stumped. Shut away ahead of time.

He had wanted to ride in the dirigibles when they started using them to beat the trains. He had wanted to say, at home, I remember this world of ours before it became as beautiful as it is now — before I went away. He had wanted to see the faces greeting him, he did not care whose — he would kiss the feet of an unwashed swagman and embrace the bole of a gum when back on unthreatened native earth, and shout for the bar at the Royal till his pay ran out, then turn for home and never again leave.

Ten minutes passed and the machine guns seemed to be losing interest. Walter's will stirred. *There's more,* he thought, *more!* So even at the finish came these heartless surges of promise. He decided to take a cautious look outside as soon as the firing properly sidled away. He would raise his sun helmet on a stick and if that worked, why, he would climb out, scoot for the ridge, and make his way back along the beach. Somewhere down there was a stretcher awaiting his tired frame. He would climb onto it, and not shift until they carried him off, out to the ships, across the ocean. He would try his hand at journalism after all, Ollie or no Ollie, and make his mark. He would live by the harbour and when Frances called would show her in, and as they gravely recalled their reckless youth she would explain no, she had never taken up with Robert Gillen, it was all a mistake, and he would say Marriage? yet agree that though their destinies were entwined there was now this matter of Art.

But when he raised his helmet it was plucked from the stick and flung with an angry rattle against the rear wall of the trench, where it rolled over to reveal a gaping tattered hole where Walter's head would have been.

How difficult it was to look at his dirty hands trembling as they picked away at the rotted sandy mortar and think of them as stiff unmoving claws. Was there hope in the realization that he was unable to do so? Hands, whether active or helpless, have a special function. They are expressive spirits even when the spirit itself has nothing to say, nowhere to go. It is hands that beckon, hands that say, *Come, we are showing the way. You may despair but we shall never. Let that be your hope.*

For weeks there had been no such time as tomorrow, only another today. Now there was just half a today, soon to be hacked clear of the rest by a means Walter dared not contemplate. But perversely his mind sprang ahead and showed him the darkness of night, and through it a Turkish patrol creeping with bayonets.

A month before, on the day after the armistice, Walter had been taking his first swim when the battleship *Triumph* was sunk by a German submarine. From water level it had been like watching a city sink into the sea. One man was glimpsed clinging like a mollusc to a sunlit propellor, another ran down the sloping deck into a mirage that ringed the waterline like a rim of tears.

Then only two days ago Walter had almost been killed while swimming at the same spot. If only he had been, he would have been spared this torment. A moment of animal ignorance — that's what he needed now. Death without all this knowledge, without thought. The swim had come at the end of a week of heat which these Australians no longer pretended was "nothing" compared with the scorchers of home. When not digging, or crouching tense in a dusty gutter at the edge of shimmering scrub, they would eat, forcing down gobfuls of red melting beef and sweating cheese, and then they would sleep. The heat was so intense that at noon one day Ollie Melrose had punched a hole in a tin of Fray Bentos and derisively poured out a lurching stream that attracted green blowflies bigger than any seen at home. The meat gave off the odour of a tidal swamp. To swim after such experience was everything. Twenty heads like floating melons cheered when the brave mail boat chugged around the point pursued by gulping white shots. Then came a pause in which the distant Turkish gunners could easily have been loading up for the swimmers, but who cared? They smacked the water, gargled and sculled peacefully around, diving like ducks to search for souvenir pellets of shrapnel from earlier salvoes.

This is what Reg Hurst had dreamed of: to be free of the body's prison after exertion. This thin remembrance, an exaggeration of feeling. Was that all Hurst had asked for — sentiment? Walter stroked six feet down to where he felt water pressure on his ears and thus failed to hear an explosion that sent the others splashing ashore. He groped for a large section of shrapnel casing, a real find, and stood there holding it, his feet on the stony bottom. After a minute he shot to the surface, took a series of noisy breaths while looking out to sea, then dived again. The next shot was closer: he wallowed out of the water to see his mates dancing and waving.

"We thought you were done," said Boof when he reached them. Walter turned to see a burst of shrapnel churn to emery paper whiteness his swimming place of moments before. Ollie alone berated him for his carelessness — the Ollie who recognized but could not accept the Australian addiction to understatement.

After the next shot Walter raced back to the water's edge to collect his shorts and shirt which he had left weighted down with a stone in hopes of drowning the lice.

They agreed to go their separate ways and meet up later in a dugout belonging to one of Ollie's countrymen. Walter traded his souvenir for two tins of condensed milk from Pig Nolan, who set off to swap the ruptured shell for rum from the English sailors who would appear at the landing stage after dark. Walter then made his way through the gullies behind the beach until he emerged at a busy part of the shore several hundred yards farther on.

For the rest of his life, for how ever long was left to him, ten minutes? a second? he would hold to the miserable series of events marking that evening as the most wonderful holiday of his existence. From out in the scrub came a growl of noise, an animal cry, though what animal could be left alive in this place? It had nothing to do with his lying here, hands covering his face, it was not meant for him because no other cry came.

"Hey, Wally! Over here!"

Walter had doubled back that evening after his swim to find Ozzie Deep acting as guard at the water cart.

"So it's you, you bastard. You're always guarding something."

"Go on", said Ozzie.

When Walter asked about the *No Drinks* sign Ozzie looked quickly around and muttered: "Take your fill, but hurry." Walter gratefully gulped the rare liquid but suddenly spat a mouthful into the dust. It tasted of chloride of lime, reminding him of the dead.

A chain stretched from the mug to the tank. Ozzie as he played with the dull metal links was like a begging monkey. He wore the defensive look that truly kindly people often adopt, a mixture of willingness and thwarted experience.

"A smoke?"

They talked while the sun sank into the sea. Past the sandbags protecting the cart Walter could see a busy stretch of beach, the part called Anzac Cove. He remembered Reg Hurst's description of how men had clung like cockroaches under the low cliff on the day of the first landing. Now they threw stones at each other, stripped and swam, played leapfrog. Not the same men — a different generation with no direct memory but a fund of queer stories concerning the events of two months previously.

"Doherty has stopped bothering me," said Ozzie.

"How's that?"

Ozzie looked awkward: "He got himself killed. It turned out he weren't so mean after all. He went up the gully behind Pope's Hill to bring back a wounded man. The Jackos let him have it but he kept going. He's somewhere over there." Ozzie nodded at a row of stretchers queueing for a hospital tent. "So's the one he saved. Did you know Keith Fryer at home?"

"The station manager? There was a scandal with an English governess."

"That's him. He lately worked for the Gillens out Condo way. Don't go," Ozzie grabbed Walter's arm: "He's dead too."

The wounded lay in an alleyway of sandbags awaiting their moment. Abandoned here by overworked bearers they took on the aspect of groups of sick in Bible pictures. Limbs dangled from the edges of stretchers. A man sat up and called for water. Bandages emphasized the startling brightness of seeping blood.

The man who had called for a drink now waved an arm and yelled: "Come on, you lazy bludger!"

"He's been there an hour and I've given him two drinks already. Don't go, he's a whinger."

"But I know him."

"Don't we all."

"Walter! Hey Wally!"

"Shut up! This stuff's like gold!" yelled Ozzie. Then he relented. "All right, take the swine this but make sure you bring the cup back."

The wounded man was Blacky Reid.

"Wally, old pal," said Blacky as he gulped the water. "That weasel —" he pointed at Ozzie. "I've been hit," he explained, and drew back the blanket to display caked blood and old rags. "My piles are killing me and I've got some sort of fever. Then this, a touch of shrapnel, just as I was getting ready to come down here about my bum. My arse is killing me!" He dropped his voice: "We're going to be friends when we get back, aren't we? You and me?"

"Like always," said Walter.

"He thinks I'm putting it on. Just you wait!" he wheezed at Ozzie. "Did you know it was safer in the trenches than in the hospital? They say a doctor died during an operation."

"Go on, you're lucky. You'll be well out of it." He now saw the problem — Blacky was desperately afraid.

"You remember Martha Bryant, don't you? She and I got married, secretive like, the day before I left. Her first old man kicked the bucket, so it was now or never."

"Congratulations."

"Ah, well, it was what she wanted."

Walter watched as Blacky the reclining farmer cupped a hand and tried to light a cigarette.

"How's old Pig to you now?"

"He's changed. He's polite. I don't know why — what does it matter?"

"Nobody likes him any more. It ain't right to profit from your mates. He needs friends."

"Like you?" ventured Walter. His intended meaning was moralistic — "as you, Blacky, have decided you need friends."

"I'm no friend of Pig's. You think I'm worse than sin, don't you. You believe all that stuff Ma Pepper goes on with, 'Blacky oughter hang', and so forth. No, I'm not like that. Bugger this cheroot, can you make it work? Light it for me, there's a pal. You've never seen me plain, have you. But you've changed too," he rambled on, "you're not such a biting whelp any more. You used to bristle all over the place."

"Did I?" Walter passed Blacky the cigarette. A different part of the beach was visible from here. A sergeant smoking a pipe walked to a position just in front of the lapping waves, seated himself on a folded newspaper, and took up a book that had been all along lying on the rubble.

"They're mad," said Blacky, referring to the throng on the beach. "Five minutes ago the bloody place was shelled."

"It never falls in the same place twice."

"Like hell it don't. Where've you been all this time?"

"Keith Fryer was here," said Walter, gazing around.

"He still is. That's him under the blanket." Blacky indicated a stretcher on the other side of the alley.

"I knew the English woman he took up with. I met her in the hospital when I was sixteen."

"Edie Davis? Poison."

Blacky was an expert on district gossip, old and new. Even now he raised himself on an elbow in a dark rush of interest: "Y'know, they always reckoned she —" But he weakened, and lay back placing an arm over his eyes.

"By the way, how's your love affair?"

Walter scraped the tin mug in the dirt. Mere talk could no longer touch him. Besides, Blacky's tone was sad and wistful. Each slow word of the question sought an image of a disappeared world. While inhabiting that world both had believed they shared nothing. Yet now it was not only all they had in common — that departed world was all they had.

"Finished," said Walter.

"Sorry to hear it." But the old malice flickered like a bed of coals in the early hours of morning: "Perhaps she was too quick for you. Women are like that, always out ahead somewhere. Sometimes I think we marry 'em just to slow 'em down."

This effort of Blacky's to be his old self showed how far gone he was. He turned even paler, those black brows pathetically huge.

"Hey, Ozzie!"

"You come here."

Walter cadged a last drink for Blacky and asked Ozzie to keep an eye on him.

"I can't be sure, but he seems about to faint all the time."

"That's nothing."

"Will you watch him?"

"If you ask me to. No other reason. All right?"

Over on the beach the book-reading sergeant stood, dusted the seat of his pants, and yawned. A slight breeze stirred the pages of the pink-covered paper which he left carelessly behind. "There's a *Bulletin* over there," Walter told Ozzie, "I'll be back in a second."

Two Australian privates, each carrying a tin can, moved at a slow walk along the edge of the water with their heads turned intently downwards. Every few seconds they swooped on small objects in the water and placed them in the cans. Any moment now they would sight the *Bulletin,* more prized than any shell, stone, chip of wood, spent bullet, or even money — and grab it before Walter could get there. So he sprinted. The *Bulletin* was rich with tales of an existence that once had belonged to all three. They lumbered from opposite directions, the two soldiers like clumsy seabirds in their heavy khaki with damp rings on their trouser cuffs.

"Hey, that's ours," one belatedly whined. Walter clutched it and retreated.

"Where's my cup?" called Ozzie.

"C'mon Wally," contributed a remarkably recovered Blacky, "give us a look." But a doctor arrived and Blacky was carried off groaning.

The first item Walter saw in the *Bulletin* was the last he read, for the news it contained set him thinking. "Son killed," ran the headline: "The son of a Paddington identity Mr M. Milojevic, a teacher of languages, has been killed in action. The son enlisted under the name of George Mullens. He died, said the father, for his beliefs."

There was no truth in this. Mullens had been trapped just as Walter was trapped. Held for an eternity below ground with the only way out an ascent to heaven through the blue corridor above. Heaven!

In the stinking Gun Pits Walter dozed for a while, feeling nauseated from the endless nervous waiting. He searched all pockets but discovered his tobacco tin gone. Then it occurred to him that he had been in this trench before. Mad as it seemed, once before in this life, or an earlier one. The idea strengthened. Here was proof that the inexorable process of finalization was not all-conquering. Chinks appeared in the bricked-up solidity of the world.

Yet on the beach that evening a scene had presented itself that showed the inexorable process all too visibly, with no fanciful routes of escape. After putting the

Bulletin down Walter had seen an officer, a New Zealander, sitting beside a pack with his back turned resolutely to the sea. He seemed to be listening for something that would never come to this part of the world — the whistle of a train, the clang of a tram, the honk of a motor bus. For a minute the military purpose of things stepped back from the stacked stores, from the barges, from the stepped dugouts climbing the slope, the water tanks, the men gathered around the brigade depots like crowds outside a ticket office, from those who strolled along the beach in convivial groups — authentic holidaymakers.

But then it advanced: the reminder that nothing here, not even the stones, was free from a military purpose. The stink of decaying flesh.

The privates with their tin cans looked up and spoke. The officer took out his pipe and puffed busily. Walter remembered the ramshackle theatre of his dream, where he had laboured in a terrifying atmosphere of love. Now he saw a broad moving belt that inched its way up the beach with a load of men and stores, and deposited them at the grinding face of the front. There was no waking from this vision, for it was the truth. If a man's mind pulled away to one side it made no difference. He was in the service of a momentum not his own, a machine that finally spewed him out, used up, as waste. Only a faulty part could win respite, a broken but not destroyed body. No matter which way he turned the idea over Walter saw that a price was required for being part of the contrivance of war. And that fact made being here not just cruelly unfair, but mad. No other activity in life took away completely what was offered without giving something back. It was a dead end. Here hands clawed gravel or clay, clutched at slithering tree roots, or ran desperately across the face of ancient brick — as if hands could take the body where the mind demanded.

Then upon these thoughts once more impinged the voice. Now it was like the echo of a stone tossed into a gorge that reverberates after the stone has rolled to a stop. The voice calling Walter's name — flint striking a spark that whizzes brilliantly towards the eye, but on arrival is nothing but a cold fleck of insensible matter.

"Billy!"

The familiar figure advancing along the beach, scuffing toecaps on shingle, was his friend after all. He had changed: white-faced with a troublesome set to his jaw. A listless wave.

"You just missed Blacky. He looks like being out of things altogether. Half his luck, eh?"

"Out of things? That's a laugh!" Billy threw himself down. The stones must have hurt, but from the way he acted they might have been soft sand.

"Are you all right?"

"I thought things had changed." He tossed a handful of gravel towards the water. "But they haven't."

"You look as if you've had a close shave."

But it was something else. The breath of danger never affected Billy like this. The constant fear, the way under everything one never stopped being frightened: was this the trouble? Most men here were either glum, touchy, or wildy elated, yet whatever showed on the outside, within was the knowledge that all moved to the one commanding drumbeat. But Billy was different. Could it be bewilderment? He withdrew a fist from his pocket, breathing noisily.

"Read this."

It was the cable message announcing Diana's death by drowning.

An anguished half hour followed. Walter promised Billy rum, but could not find the dugout where he had agreed to meet up with the others.

"It's along here, I'm sure." He dared not ask after Billy's feelings. They found themselves on a scrubby knoll that fell away to a shattered piece of open unoccupied ground. "Something about going *up* the track. They could have meant north."

"Christ."

Their retreat found them outside the chaplains' dugout. "Do you want to talk to Potty again?"

"Like hell."

Walter was leading a bullock that might at any moment turn and gore him with a swipe of its troubled head.

Finally Walter gave up: "We're bushed."

"*You* might be," said Billy meaninglessly.

All this pounding ahead while Billy doggedly followed — it was a way of avoiding Billy's eye. But at last Walter ventured: "I wonder how it happened?"

Billy's response alarmed him because it was exactly as expected. He lunged from the darkness, and for a second seemed about to strike Walter on the face — but he knew what to do: he would take the blow, and if Billy knocked him down he would struggle to his feet and take more. But Billy did nothing. He just chopped the ground with his heels, spitting and swearing.

That was how Ollie Melrose found them, locked in wordless debate. The dugout, it happened, was around the next corner, its sandbagged entrance hidden in the dark. They had passed it twice.

"Typical," said Billy.

Pig had obtained a half-canteen of rum, but because a two gallon jar was in the offing as well he collected more money and dashed off. The remaining four crowded around the pine box that served as a table, a squat candle at its centre. Mick Aitcheson was there as well.

"Billy can have my share," said Walter, and Billy accepted it without thanks.

In a dull voice Billy described his exploits. That very day he had shot a sniper. "C" squadron had been in the line then, and Billy said how it gave him satisfaction to know that he must have saved someone's life. He turned to Walter: "It could have been yours."

The rum appeared to set him up. For a while he became the old Billy again, and when Ollie and Mick ducked out for a minute Walter dared to ask:

"Are you feeling any better about Diana?"

"I might as well be dead myself."

Ollie and Mick stepped back, buttoning their flies.

"I'll take one of them too," said Billy standing. "My bladder's a joke." He drained his rum and set the mug down with a clatter.

He left the dugout, and though they waited, and twice went outside to search, he did not return.

Of all the deaths stored away in Walter's memory that of Diana seemed the least cruel. He gave no thought to the unborn child and the thwarted prospect of life for an intelligent girl — that potential he mourned for himself — nor did he grieve for Billy's sake: and he knew the reason. Diana had died in Australia, where a body, even though there was a chance it would never be found, still was fated to be welcomed into a landscape adapted since the beginning of time to the safekeeping of faint spirits. He envied her, and longed for a grave near to where his grand-parents were buried — in that clump of writhing white-limbed gums on a knoll above the creek.

Then he had an idea.

He pulled his wallet from a side pocket and unfolded a slip of paper. He took up the slim brass-capped pencil he had stolen from the effects of George Mullens. He smoothed the paper on a taut knee and was about to start writing when a dull object lying next to a dislodged brick caught his eye. It was his tobacco tin, fallen from a pocket during his plunge into the trench. So with relief he rolled a cigarette and drew deep giddy-making lungfuls of smoke as he wrote.

"To the finder: please record position of body and write to below address stating last wish of Walter Edward Gilchrist — To be removed from this place to Australia for burial at his home."

Then he signed his name and wrote the date: June 28th 1915. He tucked the paper away, and lay back uttering a deep sigh, feeling luckier than anyone he knew, than any of the dead, that is, whose names along with their forms rotted as they sprawled on each other in "God's Acre" or unknown lay out in the scrub. He knew that his father was the man to respond to such a plea, and would spare no effort to meet the request of a dead son whose wishes he had so stubbornly blocked in life.

But what if it was different, and souls went marching on into eternity? "If there's a hell," Ollie had said after the final disaster of the night, when the rum was wasted and Pig Nolan dead, "then you and Pig will fight there."

Mick had upended the pannikin of rum and obtained a few drops for each which they licked, complaining about the time Pig was taking. Then they sat back and lit their pipes.

"I don't suppose you've heard," said Ollie. "But Walter Madox got killed at sunset. Nugget came by with the message. He was running to catch up with the others and that was that."

"A sniper," said Mick. "A confounded lucky shot."

Madox? Walter tried to hold in his mind a clear picture of a man he had known for nine months, but nothing showed except brown hair, a deferential stoop. It had always been a source of irritation to Walter that the two had shared a name.

Mick let out a stream of smoke and said: "What is it, a month to the day since we lost Frank?"

"Six weeks," Walter calculated.

"Nugget and I'll have the job of visiting his family when we get back. I ain't looking forward to that in the least."

"Who were Marjorie and Mossie?"

"Ask Nugget, he knows 'em all," Mick said diffidently.

"I met one of them once," said Walter. "Marge. Do you know the other?"

"All right, but don't tell Nugget I told you. They were always very thick, those two."

"Mossy was the mother of his kids, she lived with him up at Moree for twelve year or more. But Marjorie, just a kid herself, was the one he almost made it legal with, only a couple of years back. She refused to

390

go bush with him. So Frank went back to Mossy while Marjorie stayed in Sydney. You know what a stubborn mule Frank was. Marge was the same."

"Why didn't he marry Mossy early on?"

"A few reasons."

"I'll bet she was black," said Ollie.

After a pause Mick said: "She was, but you could never've met a nicer woman."

"Oh, my!" said Pig, stepping through the doorway and setting a stone jar down on the box.

"You keep quiet about it," said Mick, startled.

"I don't talk. But what if I did ? Frank's dead. Does it bloody matter anyway?"

"Like hell you don't talk," Walter heard himself say. In the early days Pig had gone around saying anything he liked, nudging people in the ribs, waving a fist.

"I've been leaving you alone," drawled Pig, placing both palms on the box and causing it to sway creakily. "But I could change my mind like that." He snapped his fingers.

"Leave off," said Ollie.

"There's more rum where this came from," Pig straightened himself. "At least another jar, maybe two. So come on, who's tossing in?"

Ollie contributed a shiny Turkish coin minted that very year. He had obtained it in exchange for two tins of beef on the day of the armistice.

"Yes," Pig breathed, turning it in the candlelight, "they'll like this. What've you got for me?" he asked Walter.

"Nothing."

"Not even a decent shit, I'd say."

"Now look —"

Mick took out half a crown: "It's all I've got, so

make sure I get a full share."

"It never stops, does it," said Ollie when Pig had gone. "You should have shaken his hand at Ma'adi," referring to a time in Egypt when Pig had tried to make the peace but Walter suspiciously had refused. Rightly, too, because it had all been a sarcastic joke on Pig's part.

Mick poured the rum and this time Walter took some. The taste did not even make his mouth feel clean, it seemed oily and burnt. His heart was beating fast with an inner panic that rum could not touch.

Mick, who had fallen into a reverie, suddenly sat up. A sound like wind puffing through a tree filled the air outside. Walter was about to part the flap for a look when Ollie's hand restrained him. A remote muffled explosion was followed by nearby tearing and flapping sounds, as if a dovecote had been split open and a thousand pigeons struggled to escape. "One down, ten to go," said Ollie. Another shell exploded in the sky. This time the hills echoed with the sound of wet sheets flapping in a gale.

A third explosion was followed by a gap of peculiar silence. Even the popping guns on the heights seemed to pause. Walter heard Mick nervously click his jaw, a habit of his at such moments. Then footsteps abruptly sounded on the track outside. "That'll be Pig," Ollie sniggered in relief. He slid Pig's pannikin across the box and placed a hand on the jar ready to start pouring. But when the flap was wrenched aside the face that appeared was not Pig's at all, but Nugget Arthur's.

"Was Pig Nolan with you blokes?" Nugget breathed noisily through his battered nose and horsebreaker's lumpy cheeks, "Was he? Because he's out there," he continued, jerking a thumb over his shoulder: "Hit," he gulped at last.

Ollie half-stood, Mick scrambled to his feet beside him. Walter reached for the beam over his head and was about to haul himself up: "Don't go," said Nugget, "it happened right outside the hospital."

"Is it bad?" asked Ollie.

Walter attempted to cram back into his mind a thought that demanded: *Make it bad, Lord, bad, bad, bad.*

"There was blood all over him and broken stuff. He stank of rum. But the doctors dragged him inside as soon as it happened."

Walter's prayer altered: *Make it bad enough to take him away from here for ever, but don't kill him off.*

When the shelling stopped they went to look. "He's in there," said Nugget, pointing to a halo of light that shone on the white canvas of the medical tent. "Who's his best mate?"

"I'm his worst mate," said Walter nervously. He could smell the rum somewhere about, and also the whiff of chloride of lime being used as an antiseptic.

"It's me, I s'pose," said Ollie. He followed a pair of stretcher bearers into the tent.

While they waited, ramming black tobacco into their pipes, Walter realized that the hostility he felt flowing from Pig was equally of his own making. Pig had biffed him first, but the days for vengeance had passed and here was Walter still determined to carry it on.

Ollie emerged from the tent laughing.

"Pig's all right!" declared Nugget.

"The rum," said Ollie. He rested his elbows on the sandbags and giggled. "The poor bastard. He wasn't hit by the shrapnel at all. But the jar got hit and he must have fallen over on it."

"But he's all right," insisted Nugget.

"No, he's dead." Then Walter saw that Ollie's cheeks were streaked with tears. "The sharp edge did for him. He died just now, while I was in there."

Who would shed tears for Walter's death? It would come remote from human sight, it would be reported uncertainly, and by the time it was confirmed, if ever it was, the response, even of his loved ones, would be a shrug. Thus he told it to himself as the walls closed in . . .

Nugget took Ollie by the shoulders and guided him compassionately to the ground, thrusting a pipe between his teeth and inviting him to smoke his fill. Mick slid his back down the tight-packed sandbags and squatted with his knees touching his chin, a hunched beggar in the pale light of the hospital tent. As Walter joined them he envisaged the Australian troops around him squatting in similar positions — leaning on posts, lying on their backs in dugouts, balanced under the dangerous lips of trenches in deceptive postures of relaxation. Then one of them toppled to the ground. And then another. And another.

Ollie spoke in his measured, English way: "I saw the doctor lift a shard from his groin. It was smeared all over with blood."

"Take it easy," said Nugget.

"He mentioned you," Ollie turned to Walter. "We had a laugh. Pig said, 'When I get up I'm going to cook that smart-arse Gilchrist's goose.' Then the blood poured out like a fountain. There was nothing they could do." Ollie giggled again: "If there's a hell, you and Pig'll fight there."

Instead of relief Walter experienced a kind of numbness about the night's events. Yet how truly alive he had been ! Angry, envious, sad — with companions who shared in the same emotions. Feeling implicated and helpless they had moved through the night in a state of freedom they were unaware of.

"It's time we thought about sending some money to Mossy," said Nugget in a low voice, "or those kids'll go back to their natural state."

"Marjorie's the one who won't have taken the news calmly," said Mick.

"You don't consider what it does to them, or else a bloke would have thought twice about it."

Wedged against the uncomfortable angle of the Gun Pits, almost dreaming under a baking sun, Walter recalled how they had felt their way through the night and finally reached the rest area where the remainder of the squadron, gathered in shadowy excited group was speculating on the action they were to be invo.ved in the next day, the day that had opened with Walter's run and would close with his —

He rested half-asleep with his head on an arm, and tried to convince himself that there was something attractive about the inevitability of it all. In his tiredness he found nothing left that he wanted to understand. But his mind ceaselessly tortured him, and suddenly there came upon him a vision of the interlocking hostilities of the world — nation at nation's throat, friend grappling with friend, the grid of hatred descending to impose its heartlessness on the peninsula. Lord, he began . . . but there he finished. Exhausted, he felt that the walls of the trench were creeping closer, and raised his head in a panicked realization that life had thrown him into the living proof of the stone tomb that had horrified him during his stay in the hospital at Parkes, when the doctor had loomed over him and the matron or somebody had grabbed from behind when he sat bolt upright in a living nightmare. He had found himself in that place where pain was endless and struggle futile, but to fight against it a compulsion imposed by eternity.

So he raised his head higher, scrabbled to his knees, tensed his throat ready to shout *Here!* in reply to the familiar voice that just now rang out again. Why hadn't he picked it before? He drew himself almost erect in the act of launching himself forward and out of the trench, elated at the discovery that all this time someone really had been out there in the scrub watching over him, and that someone was Billy! Billy's voice the whole time calling . . . Then a shot crashed against his ears, and hands closed around him from behind, human hands with dust-caked scabs and black hairs. In the shock of seeing them and of finding himself unable to move while his will struggled to be free, Walter wondered if it was all a dream again; and as a second shot rang out a rush of oblivion assured him that it was so.

After leaving the dugout the previous night Billy had gone straight to headquarters. Here, hardly speaking, he had collected his orders for the next day and disappeared. Skipper Fagan had chased after him a few minutes later because something new had come up, but by then Billy was over the parapet in the pitch dark and making his way determinedly through the undergrowth, far from human contact.

He had been out on the extreme right since well before dawn. When the sun came up he was lying among wild thyme that hummed with bees. A clump of low scrub protected him from sight, but did not give complete shade. Had he slept? It was quiet where he lay but from the direction of Cape Helles to the south came the constant rumble of guns, indicating that an attack was in progress in the area held by the British and French. Billy's orders were to watch for changes in the Turkish trenches to his front, for although Cape Helles was miles distant, and the only line of communication between the two armies was the sea, the activities of one invariably had an effect on the other. And Billy was now ready for anything.

He wanted to release the power and pressure he felt barely contained within: he wanted an explosion. He was disgusted with himself for having bargained, on and off, with God. In the past there had been times when he felt an understanding had been reached: God had put Diana in his path, and given him the capacity to see what his life had been like before her arrival. But it had all been to make him look a mug.

As Billy lay on his back with his forearm across his eyes he heard the nearby snap of a twig that set his heart racing, and then a hiss of breath. Slowly he shifted his arm and found himself looking into the snout of a revolver. Kneeling beside him was the scout Freame, steady as a snake.

"That ain't funny."

"They said you'd be out here."

"Don't do that. Not ever!"

"You've been asleep."

"Like hell I have, I've been awake since before first light."

"It's now twelve o'clock."

"Bullshit!" But Billy was forced to fumble for his watch.

Freame's face looked cool in the great heat. He was part Japanese, and had the silky unruffled look of someone constantly at the centre of important events. Though he asked for a drink, only the faintest shine of sweat showed on his forehead. He wiped his mouth and said: "There's to be an attack."

"Ours?"

"At one o'clock the boys will be coming through. Do you think you can get down for a closer look?"

He explained. A feint was required to convince the Turks that a big attack was under way from the Anzac area in support of the one at Cape Helles. He handed Billy his binoculars and pointed obliquely to the rear, back towards Chatham's Post, the position Billy knew was occupied by Walter's regiment. Through the glasses Billy saw bayonets shuttle in a blue chain just above ground, and at one spot a line of men seemed to be leaping from one hole to another: an obvious ruse, but almost immediately earth flew up as the defences came under artillery fire.

This was more like it. Billy was no longer on the outer. This time no-one's will but his own would be responsible for what followed. There would be no throwing away of himself at the crucial moment.

"What do they want me to do?"

The scout wriggled forward and Billy followed until the Balkan Gun Pits became visible about half a mile farther along, in a dip to the left of the scrubby ridge. Across on the right could be caught a glimpse of the sea, a long sweep of bay concluding at the low headland of Gaba Tepe. Through the glasses the Gun Pits looked harmless relics. At some time in the past they had been partly roofed with brushwood. But fifty or a hundred yards farther back from these trenches were another lot, with sinister fans of freshly dug dirt tossed out in front. Now and again a glimpse of head could be seen as someone jogged along a communication trench. Billy lowered the binoculars.

"Have you sniped down there before?" asked Freame.

"No."

"The new works are what they call the Echelon. You're to get as far around to the right as you can. Try and line up with the communication trench. Our boys will be attacking the Gun Pits. It'll look serious, and if the opportunity presents they'll go farther on. But when they've livened things up they'll be getting out. If you get into a good spot you'll be able to fire over their heads and never be seen in the fun. All right?"

It took Billy only half an hour to move into position. Although alone, all the way through the scrub he talked, wriggling where there was a chance of being seen, sprinting bent double on the seaward side where there was dead ground — talked not out loud, and not to himself, but to Diana, the companion of his extremity. "I'll lie down here. Take a breather. Now, up we go!" He elbowed his way to the crest of the ridge and sure enough, just as he had guessed, his line of sight lay along the communication trench and revealed the moving heads much clearer now, as if stones were rapidly whizzing to the surface and drifting for a foot or two before burying themselves from sight — Turkish reinforcements, their headgear the dry dirty colour of their country.

Billy unpacked his telescope and spent five minutes marking the ranges. More detailed now, the Turkish heads dropped smoothly from sight, and idly Billy imagined them swinging upside down for a reappearance, as if the Turks too had their bag of tricks in full play, and only Billy, between the two armies, was seriously dedicated to the proper business of the military. Suddenly he felt lighthearted. Death itself was an ambition, therefore what did he have to fear? He felt Diana to be no longer a separate being.

In the midst of these thoughts he heard a strained voice: "Don't shoot!" and turned to see a scratched, red-headed officer pushing aside the rifle of his sergeant, which was aimed at Billy. They wriggled up the slope and joined him.

A third man arrived to point out a line of Turks at the foot of the next ridge, slightly northeast across the gully and only three hundred yards away. Billy had missed them — they were in the wrong direction, he hastily explained, they had only just popped up.

"I've been watching them for ten minutes," said the new arrival.

Billy made a quick suggestion to redeem his pride: "Five men, five shots." Could he do it? Talking rapidly, he described how the moments of surprise and uncertainty after the first shots would freeze the others.

And that is what happened.

When Billy fired the astonished Turks wavered and fell while the officer and the remainder of his men hurtled down the few yards to the empty Gun Pits, and leapt in, huddling together like children.

As soon as the five shots had been loosed Billy slithered out of sight. Sure enough, a ferocious succession of bullets caned the gravely lip of the ridge where he had lain moments before.

He had just killed five men, but the feeling was not the one he wanted: the pressure in his head almost caused him to cry out in rage.

Suddenly there were soldiers everywhere. A second party had arrived on the tail of the first, but half had taken a wrong turning and were now trapped on the slope under fire. Billy's head was pounding. A rabbity corporal in panic grabbed his sleeve: "Jim and Colin are out there, what's to be done?"

"Bugger me — can't you see?"

Billy took six leaping strides over the edge of the ridge and dragged back one of the wounded. Then he dived out again grazing his left cheek and breathing the dust of acrid, pulverized stones whipped up from the nearby bullets while he rolled the second wounded man into the arms of a stretcher bearer.

"That was a Christian act," said a moustached officer kneeling at Billy's side. "I'll remember it. What's your name?"

For a while the men lay silently under the protection of the crest. The space they occupied was no larger than a ship's life raft: leg intersected leg, elbow rested on knee. Then the officer said to Billy:

"Come with me."

They crawled through the bushes and stopped about twenty yards farther along from Billy's sniping spot. The officer rolled onto his back, tilted his head causing his neck to stretch as if for slitting, placed two fingers in his mouth, and whistled. An answering call came from the Gun Pits. Then the officer risked a long look towards the Echelon trenches, ducked, and whistled again, this time piercingly and imperatively.

"It's all over," he said, "we can go home."

They heard the crash of feet as the party from the Gun Pits came hopping back. This time there was no fire from the Turks because an Australian machine gun had started up, spinning tiny whirlwinds across the face of the Echelon.

"See anything?"

"Not a ripple. I'll try the spyglass."

"Look, Mackenzie, we can't afford this. We've got to get going."

"I'm staying," said Billy, who was already uncapping the telescope.

"You're mad."

"You'll have to carry me out." A great plain in Billy's mind was ablaze from end to end. Dark figures dashed everywhere in panic, their silhouettes startling against towering curtains of flame: Billy alone was steady.

"They'll kill you."

"I'm staying. You wait and see, I'll be on your tail in no time."

The officer made a last effort. He gripped Billy by the elbow and smiled condescendingly.

"Piss off," said Billy calmly. "How do you know what my orders are? I've got business out here."

Then it emerged that the man had all along wanted Billy to stay. He had felt guilty at leaving him, that was all. And the truth was that Billy would be doing the men a service by watching the rear. Already the sergeant had reported a glimpse of what he maintained was a battalion of Turks moving towards the rear of the Echelon. "I won't forget you," said the officer as he left, tugging a carroty lock with respect.

At last Billy was alone. He blew dust off the sights of his rifle, took out a clean slip of flannel and wiped them. He rattled a small bottle of blacking liquid from the hollowed butt, and there, in a timeless mood of care, fastidiously painted the sights, both fore and rear. He wiped the bolt and breech until not a crumb of dirt remained, then wriggled to a more protected position.

Here he took out his telescope and began setting it up. Even without looking he knew the Turks were for the moment keeping hidden. The odd distant shot rang out, the machine gun from a mile back stuttered. Then a movement caught Billy's eye.

It was a man running, coming from the left, from the Australian lines. His route took him along the gully at the base of the ridge where Billy lay. He fairly streaked, and though he occasionally stumbled on the low undergrowth these accidents seemed merely to serve as an extra source of propulsion. His final stumble turned into a dive, and he crashed into the crumbled brick embrasure forming the near side of the Gun Pits.

Billy excitedly fiddled with the telescope and focused on the trench. He was so close that the eyepiece filled with T-joints of brick where weathered mortar left dark slits. The man must have been cautiously raising himself just then because a sweat-stained shirt intruded, so Billy lifted the telescope by slightly cocking his wrist: and found himself staring not into the face of a stranger, but at the familiar wide eyes of Walter Gilchrist.

"*Wally!* Up here, quick!"

The Australian machine gun started again, only this time it sprayed around the mouth of the Gun Pits as well.

"*Wal-lee!*" Billy shouted with his mouth almost touching the ground. Bullets whipped the low shrubbery along the skyline, which was inches from his scalp; it was machine gun fire from the opposite direction, from the Turkish lines. They must have heard Billy shouting, or else seen Walter's run: or both.

It was hopeless.

But the calm deep within Billy spread until it

controlled his physical being as well. It was within his power to do something for Walter, but he hesitated.

There was a pattern to the Australian shooting. As long as the machine gun fired it was safe for Billy to raise his head. These were the very moments, though, when Walter was unable to raise his. This see-saw of opportunity seemed endless; ten minutes or half an hour passed: every now and again Billy shouted, but with little hope of being heard because no answering call came from the trench. Only once did Billy dare to raise the telescope, and saw Walter again, full face, staring straight at him like a blind man.

Billy remembered how Walter had crept up on him in their childhood games. But they had never been games to Billy. Never quite. Why had Billy never been able to understand, no matter how many times Walter explained, how it was that his name, printed BILLY on a slate, became YLLIB when held up to a mirror? Nor why the surface of water curved instead of lying flat in a full glass, nor how a piece of wire attached to a dynamo could cause a salty agitation on his tongue without any change occurring in the wire. The terrified face how held in his telescope had laughed at him for not comprehending such everyday laboratory tricks. The terrified face had once reacted just as dumbly when Billy talked about his straightforward acceptance of heaven, hell, and an invisible God that could be spoken to.

I am invisible now, thought Billy with elation. Each time the Australian guns pinned Walter down he raised his head and assessed the situation. He was able to see as far as a bend in the wall past the position where Walter cowered, his shoulders white from the storm of pulverized masonry. Billy's duty was plain, should he choose to obey it. He could easily pot any Turk who dropped into the far end of the Gun Pits, and even if he missed he would be able to pin them down for long enough for Walter to take a chance, scramble out, and sprint for his life up the slope to safety.

But having made this plan Billy worked out a good reason for not following it. He could fire only when the Australian machine guns were firing, but the chances were bad for Walter in that case.

So, whichever way he thought of it, Walter ended a dead man. When this idea was clear in his mind Billy made an astonishing discovery. The mental agitation that had plagued him all night and throughout the morning had completely disappeared. It was as if his rage had mounted to its unbearable point of pressure and resolved itself at some moment of fury without his knowing.

When he looked at Walter again he saw a trapped hand patting the bricks. What was going on? Nothing but Walter's hand feebly wandering, reaching high up the wall without seeing anything, just touching, smoothing the rough age-old blocks with his palm and feeling the bumps with his fingers, almost wonderingly. Billy had no time to reflect on what it was in the gesture that alerted him, that woke him up. But suddenly he knew that someone else was in the trench, and that Walter had no idea.

"Walter, Wally run!" For a second Walter dropped from sight. The firing came from everywhere but Billy ignored it. *"Wally, where are you?"* His voice dragged at the dry walls of his throat.

Then Billy saw them, two Turks and a German sergeant bent double moving along the trench at a speed that astonished him. By the time his sights were aligned the first man was springing at Walter with a curiously gentle leap. Billy fired — Walter rising into his sights like a runner from the blocks, like a startled kangaroo from grass — reloaded and fired again, then dropped the rifle and heedlessly consulted the telescope while Turkish marksmen sought him out. He found himself again looking into Walter's eyes, but they were blood-soaked now and sightless. The biggest Turk abruptly slung him over his shoulder like a carcase, Walter's arms drunkenly loose but swinging in time to the lurch of his captors as they lugged him away.

With their departure calm descended on the Balkan Gun Pits. Both sides seemed to abandon their interest in the place, and Billy, scooping up rifle and telescope, also wanted to be free of it.

21
Piano Music

The morning after receiving Ollie Melrose's letter Frances played the piano for the first time in six months. Ugly scales echoed through the house until the keys ran slippery with sweat. In the darkened living room, where drapes were drawn against the heat, she at last felt ready to do away with the humble being she had become. And all because of a letter! She was prepared now to play something serious. But first she stepped to the window and peered into the mid-morning glare, nervous that the piece she wished to attempt — something by Mozart — was beyond her, knowing that her mother would be listening and wondering about the transformation thus signalled. She was nervous too that the mood suddenly filling her might be only a whim, and that at any moment she would find herself plunged back into the unfeeling gloom that had possessed her since Diana's death, that had darkened even more two weeks later when Walter's disappearance was announced in a small item at the foot of the *Herald's* twenty-eighth casualty list.

Where had he gone? He was not reported dead or alive, wounded or dying, but "missing" in peculiar circumstances. Though she had stopped caring about Walter, Frances became obsessed by the spectral quality that seemed to surround his fate, as if he had been made quite special at last — uniquely beyond her grasp. Then a few weeks later his name appeared again, this time in a list of prisoners supplied through the American consul in Constantinople, and her mother had urged her to write. But instead she had dashed off a note to one of Walter's friends, and must have said more than she intended for the reply peered straight into her soul:

"A bad conscience makes a bad friend. Send him socks and chocolate but do it under any name but your own. It's lonely enough in Turkey at the best of times, take it from one who knows. For a man on his own, letters from a girl who 'don't mean it' would be a siren call with nothing but the abyss between."

It seemed to Frances that Ollie Melrose, who signed himself ornately as "Oliver", whom she had never met, whose reply came from Egypt where he was convalescing from wounds, understood her better than anyone at home. Besides, he had asked her to send a photo of herself: "Just look in the right-hand drawer, in the left corner, under those gloves and handkerchiefs, etc., and you will find one." Frances was cheered most of all by his daring to express a mixed opinion of her while still showing liking and curiosity.

But his advice went against the view of her mother, who was still urging Frances to "write and show friendship". She could not understand how Frances was able to throw herself into Red Cross work yet ignore the plight of the one man who was not a stranger. Just yesterday she had greeted a hundred returning soldiers at Woolloomooloo and won their devotion.

"I'm giving it up," said Frances when her mother entered the room and asked why she was not in uniform:

"I don't understand. Mrs Brewer's taking us in the car. Sidney will be driving."

"I've finished with war work. Honestly, I've done my share."

An astonished Mrs Reilly sent Helen to make tea. "I won't talk about it," she resolved. "I can't!" But a moment later she said: "*You* were the one who took the lead. It was your enthusiasm!"

How could Frances explain that almost at the instant of Walter's disappearance she had elected to disappear herself? But now she had been sighted, a stranger had seen her as she truly was. How remarkable! She felt alive again. "There are hordes doing it. I'm not needed. Besides, hardly anything we've done has reached the soldiers. It's all piled up somewhere."

"Is that the real reason?"

"I don't know."

"Then what is?"

"I can't say. I don't even know what got me started." But at this Mrs Reilly shook her head, because both knew how things had been in the weeks following Diana's death, when Frances had come downstairs after days of staring at the ceiling and immersed herself in Red Cross work. Mrs Reilly had suspected all along — Harry's notion, really — that her daughter's energetic devotion to the cause sprang from uneasiness at her part in Diana's fate.

"What does Harry say? 'Quod omnia something', we're all touched by the war."

"Quod omnes tangit," Frances recited, "ab omnibus approbetur."

"You can't just let it drop."

"No-one will notice."

"They've just made me secretary," Mrs Reilly

complained. At this her daughter giggled, whereas only yesterday she had stood soulfully on the wharf holding a basket of wilting flowers.

"That saying of Harry's is ridiculous," said Frances. "Why should we *approve* of something just because it affects our lives?"

"He's coming this afternoon. Please don't start an argument."

Frances had changed her mind about Harry, and was glad she had never been bold enough to repeat Sharon's scandalous accusations to her mother. They were true without doubt, but under Harry's fuzziness and querulous deceit she had found something to respect. On her arrival home after the drowning he was the only one who refused to pretend that nothing had changed. So they went on disliking each other, but with respect instead of disdain for the battle each needed to fight in silence. In that way dislike turned into something else. Frances tolerated and began to enjoy his "helping out" with the heavier Red Cross loads whenever he had the opportunity — almost continuously these past two weeks of his annual holidays.

"Do you know who Harry thinks he saw at the ship yesterday? Billy Mackenzie."

"But we met them all."

"Not the ones at the other end. The cases for the hospital were seen by the ladies from Vaucluse. Harry was very sure, except that Billy's hair was close cropped and bristly. He looked like a German."

"Wouldn't we have heard? Why didn't you say so before? Couldn't you have spoken to him ?" Her mother leaned forward: "We should have sought him out."

Frances chose this moment to break finally clear of the shell of grief that had enclosed her since June.

"He blames me for Diana," she said firmly. "I know that he thinks nothing would have happened if it hadn't been for my . . . my . . . " Frances took a sip of tea, then nibbled a biscuit, leaving her mother an awkward witness to the confirmation of her own suspicions.

"Who would think such a thing!"

"He must," said Frances quietly, "I think it myself."

"You shouldn't."

"I left the door open and Diana caught cold. She would not have got pneumonia otherwise. The holiday was spoiled and I insisted on going home. But worse than that."

"Worse?" Mrs Reilly was alarmed. All this she had thought herself, and had discussed her feelings many times with Harry. Now it seemed there was to be another revelation.

"It's the way I am. I drew her into it."

"Into what, for God's sake," breathed Mrs Reilly.

"Into life. My life. I feel as if Diana was forced to make amends because I'll never be able to."

"I won't listen to — "*this madness,* she wanted to say.

"It's all right, mother. I know I'm to blame, but I've finished worrying. I really have finished."

"Something Oliver Melrose said made the difference, didn't it. May I read the letter? Or was it catching sight of Billy? We'll have to go and see him, you know."

"I can't change," said Frances, raising her head in decisive resignation, "I can't."

Her mother took her daughter's hand. "You've

changed already. Today is the first time in months I've heard you play the piano. You've recovered your old self."

"That's what I mean."

There they sat without talking until the doorbell clanged and Mrs Reilly leapt up in alarm because she had not yet tidied herself.

Helen ushered in Mrs Brewer. She was a large puffed woman with a heaving red cross fixed almost horizontally to her starched bosom. Recently a photograph of four of her sons, all in uniform and overseas, had appeared in the *Herald* under the heading "The Brewer Brothers of Balmoral".

"'Won't Sidney come in for a cup?" asked Frances. She rather liked the languid fifth son whose weak lungs made him a prisoner to his mother's national spirit.

"He's keeping the engine running," replied Mrs Brewer, glancing at her watch.

"Mother won't be long."

"What about you, my dear? The troops must be properly kitted."

"I'm not . . . well today. Do you mind?"

"Sometimes," said Mrs Brewer sharply, "I'm unwell myself."

Then the doorbell rang and Helen announced a second caller, grasping Frances's sleeve and dropping her voice to a hoarse whisper while Mrs Brewer looked on: "She won't come in, nor would she give her name. She looks like a domestic. Should I send her away?"

Frances went to the door to find a thin girl her own age wearing a ridiculously smart hat and a white muslin blouse with grubby cuffs.

"Are you Miss Reilly? I couldn't ring. I've never used a telephone before. I've come down to find Billy, but I can't find him nowhere," and as she spoke she stood on her toes and peered over Frances's shoulder into the dark hall as if someone might be lurking there. "I'm Ethel Mackenzie," she continued, extending her hand, "Billy's cousin."

When the others had gone, leaving them alone, Frances commented on the heat, but Ethel, after unpinning her hat and running a finger along its dyed blue hen's feather, said it was not too bad — compared, that is, with home, where the New Year was always a scorcher. As the Brewers' car noisily departed up the road Ethel cocked her head quizzically and after a moment announced: "I thought it was a calf or something."

Helen brought a glass of lemon cordial which Ethel downed without a pause, then she twisted around to admire the room while gripping the empty glass in both hands.

"Do you work for the Red Cross too?"

"Whenever I can," said Frances.

Helen waited to be handed the glass.

Ethel laughed: "As if we'd have time for it up home. The war's for those with nothing to do."

Frances wanted to object, and suggest all those tasks towards which her life had once seemed to be serenly tending — the labour of music, which that very morning she had taken up again; the timeless effort of art. But she was irritated to find that Billy's cousin forced her to be plain: "To tell you the truth I'm about to give up the Red Cross work altogether."

But if she disliked Ethel, as she decided she did the

moment she set eyes on her, why should she seek her approval?

When Helen left for the kitchen Ethel changed seats. Frances found her hand suddenly in the grip of one that was chafed and red, though the fingernails were surprisingly well kept — better than her own.

"I didn't come looking for Billy," Ethel confessed, "I know where he is. I've come to warn you about him. He's not the same. I saw him this morning at the hospital where he's kept. They've shaved his hair off, you can see the scar plain as daylight."

"I don't know anything. What happened?"

"He said he'd written."

"No."

"He swore." Ethel sucked in her upper lip and stared thoughtfully at her hat which was occupying a chair all to itself. "Then perhaps it's all right. Gosh, what a lovely piano!"

"The wounded men don't shock me. I've visited the worst cases." Frances stood and searched for a box of cigarettes, holding them out to Ethel who shook her head.

"I'm at sixes and sevens. He told me he'd written to you with a — he started blaming people — he used words I can't repeat."

Frances now found herself in the chair previously occupied by Ethel: "I know what he's thinking. He blames me for Diana. Isn't that true?"

Ethel hung her head and wiped dust from her toecaps with the side of a finger.

"Isn't it?"

"Not you — everyone."

"But he mentioned my name particularly," Frances stated with force: "Didn't he?"

414

"Yes."

"You don't have to pretend — I'm strong, you know."

"Oh, I know that," said Ethel, at last looking up. "You're much stronger than me. I've always envied you, ever since I saw you once at the station. I told Walter about knowing you by sight. Did he ever say anything?" When Frances nodded Ethel smiled and said: "Girls aren't the only tittle-tats."

Frances blew smoke in a narrow firm stream, adopting the manner of Sharon Keeley: "I believe we're better at keeping secrets than men."

"Yes, we are!" said Ethel excitedly. She accepted a cigarette after all. Her entire life, she said, had been spent in the company of males. They carried on about their own trustworthiness only because so little mattered to them, and talked their heads off without realizing it.

"What did Billy really say?"

"That he was going to make you pay. He said he'd written you a letter, some kind of threat, but if he didn't then what is there to worry about? He rambles on with whatever comes into his head, and does an awful lot of staring."

"I've already paid — if only you knew." But to herself Frances sounded false, and saw that Ethel thought the same. Her blue eyes were hooded in a family likeness to Billy's, but with a penetrating instead of sullen gaze that unsettled Frances and drove her to the truth: "No, I'll never pay I suppose. How could I?"

"That's supposing you've got something to pay for. I've heard the story," Ethel reached across and touched Frances briefly on the forearm, "and if anyone's to blame it's not you."

"Thanks, but you don't know the half of it."

"I don't need to," said Ethel.

"What's Billy's wound? Someone saw him walking. It can't be bad."

"He was shot in the head, leaving a sort of pink bare patch." Ethel demonstrated by tugging back her hair. "He used to be such good fun. But now that he's not in his right mind he's like a stranger. It took him a minute to remember my name."

The telephone jangled, causing Ethel to give a small squeak of surprise and cover her mouth: "I thought it was the doorbell. Sometimes when I talk about people they suddenly turn up. Oh dear," she giggled.

"Happy New Year," said the man in the bow tie who stood next to Billy at the railing of the ferry.

"New Year?" Billy replied, stepping closer and peering into the man's face. He scrutinized polished cheeks above bushy whiskers, and dwelt for an eternity on the intricate plaid patterning of the coat which the man had slung across one shoulder in the heat.

Then the man was gone, and blue water turned to green as it arrived swollen alongside the ferry. A seabird glided down and clawed the top of a pile before alighting. The ferry stopped, trembled, and set off again, rounding a familiar rocky point. Bushlined shore slid past, filling Billy's gaze with tangled scrub as if the boat had chugged into a creek on the other side of the mountains. It was not the New Year yet, but the day before. What was the day before called? Billy's mind worked differently now, the simplest answers eluding him. Even to move his arms and legs, especially on the left side, took an effort of thought. But while memories were hard to grasp, feelings came easily. Rage and bewilderment sped through his mind like wintry clouds. Sometimes he believed again that he had killed Walter during those last moments at the Balkan Gun Pits. He was forced to relive the agony that had possessed him in the months that followed, before word of Walter's imprisonment had come through.

Two children came onto the deck to stare at him. Billy tapped the bewhiskered man on the shoulder to ask what day it was, but when he turned around it was someone else. The ferry jarred against another set of wharf pilings and set off one of those dull, nauseating headaches that often made him weep.

Then he found himself thumping across the flimsy footbridge at the head of Mosman Bay having missed his stop and been told of a pleasant walk around the treeclad foreshore. He climbed stone steps clear of a band of tide-smelling air and entered leafy shade. Here he paused and unbuttoned his fly, sending a stream of water onto fat green leaves and enjoying the sound it made. He felt better. A swarm of bees had established a hive on a branch above his head, their combs grey as soap in the sunlight. A few yards away a man and a woman sat on a rock pretending not to notice. When Billy walked past, the man tipped his hat to the uniform while the woman stared red-faced into her lap.

Farther on Billy sat on a fallen log to puzzle over a picture that suddenly entered his mind: a butcher carrying a bloodied side of beef off into nothingness, the beef wearing clothes. Next Billy found himself flat on his stomach on the path, tracing a spiral on the sandstone gravel with a short stick. An ant crawled up his trouser leg but what did it matter? Then someone was poking him in the ribs with a cane.

"Are you all right?"

It was the man in the bow tie. Billy suddenly recognised him, and almost spoke his name. He had met him near here before, at the Reillys'.

"What do they call the day before New Year's Day?"asked Billy from his back. "You know — today."

"New Year's Eve."

Billy sprang upright and dusted himself, shaking the man's hand and winking to show that he too was aware that to lie prone on a path at the height of a midsummer's day was none too sensible.

"Are you sure you're all right?"

"Capital."

"May I talk with you?"

Billy shrewdly pointed out that the man had come from the opposite direction and would be wasting his time. Then he stepped off with a smart salute. But around the next bend he came to a fork in the track and slowed with a chuckle for the nosy Harry Crowell to catch up. Billy congratulated himself on getting the name right. Somehow it proved that he was going at things in the right way, despite his sense of falling asleep and then waking in a place or in the midst of some action he could make no sense of. When he was sure that Harry had glimpsed him he quickened his pace, ducked behind a bush, and watched his pursuer stride past just a few feet away. Then he doubled back to the lower track and made his way swiftly to the Reillys'.

When Billy saw the house he realized his mistake — he had forgotten his rifle. Therefore he broke into a run but tripped over, then picked himself up and limped

418

swearing across the grass where a year before Robert Gillen had played at being a cowboy. A second later he was through the back door and into the kitchen, where he leaned on the table to catch his breath.

Laughter and piano music reached him from the front of the house. He was in good humour. He felt at ease in a familiar place. What could be more pleasant than to saunter through to the living room and enjoy the entertainment?

Ethel saw him first and stifled a shriek.

Frances looked up from the music and said quietly, "Please give me the knife." Billy seemed to realize only then that the object he had collected from the kitchen table was a carving knife. He held it out, then changed his mind.

Frances accidentally struck a key as she stood.

"It's New Year's Eve," slurred Billy. "What about a medley?"

"Let's sit and talk." Ethel had recovered herself enough to exchange glances with Frances. "Have you written to Uncle Hugh?"

"Who," Billy seemed to say, "who hoo is Hugh?" Then he said it again, for they must understand that this was an echo from inside his head.

"Your father."

Billy rested the knife on his lap. The faces opposite seemed unaccountably hostile; one framed by dark hair, severely frowning, the other sending quick glances towards the door like an untrustworthy kelpie about to dart free. To prove his good intentions Billy placed the knife on a low table, but when Frances moved towards it he shifted his hand warningly and she sank back in her chair. If only they understood the effort needed to sit here, thought Billy, they would treat me better.

"We missed you yesterday," said Frances striving to be sensible. "Were you well looked after? I suppose the flowers lasted no time at all. Have you heard any news of Walter?" Billy stared at her. He wondered why another person was not in the room — that tall olive skinned woman who played the piano, whose daughter had been Diana's friend.

"Flowers?" he mumbled.

"Our baskets wilted in the heat even though we sprinkled them with water. The ladies here go into their gardens cutting them at dawn. You can't imagine the trouble they take. Such a waste," she concluded, addressing the remark to Ethel because Billy was not listening.

But he was listening. Trapped in an airless room he heard the faint rumble of guns along a horizon of steel and shuddered in recollection of the scenes that had greeted him in August, when he was sent to be a sniper among the hills above Suvla Bay. Then as now the sound seemed to rise through his blood rousing the awfulness of terror until it intensified into a shout:

"It's a tram!" Frances yelled, her face inches away: "Only a tram." Her hands gripped his shoulders as the tram whined past the house and down to the wharf.

"You poor man," murmured Frances, at the same time nodding to Ethel who snatched up the carving knife and carried it from the room. Frances felt Billy sink listlessly under her hold. For a moment it seemed he would be calm. But her closeness, her curves and odours, at last awoke him to her identity — that person who had thwarted his one attempt to escape from the prison of himself.

Enraged he rose from the chair and knocked her down with a blow to the side of the head.

Ethel heard Frances's scream from the kitchen and ran back through the unfamiliar rooms taking a wrong turn into the shuttered dining room where the table was covered in dark velvet like the resting place of a coffin: then she slithered on the hall carpet, still holding the knife, hearing the maid Helen thump downstairs as the front doorbell suddenly rang and a fist pounded on the leaded glass demanding entry, and at last she entered the gloomy parlour to see Frances spreadeagled on the floor with Billy crouched over her, his hands clamped on her neck and his shoulders powerfully arched as if he were tightening a bolt or advancing a ratchet to its utmost. Frances's wide eyes stared past Billy's shoulder straight into Ethel's, her face swollen and dusky. The only sounds were Billy's heavy breathing and a rasp of noise from Frances. Then Ethel threw herself at Billy's back. Billy reared up, flinging her off as if she were a terrier, and the knife, still gripped in Ethel's determined hand, tore through the carpet before its point stuck fast.

Now Billy swung his fists at Ethel and the horrible welt on his head darkened. Frances, gulping breath in the corner where she had crawled, wondered why it was that Billy's ferocious swings seemed unable to reach Ethel's face. Then she saw that Harry Crowell had sprung from nowhere to grip him around the waist with his powerful arms.

A second later Billy and Harry were fighting. A pair of glass vases crashed to the floor. Two weighty encyclopaedias toppled one after another from the bookshelf, then lay with their pages doubled up like crushed noses. Harry sat on the piano, striking a deep chord. Ethel hugged Frances in the corner. When Billy finally lay slumped in a chair, as if dozing, they heard

Helen shriek "Police!" into the telephone.

Billy's nose had flooded red. The head wound which had been split open during the fight wept a watery pink substance. Ethel held towels to his lolling face while Harry tied double knots in the silk curtain cords that bound him hand and foot. When at last Billy's eyes opened he did not speak, but looked at each of them with the air of a person who has made the effort of his life to correct a wrong, but has failed, leaving all as it was before.

Whistles and bells greeted the New Year — hooters, fireworks across the still water, banged saucepan lids, and someone on a rooftop crowing like a rooster. At the Reillys' no such response was forthcoming. Mrs Reilly sat at the piano with the windows open to the moonlit garden, allowing a Chopin nocturne to flow across the unheralded stroke of midnight.

Harry stood on the dewy grass smoking a last cigar. The doctor had come and gone, Ethel slept in the spare room. Frances, following a drugged dreamless slumber, awoke, listened to the music, and after a while climbed from her bed and went to the window. She had been forbidden to watch Billy leave but had forced herself — and had seen a bag of equipment being carted away, mason's tools or cricketing gear strapped in canvas; something inert and useless, its purpose abandoned. The men who tied him into his straitjacket were gentle but they were used to the work, and it seemed horrible. Now Billy was in the asylum.

She cried. The effort caused her throat to ache unbearably. She sat in the open window bathing her arms in coolness as she had countless times before, and saw Harry's cigar tip glow and fade, and then his shadowy form moving back into the house. In the quiet following the fight, during their half hour wait for rescue, Harry had announced his intention to go to England as a volunteer munitions worker. His face had been stern — nothing like the old nervous Harry at all. It was the war. How people needed it! Even when they saw that it destroyed people they needed it. Why else would patriotic soldiers missing an arm or a leg wave their crutches from recruiting platforms? Even Billy, that sullen madman, half the time unconscious of his surroundings, carried the war with him and still tried to obey its simple imperative. Ethel alone seemed to understand the mood Frances now found herself in. They talked about taking a holiday together — of going somewhere where there were no people. Ethel said she wished she had dreamed Walter and Billy dead, it would have been better. Walter would return, she knew, when the war was done, and his unhappiness would take a different form from Billy's but it would be just as awful.

The piano music stopped. Mrs Reilly walked to the gate with Harry. Frances heard one word, "Gallipoli", before Harry set off on his walk home. Her mother drifted back towards the house, pausing for a moment to stamp on the cigar stub smouldering in the wet grass. Frances was unable to call to her, but thankfully she began again the beautiful music which Frances at last knew was beyond her own reach — those notes of ivory and glass that had been created in a distant world no different from this one, where contact between people, beginning in kindness and curiosity, suddenly burst into a crescendo of cruelty and destruction.

"Dear Miss Reilly," Oliver Melrose had written, "I was surprised, not to say pleased, to get a letter from you, as I was quite unaware that Walter had mentioned my name. Your letter was pleasant, interesting and sane, so different from those of the misguided but well-meaning girls who write to 'lonely soldiers' without saying anything, or else making them feel lonelier. Perhaps you don't know that I'm in Egypt at present; wounded . . ."

Frances shifted position on the windowledge. She touched her raw throat and drew her legs up, wrapping her arms around them. Then with care she rested her chin on her knees. Along a reach of harbour she saw the dark shape of a barge being propelled by a tug. How many months had passed since her last dream of sailing away? What would she do with herself? The tug entered a shaft of moonlight and darkened even more. How odd that light should do away with mysterious detail, leaving only a hard black outline. She was tired, and dozed for a second before waking with a start. Then she made her way back to bed.

"Concerning Walter," the letter had concluded, "about whom you ask most nicely. He went missing at the point I was getting to know him. It was the devil's job to make his acquaintance, and we used to fight, but in that unpleasant place the fights never last. He went the way of thousands and when he was gone nobody gave him a thought. Does that sound hard? There's no morality in all this. When word came through of his capture we cursed his luck, being out of it, but then gave a thought to the Unspeakable who fenced him in, and felt a little sorrier. That's about the depth of things in this surprising world, at least till the present madness runs its course. Come to England when it's done, I'm going to settle there, and we'll pretend that nothing has happened. Have you ever run gaily over an ant heap, dashing towards a pretty flower or (pardon me) to the arms of a lover? Your dainty tread, etc. Until then we are the ants.

"This isn't the kind of letter you want: but we never get what we want, or if we *do,* we find it was not worth waiting for. If I have been lengthy to the point of boredom, forgive me, for as I said before: I was blown up by a bomb, which is as bad as being blown up by a woman — but not so interesting.

"If you write again, please send letter to the above address; the hospital will forward it to me, as I may be back at Gallipoli, or I may be — who knows?

Yours sincerely,

Oliver Melrose."

Acknowledgments

Although derived from many real events, *1915* is a work of the imagination. The following, however, willingly recounted their experiences at Gallipoli, fully aware that their stories were destined as background to fiction: Mr Albert Platt, M.M. (7th ALH) of Parkes, Mr Len Bennett (1st Field Ambulance) of Yass, Dr A.T. Dunlop (Medical Officer, 18th Battalion), Mr H.A. Clapson (23rd Battalion), and Mr Clive Newman (9th ALH), the last three all of Canberra. I am particularly indebted to Mr Newman for a wealth of vividly remembered detail.

I also wish to record my debt to the late Mr Tom Dunford (6th ALH, Palestine) of Parkes, and especially to the Parkes and District Historical Society through the generosity of its President, Mr W.F. Nash.

I was directed to valuable sources by Dr Bill Gammage; made use of many books, diaries and letters held in the library of the Australian War Memorial, Canberra; and viewed material in the La Trobe Library, Melbourne, thanks to the assistance of Patsy Adam Smith. I am grateful to Geoffrey Lehmann for invaluable comments and criticisms.

While writing this novel I was the recipient of a Senior Writer's Fellowship from the Literature Board of the Australia Council (1977-78).